"A fast-paced,
–LISA DU

NEITHER MAN NOR ANIMAL

"Murder's all over this mornin's papers. Fleet Street's bound to get the details before much longer." Woburn looked me straight in the eye. "Reginald Mackleston was dis-membered." He leaned forward. "In all my years on the force I have never seen anything like it."

"Dear God!" The color drained from Miss Luce's face. She clutched at my sleeve.

Even I found the idea unnerving—but I had to know the specifics. "You mean he was butchered?"

"No," Woburn said forcefully. "I mean he was tore limb from limb. Someone—or something—ripped him apart."

Miss Luce's appalled expression gave mute testimony to her distress. As the horror of his words sank in, my mind conjured up Poe's "Murders in the Rue Morgue." "Might it have been the work of a savage beast?"

"I think it's the work of the devil himself," Woburn muttered. "In any case," he addressed us once more, "no zoos have reported escapes."

"Perhaps a private collection?" I suggested.

"Look." A note of desperation crept into his voice. "In the old days when criminals were drawn and quartered, it took four strong horses lungin' to pull a man apart. You tell me the animal that could do that...."

WHAT ROUGH BEAST

H. R. KNIGHT

LEISURE BOOKS NEW YORK CITY

A LEISURE BOOK®

February 2005

Published by

Dorchester Publishing Co., Inc.
200 Madison Avenue
New York, NY 10016

ISBN 0-8439-5456-6

WHAT ROUGH BEAST

Preface

1 November 1926

It is with a heavy heart that I take pen in hand to write these words. I have suppressed the facts of this matter for over twenty years, though they tell of perhaps the greatest adventure of my life—an adventure some will surely dismiss as mere fiction. I only wish it had been.

Herein at last I shall set down my first encounter with those terrible powers that lurk beyond the borders of natural science. I was lucky to survive; others were not so fortunate.

Only now is it safe to break my long silence, since I have just received news that one of the greatest showmen in the world and a dear friend of mine has passed on.

I could not reveal the truth whilst he lived, because I feared it would damage his reputation and possibly curtail his livelihood. I refer, of course, to the great magician Houdini. Now he is past harm and in a place where all is peace and forgiveness. One way or another, I am sure we shall be in communication again soon. One of the deepest regrets of my life is that we had not spoken for nearly two years when he died.

Sir Arthur Conan Doyle
Bignell House, Bignell Wood
Hampshire

Chapter 1
Mischief at the Palace

I shall never forget the time I first laid eyes on Harry Houdini. I had no way of knowing this meeting was to change the course of my life. It was in the autumn of 1903. The Great War and my great losses in it were still more than a decade away. I had spent the better part of the season in constant attendance on my wife, Louise, during the final stages of her illness. We had a nurse, but for reasons of my own I insisted upon taking responsibility for her care.

The slow, inexorable advance of the consumption that wasted her body had been excruciating to watch. Her life was not ending with dignity. Rather, it dragged on in whimpers of pain and the humiliations of the sickroom. I could only hope that the clergy were right and a better world awaited those who were forced to suffer so in this one. Some days I would have given much for proof it was true. Unfortunately, I had given up all hopes that such evidence would ever appear.

With nothing to do but await the inevitable end, I felt like a trapped animal in my own house. I snapped at Nurse and was brusque even with my son, Kingsley. He was eleven and already a forthright, manly lad. Now, however, I could scarcely brook the silent misery in his eyes.

I had not set foot outside of the house for many weeks when I received a letter from my publisher. He needed to meet with me in London to finalize the details of an American lecture tour scheduled for the following year. The joy I felt at finding a reason to escape soon faded. It was replaced by guilt over my eagerness to abandon my dear invalid. I had drafted a refusal when my wife, in one of her rare lucid moments, insisted I go.

"The change will do you good." She smiled weakly. "One of us needs to remain strong."

Reluctantly, I agreed to a short trip and determined to take Kingsley along. He, too, needed a respite from the pall that hung over our home.

London was a tonic for both of us. We had reached an unspoken agreement for one day to put aside the grief that had worn us down so. After finishing my business, I gave us both a treat. Houdini was performing in London. I had long been fascinated by the idea of a man who could escape anything. So I took my son to see him at the Palace Theatre. Once an opera house, of late the Palace had been given over to variety entertainments. As we left our hotel, we spied one of the brand-new motor taxis.

"Oh, may we hire it, Father? May we?" Kingsley jumped up and down in his excitement.

I motioned the driver over and we climbed aboard. Once we were settled on the leather bench seat, the driver pulled into the stream of horse-drawn carriages, wagons, and cabs. I was surprised at how high off the ground we sat. We rode like a rajah on his elephant and surveyed the rush of traffic below us. Despite the vehicle's constant vibration, its instantaneous acceleration and quicksilver maneuverability fascinated me. Our driver dexterously wended his way among the less agile conveyances around us. Horses shied at our approach or showed their suspicion by pinning their ears back against their heads.

"Get off the road with that thing!" one driver called angrily to us.

Pedestrians looked up in alarm or curiosity as we passed them. From our vantage point, the crowd on either side of the roadway seemed like a swirling flock of raucous fowl. Stiff corsets forced the ladies' figures into swanlike S-curves. Broad-brimmed hats mounded with feathers enhanced the resemblance. The sober blacks of their escorts' dinner jackets and stiff shirtfronts rendered the women even more flamboyant by contrast. The chatter and laughter mingled with the clop of horses' hooves and the rumble of carriage wheels.

"It's rather wonderful, isn't it, Father?" Kingsley confided.

I nodded to him and resolved to own one of these machines soon.

As we continued, our vehicle's gentle shuddering relaxed me. My mind began to drift. For the first time in many weeks, my thoughts wandered back to the days before my wife's illness. My youthful adventures as a young doctor aboard ships sailing to far-flung corners of the Empire seemed far behind me. I now devoted myself to my historical novels. I played cricket with James Barrie's team of writers, boxed, and golfed when time permitted. Still, something was missing from my life.

It had been ten years since I'd published the "Final Problem" in the dear old *Strand* magazine. The outrage and mourning following this "death" of my creation Sherlock Holmes had shocked me—and, I confess, given me some gratification. Angry letters had flooded my publisher. Crowds of people wore black armbands for weeks. Only the death of Queen Victoria seven years later equaled the tumult. Now, save for the occasional appeal from H. Greenhough Smith, editor at the *Strand*, I thought that was all history. I was about to find out just how wrong I was.

When we arrived at Cambridge Circus, its dozens of newly installed electric streetlights dazzled us. Blinking, we picked our way through the crowds that surged around us.

"Keep hold of my hand," I warned Kingsley. He seemed happy to do as I bade him.

On the ground there was an absolute crush of couples in their finery. We pushed on through scents of lavender and tea rose. I felt a pang at the thought of enjoying myself while my poor Louise endured her final agonies. But the joy on Kingsley's face convinced me I was doing right.

His eyes went wide at his first glimpse of the theater. It was a magnificent structure in the Spanish style with rows of tall, arched windows and a spire at each domed corner.

The more desirable seats were all sold out, so we had to content ourselves with sixpence seats toward the rear. To compensate, I rented us each a pair of opera glasses for a close-up view of the show. As we started down the lushly carpeted stairway, I felt an elbow in the ribs. I turned to see a laborer in his coarse wools push past me with a grunt. He swaggered to his seat with his sweetheart, who wore a shawl and clogs. A whiff of unwashed bodies and cheap perfume trailed in their wake.

I hastened Kingsley past the copper-colored marble pillars to our seats. From this vantage point I observed the people around us. Houdini evidently attracted an eclectic following. Well-to-do young wives in their pastel silks and satins jostled and were jostled by their poorer sisters in dark chintzes or lustrings. Gentlemen in silk hats threaded through knots of working men in cloth caps and open shirtfronts.

Once the show began, we endured the juggler, the strong man, the singers, and the *tableau vivant* while we awaited the main attraction. At last the great magician strode onto the stage in full evening dress. The applause rolled in waves across the vast auditorium. I examined him through my opera glasses. His face was broad, with a high forehead and a thatch of dark, unruly hair. A humorous mouth softened his expression somewhat, but the strong jaw, firm lips, and furrowed brow all bespoke determination.

"Ladies and gentlemen," he announced, as he took his place in front of the red velvet curtain, "tonight you will see things that defy explanation."

He was as good as his word. He plunged into tricks with cards and coins. At one point, he swallowed six needles and a length of thread. When he spat them back up, all six were threaded on the strand. He looked as delighted as a child after each successful sleight of hand. His enthusiasm was contagious. The crowd chuckled and enjoyed themselves fully.

He began the second part of his act by stepping to the front of the stage and lifting his arms for quiet. Only when the crowd was absolutely silent did he speak. "I will prove to you that nothing made by man can ever hold me."

He proceeded to astonish us all with a series of escapes. In full view of the audience, he struggled from the coils of a length of rope, using only his fingers, teeth, and the incredible flexibility of his body. A representative of Scotland Yard locked him in a pair of handcuffs—the same ones that had restrained the bludgeoner Edgar Edwards on his way to the gallows. In moments they clattered to the floor. Houdini triumphantly flung up his bare wrists for all to see.

Next, he was bound hand and foot, tied in a bag, and deposited in a chained trunk. His assistant, a short woman in tan tights, stepped behind a curtain on stage. In the blink of an eye, she vanished and Houdini stood in her stead. The trunk was unchained. When Houdini cut open the bag, his assistant's head of curly brown hair popped up through the slit.

At last came the part I had awaited eagerly. While his assistant rolled a curtained cabinet on from the wings, Houdini strutted to center stage. He announced, "I will pay ten pounds to anyone who can shackle me so that I cannot escape."

The crowd waited in expectant silence. This challenge was his trademark. He offered it at every show.

"Come on," the magician exhorted. "Anybody think he's up to it?"

A burly man stood up in front of us. A pair of manacles dangled from each hand.

"You won't get out o' these," he shouted.

Houdini invited him up on stage with an enthusiastic gesture. Here is a confederate, planted in the audience, I thought. As the man made his way to the stage, I revised my opinion. He was an uncouth sort, obviously the worse for drink. I caught a glimpse of the manacles as he staggered down the aisle. They hung heavily in his hands and clanked ominously with each step. I speculated on where he might have got them. His peculiar, rolling gait was suggestive. With this fellow, Houdini might well have met his match.

The man climbed onto the stage. "C'mere," he bellowed.

The fellow grabbed one of the magician's hands roughly. Houdini, however, shook his head and said to the audience, "I will examine the apparatus first."

The man growled something, but Houdini insisted. First he looked the manacles over. Then he shook each one in turn, listening carefully.

"The locks have been fudged," he announced. "But with a little extra time, I can do it."

"Ain't nothing wrong with those locks," the surly giant beside him insisted.

Houdini lifted one of the irons head-high and spoke quietly for several seconds. None of us could hear what he said, but the man's face grew red.

Finally, the magician closed his eyes, took a breath, and proclaimed, "Houdini is ready."

The man spun Houdini around, yanked his arms behind him, and drove him to his knees. We all heard them thud loudly on the boards of the stage. Several in the audience groaned in sympathy.

"This is not a challenge to break my bones," the magician protested.

I saw the ruffian grin as he manacled Houdini's hands behind him. He padlocked the magician's ankles together. Finally, he scooped off the floor the handcuffs Houdini had recently escaped from and bound the magician's wrists to his ankles. Thus effectively hog-tied with bonds of steel, Houdini could barely kneel upright. His assistant opened the door of the curtained cabinet and rolled it up to surround the bound man. Before she could close the door, the ruffian on stage pushed his way inside the cabinet. We heard a loud thud and one side of the enclosure bulged. The challenger stumbled out of the door and the cabinet rolled backward.

Houdini lay on his side, still fettered by the manacles. I examined him through my glasses. His face had grown flushed. The angle at which he had fallen and the constriction of his bonds evidently hampered his respiration. Obviously, the hooligan beside him had knocked him over. Kingsley looked up, concerned.

"Shouldn't someone help him, Father?" he asked.

"It's all part of the act," I reassured him, but privately I didn't like how shallow Houdini's breathing had become.

The magician's assistant rushed over to help, but the challenger forestalled her. "This is a test," he said, and laughed. "Get on with it." Then he placed himself between the magician and his assistant, who seemed little more than a girl. She flung up her arms as she expostulated with the lout on stage. When he merely laughed at her, she hurried into the wings. I sat forward on my seat. Would no one help the man?

Mutterings of disapproval began to roll across the auditorium. I examined Houdini through my glasses once more. He gasped and perspired—the man was in real distress. But he struggled valiantly to right himself. Eventually, he got himself up on one elbow when the challenger stepped in front of him. The ruffian bent down and whispered something to Houdini. The magician looked up, surprised. Then the cad once more kicked Houdini's arms out from under him. He hit the boards with a groan. Cries of "Foul!" and "Play fair!" vied with raucous laughs of approval from the lower sort in attendance.

I could stand it no longer. I rose from my seat, dashed up the aisle, and leaped upon the stage. I made for Houdini. The brute forestalled me, fists clenched. I had no desire to engage in a public brawl, but Houdini needed help, and quickly. Then a strategy presented itself. I turned toward the audience.

"Ladies and gentlemen," I began, "my name is Arthur Conan Doyle." The room fell silent. Houdini's assistant stood on the sidelines. She wore a worried look.

"Prove it!" one man challenged.

"Hush, let him speak," a woman called.

I ignored these sallies and continued. "Since we are lucky enough to live in a free society, let's put this to a vote. Do we allow a ruffian to mistreat a guest in our country?"

A rumble of discussion rolled across the audience. The first man bellowed again, "Why should we listen to you?"

In the heat of the moment some people, I regret to say, echoed his sentiments with their jeers. Many in the audience looked uncertain. How could I verify my identity? I glanced down at Houdini. Perspiration dotted his face as he struggled to right himself.

The large man on the stage approached until he loomed over me. "This here's none o' your bloody business."

He swung a haymaker at my jaw, but I tucked my chin. His blow slipped off my hunched shoulder. I spun and used his own momentum to push him off balance. He staggered halfway across the stage. A gasp ran through the spectators. When the man regained his balance, he shook his head and stalked back over to me, murder in his eye.

I had a burst of inspiration. I spoke loudly, so that everyone could hear. "Behave yourself, Mr. Wilcox. You're in enough trouble with the authorities."

He stopped up short and his jaw dropped. "That don't scare me none." He turned to the audience. "He's talking crazy."

People shifted in their seats. Their mutterings sounded like low thunder. I saw more than one hostile glance directed toward me.

"You have the walk of a seaman," I said loudly. "The anchor tattoo on your arm and your use of naval slang confirm my diagnosis. My nose tells me you have been to a public house for several drinks, but not to a hotel for a bath. You are recently off a ship, or you would have freshened up and lost your shipboard waddle. You have enough money to attend a show at the Palace and to buy a brand-new suit, but not the level of diction one usually associates with these acquisitions. Your accent betrays you as having been born in the Portsmouth area.

"This morning," I addressed the audience, "the *Times* ran an appeal from the police for information of the whereabouts of a Robert Wilcox, from Portsmouth. He had been manacled in the brig of his ship, the *Saxon Warrior*, for stealing money from his mates' lockers. He somehow escaped and jumped ship. The *SW* stamped upon the manacles you used confirms my theory."

"It ain't true," the lout beside me insisted.

Chuckles and shouts of derision issued from the crowd. "It's bleeding Sherlock Holmes!" a large man down front cried. I gave an inward sigh of relief. Fortunately, I could play at being Holmes when necessary. Still, there was an unruly element to contend with.

"Conan Doyle," one person called, "when are you bringing Holmes back?"

Calls of "What'd you kill him for?" and "Bring him back" drifted up through the limelights. These scattered outbursts soon resolved themselves into one unified chant. "We want Holmes," they called over and over again. The sound rolled across the auditorium and echoed back at me from the walls. Many of the faces looked decidedly unhappy with me. Peering into the audience, I could barely make out Kingsley's small form, squirming uneasily in his seat. Some of the crowd left their seats and advanced on the stage. They looked angry.

I glanced at Houdini behind me. His face had grown pale and his hands were slowly turning blue from the constriction of the manacles. I saw only one way out of this dilemma for both of us.

I raised my hands. The crowd grew silent. "You shall be the first to know," I called. "I have begun the first of a series titled 'The Return of Sherlock Holmes' for publication in the Christmas issue of the *Strand*."

For a moment all was silent, then there was such a wild cheering as I expected to hear only on Judgment Day. Men threw their hats in the air; ladies fanned their faces with handkerchiefs.

I took advantage of the ease in tension to bend down and lift Houdini upright. He gave a sigh of relief and winked at me. I turned away from him to confront Mr. Wilcox, but the stage was empty except for Houdini's assistant. The man had made good his escape.

I turned back to the crowd and was surprised to see cheering break out again. At first I thought they were applauding me for helping Houdini. Then I realised that all the men who waved wildly and the women who applauded were looking past me. I turned around to see Houdini standing triumphant behind me. He held aloft all three sets of manacles, still locked shut in his left hand. In the midst of the applause, he shook my hand vigorously and patted my back. "Sir Arthur Conan Doyle," he announced, urging the audience to an even greater ovation. "A true gentleman."

Somewhat embarrassed, I retired to my seat.

Kingsley's face was glowing. His eyes glistened and his lower lip trembled. "Well done, Father," he said. I gave him a quick hug. The cheering continued long after Houdini had bowed and the curtain had fallen.

Eventually, the enthusiasm wore itself out and we made our slow way toward the exits. People kept stopping to shake my hand and express their admiration. At the door, I returned our opera glasses to the vendor. As Kingsley and I turned to leave, I felt a hand on my arm. To my surprise, it was Houdini's petite assistant who clutched at me. I noticed she had a wedding band on her third finger. She also wore a small silver crucifix on a chain around her neck.

"Please, sir," she said. "Harry would like to thank you."

She led us behind the stage to the dressing rooms that ran along the left side of the building. Houdini occupied a large suite on the ground floor, as befitted the headliner. We found the master magician collapsed in a chair and applying a salve to his raw wrists.

As soon as he saw us, he leaped to his feet and once more grabbed my hand in both of his. He had a firm grip despite the ointment on his hands. "Great to meet you!" he exclaimed. I was startled to see how much shorter he was than my own six feet, four inches. His head came to just my shoulders, yet he had absolutely dominated the stage. His smile suffused the man of mystery with a boyish charm.

He turned to his wife, for so I surmised the woman beside us to be.

"I'm sorry, Harry," she said contritely. "I tried to charm that guy, but I just couldn't get him to come into the wings."

Houdini gave her a little hug. "You did your best," he said. Turning to me, he said proudly, "That's my Bess. She'd have fixed him good. Isn't she something?"

Naturally, I assented, but he must have read puzzlement on my face, for he looked back at his wife and said, "Show him how we handle weisenheimers."

Bess Houdini blushed, looking even more like a little girl.

"Go on," Houdini insisted, "show him."

Shamefacedly, she reached around behind her and produced something small and dark, about the size of a child's sock. It was a leather-wrapped cosh; I believe the Americans call it a blackjack.

"Only because he kicked my Harry," she said in a small voice. The blackjack disappeared once again into the secret pocket behind her back.

"What'd I tell ya?" Houdini crowed. "Quite a gal, huh?"

"I had no idea life on the stage could be so rough," I said.

Houdini shrugged. "That's showbiz."

I was struck by the difference between his language on stage and off. During a performance he spoke in a cultured, obviously trained voice. Off stage his vocabulary was casual in the extreme and he spoke English with the American nasality I have come to recognize with such affection. I also noted the shifted vowels of some regional accent. Clearly, for the public arena he had worked hard to eradicate all traces of his origins. "Houdini thanks you," he said, and yet again grasped my hand. "Sir Arthur Conan Doyle. You really saved my bacon!" He continued to pump my hand. I began to feel uncomfortable with his effusion.

"That was great. For once, Houdini didn't mind being upstaged." Despite my embarrassment, I couldn't help noting his peculiar habit of referring to himself in the third person. Finally, he released me. "How'd you ever figure out all that stuff about that guy on the stage?"

I shrugged. "In my younger days I toured as a ship's doctor—once on a whaler, once to West Africa. When one has spent time around sailors, these things come naturally."

"Naturally, huh?" He eyed me intently. "Not for everybody."

He finally noticed Kingsley hanging in the doorway. "Is this your boy? Come in, come in, sonny. Did you like the act?"

"Ever so much, sir," Kingsley replied. "We've been to magic shows in Portsmouth, but they were nothing like this."

The magician lifted his head high and tossed it, like a proud racehorse. "Yeah," he agreed enthusiastically, "there's only one Houdini. Wanna see more?"

"Oh, yes." Then Kingsley's eyes shifted to me. "That is, if it's quite convenient."

Houdini threw his head back and laughed uproariously. "You have raised a little gentleman, Sir Arthur."

I smiled down at him. "Please call me Conan Doyle—all my friends do."

"We're going to be friends, then?" he asked.

"I should enjoy that."

"Great—me, too. Now, on with the show."

He must have entertained us for a good half an hour with sleights of hand and carnival tricks. But the highlight from Kingsley's point of view was when the master magician taught him how to eat fire.

"Always hold your head back, like this," he instructed, dipping a lit match into his gaping mouth and retracting it. "See? The flame rises out of your mouth instead of burning it. Breathe out gently, keep the heat moving away from you. Then close your lips hard. That puts out the flame."

Kingsley was thrilled, and under Houdini's instruction soon became proficient.

"Now you gotta let me take you to dinner," Houdini said.

Kingsley's eyes positively glowed at the thought. But much as I hated to, I had to refuse.

"Why?" The man looked heartbroken. "Have I bored you?"

"Not at all," I hastened to assure him. "If anything, it is we who have overstayed our welcome. No, I must get back to my rooms tonight."

"Why is that?"

"Because I have promised several hundred people to resurrect that damned Holmes in time for the Christmas edition of the *Strand*, and I need every second if I am to make their deadline."

Houdini chuckled. "You may hate me, but millions will thank me this December, I bet." He shrugged. "Okay, I'll let you go. But you gotta come back tomorrow evening. We can make a night of it."

"Well . . ." I really did not want to impose. Besides, I'm not the sort who makes friends on the spur of the moment.

Houdini eyed me speculatively. "I'll let you in on something. That sailor—somebody hired him to louse up my act."

Here was a surprising development. Then I recalled that the man had whispered to Houdini just before he kicked his arms out from under him. "What did he say to you on stage?"

"He told me, 'This'll teach you to interfere with Mr. Maximillian Cairo.'" Houdini bristled at the memory.

"Well, well . . . ," I said. These were deep waters indeed. The name Cairo was infamous. It summoned up the image of an explorer, a dabbler in the occult, and a writer of notorious verse.

"A friend of mine," Houdini went on, "has got herself mixed up with Cairo. I promised to help her out. If you got the stomach for it, I can promise you some excitement tomorrow." An idea occurred to him. "Maybe you'll get an idea for that story you gotta write."

I did not like this turn of events. "Consider," I said, "how readily the thug revealed Cairo's involvement. Doesn't it seem as if Cairo might be deliberately baiting you?"

Houdini shrugged. "So what? He'll get more than he bargained for, I bet."

"Are you aware," I asked, "that he has been called the most debauched man in London?"

Houdini shrugged.

"It is considered risky to cross his path," I added.

"I'm not worried," Houdini insisted. "All those fakers spread rumors like that." He craned his neck to look up at me. "Meet me here after my show tomorrow night, if you feel in the mood for an adventure."

Chapter 2
A Strange Errand

The next morning, I breakfasted early with Kingsley. I am afraid I wasn't much company, weighed down as I was by my promise to resurrect Holmes. The previous night, for the first time in my life, the writing had not gone well. Often I dash off a short story in a matter of an hour or less. However, try as I might, the words had refused to come.

I readily guessed what my problem was: I had been distracted by Houdini's mysterious offer from the night before. I knew it was ridiculous to even consider it. I had to return to my wife's sickbed. But even as I finished my kippers and eggs, the hint of danger tantalized me. My last real adventure had been when I had volunteered to run a hospital in South Africa during the Boer War. That had been four years ago. I longed to pit myself once more against an adversary and feel the thrill coursing through my body that reminded me I was still alive.

Nonsense, I told myself. Louise needed me. Much as Houdini's invitation intrigued me, I resolved to put the matter from my mind. Instead, I attempted to concentrate on the new Holmes story as we packed our bags. Inwardly, I groaned at the thought of forcing myself to concoct yet another of those tedious little puzzles that the public had grown so fond of.

Kingsley had been silent a good portion of the morning. As he closed and latched his valise, a furrow divided his brow. Something was troubling him. I abandoned all pretense of working on the Holmes story.

"What is it, Kingsley?" I asked.

"You know, I think Mr. Houdini is a proud man," Kingsley began slowly.

"Doubtless."

"He never would have asked for help on the stage, would he?"

"Perhaps not." What was he getting at?

"Suppose he wants your help again tonight, only he was too proud to ask."

Out of the mouths of babes, I thought. I should have seen it myself. Houdini was a stranger in London. He had no idea how dangerous Cairo could be. Rumors of occult rites, orgies, drug use, and worse swirled around the man. Why, just last year a fellow had died during one of Cairo's rituals. The police had not found enough evidence to prosecute. Still, the affair had never been satisfactorily explained.

With these thoughts whirling through my head, it took a moment to realize that Kingsley was still talking.

"What was that?" I asked.

"Nurse can look after Mother," Kingsley repeated. "Nurse says she's perfectly capable of doing her job and that you're just underfoot."

Could this be true? Was my solicitude actually hampering the care of my beloved invalid? It was only a matter of a day. If Louise's condition worsened, Nurse had strict orders to wire me.

"Mr. Houdini is counting on us," the boy said seriously.

My conscience still pricked at me, but I grew resolved. I would accompany Houdini this evening and return home the following morning. However, that still left me with the problem of what to do with Kingsley. I had not missed the fact that he had said, "counting on us." Whatever Cairo was up to, it could not be suitable for a child. When I told Kingsley as much, he raised a loud protest—quite unlike his usual good nature.

His mother's illness must have been weighing on him even more than it had been on me. After a moment's thought, I had an idea.

"I wonder if you are mature enough."

He turned back, puzzlement in his eyes. "Mature enough for what?"

"If I am staying on here, I shall have to trust you to travel alone."

He began to understand. "All by myself?" His eyes lit up. "On a train?"

I nodded soberly. "I'm just not sure . . ." I let my voice trail off dubiously.

His words tumbled out in a rush. "I'm ever so grown up now. And Michael in my class has been all the way to Leeds by himself to visit his grandmother. And traveling alone on a train would be such a jolly sort of adventure. Please?" Here he paused for breath and stared up anxiously at me. I pretended to consider.

"Very well," I agreed solemnly.

The glow of triumph soon faded from his eyes, however. He cast me a reproachful look. "But it won't be as much of an adventure as yours, will it, Father?"

I took Kingsley to Charing Cross Station, where I booked him a first-class ticket on the next train to Surrey. I left the boy resigned to his fate in a private compartment with a copy of a magazine and a bar of chocolate.

Back at my hotel, I arranged to stay another night and retired to my room with paper and pen to write. For the second time in my life, however, my muse deserted me. I kept seeing the tantalizing smile on Houdini's face as I had left him. Eventually, I gave up and went down to dinner. When I returned to my rooms, a telegram awaited me from Nurse, assuring me that Kingsley had arrived home safely.

By the time I arrived at the Palace, Houdini's show was letting out. I pushed impatiently through the crowd to the dressing rooms and rapped on Houdini's door. When it swung open, I was relieved to see that he wore evening clothes, just as I did. If we were overdressed, at least we would be overdressed together.

"Sir Arth—I mean, Conan Doyle! You came!" For all his enthusiasm, the muscular little man spoke in a low voice. Looking back over his shoulder, he ushered me into the hallway. "Bessie's changing. Let's get going before she sees you."

Closing the door behind him, he explained, "She wanted to come along. I told her it was just another boring séance. I'm not sure she bought it."

So saying, he grabbed my arm and hurried me toward a side exit. "She finds out I'm taking you along as a safeguard, she'll know something's up. And if that guy Cairo is as dangerous as you said, I sure don't want my Bessie mixed up with him."

I heartily concurred. I should not want any wife of mine in a party that included Maximillian Cairo. "So it's a séance we shall be attending?"

Houdini nodded. "We gotta hurry or we'll be late."

We came out upon Oxford Circus and made our way around to Shaftsbury Avenue. Houdini raced to one of the hansom cabs lined up to take advantage of the crowd of theatergoers. As we climbed aboard, he shouted an address to the driver. I recognized it as Cairo's residence. The address had been frequently listed in newspaper accounts of his questionable soirées. It was north of Euston Station—not one of the better parts of the city. Houdini jumped in beside me and we were off.

The horse's hooves clopped over the roadway and we swayed along behind. We rode through Soho, Bloomsbury, and turned east on Euston Road. As we passed a gaslight, Houdini glanced at a pocketwatch in the pale-yellow light. He sighed with apparent satisfaction, and settled himself back into the leather seat. I, however, was not easy in my mind about Cairo. I briefly apprised my new friend of all that I knew about the man.

"He won't fool us," Houdini vowed. "I know that racket inside and out."

"What, are you a medium, too?" I asked.

Houdini chuckled. "Not anymore. I'm not proud to admit it, but I ran a medium act in Kansas when I was a broke kid. It was good money, too. But I couldn't keep doing it."

The laughter vanished from his voice. "Those poor people, so desperate for some word from their loved ones. And me scamming them with my lies. I hated myself," he admitted matter-of-factly. "I swore that even if I starved, I'd never do it again. And I'd never let anyone else do it, either, if I could help it."

He gave a sigh and continued briskly, "Anyway, tonight we're on the other side. We'll get the goods on that faker all right."

I hoped our task would be as simple as my friend expected.

The horse's hoofbeats took on a sharper sound. From the vibration in our cab, I could tell we had left pavement and were now on cobblestones. I leaned forward to peer out the window. We rattled through an older section of the city. The electric illumination of the more fashionable districts gave way to gaslights. Only infrequently did their pale-yellow glow illuminate the narrow streets flanked by shabby storefronts. From one of the dark side streets came a cry of pain or fear. I called for the cabman to stop. Instead, he urged his horse to even greater speed. Leaning forward, I saw our horse's shoes strike sparks off the stones. The jolting grew even worse.

We passed what I at first took to be a heap of rags beside a building. The pile stirred and I realized it was one of those who "carry the banner"—one of the legion of men without shelter for the night. Disgraceful, I thought, for the most prosperous empire the world has ever known to abandon any of its citizens to such a fate.

Houdini shifted in his seat. He was a dim outline beside me. I recalled that we had serious business tonight.

"You called Cairo a faker," I said. "Are you certain?"

Houdini shrugged. "I was when I did it. I've never seen one who wasn't."

"But why take an interest in this particular fellow?"

"He's set his traps for a friend of mine. Her name's Mrs. Pangbourne." Houdini's voice betrayed anger. "He promised to contact her dead husband."

He continued, "She was widowed only last month, so she's ripe for this kind of scam." His voice rose. "That chiseler! Once he gets his hooks into her, he'll stick her for all he can get." He paused to collect himself. After a moment, he went on a little more calmly. "Mr. Pangbourne and I did business together. He was a friend. When she told me what she was up to, I knew she needed protection."

I sank back in my seat. Cairo was an unpredictable fellow who positively reveled in his notoriety. What had I let myself in for this evening? I tried to take comfort from the fact that I wasn't facing him alone.

A year or so ago, curious to see what all the fuss was about, I had purchased a copy of his infamous book of verse, *Moist Folds*. It was nothing but the vilest smut masquerading as poetry. I had burned it, half-read, in the fireplace before the women or children in my household could set eyes on it. God alone knew what such a scoundrel was capable of.

While I mused thus, the cab slowed and pulled up at a block of flats. We were in a desolate section of the city. Few lights shone through the dirty windowpanes on either side of us. I'd not seen a cab pass since we had entered this district. How were we to get home? I certainly did not relish the idea of walking through these slums.

Over Houdini's objections, I insisted upon paying the cabbie myself. While Houdini examined the building, I surreptitiously tore a five-pound note in two. Giving half to the driver, I spoke lowly. "Rap on this door for us at midnight," here I pointed to the building opposite, "for the other half." The man glanced around at the neighborhood. At last his eyes returned to me and he nodded stoically.

The cabman drove off a little hurriedly. I hoped he would keep his word and return for us. Since there was nothing else I could do in that direction, I turned my attention to our surroundings. The building itself had a certain faded Palladian grandeur, with its carved wooden pilasters pretending to support a dark pediment above the portal. Houdini strode to the entrance, grasped the brass knocker, and rapped thrice on the cracked wood of the door.

After a moment, it swung inward. The light from inside revealed an apparition that momentarily took me aback. It was a man dressed all in black. He was tall, and thin almost to the point of emaciation. Light from behind formed a halo around his closely cropped hair. His eyes were dark hollows above sharp cheekbones. Moisture glistened on his thin lips. His eyes narrowed at the sight of us.

"We're guests of Mrs. Pangbourne," Houdini said. The man looked us up and down coldly. His continued silence made me uncomfortable. Without warning, he slammed the door shut in our faces. We stood alone on the stoop and stared in amazement.

Houdini tried the knob, but the door had locked as it shut.

"We don't appear to be expected," I remarked. Were we going to have to walk through these neighborhoods in search of a cab after all?

Houdini did not answer. Instead, he grasped the knocker and beat out a tattoo upon its strike plate. When this elicited no response, he turned to me. His face was flushed with anger. "You see?" he vociferated. "He's afraid to face Houdini."

Before I could reply, the door swung open. Once more our sepulchral greeter stood before us. "He says you may enter," the man intoned as he stepped aside. He might have been an undertaker admitting the bereaved.

I passed him closely enough to notice that his pupils were narrowed to the pinpoints of a drug addict. What sort of a situation had my companion let us in for?

We were ushered into a handsome library with a massive oak writing desk and floor-to-ceiling bookshelves that positively creaked with volumes. An Oriental carpet covered the stones of the floor. The rug's reds and purples and blues twined together to form a pattern of great intricacy. These sumptuous furnishings were in sharp contrast to the decaying neighborhood outside.

"He will be with you shortly," the cadaverous one murmured as he departed.

I turned to Houdini. "Apparently, your friend neglected to tell Cairo we were coming."

Houdini merely shrugged. "What's it matter, as long as we got in?"

I confess, I was not at ease. We were intruding upon a private party. Our host was a man reputed to be capable of anything.

At this point, however, we had to see it through. To pass the time, I examined the books that surrounded us. Houdini followed suit. I recognized French, German, and Latin titles. Few were familiar to me—many were ancient. They appeared to be various treatises on magic and witchcraft. One in English I picked up at random was *The Sacred Book of Abramelin the Mage.*

"My God," Houdini called softly from across the room. He brought over a roughly bound pamphlet, the fragile pages of which gleamed in the light from the gas sconces on the wall. "This is a copy of the *SeferYetzirah* in the original, unpointed Hebrew script. If he's studied the Cabala, he's more dangerous than I thought."

"Gentlemen, your interest flatters me."

Houdini and I spun around to face the source of the silky voice that sounded behind us.

Chapter 3
A Mixed Company

We stood there, each holding a book. A doorway, cunningly disguised by the geometric pattern of the wallpaper, had swung open. In it lounged the man I took to be our host.

He wore evening dress, but what struck one immediately about him were his eyes. They were dark brown and positively snapped with energy. When they locked on me, I felt as if I'd been given a jolt of electricity. I could hardly get my breath. Had he heard Houdini's rash words?

Cairo's gaze released me and shifted to Houdini. Feeling slowly returned to my limbs. What manner of man was this?

Cairo looked to be in his early thirties. His features were regular, if not striking. He was dark complected and his frame, though powerful, was beginning to flesh out from self-indulgence. He had a strong chin and a Roman nose. His hair was coffee brown and receded at the temples.

If his gaze had any effect on Houdini, my companion gave no sign. He put down the book, strode forthrightly up to him, and held out his hand. "I am Houdini," he announced. "And this is my friend, Sir Arthur Conan Doyle. We're here for the séance," he added.

The man studied us a moment. "I am doubly honored by your presence. Sincere inquiries are always welcome." His eyes mocked us. "However, I should warn you, this could be a very dangerous evening for you both."

"Dangerous how?" Houdini demanded.

"The forces I call on are quite powerful," he explained. "Anguish, madness, even suicide await those who trifle with them."

"We'll risk it," Houdini said curtly.

Cairo's threats merely hardened my resolve to see the evening through. Still, I could not put out of my mind the chill I felt when our eyes had met. Open antagonism would simply put him on his guard. So I attempted to change topics. "We were admiring your library," I said.

Cairo turned to me, amusement on his face. "Yes," he agreed. "I fancy that on occult matters it is the best in the world. More comprehensive than the Vatican's. Though I must confess, their collection of pornography puts mine to shame."

Here I felt obliged to lead the conversation to a higher plane. "Be that as it may, we are most grateful to you for your hospitality this evening."

Houdini gazed unblinkingly at our host. "Yeah, I can't wait to see you perform."

"Perform?" Cairo's eyes widened in mock surprise. "Mr. Houdini, you perform; I serve humanity."

Houdini drew himself up to his full height and threw out his chest, like a bantam rooster fluffing out its plumage. "Oh, yeah? I bet your service pays the bills as well as my act does."

Mr. Cairo smiled indulgently. "Since you are a fraud yourself, you find it impossible to believe that others are sincere."

"A fraud?" Houdini flushed a deep red. "At least I don't hire guys to beat up on the competition." He advanced on Cairo. It looked as if he intended violence.

I hastily interposed myself between them. "Gentlemen," I said sternly, "remember why we are here. We came to observe Mr. Cairo's phenomena."

I turned to Cairo. "And you would do well to avoid threats. After all, you did send a minion to tempt us into judging your claims."

Cairo shrugged. "I make no claims. In fact, I deplore vulgar notoriety." His eyes widened in mock innocence. "Unfortunately, I find myself besieged by admirers." He waved one hand languidly. "What is one to do?"

By now Houdini had hold of himself. "You're right, Conan Doyle." Turning to our host, he said stiffly, "I give you the benefit of the doubt until I see your act—I mean, until after the session."

Cairo inclined his head. "As you say." His gaze slipped over to me. "It is always a mistake to theorize in advance of the facts." His voice was mocking as he quoted my own creation back to me. "In any case, you have been warned."

With that, he disappeared through the door. Houdini charged after him. I followed more thoughtfully. The fellow had obviously been taunting us. Why? Was he merely throwing down the gauntlet? Or had he some deeper purpose?

At the doorway, the scent of eastern spices wafted to my nostrils. The room beyond was large but nearly bare of furniture except for a circular dark oak table in the center with seven chairs squeezed around it. A saucer of smoldering incense sat in its center.

Some half dozen people stood talking in small groups. Tea and sherry were laid out upon a sideboard at the end of the room. Ornate Oriental hangings covered the walls. The light fixtures were of wrought iron in a Moorish design. Gaily colored cushions littered the floor in lieu of more traditional furniture. The room was a riot of purples, oranges, reds, and blues. The whole impression was of an eastern potentate's reception room.

A formidable-looking woman in her sixties detached herself from a pale, rather slight young man. She looked obdurate as she bore down on us. Her long-sleeved dress was black with a banded collar. Cascades of black lace fell over her ample bosom.

"Mr. Houdini," she exclaimed, "I told you there was no need for you to interfere."

"I'm just here to protect you, Mrs. Pangbourne." He spoke in a conciliatory tone.

At this she withdrew a step. "I am perfectly capable of looking after myself," she announced. "And I particularly do not wish any unpleasantness tonight."

"Me either," Houdini insisted.

One glance at Mrs. Pangbourne's hands told me they were unaccustomed to housework. They argued for her staff containing at least a cook and a maid. Add to that the elegant widow's weeds and the conclusion was inescapable. Mr. Pangbourne had probably left her extremely well situated.

I looked up to see her casting a baleful eye upon me. "And have you found it necessary to employ a henchman?" she inquired of Houdini.

"Not at all," he said, and smiled. "Let me introduce a friend of mine. Mrs. Pangbourne, Sir Arthur Conan Doyle."

The woman blinked at me. "*The* Conan Doyle?" she inquired. "The writer?"

"The very same," I admitted.

At this she rushed forward and clasped my hands in an effusion of emotion. "Do forgive me. I am so very glad to make your acquaintance. My poor, dear Edgar never missed one of your adventures. How he would have loved to meet you."

"I'm sure it would have been a pleasure for us both," I said.

I studied her face. It was a kindly countenance with lines of determination around the mouth. But her eyes were rimmed with red and reflected the pain of her recent loss.

Houdini took her arm gently. "Mr. Pangbourne was

with Lloyds of London. He took care of my life insurance." Houdini shook his head sadly. "He was a good man, and I'll miss him."

Mrs. Pangbourne snatched a black-bordered handkerchief from her sleeve and held it to her eyes. When she looked up, hope filled them. "Suppose it is true—that this man can put me in touch with Edgar." Tears welled again. "I would give anything for even one word from him."

"Dear Mrs. Pangbourne." Houdini turned her gently to face him. "Me too. But we can't let our hopes cloud our judgment."

The woman abruptly withdrew her arm from Houdini's grasp. "Mr. Cairo warned me that you would be a skeptic," she said stiffly. "He said doubters can poison the atmosphere and ruin any communication with the Higher Planes."

"I promise," Houdini said seriously, "to keep an open mind. If Cairo's the real thing, I'll be the first to say so."

"Well . . ." The lady appeared somewhat mollified.

A female voice behind us broke in. "Delia, you have monopolized our mysterious strangers long enough. Are they the wet blankets, come to smother our fun?"

I turned around and found myself looking into a pair of startling sea-green eyes.

"Really, Justine, the things you say," Mrs. Pangbourne clucked. "This is Mr. Houdini and Sir Arthur Conan Doyle. Gentlemen, Justine Luce."

Justine was a most attractive woman in what I judged to be her late twenties. A glorious mass of honey-blond hair lay piled atop her head. Her full lips had a sensual quality and curved upward in natural good humor. She wore a mauve suit. A touch of burgundy braiding on the short jacket and swirling skirt saved them from severity. Her blouse was silk, but not encumbered with the lace waterfalls affected by the more flamboyant members of her sex. The effect was both businesslike and feminine. She shook Houdini's hand in a forthright manner.

My companion examined her with frank appreciation

in his eyes. "I promise, we don't want to ruin anything," he said. "We simply want to find out the truth."

"Oh, truth!" she groaned. "The truth is inevitably dull—sums and balance sheets. What I've come for tonight is escape." After a moment's thought, she added, "And hope."

"Hope of what?" I inquired.

"That the next life will be better than this one." She looked quite sincere.

I must admit this young woman intrigued me. Her last, sad comment was at variance with her air of spirited independence. And while she carried herself with confidence, she exhibited none of the excesses of dress or bearing that often characterize young ladies of means. Not for her were the eighteen-button gloves reaching to the shoulder, nor the silly affectation of a fluttering Oriental fan.

Her personality appeared vivacious and outgoing, signifying someone at ease in the highest circles, yet her dress exuded simplicity and common sense. The two did not seem to go together. Had circumstances forced her to economize?

She turned and extended her hand to me. Her grip was firm. "Pleased to make your acquaintance, Mrs. Luce," I said.

"Miss Luce," she corrected me. "I have yet to subject myself to the serfdom of marriage."

I was taken aback. "Surely," I said, "there is no more noble occupation than the regulation of a family life."

"Doing the washing until your knuckles bleed? Getting dinner for a lout who never speaks except to complain? One is merely an unpaid servant. And beaten if one proves unsatisfactory."

"I agree the law owes protection to your sex," I said, showing my progressive side.

She leaned forward and looked frankly into my eyes. "Would you be content to take such treatment and wait for a rescue?"

For once I was at a loss for words.

As I struggled with my conflicting emotions, Miss Luce said simply, "What we want from the law is the power to help ourselves—to make our own way."

At last I found my tongue. "But surely not at the cost of forsaking your rightful sphere."

"What of you?" She tilted her head to one side and eyed me quizzically. "What is your rightful sphere?"

I was unprepared for such a question. "Well, it's—" I thought of my study, the cricket field where we practiced, my publisher's office. What could I say that would encompass my entire life?

When I did not speak, Miss Luce suggested, "Isn't your rightful sphere whatever you have the courage and resourcefulness to make it?"

"I suppose that sums it up," I admitted. Clearly, a keen mind was at work behind those marvelous eyes.

"Do I deserve less?"

Again, she had left me with no answer. I threw up my hands. "I yield," I said, "and flee the field in complete disorder."

"Justine," Mrs. Pangbourne interrupted sharply. "Do not tease Sir Arthur."

"It's all right, Delia," she said. "I imagine Sir Arthur dismisses all my opinions as the fabrications of youth and inexperience."

"No," I protested, "truly I do not. Perhaps a trifle—"

She raised a hand to forestall my explanations. "Regardless of our differences, I remain a staunch admirer of yours. I am certain you will still be read avidly when your contemporaries are completely forgotten. It truly was a pleasure to meet you."

She flashed me a dazzling smile, nodded to Houdini, and floated gracefully across the room.

I turned to my companion. "There," Houdini announced, "goes one heck of a gal."

I nodded. At last I had met one of the "new women" I had read so much about lately. They were supposed to be the very vanguard of the modern age. With bemused interest, I watched Miss Luce pour herself a glass of sherry from the sideboard.

Her opinions ran counter to common sense and even basic biology. Oddly enough, however, I found my interest piqued. Such a woman would truly be a helpmeet—eager to shoulder her share of the burdens of life. And also her share of the decision making, I realized ruefully.

I chuckled at the thought of the arguments that would inevitably ensue from such an arrangement. No, I preferred a tranquil household, where no one challenged the natural order of things. Still, I was intrigued. From whence came her extreme views? I strongly suspected that some man had once behaved abominably to her.

Miss Luce had drifted over to an elderly gentleman with receding white hair. I recognized him as Sir William Bowers, the distinguished chemist. His bushy brows lowered over deep-set eyes. Over the sixty years of his life, a frown of concentration under his mustache had become habitual. I was pleased that we should have the benefit of his long experience as a scientific observer.

Houdini spoke in my ear. "I'm gonna check up on the others. See if Cairo's got a shill here." He strode across the room to join Justine and Sir William.

The last of the group, a slim wisp of a young man, stood alone. He held a glass of wine in one hand. There was something vaguely familiar about him. I strolled over to introduce myself.

He had small, pale features under softly curling brown hair. "Name's Mackleston," he said as I took his hand. His grip surprised me. It was firmer than I expected.

"How did you meet Maximillian Cairo?" I asked after I had introduced myself.

"M'father mentioned him at the breakfast table," he said cheerfully. "Disapproved of him pretty strongly. Seemed like it might be fun to meet the fellow." He laughed nervously. "I met him through Gaylord over there." He indicated with a nod the cadaverous man who had admitted us. "Actually, Cairo and I hit it off right away. He's a queer chap, but quite entertaining."

"Who is your father?" I inquired.

"Lord Vollmer."

I recognized the name. Vollmer ran a department in the Foreign Office. King Edward was frequently exasperated with his lack of tact. His Majesty had once confided to me that it had taken nearly a month to soothe the German ambassador after one of Vollmer's gaffes. Growing up under the thumb of such an arrogant man would not be pleasant.

"And what induced you to come here tonight?" I asked.

"Cairo," he said simply. "I want to study with him. This seemed a good place to begin."

"Study what?"

"Metaphysics." The man shrugged. "So many of these fellows claim to have heaps of occult knowledge. But is it the real thing? That's what I want to know. With him," he looked over at Cairo, "I think it might be."

I felt some unease at anyone deliberately placing himself under Cairo's influence.

My attention was drawn to the far end of the room where Cairo huddled with Gaylord. Our host appeared to be giving instructions, for the other man listened intently. Both glanced frequently toward our party, particularly at Houdini and me.

At last the man in black nodded and turned to leave. Cairo's hand brushed his arm and lingered there for just the briefest moment. Gaylord paused, and a faint smile passed across his face before he continued on his way. It was obvious that an unhealthy attachment existed between them.

Gaylord seated himself at the table while Cairo made his way to the center of the room. For the first time, I noticed that he walked with a slight limp. He appeared to favor his right leg. Was this a congenital defect or a recent injury? I wondered. And did it somehow relate to the scene we were about to witness?

Cairo stood where he was until every eye was on him. Only then did he speak. His gaze singled out Mackleston. "You wish to learn from me. Here is your opportunity, if your soul can stand the revelations."

Mackleston leaned forward, captivated. Cairo turned to Mrs. Pangbourne. "You desire to contact the Higher Planes. Well, so you shall, but only if you can cast aside your preconceptions."

Uncertainty filled the good lady's face. She glanced from one of us to the other, seeking a clue as to how to respond.

To Miss Luce, Cairo's voice grew silky, his smile tempting. "You are bored with the workaday world. I shall open a new world to you—one of bizarre delights and nameless dreads."

Miss Luce vouchsafed him a cool smile, but her eyes sparkled at the challenge.

"Sir William," Cairo continued, "you wish solace. Can an erstwhile pain be assuaged?"

Sir William stared at the floor, his expression unreadable.

At last he turned to me. I confess I met his eyes with some consternation. The deepest secrets of our souls seemed open to him. "And you, Conan Doyle, why are you here tonight?" His smile mocked me. Before I could answer, he said simply, "Let us begin."

He had completely ignored Houdini in his little speech. I looked to my companion. He remained silent, but his eyes glittered with suppressed emotion.

"I must ask you all to remove any articles of jewelry on your persons," Cairo announced solemnly. "The vibrations of precious metals can interrupt the flow of energy. Please deposit them with Mr. Gaylord."

Gaylord passed among us with a large black lacquer box painted in intricate Oriental designs. It was lined with purple satin, and he held it open to me. The only jewelry I wore was my gold wedding band, but I hesitated to trust it to the keeping of Cairo or his confederate. After all, it was my sole remembrance of Louise. And I was not the only one with reservations. Others traded uneasy glances.

Cairo noted our reluctance, as well. His voice rang out briskly. "The prerequisite to success is faith. If yours does not extend even this far, there is no point in proceeding."

"Oh, you all are being absurd!" It was Mrs. Pangbourne who spoke. She pulled a large ruby ring off her left hand. "I, for one, trust Mr. Cairo implicitly," she announced as she held the gem out to Mr. Gaylord. Cairo bowed slightly, an ironic smile on his face. Mr. Gaylord drifted over to her and she dropped the jewel into his box. Sheepishly, the rest of us followed suit.

As he held out the small, ornate casket to me, I had noted something curious. Around his fingernails lay thin crusts of color. The smell of turpentine lingered faintly about his hands. This implied something extremely interesting. His dramatic appearance supported my suspicions. I dropped my ring into the box and pondered his retreating figure. What use might Cairo make of such a person?

I edged across the room to Houdini. He leaned toward me. I lowered my head and he spoke lowly in my ear.

"What do you think about him?" He indicated Gaylord with a slight nod.

"I believe Mr. Gaylord is a painter."

Houdini maintained an impassive face. "That could be important," he murmured.

I was at a loss to understand how, but I continued, "Unless I miss my guess, he has done some work in oils as recently as this afternoon."

My companion nodded imperceptibly. He replied quietly out of the side of his mouth, "Good. This explains a lot. Did you notice Cairo's limp?"

"Indeed I did," I assented quietly.

"Those two things tell me all I need to know."

I was about to inquire just what it was they told him, but our host's thrusting himself into our midst curtailed further conversation. "My protégé Mr. Gaylord," Cairo announced, "will now, at great personal risk to himself, call upon the spirits of the dead."

There was consternation among the participants and much low discussion. Finally, Mrs. Pangbourne spoke hesitantly. "But, Mr. Cairo, I thought you were to lead the session." Disappointment filled her voice.

Houdini appeared at my elbow. His eyes were bright and he trembled like a setter on a leash. He lifted his head, and I bent down to listen. "You see?" he breathed. "It begins. He fears me and so he sends a scapegoat to the slaughter."

Cairo raised his hands for silence. "Never fear, Mrs. Pangbourne. I shall not abandon you. But the work of a medium, while by no means easy, is necessarily that of a passive receptacle." Here my eyes flicked to Gaylord. I noted with distaste that he smiled as if at some private joke. Mr. Cairo continued, "He must surrender his will to those subtle vibrations that ordinary people demean with the term 'ghosts.' I assure you, I have personally initiated Mr. Gaylord into these mysteries."

Houdini nudged me. "This guy has been around," he said lowly. "See how he distracts us." The magician inclined his head toward Mr. Gaylord. "Notice his partner."

I looked from Cairo over to Gaylord.

"He's just sitting at the table," I whispered.

Houdini nodded. "Exactly," he chortled softly. "This is all penny-ante. Hardly worthy of Houdini's presence."

Cairo continued. "My own researches into the occult are far more advanced. There are distinct dangers, ladies and gentlemen. I shall serve you far better by remaining ready to counter any malign influences that threaten our spirit-circle."

He nodded to a servant, who dimmed the lights. As we began to take our places around the table, Cairo interrupted us.

"Houdini," he said, "I am sure you wish the closest possible view of Mr. Gaylord. You shall sit upon his right hand; Conan Doyle, please sit upon his left."

Houdini appeared surprised.

I spoke softly. "Do not be fooled. Cairo is still arranging us for his convenience. I have observed that Mr. Gaylord is left-handed."

Houdini shrugged. "It doesn't matter." His face relaxed into a knowing smile. "I could expose him here and now, if I wanted."

"How can you unmask his deception without seeing it first?"

Houdini didn't answer. All he would say was "When Cairo starts, watch his feet."

Chapter 4
Spirits of the Dead

When everyone was seated at the table, Cairo dimmed the lights until all was in darkness except for a small, flickering lamp suspended low over the group. The oil in the lamp must have been perfumed, for a faint smell of cloves drifted up from the wick. Cairo squeezed himself in between Mrs. Pangbourne and Sir William. That put him directly across from Mr. Gaylord. Our hands glowed palely in the faint circle of yellow light. The walls around us had disappeared. I had the eerie feeling that our little circle huddled against a vast emptiness at our backs. A prickle of uneasiness crawled down my spine. Cairo spoke quietly.

"Please grasp the hand of the person on either side of you."

We did as instructed. I took Mr. Gaylord's hand in my right, Miss Luce's in my left.

"Wait a minute." I recognized Houdini's voice, though in the dim light I could no longer see his face. "I gotta know that everybody really is holding hands. If you are, say so—starting with Conan Doyle."

"I have a hand in each of mine," I asserted.

Everyone around the table followed suit. I counted six different voices.

"Would Mr. Houdini care to take any other precautions?" Cairo's voice sounded acidly from across the table.

My companion was silent. Evidently, he was considering. I remembered his adjuration of earlier and spoke up. "If you have no objection, Houdini and I would like to cover each of Mr. Gaylord's feet with one of our own."

"Well, really!" Mrs. Pangbourne expostulated. "You might think they were common criminals."

"Not common," Houdini observed sardonically. "What do you say, Cairo?"

A world-weary sigh emanated from across the table. "Please inform me when you have things arranged to your satisfaction."

We shuffled around until we each had one of Mr. Gaylord's shoes pinned between one of our feet and the floor. Just to be sure, I shifted my foot until I felt his leg to be certain that he had not presented me with an empty shoe. Satisfied, I maneuvered my heel back to the floor. There I had the leverage to maintain a good grip.

I felt a slight pressure on my right hand. I sensed movement beside me. "That was worthy of Holmes." Miss Luce's rich alto voice caressed my ear. Her lips briefly brushed my lobe and then withdrew. These words, softly spoken in the dark, produced a strange feeling of intimacy. It took effort of will to recall myself to the task at hand.

Cairo began the session by leading us in a series of slow, deep breaths. "To fuel the body for the efforts to come," he explained. He adjured us to empty our minds of all thought, to free ourselves to receive impressions. I tried to comply. After all, we owed the man a fair chance.

Cairo began to speak. His voice was surprisingly melodious as he described a scene to us. Though I cannot recall his words, the images he conjured in my mind remain indelible. He spoke of a land of perpetual twilight, of peaceful mists and gentle valleys. He spoke of subdued colors and deep calm where millions of souls found respite from the clamor and hurts of the waking world. A great tranquillity seeped through me. For the first time in many months, the thought of Louise did not bring me pain. If only his words were true, she would soon be at peace.

What we call death, Cairo gently insisted, is not the end but merely a transformation to a more abstract form of existence. In fact, these different levels are part of our daily lives. Light itself, he pointed out, is merely a delicate resonance that our eyes are tuned to perceive. Mr. Marconi's radio waves transmit messages invisibly through the air from distant ships to the shore.

So also could vibrations from this other plane reach us. But these emanations are very subtle. They need to be enhanced before all but the most sensitive can sense them. Our circle, focusing all its energy, all its belief and hope, would amplify the emanations to make the messages audible.

"When a dear one has passed over," Cairo said, "it can take a while for him to fully succumb to the healing air of his new home. Sometimes he yearns to contact those recently left. Grieving friends and relatives naturally desire the same. These mutual longings can work wonders. If their efforts are sincere, they can actually form a bridge between the two worlds."

Cairo's voice grew forceful. "But concentration is necessary. If any one of you gives less than his most heartfelt effort, the exertions of the others will be futile. All must focus your energies that we may be granted a glimpse of that far land."

He stopped speaking, and the silence was complete. I did not want to be the cause of failure. On the other hand, I couldn't escape the suspicion that all this was merely an elaborate stage set. Nevertheless, for the sake of the experiment I tried to fix all my thoughts on a silent call to those great powers that guide our destinies. Several minutes passed. Beads of sweat popped out on my forehead from the effort of concentrating.

At last, Cairo spoke again. "I sense a great thing has happened here tonight. You have merged your separate identities into one willing receptacle."

Despite my reservations, I did feel a certain kinship with the others in the circle, as though we had formed a party of explorers to venture into an unknown land.

Cairo's voice swelled in exaltation. "We present ourselves in sincere and humble reception. Are there spirits among us?"

I waited tensely in the silence that followed. Had we achieved the necessary union? Were we simply being manipulated? No one breathed.

Without warning, a loud rap broke the silence. I jumped and heard several gasps around me. I gathered my wits. This was no time to succumb to fear. Once more a sharp crack sounded. I realized it came from the table. Another and another swiftly followed until the table rang with the pounding. I felt the very wood vibrate through my arms. Then the raps diminished until there was silence.

"Oh, my goodness!" I heard Mrs. Pangbourne exclaim. Someone shushed her. We sat there nervously, eyes straining into the darkness, ears alert for the slightest noise. Next an extraordinary thing happened. The table tipped toward me and settled back down. It rocked from side to side, more and more violently. Finally, it left the floor in a frenzy and launched straight up into the air.

Frightened cries broke from around me. Miss Luce clutched at my hand. I gave her a small, reassuring squeeze and felt her grip tighten even more. I had to strain to keep hold of Miss Luce's and Mr. Gaylord's hands as the table rose above head height. Somehow I retained the presence of mind to note that I still had Mr. Gaylord's foot clamped between my shoe and the floor. The table hung suspended above our heads a moment, quivering slightly. Then it fell to the floor with a crash. Shouts and screams peppered the air around me. Beside me Miss Luce giggled.

From overhead came the sound of a sigh. It repeated,

louder this time. Several different voices joined in until low, unearthly moans filled the air around us.

A soft blow at the back of my head made me jump. A puff of air fanned my cheek. I heard quiet thuds and exclamations as others around the table were struck.

"What in the world?" Sir William's outraged voice sounded.

All at once I understood. "No cause for alarm," I called. "It's just the cushions. They're being flung about."

As I spoke, all movement stopped. In a moment Cairo's voice, deep and resonant, rolled over us. "Are any spirits present?"

The chorus around us grew still. A faint voice drifted from the direction of Mr. Gaylord. "Delia," it quavered. "Delia, are you there?"

I confess that, coming from beside me as it did, the voice lifted the hairs on the back of my neck. Mr. Gaylord's hand was slack in mine. Near me, someone's teeth chattered. Mrs. Pangbourne's timid voice rose. "Edgar, is that you?"

The voice grew stronger. "Delia, I have reached you at last. I have tried for so long."

"Oh, Edgar, Edgar, I am here."

"Delia, I miss you."

The poor woman's voice broke with emotion. "I miss you, too, my dear, dear husband."

"Remember me to Ann and Stephen."

"Oh, I shall. Indeed, I shall. They'll be so pleased to hear from you."

"And tell young Edgar not to worry. Our quarrel was so foolish. His wife is a fine woman. I should have welcomed her into the family."

"He will be so relieved. But, Edgar, are you all right? What can I do for you?"

Mrs. Pangbourne was absolutely convinced she spoke to her dead husband. My mind filled with wonder. Had we truly crossed that Great Void? The ghost's voice broke into my thoughts.

"Do not mourn. It is pleasant here. All is peace and kindness. You shall see when you join me."

"Then we shall be together again?"

"Yes, for love never dies."

"How long? How long before we see one another?"

"Time has no meaning here. A century is as the blink of an eye. But we will be together soon and for all eternity."

"I don't know if I can wait. I want to be with you now."

"Now is not your time," the ghost rebuked her. "You have important work to perform on your side of the veil. With what you have learned tonight, you must comfort the bereaved. Let people know that death is nothing to fear."

"Oh, I will, Edgar, I swear it."

"That is good." The voice was softer now. "My time grows short. But there is one last thing I must tell you."

"What is it?"

"Our property in Brighton. It will be devalued within six months. Now is the time to sell. Donate the money to a worthy cause."

"But how shall I choose?" Panic filled her voice. "You always managed these affairs."

"I am not allowed to interfere in such matters. You will make the right decision."

"I'm afraid I just don't know . . ." Her voice trailed off.

I shifted in my seat. I was torn. There was something so appealing about this view of death that I almost hoped Cairo wasn't a charlatan. On the other hand, Houdini's suspicions of the man's motives appeared all too accurate. But how had he duped us? Houdini and I had Mr. Gaylord effectively bound hand and foot between us. The people on either side of him immobilized Cairo's hands. How had pillows been tossed? From whence came the sighs we had heard? I thought of Houdini, only one person away from me. Why had he remained silent throughout the proceedings? For all his bravado, was he, too, baffled?

Mrs. Pangbourne had subsided into fretful mumbling.

All at once, her voice came back clearly. "I have it!" she announced to the ghost. "Mr. Cairo. I shall bestow the money on Mr. Cairo's institute."

"As you will." The voice became faint. "I grow weak, but I must take back with me one last glimpse of you. Do not move, my dear. I shall materialize for you."

A pale form floated very slowly into the light. It was strangely distorted, yet recognizable as the face of a man. The features were blurred, as if perceived from a great distance. The apparition spoke. "Yes, I see you. Am I visible to you?"

"Oh, Edgar." The woman's voice was racked with sobs. "Yes, I see you. Come back. Come back to me, Edgar."

The form began to withdraw and the voice was barely audible.

"That I may not do. But have faith, and I shall visit you again. Do not grieve for me. We are close—closer than your eyelid to your eye."

The materialization vanished, but the voice grew strong again, sending a thrill down my spine. "I am sending you my love. Do you feel it? Do you feel the warmth of my affection washing over you?"

"Oh, yes. I feel it. I feel your love."

"I must go . . . I must go . . . I must go . . ." The voice faded out.

On my left I heard drawn a long, shuddering breath and Gaylord pitched forward, apparently unconscious, into the tiny pool of light in the center of the table.

Chapter 5
Cairo Plays His Trump

The lights came up to reveal Cairo already bending over his friend. "I told you these efforts were dangerous," he hissed. I helped him drag Gaylord from the table and over to a line of cushions that had not been disturbed. We knelt over him.

Gaylord was pale; his breathing was shallow and rapid. Everyone crowded around.

"Give him air, please," I insisted, as I loosened his collar and cuffs. I was unsure whether his indisposition was physical, mental, or spiritual, but I did what I could. First I felt for his pulse. To my surprise, it was strong and regular.

I examined him closely. His muscles held a tension one would not expect from a swooning body. Yet it was not the rigidity associated with a seizure. I opened an eyelid. The pupil responded normally to light. I could have sworn it focused on me a moment before it rolled up in his head.

"I'm sure he'll be all right," I said dryly to Cairo.

Obviously, Gaylord was feigning. Were the phenomena we had witnessed a sham, as well? I looked to Houdini, hoping he had an explanation.

To my surprise, the magician had remained where he was and tilted his chair back on two legs. In that precarious position, he lounged with his feet upon the table. All the while he gazed at the ceiling, a peaceful smile on his features.

Slowly, all eyes in the room turned toward him. When he had our complete attention, he said, "Penny-ante."

He continued to stare serenely upward. Every person in the room stood frozen in surprise. Cairo's countenance flushed with anger. He rose slowly, like a cobra rearing to strike. "You miserable little mountebank. How dare you presume to judge me?"

Houdini pushed off the table with his feet. Though the chair clattered over backward, the magician somehow contrived to land on his feet. He rubbed his hands together. Smiling broadly, as though Cairo had not even spoken, Houdini inquired, "Ready to start?"

"Start what?" It was Sir William who spoke. "Do you claim to explain these mysteries?"

A smile curled Houdini's lip. "No mystery here—just a few tricks."

"This is intolerable," Cairo spat. He advanced on Houdini. "You invade my home without invitation, you insult me at every opportunity, and finally you slander me in front of half a dozen witnesses."

I did not like the look in his eye, so I stepped up behind my friend. When Cairo saw me looming over Houdini, he stopped short. I gazed about us. Mrs. Pangbourne's face was a mask of distress. Miss Luce, on the other hand, appeared amused. Sir William stood, arms folded above his ample paunch, disapproval clearly stamped on his face. The slim young man knelt to examine the underside of the table.

Houdini stared up coolly into Cairo's face. "Mrs. Pangbourne invited me," he reminded Cairo. "And since when is telling the truth called slander?"

Cairo stood only inches from the magician. "You will

leave my home immediately! All of you. And you will never be invited back."

"Oh, Mr. Cairo," Mrs. Pangbourne wailed, "you mustn't say so." She turned on Houdini and threw her hands in the air. "How could you!" she exclaimed. "Now Edgar is lost to me a second time."

Houdini ignored her outburst. "I'll go, if that's what you really want," he said agreeably to Cairo.

I had to lean close to hear Houdini's next words, for he dropped his voice to a murmur. "But I warn you, Cairo, if I leave now, I add a special section to my stage act—how the great Cairo hoaxes the gullible. I'll expose all your tricks. After London, I go on to France, Germany, and Russia. You'll be the laughingstock of Europe."

Cairo trembled silently. His eyes glittered with hatred. Suddenly, I remembered his assistant. I turned to make sure Gaylord was not sneaking up on us. I needn't have worried. His long form reclined on the cushions across the room as he watched our little tête-à-tête impassively. He had certainly made a quick and thorough recovery.

"My friend," Houdini gestured with his hand, "we both work the crowd for what we can get. You got a right to charge a reasonable fee for your act. But I won't let you bankrupt anyone, or fill that poor woman's head with false hopes."

"Who says they're false?" Cairo snapped.

"Save it for the act," Houdini advised. "One more thing. You ever send a goon to rough me up again, and I'll put you out of business."

Cairo was not abashed. In fact, a tiny smile flickered about his mouth.

"If you're smart," Houdini continued, "you'll wait until the excitement from tonight dies down before you try again. And next time, don't be so greedy."

Cairo ignored Houdini and turned to face the rest of the room. Curiosity was writ large on every face. For the crowd, Cairo dismissed Houdini with a flip of his hand.

"Further talk is useless." He strode away. "None are so blind as those who will not see."

He threw himself on the cushions next to Mr. Gaylord and the two soon lost themselves in a whispered conversation. What were they planning?

The slim young man rose from his study of the table. "Everything's aboveboard here," he ventured.

Houdini ignored him and strode briskly to the table. "Okay, let's get this over with."

Sir William stepped forward. "I say, Houdini," he began. "Can you really prove Mr. Cairo is a fraud?"

Miss Luce stared curiously at the magician. At her elbow, Mrs. Pangbourne looked fearful.

"Sure thing," Houdini said. "Everybody, go back to where you were and hold hands." He seated himself in Cairo's place.

"But what about Mr. Gaylord?" Mrs. Pangbourne protested.

"Gaylord has nothing to do with the trick."

I noted with some amusement that Mr. Gaylord's look of unearthly menace dissolved into a pout. He stood up and stomped over to the sideboard.

Sir William and Mrs. Pangbourne took their places on either side of Houdini. Miss Luce and I returned to our chairs across from them. When everyone had taken his seat, Houdini instructed us all to clasp hands. "Now," he said when we had complied, "let's see what we got here without all the atmosphere and two-bit patter." He beamed a smile at each of us in turn. Suddenly, a sharp rap shook the table. Another followed, and yet another. Unquestionably, he was re-creating the first manifestations we had experienced. A strange look came over Sir William's face. He bent down. When he straightened up again, his features were suffused with anger. "You're just kicking the tabletop," he accused Houdini.

His statement was met with a veritable tattoo of poundings. In the silence that followed, Houdini nodded. "You got it, Sir William. Since you all focused on Mr. Gaylord, the real crook got away with it."

Then the table tipped and righted itself. "You see," Houdini continued, "by pushing my foot against the edge, I can make it tip. Now, for this next effect, you all have to close your eyes. Don't open them until I tell you."

I suddenly realized that Mr. Gaylord had disappeared. What was he about? A hasty glance around assured me that Cairo still lounged in the corner of the room. He appeared deep in thought. I caught Houdini's eye. His gaze flicked over to Cairo and back to my face. He gave a little shrug and went on.

"All except Conan Doyle, that is. I want a witness. 'Cause when I explain to you how simple it was, you won't believe me."

I nodded. Not only did Houdini want a witness, he also wanted someone alert in case Cairo tried to interfere.

Accordingly, everyone but I clenched their eyes shut and waited. Houdini gave me a wink and leaned back slightly in his chair. Slowly, the table began to rise. Our hands rose with it. I bent down and saw that underneath the table Houdini had both legs stretched out and was lifting it with his feet. He got it almost up to head height and held it there. But the effort was noticeable, for his legs trembled with the strain—just as the table had during the séance. Houdini dropped his legs and the table fell with a crash. Though they were prepared for it, the noise still wrung exclamations from our party. At the moment of impact, Houdini crossed his hands and slipped free from Mrs. Pangbourne and Sir William. Unnerved by the jolt, they immediately grabbed at each other's hands. Houdini silently stood and backed away from the table. He leaned forward between them.

"Do you all have hold of the person next to you?" Everyone assented. He grinned.

Houdini began to walk rapidly around the table, uttering sighs and moans. Occasionally, he would stop and lean between two people so that the sound seemed to come from the very middle of us. Silently, he walked over to the wall and grabbed an armload of cushions. Continuing his perambulation around the table, he tossed the pillows into the air so that they landed gently against the participants. The poor people once again flinched and gasped as they were struck. All, that is, except Miss Luce, whom I caught sneaking a peek. For my part, I felt embarrassed at how gullible I had been.

"Conan Doyle," Sir William called out. "Are these acts comprehensible to you?"

A broad smile stretched across Miss Luce's face. I could scarcely keep the rueful laughter out of my own voice. "Perfectly," I assured him. "There are no spirits here."

As I spoke, I glanced at Cairo. He sat against the wall with his knees drawn up. His face wore an expression of boredom, but his eyes never left Houdini.

"My dear." Houdini's voice creaked with apparent age. "Delia, are you there?"

Mrs. Pangbourne gave a start. "Edgar, you did come back."

"No, my dear, I am afraid"—here Houdini's voice resumed its normal timbre—"that I am just a hoax. You can all open your eyes," he announced.

When they did, Sir William and Mrs. Pangbourne were startled to discover they held each other's hands. Houdini patiently explained each of the effects. "And so," he concluded, "he had us remove our jewelry to give no clue whose hand each of us really held."

"Oh, dear . . ." Mrs. Pangbourne looked distressed.

At Houdini's mention of our jewelry, I glanced at the side table and got an unpleasant surprise. The box that held our rings and so on had vanished. Had that been Cairo's whispered instructions to Gaylord—to make off with our valuables? I resisted the impulse to protest. Better wait, I thought, and be sure what he's up to. Apparently, no one else had noticed yet.

"Brilliant," I congratulated Houdini. "And neither Miss

Luce nor Mrs. Pangbourne has nails long enough to give away the game."

Sir William stepped forward, a sheepish look on his face. "I say, Houdini. How is it you saw through a fraud that I, a trained scientist and observer, failed to detect?"

"Ah, Sir William," Houdini replied gently, "those molecules you watch, they don't cheat. To catch a charlatan, you need a master deceiver." And with that, he bowed.

Sir William smiled ruefully and shook his head. Drawing a cigar out of his pocket, he proceeded to cut and light it. Clouds of blue smoke issued from his mouth.

Mackleston lounged over and stood before us. "Much obliged," he said. "Almost was taken in m'self."

From across the room came the sound of slow clapping. We all turned to see Cairo applauding languidly. His brows arched.

"Congratulations, Houdini. You have proven that you have the intellect of a penny-museum performer." He rose slowly to his feet.

"Well, at least it is appropriate to the occasion," Miss Luce remarked acidly.

Cairo shot her a venomous glance. "No doubt, given enough time and preparation, you could duplicate the miracles of Jesus Himself. But it doesn't necessarily follow that He was a fake. Perhaps you can approximate my manifestations with cheap tricks. It proves nothing."

Mrs. Pangbourne surged forward eagerly. "And you still have not explained Edgar's appearance," she announced triumphantly. "We saw him with our own eyes."

In fairness, I felt compelled to agree. "I am afraid she's right, Houdini."

Houdini appeared crestfallen. "What you say is true, Sir Arthur." He hung his head. "How could I have missed that? I guess I failed." He turned to Cairo, who now looked smug. "I offer the hand of Houdini in apology." He stepped forward, arm outstretched. With a thin smile Cairo extended his own hand. Houdini grasped it and lunged forward.

Cairo uttered a shout of surprise as Houdini brought his foot down hard on the man's right shoe. I believe the women jumped. I know I started at the suddenness of it.

"What do you think you're—?" Cairo began. Houdini planted his palms on the man's chest and thrust at him.

To my surprise, the shoe split in two crosswise and Cairo staggered back a couple of steps. I recalled his limp and began to understand. "His foot!" I fairly shouted. "Look at his foot!"

The whole company crowded around to gawk at Cairo's bare, white foot poking out of half a shoe. Houdini bent down and triumphantly held up the other half of the shoe he'd trod on.

"You see," he explained. "A secret catch releases the two halves of the shoe."

"But my husband's face..." Mrs. Pangbourne protested weakly.

Without a word Houdini turned to Cairo, who smoothed his hair and straightened his clothing. He eyed the magician warily as Houdini approached. Nothing could have prepared him for what came next. Houdini charged in, dug a shoulder into Cairo's midriff, and hoisted him off the floor.

Ignoring his gasps and struggles, Houdini carted the man across the room. With the differences in their heights, he looked like a fireman rescuing a stilt walker. The magician dumped Cairo unceremoniously onto the table. Cairo's legs splayed out in front of him. Houdini grabbed his right leg and lifted the bare foot up for us all to see. On the sole was a crude painting of a face, somewhat the worse for wear. Still, it was recognizable as the very one we had observed in the séance.

"Copied from the drawing of your husband in an obituary," Houdini explained gently to Mrs. Pangbourne. "That obituary was also where he found most of the 'personal and confidential' information he trotted out for you."

Sir William removed his cigar from his mouth and leaned forward to peer at the tiny painting. A moment later, the magician dropped Cairo's leg. "Only the phosphorescent paint would show up in the darkened room, as long as he kept his foot out of the light." He turned to me with a triumphant gleam in his eye. "You gave me the clue to this trick. Now you see how Cairo can use an artist like Gaylord. And why he favored his right foot—to protect the painting."

Mrs. Pangbourne pulled a handkerchief from her sleeve and held it to her face. "Edgar," she sobbed. "Oh, Edgar, I've been such a fool."

Houdini planted his fists on his hips, turned to our host, and called out, "What you got to say now, Cairo?"

Cairo pushed himself off the table. "Little man, you don't know the powers you challenge." Without warning, he launched himself forward. His hand darted for Houdini's throat. Before I could react, Houdini snatched the cigar from Sir William's hand and brought the lit end squarely up into Cairo's palm.

Cairo sucked in a breath and his eyes widened in pain. But he did not withdraw his hand. Instead, he looked Houdini full in the eye and pushed down farther on the cigar. The glowing end sizzled against his skin. Cairo's eyes had a dreadful intensity. His mouth twisted into a grimace. Still he did not withdraw his hand. Rather, he increased the pressure until the cigar crumbled into brown bits. Houdini was left with a stub in his hand.

Cries broke from the others as they surged around the two antagonists. Cairo ignored them all. His eyes held a challenge for Houdini alone.

Houdini shook his head. "You got guts, but no sense." Nevertheless, I could tell by the tremor in his voice he was shaken.

I reached for Cairo's wrist. "You must let me dress that burn," I insisted.

In answer, Cairo showed me his palm. I stopped short. Nowhere did I see the charred flesh I expected. In fact, except for a slight redness at the center, his hand appeared quite normal.

"How on earth . . ." I expostulated.

"Precisely the point," Cairo said. "My powers are not of this earth." He looked back to Houdini. "Are you still certain that I am a fake?"

He raised his hand to the stunned group that now surrounded us.

Houdini eyed the man suspiciously. "In India I once saw a man walk across live coals. Afterward, his feet were unharmed. It's a good gag, but it's still a trick."

Cairo hobbled across the room. When he turned back, his eyes held no trace of animosity. Gone were the grandiose mannerisms, the affected delivery. He gave no thought to straightening his appearance, but spoke matter-of-factly. "I underestimated you, Houdini. I shall not make that mistake again."

Houdini watched him warily. Gaylord appeared at the doorway. "There is a cabman outside," he announced. "He says he is here to pick up Messrs. Houdini and Conan Doyle."

"Great." Houdini turned to me. "That was smart of you." He addressed the ladies. "You need a ride?"

"My carriage is here," Sir William offered.

"One moment," Cairo interrupted our progress toward the door. "Hear me out."

Houdini paused and looked back with amusement at the man.

"I have no doubt you could make good your threat to humiliate me across Europe."

"Look," Houdini protested, "I already promised you—"

"Yes, yes," Cairo interrupted. "But you won't be able to resist telling your friends how you bested another fraud. Word will travel." He fixed the magician with a piercing stare. There might as well have been only he and Houdini in the room.

"All this," his gesture included the furnishings, the table, and those who watched, "is merely a show that supports my real work. And that work is quite literally beyond your comprehension."

He appeared deadly earnest. "If you discredit me, I shall have to establish myself all over again. My precious work would be interrupted. I simply cannot allow that to happen."

Cairo strode forward until he loomed over my companion. "I offer you a challenge. I have forged a body of occult knowledge that will transform the world. Come here tomorrow evening and I shall reveal the true nature of my work."

When Houdini demurred, Cairo's eyes blazed. "Do you realize the honor I am conferring upon you? I have never allowed such an opportunity before, never!"

The man was obviously in the grip of a powerful emotion. At first I thought he was angry. With a shock I realized I was mistaken. What so transformed his features—in the curl of his sensual lips, in the flush that suffused his entire countenance—was barely contained ecstasy.

"If you see with your own eyes, you will not dare to dispute my claims!"

Houdini, unprepared for this rush of emotion, fell back a step. So, I thought, must a great revivalist preacher like John Wesley have awed the crowds.

Cairo leaned down. In a voice barely above a whisper, he demanded, "Do you dare?"

For a moment, Houdini was at a loss for words. When he could speak, he growled, "Anything you could show me, I've seen twenty times already."

"Even the cigar?" Cairo taunted.

Houdini's face grew dark.

"If you wish to match wits with me," Cairo said, "return tomorrow evening at nine."

Across the room, Mr. Gaylord pulled aside a hanging. Behind it a section of paneling gaped open. Cairo spun on his heel and hastened through the opening. Gaylord followed and the tapestry fell behind him. I heard the panel slam shut and the rasp of a substantial bolt being thrown.

Chapter 6
The Remarkable Miss Luce

"That rascal still has all our jewelry," I remarked to the party.

Houdini nodded with a puzzled look on his face.

"What shall we do?" Mrs. Pangbourne inquired helplessly.

"Come now, Delia," Miss Luce reassured her. "We are all witnesses. He stands no chance of keeping our valuables." She ended on a practical note. "We can always bring in the police." She turned to me. "What would you recommend?"

I was flattered that she looked to me for guidance. But I also detected a note of challenge in her voice. Her green eyes flashed with devilry.

I was torn. Cairo's offer intrigued me. On the other hand, I had Louise to attend to. "I am afraid I must beg off," I answered sadly. "An illness in the family compels me."

I looked up to see Miss Luce studying me with some curiosity. *You refuse an adventure?* her look seemed to say. She turned to the others. "I am inclined to return tomorrow night."

Houdini looked around. "How about the rest of you?" he asked.

Mackleston spoke up. "With the Season over, London's been rather a bore. Wouldn't dream of missing it."

Sir William readily assented, as did Mrs. Pangbourne, though reluctantly.

"All right," Houdini agreed. "If he wants more trouble, I'll be glad to give it to him."

The ladies and Mackleston accepted Sir William's kind offer of a ride home. Before they left, Houdini suggested they meet the next day.

"We can plan a strategy," he said. Then a frown creased his brow. "Only trouble is, the rooms I've taken are pretty small for so many people."

"My chambers are at your disposal," I hastened to offer. "I have a large sitting room at the Langham." I was unhappy at abandoning the party and wished to lend what support I could.

"But you're leaving," Houdini protested.

"My train doesn't depart until four in the afternoon," I explained. "As long as we finish our business by three, I am at your disposal."

They all assented, and we agreed to meet at two the following afternoon.

The next day, I breakfasted early and packed my things. Since my morning was free, I endeavored to settle down and write the new Holmes story.

Once again inspiration forsook me. I stared impotently at the sheet of foolscap in front of me, the ink drying on the upraised nib of my pen while I struggled vainly for an idea. Frustration gave way to anger. How was I to support a household if I could no longer rely on my imagination?

The morning dragged on thus until lunchtime. Flinging down the pen, I gave up. After a hasty repast, I retreated to the solace of one of Scott's Waverly novels. I confess I was profoundly disturbed. Usually ideas flood my mind faster than I can get them down on paper.

Eventually, I even gave up attempting to read and went down to make arrangements for tea when the party should arrive. Afterward, I returned to my suite. For once I did not enjoy the company of my thoughts. It was with distinct relief that at half past one I heard a knock upon the door.

To my surprise, Miss Luce stood there. She wore a pale-green suit that brought out the color of her eyes.

"I know I am dreadfully early," she apologized, "but there was a lull at the office and I had to slip out when I could. Besides," she admitted hesitantly, "I couldn't resist stealing a few moments with the great author all to myself." She looked me in the face. "If I am a pest, you must send me straight away."

"Not at all," I assured her. Her arriving unescorted at my doorstep was a bit unconventional, but I was grateful for a distraction—even from a suffragist. I ushered her over to a seat on the maroon-colored sofa.

Seeing her a second time confirmed my good opinion of her taste in clothing. Her excesses were limited to her convictions—they did not extend to her manner of dress. Her skirt did not affect layers of ruffles. Her jacket was well cut, if plain. Her white blouse was silk, and she wore a simple matching hat, unadorned with the usual garish conglomerate of feathers. Much of fashionable ladies' headgear seemed more suitable for one of Buffalo Bill's Wild West Shows than for a promenade in Hyde Park.

"The great author finds himself singularly unproductive today," I confessed.

"Not going well, is it?" Those marvelous eyes exuded warmth and sympathy.

"No." Here, I am afraid, my frustration burst forth. "I've promised to resurrect that damned— I beg your pardon . . ."

She smiled. "Don't apologize. I find artistic passion quite a refreshing change from the predictable boredom of the business world."

"I meant to say," I amended, "that nuisance Holmes. I can't, for the life of me, come up with a plot."

"Perhaps you need a fresh source of inspiration."

"Perhaps," I agreed moodily. Abruptly, I came to myself and saw Miss Luce studying my face intently. Here I was, ignoring a guest. "Sorry I can't offer you refreshment. We shan't have our tea for nearly an hour."

"No matter," she said. "I actually had a serious reason for my call."

This rather took me aback. "Pray, state it."

She looked down. "I do not wish to intrude, but I am acquainted with Mr. Balfour. He has told me of the unfortunate situation regarding your wife."

At the mention of my old friend, I regarded her with puzzlement. How came this woman of modest dress and extreme opinions to enjoy the confidence of our staunchly conservative Prime Minister?

"As soon as I heard," she went on, "I recalled a specialist in Harley Street who treats consumption. He has succeeded where many others have failed."

Louise's case was far too advanced for me to feel hopeful, but I dared neglect no chance, however remote, for a cure. "What is his name?"

"Dr. Burton." She handed me a slip of paper. "Here is his address."

I was touched by her concern and her compassion. Again, I wondered what she could have suffered to produce her extreme views on the societal role of her sex.

"How is it that you know Balfour?" I inquired.

"He is one of my clients."

"Clients?" I asked. "What company employs you?"

"No company employs me. I am myself an employer."

"Indeed?" I should not have been shocked, given her politics and independence. I studied her hands for some clue as to her occupation. The nails were short. Bathing had not entirely eliminated a faint smear of ink along the little finger of her right hand. The cuff of her right sleeve was shiny from long hours of writing. She kept her own accounts, then. Did this bespeak simple independence or a deep mistrust of the world?

As I examined her hands, I noticed something curious. While they were presently well cared for, old scars and calluses on the knuckles spoke of years of scrubbing. Given her views on marriage, it had most likely been done for a living.

This took me aback. She did not dress like a charwoman, and her level of address was certainly not of the working classes. How had she been forced into manual labor? I postulated a fall from station. And now she runs her own business, trying to recapture her former situation in life.

Her nails were unsplit and healthy looking—her hands had had years to heal. Furthermore, her business, whatever it entailed, must be well established to attract clients of the caliber of Arthur Balfour. Therefore, her loss of position must have occurred when she was quite a young woman, barely out of her teens.

At that tender age, it was most likely that the death of a protector had left her without resources. What protector? Given the young age at which this surely occurred, probably a parent.

I looked up to find her regarding me curiously. "Is something wrong?"

I realized I had been staring for some moments. "Not in the least," I assured her. I couldn't resist showing off my little deductions. "It must have been quite frightening to have been forced to rely upon your own resources at so early an age."

Miss Luce gasped. Her hand flew to her throat and her eyes widened. "How—? To whom have you been talking?"

Her color heightened and there was something akin to fear in her eyes. I was heartily ashamed of myself for startling her so. I should have realized those memories might be painful, even after all the years that had passed.

"Do forgive me," I begged. "I promise I've made no inquiries. It was your hands."

She looked down at them. "They reveal that much?" she asked ruefully.

"No, no," I assured her. "Writing mysteries, I have grown used to drawing inferences, that is all." I then related my train of reasoning.

She listened with interest, her color returning to normal. When I had finished, she leaned forward. "That was remarkable."

"A mere commonplace," I assured her.

She rested her chin on her delicate hand. "Since you have deduced so much, you may as well know the rest. My father gambled away most of his inheritance and managed to drink himself to death on what remained. He left me when I was barely more than a girl—as you surmised—well educated but impoverished, and totally unsuited to find my way in the world."

"Were there no eligible suitors?"

Her green eyes flashed and she sat upright. "None I loved. And I would not allow myself to be auctioned off like livestock."

I could entirely sympathize. "So you went into domestic service?"

She nodded. The thought made me cringe. "Surely there were other avenues open to you," I protested. "Perhaps, as a governess . . ."

She shook her head sadly. "No wife wants a young, presentable woman sharing her household."

I took her meaning right away. It would take a secure woman to allow such a beauty in close proximity to the males under her roof. Indeed, Miss Luce looked radiant today. Her eyes sparkled; her skin glowed with health. She wore her hair in a tumble of amber curls loose at her long, delicate neck.

"I suffered some difficult times," she said simply, "until I managed to secure a position. I did everything—cleaned, cooked, made fires. From there I worked my way up to better situations. At last I found myself much in demand—though not always for reasons I would have preferred."

I had visions of a desperate old man pleading urgently outside her bedchamber door at midnight. In the daytime, it would be the eldest son taking ever-greater liberties. I began to understand her politics. Extreme experiences provoke extreme views.

"You were forced to change employment fairly regularly?" I hazarded.

She stared off into the distance. "A good many people in this world are . . ." Here some memory overcame her and her eyes filled with pain. ". . . unkind."

She gave her head a little shake and forced herself back to the present. "But it has turned out for the best, since I acquired a broad range of contacts among both employers and servants."

I wondered what incident could still torment her even years later. My heart went out to her, but her voice grew businesslike once more. "In a few years," she continued, "I saved enough money to open a small servants' registry firm in Westminster."

I was impressed. To save anything on a servant's wages spoke of extraordinary determination.

She went on. "I still had a few contacts among the polite world, Mrs. Pangbourne and Mr. Balfour among them. They formed the first clients for Reliable Domestics."

"Reliable Domestics?" I was surprised. "Is that you? I seem to hear of them everywhere."

"Yes, the business has thrived." She smiled. "I had wished to name it after myself, but Luce Domestics is not a name to inspire confidence, is it?"

I chuckled. Extremist or not, she had a sense of humor. I liked this woman. She was pluck to the backbone.

In the midst of our pleasant conversation, thoughts of Louise came unbidden. Here I sat bantering with a young woman while Louise lay wasting in her sickroom. And Kingsley had to suffer through it all without my support. I felt a pang of guilt at my secret shame. What right had I to any sort of happiness? I noticed Miss Luce staring at me.

"What is it?" I asked.

She leaned forward. "You seem so unhappy."

I shifted uncomfortably. "We all have our burdens, I imagine."

She sat up straight. "I am sorry. I have no right to intrude." She looked away. "It's just that sadness in your eyes." She sounded wistful, as though she yearned to share confidences.

I would have judged such a comment from a man as an encroachment. But this woman was so basically decent that I could not bring myself to be put off. After all, she too nurtured a secret sorrow. What a relief it would be to confide in someone.

"You have heard about my wife," I said at last. "What no one knows is that it began in the fall of 1893. And I—a doctor—was oblivious. She grew weak and fretful. She began to experience night sweats. Not until I found blood in her sputum did I suspect the truth. A lung specialist confirmed the diagnosis. She had consumption."

I looked up at her, expecting to see accusation on her face. To my surprise, it showed only compassion. "You can't blame yourself."

"Oh, can't I? It was I who prescribed exercise when I saw her weakening. It was I who forced her to go on those tricycle rides—even in the rain—to strengthen her constitution." I repeated bitterly, "Strengthen her constitution! All I did was hasten the moment she must die."

Her expression remained composed. "What did you do once she had been diagnosed?"

"Do? What could I do? We traveled. Italy, Switzerland. I chose the most healthful climates, the best air. During our travels, I wrote furiously to afford them."

"And you nursed her?"

"Of course I did! Until this trip to London." I am

afraid there was a catch in my throat. I looked away for fear I would break down entirely. "I shouldn't have come. What if—?"

She stopped me with a hand on my arm. "You've done all that is humanly possible."

She drew a breath. "When Mr. Balfour told me of your situation, I suspected—" Her hand tightened on my sleeve. "The pressures on you must have been tremendous. And I would imagine you have denied yourself the releases other, lesser men might take."

Tears sprang to my eyes. I hunched away in shame. I heard the soft rustle of silk as she shifted toward me. Her delicate scent invaded my nostrils. She smelled faintly of violets.

"What a pathetic thing I am," I groaned.

"No," she murmured in my ear. "You are remarkable. Last night I was terrified. When you squeezed my hand, you saved me from hysteria."

Her praise made me even more uncomfortable. "Not at all. It was Houdini who saw through the deception."

She leaned toward me. Her curls brushed the back of my neck. "Ah, but he knew what was happening. It was you who faced the unknown without flinching." I felt her warm breath on my ear. "It was you who showed real courage."

She leaned even closer, and her voice thrilled me with its warm sympathy. The blood coursed through my veins. Her voice was soothing and—dare I say?—almost seductive. I felt a soft touch upon my shoulder. "If there's anything I can do—anything . . ."

Before I realized what had happened, we were in each other's arms. Her eyes were large and luminous. I saw compassion—and more—in them. Her lips parted as she gazed up at me. We clasped each other tightly and I felt her soft flesh beneath the fabric of her suit.

"You poor man," she murmured. She understood what I had endured. God, how I yearned for the solace that only a woman can provide—that merging of spirit, mind, and body that makes each of us, for an instant, fully human.

A knock sounded at the door. Her eyes widened in shock. I bolted upright and thrust her from me. A man entered carrying a tea tray. "Where would you like it, sir?" he asked, then stopped and stared at the strange tableau we presented. We stood at opposite ends of the couch avoiding each other's eyes. Miss Luce straightened her disheveled clothing. I realized to my dismay that my vest and tie were askew. I could only imagine the state of my hair. There was a long, uncomfortable silence. At last I gestured to a table in the center of the room, and he got to work. Cups tinkled on saucers as he took forever to arrange the service.

Still the two of us sat motionless and silent. Once more my wife's wasted countenance rose before my eyes. I saw her dependence on me in her face. My shame knew no bounds. I had nearly betrayed a woman's most sacred trust. My face grew hot.

The servant stood there, still fiddling with the cups and saucers. "For God's sake, be done with it," I shouted. He left with a mumbled apology.

After he had gone, I could not meet Miss Luce's eye. Mortification overwhelmed me. I, whom she had just lauded as courageous, had given in to my basest instincts. I struggled for words. "You must forgive me," I began stiffly. "I have not been myself for some time. I did not intend any impropriety. That is, I didn't mean to give the impression . . ."

My words trailed off as a horde of conflicting emotions swept through me. After a moment, I risked a glance back at her. Her face was suffused with scarlet.

"I am sorry." Her voice was strained. "I have just recalled an urgent appointment. I shall have to miss the entertainment this evening."

She rose and hurried for the door. I tried to intercept her. "Please stay. I couldn't forgive myself if I have—"

"Don't be foolish," she cut me off. "I can't neglect my business for every fancy that comes along. No, I'll show myself out. Convey my apologies to Mrs. Pangbourne and Mr. Houdini."

I felt helpless as she fled the room. The door slammed behind her.

Only the server's arrival had saved me from a dreadful indiscretion. Moreover, the humiliation on Miss Luce's face haunted me.

I sank to the couch. At the moment when I had most needed my self-restraint, I had failed us both. Now I feared the air was poisoned forever between Miss Luce and me.

"Conan Doyle, you okay?"

The words jerked me from my thoughts. I looked up to see Houdini standing before me.

Chapter 7
Houdini Takes Charge

"Door was open," Houdini explained. "When no one answered my knock, I barged in. Am I too early?" He watched me curiously.

"Not at all." I bounced to my feet, trying to hide my discomfiture. "I—I merely have a lot on my mind today."

He nodded thoughtfully. "I passed Miss Luce on the way up," he said. "But she was going so fast she didn't even see me."

"I believe she has an important errand," I said uncomfortably.

Houdini smiled. "Probably for the best. We're better off without that kind of distraction."

"Tea?" I asked, ignoring his last comment.

Houdini gazed steadily at me. I had the unpleasant sensation that he read my thoughts and sat in judgment on me. Then he shrugged, and the moment passed. "Sure."

I poured the tea with shaking hands, and we settled down to await the rest of our party. After a moment, I realized something. If I visited the physician Miss Luce had recommended, I was sure to miss my train home.

I couldn't possibly get out of London before midday tomorrow. Though it meant abandoning Louise for another night, I must pursue any chance of a cure for her. Furthermore, I must admit I felt a thrill at being able to see the adventure through to its conclusion. I could accompany Houdini to Cairo's flat tonight.

I would send Nurse a telegram explaining the situation. She was under strict instructions to wire me should a crisis approach. When I informed Houdini, his joy was gratifying. He fairly danced around the room. "Now we'll show that Cairo," he said.

A knock at my door interrupted Houdini. I opened it to find Mackleston there.

"Oh, hullo," he said. "Am I early?"

"Not at all," I said as I took his hand. His grip was slack and he appeared to weave.

"Are you feeling well?" I asked, studying his slight form.

"Yes, quite, quite." He dropped my hand and drifted over to an armchair.

Clearly, he would be no help in planning a strategy for tonight. He appeared intoxicated, but I smelled no alcohol on his breath. His light brown hair lay in untidy curls on his head. His dark brown eyes gazed dreamily at me. He collapsed into the armchair and produced a pipe from the pocket of his blazer, which he lit before crossing his long legs. A thick, cloying smoke drifted from between his loosely parted lips. The smell was vaguely familiar.

"What's that you're smoking?" Houdini called with some annoyance in his voice.

Mackleston giggled like a child. "Special blend of Cairo's" was all he said. Then he leaned back and stared at nothing in particular, as far as I could tell.

After a moment, he roused himself. "Got any brandy? A spot of that would do nicely."

By now I recognized the smell. I poured a cup of tea and offered it to him.

"I want brandy." Mackleston said.

"The tea," I insisted, "is all the stimulation you will need."

Abashed, Mackleston clamped his thumb over the bowl of his pipe to extinguish the spark and took the saucer I held out to him. It rattled slightly in his hand.

"There's a good fellow," I said.

Houdini had retreated to the tea service and filled two more cups. I joined him there. "Hashish?" he inquired softly.

I shook my head. "Opium. As soon as his cup is empty, refill it."

Mackleston drained his cup. Houdini carried the pot over to him.

"How is your father this morning?" I inquired of Mackleston.

"He's fine," the young man replied glumly.

"Ah, yes, Lord Vollmer." Houdini refilled his cup. "It must be great to know that you'll be Lord Vollmer one day."

"Not I," the young man countered carelessly. "That's m'older brother. He's the responsible one. I'm the black sheep." He looked up and a smile transformed his face. He suddenly had an endearing quality—somehow both defiant and vulnerable.

"Well, when he finds out you helped us get the goods on that quack," Houdini said, "I bet he'll be impressed."

"Not likely," Mackleston replied lightly. "The old fellow don't care if I live or die. So long as m'brother stays healthy, that is."

"Oh, now, surely—" I protested.

He turned serious eyes on me. "It's no secret. Ask Justine. She'll tell you."

Here was a topic I was not eager to have broached. "Ah, I am afraid that Miss Luce will not be joining us this afternoon."

"Is that a dead cert?" Mackleston asked.

"I am afraid so," I admitted.

"Damn," he said morosely. "She's a load of fun—not a bore like those other girls."

"Yes, well," I strove to change the subject. "I hope the rest of our party arrives soon."

Fortunately, we hadn't long to wait. The awkward silence that followed our brief discussion of Miss Luce was soon broken by the arrival of Mrs. Pangbourne, still in her widow's weeds and snuffling into a black-bordered handkerchief. Sir William Bowers, his white hair carelessly combed, followed her in.

Houdini arranged the chairs of the room in a circle and strode into the center. I chuckled to myself. Ever the showman, even in a small room he managed to contrive a stage.

"My friends," Houdini announced, "this evening we shall do a great service to the world. We shall once and for all expose a cheat and fraud."

"Mr. Houdini." Mrs. Pangbourne clasped her handkerchief nervously.

"Yes?"

"How can you be so quick to judge poor Mr. Cairo? It was you, a doubter, who poisoned the atmosphere. That's why he was forced to descend to trickery."

Houdini gaped at her. She held her chin high and continued. "Numerous friends of mine have had genuine spiritual experiences in his company."

"In that case," I suggested, "we shall give Mr. Cairo the means to vindicate himself."

She appeared somewhat mollified. By now Houdini had recovered sufficiently to speak.

"Of course, the main thing is to get at the truth. I hope we can all agree on that?"

Four heads nodded their assent.

"Good. Let me get you ready for what you'll see tonight." He glanced toward Mrs. Pangbourne. "That way, if he proves himself, he'll do it once and for all."

She sighed and said, "Yes, yes. Get on with it."

"Okay." Houdini's tone became matter-of-fact as he continued. "The first thing is: Keep your wits about you. Don't be fooled by the show." He spread his hands in front of him. "A voice comes from a human throat. If something flies through the air, somebody threw it. Think who could be making the sound, who had a hand free."

He paused to let these words sink in before continuing. "Second: Whatever he hides is the core of the trick. If his hands are under the table, however briefly, there is a reason. If the room is darkened, it's to hide something."

"What about tying the fellow up?" Mackleston contributed. I was pleased that he seemed to be recovering from the narcotic.

Houdini smiled. "I bet he won't allow it, especially if I do the tying. But it's a worth a try. By all means, bring some rope."

The magician raised his hands to shoulder level. "Now, everybody listen carefully. I want you to understand how these guys operate," he said.

As we gathered around, he continued. "The one thing that always gets you is how they come up with information they couldn't possibly know."

Houdini spread his hands. "It's easy—old newspaper articles, obituaries. The guy may even slip a few pounds to one of your servants to get the dope he needs."

Houdini looked at each one of us in turn. "You each have to come up with some fact that nobody but the dead person knows about you." He gave a triumphant grin. "I always ask what my mother's pet name for me was. That gets 'em."

Sir William opened his mouth to speak. "No!" Houdini admonished sternly, "don't tell any of us. Keep it to yourself until you need it."

"But how do we use this piece of information?" Mackleston wanted to know.

"Ask to speak to the dear departed yourself," Houdini answered. "Then ask the question nobody else could know. Remember," he continued with another wary glance at Mrs. Pangbourne, "if this guy is a cheat, he's using your grief to line his pockets."

Mrs. Pangbourne was not paying attention. Instead, she looked around. "Where's Justine?"

I dreaded having to answer, but Houdini came to my rescue. "Something came up," he said brusquely. "Business, I guess. She won't be coming."

"How odd," Mrs. Pangbourne commented. "She was quite keen on it at lunch." She turned to Houdini. "When did you speak to her?"

He shot me a desperate glance. I drew a long breath and began, "Actually, I—" only to be interrupted by Mackleston.

"Point is," he said, "she should see it through with the rest of us. Not sporting, otherwise." He added with a puzzled look on his face, "Come to think of it, not at all like her."

"No, it isn't," Mrs. Pangbourne mused thoughtfully.

A knock sounded at the door. Houdini opened it to find a messenger with a telegram in hand.

"Mr. Houdini?" the messenger inquired.

"I am Houdini," the magician announced. The messenger handed him the envelope and left. Houdini tore open the letter and read it aloud: "'To the impostor Houdini and his lackeys: Holy Rites begin promptly at nine. Premises open for examination from six o'clock on. Imperative Miss Luce and Doyle present or the challenge is off. Doyle, you old goat.' Signed, Cairo."

As you can imagine, the message caused an uproar. I noted several furtive glances cast my way. How could Cairo possibly have known what had passed between Miss Luce and myself? And how dare he misrepresent my intentions!

Houdini tried to calm our party. "Cairo's trying to shake us up. Don't give him the satisfaction."

"But is there even any point in going now?" Mackleston wanted to know.

"Evidently, without Miss Luce," Sir William added, "we are not welcome."

I was again conscious of several pairs of eyes focused on me. I was acutely aware that it was because of me that Miss Luce had absented herself from our adventure.

"Do not trouble yourselves." All turned to see Mrs. Pangbourne holding up a hand. "I shall speak to Justine. Mr. Cairo deserves the opportunity to exonerate himself. She must be there." The woman looked quite determined.

Perhaps I could help. If Miss Luce was apprehensive about meeting me, I saw a way to ease her fears. "Would you be kind enough to deliver a message for me?" I asked, my voice not as strong as I might have liked. "Please tell her that I particularly wish her to join us."

"Certainly." Mrs. Pangbourne gave me a peculiar look but inquired no further.

"That's good enough for me," Houdini said. "Let's count on her being there." He turned to me. "I'll barely be able to make it from the theater in time for the 'Holy Rites.' Can I leave examining the room to you and Sir William?"

We readily assented. Houdini gave us strict instructions. "Sound every square inch," he insisted. "Push, pull, and pound. If there's a secret room, you gotta find it."

As the party broke up, Houdini drew me aside. "Be on your guard at Cairo's," he warned.

"I shall," I promised. "The fellow's reputation assures that."

"It's more than that," Houdini said. "I didn't want to scare the others, but you should know this. On my way up, I spotted that guy Gaylord in your hotel lobby. He sat with his back to me, but he was in front of a window. I saw his face in the reflection."

"You think Cairo sent him over to spy out our plans?" I was alarmed. I hadn't thought to check the door for eavesdroppers. On reflection, however, I realized all he could have learned was that we were on our guard. And that fact he already knew.

Houdini looked worried. "Bess'll want to come along for sure if she finds out I'm heading back there." He thought a moment. "Maybe I can convince her Mrs. Pangbourne insisted I give the guy one more chance. Make it sound really dull. And then I'll find a good show for her to see while I'm gone."

"So you're finally convinced that Cairo can be dangerous?" I asked.

"He's on the ropes now. If I show him up again, he loses his bread and butter."

"You think he might try to rid himself of the witnesses to last night's debacle?"

"With a guy like that, who knows?"

Chapter 8
The Sanctum Sanctorum

Houdini's warning gave me much food for thought. Were we headed into a trap at Cairo's tonight? I sternly resolved to put such thoughts behind me, at least until I had consulted with Dr. Burton. A short cab ride brought me to his office in Harley Street. There I informed his receptionist that Miss Luce had referred me. I was told that the doctor had left on his rounds and would not be back until tomorrow. I made an appointment for early next morning. I then returned to my hotel and arranged to extend my stay.

Sir William arrived promptly at five. All day the sky had been overcast. A damp chill in the air warned of rain. As I climbed into his cab, thunder murmured off in the north. The faint gray light soon faded. Before long, thunder cracked around us and large drops began to fall. Our horse clopped on amid swirls of people scurrying for cover. We huddled back in the seats to avoid the wind-whipped drops that blew in through the open front of our conveyance. I pulled down the leather shutter that protected the side window. Our cab smelled of damp fabric and old cigar smoke.

Ordinarily, I would have been eager for the companionship of such a renowned chemist, but today my mind was filled with anxious thoughts. I couldn't help holding out hope that in Dr. Burton I had at last found someone who could help my poor sufferer. How I longed to see Louise's gray eyes free from pain. I would have given anything to restore her gaunt face to its pretty, round look of health.

Unbidden, scenes of our life together came to me. Often, just as I had exhausted myself at my writing desk, she would miraculously appear with a cup of tea. How comforting was her plain common sense. How happy I had been to know that she was around the house, cleaning and sewing!

Yet, deep in my heart, I feared it was too late for any human agency to help. It was with trepidation that I anticipated my meeting with Dr. Burton on the morrow.

The memory of my behavior with Miss Luce added to my anxiety. Was this how I repaid my wife for her years of selfless devotion? Worse yet, I still found Miss Luce fascinating.

Very well: If my character was being tested, it would not be found wanting. I would earn Miss Luce's friendship once more. I would prove that I could sustain a relationship unsullied by the lower passions. Only thus could I redeem myself in her eyes and my own. But would I even be granted the chance? She might well not show up tonight. In that case, I should never see her again. Moreover, Sir William and I were embarking on a fool's errand.

I recalled Cairo's insolent telegram. How could he have known what had passed between us? Might she have confided in him? No, I wouldn't believe it of her. Besides, there had not been time.

I looked up to see Sir William lost in his own thoughts. His deep-set eyes stared unseeing out the front of the cab. His thinning white hair stirred in the cold air as we rolled along. At the séance Cairo had hinted that he, too, had some private sorrow. I wondered what it could be.

By the time we pulled up at Cairo's flat, a downpour drummed on the leather roof of our cab and ran in rivulets down the horse's rump. The streets had become shallow streams. Rain fell with such fury that it raised a mist off the surface of the waters. Sir William and I dashed along the slippery brick walk to the narrow protection of the doorway. Before I could knock, the door swung inward.

Maximillian Cairo stood before us. A black brocade smoking jacket with a pattern of red fleurs-de-lys covered his broad shoulders. Charcoal flannel trousers completed his ensemble. I half expected him to make some allusion to his outrageous telegram or my recent encounter with Miss Luce, but he did not. He merely surveyed our drenched state with a humorous glint in his eye.

"How appropriate. You arrive for the rites purified by a celestial baptism." He blocked the entrance while it continued to pour down on us.

"For God's sake, let us in," Sir William expostulated.

Cairo bowed. "Your servant." He stood aside and we rushed, dripping, into his narrow entry hall. "I do hope all your party will be attending. Otherwise, you will have endured a drenching for naught."

Sir William looked concerned. I knew what he was thinking—could Mrs. Pangbourne indeed persuade Miss Luce to come? If not, would we all be summarily ejected? Before these doubts could plague me further, Cairo pushed past us, a "Follow me" tossed over his shoulder. He strode down the dark hallway without even offering to take our coats. We were hard-pressed to keep up. I was surprised when he led us past the brightly lit library and the hidden door to the séance room.

I pointed to the concealed panel. "You're not holding the ceremony in there?"

Cairo threw a look of disdain at us. "That is for mummery." His gaze narrowed. "Do not let your victory last night make you complacent. You are about to enter my Holy of Holies."

He led us into his kitchen. At the far end he unbolted a rough, wooden-plank door, pulled it open, and disappeared into the darkness. A moment later, faint light glowed from within. Sir William and I traded puzzled glances and followed him.

The doorway gave onto a steep flight of stone steps. The stairway was dim and lacked a banister rail. I picked my way down, step by step. Sir William followed some distance behind me. At the bottom, we found ourselves in a small room with stone walls and floor. It smelled of damp and mold. Sir William looked about curiously. A small rug lay in the center and a couple of tables held candles on the wall opposite the door. There were no windows.

Cairo gestured at the room. "Here you are. My sanctum sanctorum."

"Looks like a fruit cellar," Sir William observed, and glanced over his shoulder at the door.

Cairo glared at us. "Yes, and to the unsophisticated, sugar and strychnine look alike. Don't be fooled by appearances."

I ignored his veiled threat and turned to Sir William. "Shall we begin?"

The chemist nodded and produced a small tack hammer from the folds of his coat. He began to sound the walls. I walked over to one of the tables and examined its underside minutely.

From the corner of my eye I caught movement and looked up to see Cairo mount the steps briskly. I had a suspicion of what he was up to, so I strode after him. I was too late; the door closed in my face. The bolt rammed home. We were left alone in the faint yellow glow of the candles. Sir William looked up, startled.

"Has that scoundrel locked us in?"

To make certain, I tried the door. The thick planks rattled against the bolt. "I am afraid so."

"Well, I'm damned!" Sir William dropped his hammer and plunged his hands deep into his pockets. A worried look grew on his face. His mustache and bushy brows made him look like an anxious old walrus. "How long do you suppose he means to keep us here?"

"A few hours at most. The others will arrive by ten."

"If he allows the others inside."

He was right. If Miss Luce was not among the party, Cairo might well turn them away at the door. The room was mostly in shadow. As I stood at the locked door, the dark corners seemed to close in on us.

"I say, Conan Doyle." Sir William's voice sounded small. His face was a pale glimmer in the candlelight at the base of the steps.

"Yes?"

"You don't suppose Cairo intends to leave us here for good, do you?"

"Why on earth would he do such a thing?"

"He could be mad."

I recalled the incident of the cigar last night. A small prickle of fear ran down my back. Unbidden, Poe's story "The Cask of Amontillado" crept into my mind. This room, I realized, made an admirable dungeon. I tried to shake off the feeling. Cairo was arrogant, yes, but not deranged. Still, a small voice in the back of my mind whispered that all he had to do was deny we had ever arrived. A man of his resourcefulness would have no trouble putting off the police until he could dispose of our bodies.

Nonsense! I was merely letting the dreary atmosphere around us get the better of me. I resolved to continue our search. At the doorway I looked for hinges, hoping to find a way to spring them. Unfortunately, the door was hung so that all hardware was on the kitchen side. The stout planks looked to be proof against anything short of an artillery barrage.

"He was quite angry last night," Sir William called up to me. An unhappy thought seemed to strike him. "Do you suppose this is where that fellow died? You remember—

the one last year? They say he saw something so horrible it scared him to death."

"This is simply a childish prank," I answered. "Cairo hopes to frighten us into giving the room a less than thorough going-over." I devoutly hoped I spoke the truth.

I descended the steps to the faint glow at the bottom. Sir William was breathing rapidly and perspiring freely. He looked from wall to wall with increasing unease.

"Do you by any chance suffer from claustrophobia?" I asked.

"A little," he admitted in a high-pitched voice.

"Can you try thinking of something else?" I asked.

"How?" he said. "I mean, we're trapped down here, aren't we?"

Clearly, his phobia was getting the better of him. I recalled that he was a scientist. "Isn't there some analysis or calculation you could make about this room? To distract yourself, I mean."

"I can't think what." A desperate tone had crept into his voice.

"What about its capacity?" I urged.

"Its what?"

"Capacity—say, the amount of oxygen in here. How long it would last?"

"Too many variables."

"Just a rough calculation," I suggested. "How would you begin?"

Sir William said shakily, "You'd start by determining . . ."

He pulled out his pocket watch and counted off seconds. "Ten breaths a minute. That means—"

"Your respiration is elevated," I interrupted. "Your computations wouldn't be valid for others." I was deliberately provoking him to take his mind off his fears.

"All right, what then? You're the doctor," he reminded me.

"Six breaths a minute is a good average."

"Fine, we'll settle on six." Even as he spoke, his breathing slowed a bit. "These are only going to be approximations," he warned me.

"I understand," I assured him, glad to see my scheme working.

Sir William went on, "Lung capacity of twelve hundred . . . well, let's say fourteen hundred forty CCs per minute. The room . . . approximately ten by ten and an average of nine feet high . . ." He knelt and calculated with his fingers in the dust on the floor. His voice grew even calmer. "Just round it up to twenty-five million, five hundred thousand CCs. Divided by breaths per minute . . . then divided by sixty."

He stood up. "Twenty-eight hours. That's how long the oxygen would last."

"If we blow out the candles," I reminded him.

"Yes, and assuming the door is airtight. Which, of course, it isn't."

"Quite," I agreed.

A gruff smile slowly softened his features. "Thanks, Conan Doyle. I do feel a bit better."

I clapped him on the back. "Good. Shall we begin our search?"

Sir William nodded. I removed my coat and folded it on the rug in the center of the floor. He bent down and retrieved his hammer with a grunt. I caught him glancing around nervously from time to time, but he kept hold of himself.

While he tried each stone of the wall, I concentrated on the tables. I pulled them out from the wall to examine them for false bottoms, hollow legs, and movable panels.

As Sir William transferred his attention to the stones of the adjoining wall, I pulled a penknife from my pocket and dug deeply into each candle to make sure it hid no secrets. Next, I climbed atop one of the tables. From that vantage point I lifted a candle and ascertained that the great beams of the ceiling concealed nothing. Then I helped Sir William test the remaining walls and roll up the rug to examine the stone floor. We even studied the rug itself thread by thread.

I have no idea how much time passed as we observed, sounded, and prodded every square inch of the room. I do know that the candles had burned low by the time we finished. We had found nothing.

Across the room, Sir William sat upon one of the tables and mopped his face with a handkerchief. "I'd swear before a jury there's nothing here. That Houdini fellow's wasted our time."

"Well, at least we can report we have eliminated some possibilities."

"If we ever see him again!" Sir William said wryly. His eyes traveled in a large circle around the room.

I didn't have the heart to answer. We had let Houdini down. I leaned against the cold stones of the wall and looked around the now-familiar room. The candles flickered in their last half-inch of wax. Our every movement cast vast shadows. I was not looking forward to the moment when the flames finally guttered out. Would Sir William be able to endure the darkness? Despite my brave words earlier, I began to wonder when Cairo would come for us. How would Houdini respond if Cairo insisted we had never shown up?

"Conan Doyle," Sir William called softly.

With a sigh I looked up. I was in no condition to comfort his fears. But I had misread his intent. He was hunched forward. His legs dangled over the edge of the table; his feet just brushed the floor. For a moment in the dim light he seemed the impulsive schoolboy he must have been forty years ago. He looked up sheepishly at me. "Sorry about earlier. Suppose I was a bit worked up."

"Not at all," I said, relieved.

He swung his feet back and forth. "This tiny space, the candles," he said. "It reminded me of the long nights I sat up with Stephen in his little room. I expect that's why I got so nervous."

"Stephen?"

"My boy," he said softly.

"I didn't know you had a son."

"I don't. Not anymore."

I scarcely knew how to reply to this. When Sir William spoke again, it was as if he were talking to himself.

"It started with blurred vision. At first, I chided him for squinting. Then came the headaches, and later the tantrums. It was a tumor, you see, in his brain. He was only ten. At the end, not even morphine could ease his agony. His shrieks . . ." Sir William's voice trailed off. Tears glistened in his eyes. He drew a breath and continued. "The fact that I could do nothing nearly drove me mad. One evening, out of frustration, I nearly assaulted his physician."

I yearned to give solace, but any words would sound empty. The loss was obviously far too recent. Now I understood why he, too, had been driven to contact the departed.

I sought to divert his thoughts. "Have you other children?" I asked.

"Three daughters." His voice was indifferent. "Grown now and married."

"Surely you can take comfort from them."

He was silent. It occurred to me that were I his physician, I would suggest travel. Leaving the scene of recent suffering can bring some measure of surcease.

"When did you lose your boy?" I began.

"Easter Sunday fourteen years ago."

This brought me up short. I chose my next words carefully. "Have you grandchildren?"

"Oh, yes," he spat out bitterly. "I have plenty of other men's sons in my life."

His vehemence took me aback. While I gathered my thoughts, he pushed himself to his feet and began to pace impatiently.

"Didn't mean that," he grumbled. "Of course, I'm grateful for 'em. But the universe is so damnably unfair."

A noise from the top of the stairs froze him in his tracks.

There was a scrape and a thud, then the door swung open. We both turned toward it. Footfalls descended. Down into our line of vision came Justine Luce, resplendent in white and gold, on Maximillian Cairo's arm.

Chapter 9
Holy Rites

I gaped, momentarily taken aback at the sight. Miss Luce's laughter tinkled across the room at some witticism that Cairo had just whispered in her ear. Then she caught sight of us.

"So," she exclaimed merrily, "here are your captives!"

Cairo's face wore a smug expression. You see, it seemed to say, she prefers my company to yours. Conflicting emotions coursed through me. I was relieved to be delivered from my confinement in the basement room, but Miss Luce's attendance upon Cairo concerned me. He seemed a poor candidate for intimacy.

Cairo bore a tray that had on it an open wine bottle and silver goblets. He paused at the bottom of the steps. With great amusement he observed us in our rolled shirtsleeves. "Gentlemen," he inquired with mock seriousness, "have you exposed my machinery of deception?"

"Outrageous!" Sir William sputtered. "Locking us in like—like a couple of hounds!"

"How else could I assure you were undisturbed?" Cairo smiled wickedly.

Bandying words with the man would gain nothing, so I bided my time. As we stood there, Houdini, Mrs. Pangbourne, and Mackleston slowly descended the steps. Each of the guests carried two lighted candles in holders, which they lined up along one of the tables across the room. Mr. Gaylord next appeared on the stairs. He carried a blazing candelabrum, which he proceeded to place on the other table. The resulting light was most welcome.

Cairo continued in his jovial manner. "What? No triumphal revelations? Ah, well, perhaps later." With that, he turned and conveyed the tray to the nearer table. Lifting the bottle, he poured ruby liquid into each of the vessels.

"Justine, my dear," he called. Miss Luce hurried over to help him. My attention was drawn to Mr. Gaylord, who lounged in a solitary corner of the stark room. His eyes followed Miss Luce with a hateful glitter as she swept over to Cairo. Clearly, he did not approve of the attentions she received from our host. Nor did I, though for very different reasons.

Cairo abandoned his jocular pose and grew serious while she distributed the gleaming wine cups among us.

Houdini hurried over to me. "What'd you find?" he whispered.

"Nothing," I admitted ruefully.

"Nothing?" Houdini looked put out. "Did you—"

Before he could finish, Cairo motioned for silence. "I have given much thought to this evening's rites." He folded his arms. "I want the experience to be beneficial as well as instructive for you all. Therefore, I have decided that tonight I shall materialize the god Dionysus."

A rumble of surprise ran around the room. "What about Edgar?" Mrs. Pangbourne wailed. Houdini grunted. Mackleston pursed his lips. Miss Luce looked intrigued.

Cairo surveyed the room. "Some of you are supporters." He gazed fondly at Mrs. Pangbourne, who returned his look with dismay. "Some of you are here out of boredom." His glance took in Mackleston and Miss Luce. Though the latter tried to maintain an air of amusement, she could not meet his gaze. "Some claim a dispassionate search for the truth—whatever that is." His eyes slid over to Sir William. "And some have come solely to dispute." Here his eyes rested coldly on Houdini. The magician glared back at him.

"You may do what you will before and after the ritual. But I warn you, any attempt to disrupt the ceremony itself will have terrible consequences—"

His eyes traveled from Houdini to me. In that moment, a strange sensation took hold of me. A shock ran though me as if my whole body had been plunged into ice water. My breath froze in my throat, my chest constricted, my limbs felt paralyzed.

"—consequences you will suffer for the rest of your lives." Feeling slowly returned to my body. I could draw a breath. A faint smile stretched Cairo's sensual lips; mockery lurked in the depths of those eyes—then they left me. He addressed the room at large and raised his goblet.

"Now, in honor of him we invoke, let us partake of his principal gift to humanity."

The company raised their cups and drank. Though weak and trembling, I had enough of my faculties left to be suspicious of the wine. Cairo had not yet drunk. He noticed my hesitation and smiled. Elaborately, he raised his cup and took a long swallow. Then he nodded to me.

Still, I hesitated. What if he intended to drug us all? His eyes lingered on me. This time I felt nothing except the sardonic mockery of his expression. I thought of my promise to Houdini. I had committed to this evening—I had accepted all the risks it might entail. Resolutely, I took a drink. I tasted nothing untoward. Nevertheless, my hand trembled as I brought the goblet down. Cairo lifted his own in mock salute.

I heard Mackleston giggle. "Just like church, then. Except this claret's a bit better than what Reverend Oliphant serves up at Communion."

Cairo smiled. "I always considered it rather larcenous

of the Christian Church to appropriate Dionysus' sacrament for its own use."

"Well, really!" Clearly, Mrs. Pangbourne was not amused.

The wine helped to restore me. I took a second sip. Later, the others told me it was a fine vintage, complex and mouth-filling; however, at the time I scarcely tasted it, so overcome was I by Cairo's effect upon me a moment before. Had I been the victim of some form of hypnotism?

No, I decided; it was more likely that I was overstimulated by the ordeal I had undergone in this room earlier. Yes, that was the answer. I took another drink of wine and forced my mind into more practical paths. I resolved to be alert for any signs of pathological intoxication. To that end, I observed the others around me.

Houdini watched Cairo narrowly. Mrs. Pangbourne stood alone in the center of the room, looking decidedly uncomfortable. Gaylord swirled his wine in a bored manner, but his eyes were restive. Mackleston stood to one side, lost in his own thoughts. Sir William looked disappointed. No doubt he had hoped to ask Cairo to contact Stephen.

As for Miss Luce, she hovered around Cairo. Occasionally, he addressed a quiet remark to that caused her to smile. She contrived numerous excuses to touch his shoulder or his arm. Certain passages in his detestable volume of poetry, *Moist Folds*, flashed unbidden through my mind. I shuddered inwardly at the thought of such a fine young woman under his spell. Perhaps if I could put things right between us, she would listen to my warnings. I resolved to speak with her as soon as possible.

I felt a hand on my sleeve and turned to see Houdini standing behind me. "Did he let you search the room?"

As quickly as I could, I quietly recounted the events in Cairo's Sanctum Sanctorum. Although Houdini listened intently, his eyes never left Cairo for an instant. At last he nodded. "You're sure there was nothing in the ceiling?"

"Positive."

"Good. Then he's got to have it on him somewhere."

"Have what on him?"

"Whatever he uses. Flash powder, fulminate of mercury, something like that. If he doesn't have it now, he's got to go get it. You want to see him squirm? Wait'll I ask to search him."

Just then Cairo lifted his head from yet another tête-à-tête with Miss Luce and called out. "I must leave you now to prepare myself for the Holy Rite."

Houdini looked triumphant. "See? See? I told you!" he whispered.

Cairo continued, "Make you ready to welcome the god of inspiration and frenzy." He downed the last of his wine and mounted the steps. I was after him in a flash, in case he intended to lock us in again. I needn't have bothered. He left the door swinging open behind him

I made my way back down the steps to Miss Luce, who stood alone by the table with the empty wine bottle. She coolly watched my approach.

"I'm glad you were able to join us after all," I began.

"Delia practically kidnapped me," she replied carelessly.

"And did Mrs. Pangbourne deliver my message?"

Miss Luce looked away. "I don't recall."

This sparring was getting us nowhere. "See here," I said, "I should very much like for us to be friends. I know we got off to a bad start—"

She flushed. "Don't," she begged, and lifted a hand.

"There is nothing for you to regret," I insisted. Then I leaned forward and whispered, "After all, it was I who let things proceed too far."

Her mouth dropped open. She planted her fists upon her hips and anger flashed in those green eyes. "Of all the arrogant—" she began.

I involuntarily drew back a step and threw up my hands. "You misunderstand."

She looked away. "Really, this is too absurd."

"I take full responsibility for what happened between us," I insisted.

She covered her mouth with a hand. A giggle escaped. "No," she said from between her fingers, "you take full responsibility for what didn't happen between us."

I stiffened. Her eyes rose to my face and then full-blown laughter burst forth from her. "You are so medieval!" she gasped.

"I say," Mackleston complained from behind me. "Let us in on the joke."

I spun around to see him and Houdini watching us. I felt myself redden.

Miss Luce's mirth subsided enough for her to say, "Oh, it's just that Sir Arthur insists upon attributing to me virtues I neither possess nor desire."

The others had gathered around and I feared I'd have to make an embarrassing explanation, but Mackleston himself rescued me. His attention was drawn to the steps. He lifted his arm and pointed to them, a peculiar expression on his face. "Look!" he breathed.

We all turned to see a brown-robed figure slowly descend the stairs. A deep cowl obscured the face. The group fell silent as the figure reached the bottom. Metal glinted in its left hand. A dagger. Looking like a medieval monk, the figure moved soundlessly toward us. Candlelight flickered on the deep folds in the cloth that swayed as it approached.

Mr. Gaylord rolled up the rug in the center of the floor and stashed it under a table.

"Cairo?" Mackleston's voice cracked. "Cairo, is that you?"

I clapped a hand on his shoulder. "Get hold of yourself, man," I said. Sir William blinked. Miss Luce stared, fascinated. Houdini watched with a curl of contempt on his lip. Mrs. Pangbourne backed up a pace.

The figure drifted past us to the table. It bent over and extinguished all but one of the candles. By the single flickering flame its shadow grew monstrous and distorted on the wall behind it. The figure turned back and advanced on us again. Instinctively, we shrank back—all except Houdini. The magician set his jaw and stood his ground. He looked for all the world like a bull pup defending its territory. The figure ignored him and continued on. At the center of the room, it plunged its hand into the folds of the cloth and produced a piece of green chalk. Slowly, it knelt and began to draw on the floor. I moved closer to see. The signs were unfamiliar but resembled obscure mathematical symbols. The figure connected each sigil with lines. The chalk scraped and wobbled across the uneven floor. When the monk arose and stepped back, it stood in the center of a seven-sided polygon with those curious symbols at each corner.

"Upon no circumstance are you to cross this protective septagram." The commanding tones rang off the stones of the room. "Neither shall you disturb the Holy Names of Power inscribed around it." The figure lifted its head and the cowl fell back, revealing Cairo's face.

Houdini called out. "That's okay, Cairo, but first I'm going to search you." With that, he started forward. Cairo lifted a hand and Houdini paused.

"I have purified myself and must not be profaned by human touch. In any case, as you shall see, that will not be necessary." Then he shrugged his shoulders, and the robe tumbled to the floor. A gasp ran around the room. He was completely nude. His oiled skin glowed golden in the flickering candlelight. On his right hand sparkled an emerald ring.

I was outraged. Mrs. Pangbourne wailed and fled to a far corner. Mr. Gaylord was impassive. A sneer of distaste curled Houdini's lip. Mackleston looked entranced. I was distressed to see that Miss Luce, too, leaned forward with fascination to examine his well-muscled body.

Ignoring us all, Cairo clenched his eyes shut and began to mumble. I heard Houdini's voice at my side. "Quickly, get in a circle around the perimeter of the septagram." He thrust Mr. Gaylord next to me. Houdini pulled Mrs. Pangbourne from the corner where she crouched, covering her eyes. She kept her eyes tightly clenched but let him lead her. Miss Luce fell into place by my side. Houdini gathered in Mackleston and then assumed a place next to Mr. Gaylord.

Cairo continued to murmur. I realized he was reciting ancient Greek. I recalled enough from my school days to catch the words for life, death, and inspiration. He paused, drew a breath, and began again.

His voice rose until his words formed a chant. He moved in a small circle, swinging his arms. The dagger flashed in the candlelight. At one corner of the drawing on the floor he paused, raised his arms high, and whipped the dagger down and across his bare forearm. Blood, looking black in the faint light, welled up from the cut. He let a few drops fall in the corner, then proceeded on to the next. He stopped in turn at each angle of the chalk figure to dribble a few beads of blood.

Then he continued his perambulation. His movement slowly evolved into a dance. His arms swung rhythmically, his body swayed and dipped, his feet padded out a beat. The emerald stone in his ring caught the candlelight and flung it around the room in green shards.

Cairo's voice rose in some sort of call, alternately pleading and commanding. His arms swung more forcefully, and his feet picked up their pace and stepped in fascinating syncopation.

As he continued his chant, his movements grew wilder and more unbridled. He stamped his feet and swept his arms about in a frenzy, almost shouting the words in the chant. His breathing grew heavy. A strange scent filled the room. At first I thought it was perspiration from his exertions, but then I recognized the odor of sandalwood. I searched the darkness in vain for a brazier or censer.

The emerald on his hand seemed to shine brighter and brighter until the entire room was bathed in a green glow. The candle in its corner flickered with a green flame. We all stood motionless in our silent circle. Every gaze was fixed on Cairo's twisting body. Now he whirled frantically and shrieked a passionate call to his god. His body gyrated fiercely, his feet pounded the floor. His eyes were wide and staring, and his hair flew in all directions at once. He looked like a lunatic—or a saint—howling and writhing in the pale, emerald light. In response to his passion, whether holy or demonic, his maleness began to swell. I watched, fascinated, at its triumphant rise. His hands, open with want, clutched at air, clutched at us, clutched at himself.

I, too, was panting. I felt acutely aware of Justine beside me. I imagined the softness of her form; her delicious female musk drifted up to me. The soft flesh of her hand in mine sent shivers down my spine.

I looked at her, drank in her beauty. Her eyes were wide, her pupils dilated in the green light. Her bosom heaved. The room filled with the jangling of tambourines, the clash of cymbals, and the blare of horns. Harsh, cawing laughter swirled around us. How ludicrous my timidity in my rooms now seemed. I was a man. I was created to fulfill her desires. And she existed to receive me.

I was reaching for her when a sound ripped across the room. It froze me and literally raised the hairs on the back of my neck. It sounded like a cross between a squeal and a bellow and came from the center of the septagram. I turned to look and saw that Cairo had seemingly vanished, and in his place stood a filthy, stamping beast with a rangy, manlike body that grew up out of a pair of goat legs. Matted fur covered the beast. Its cloven hooves charged up to the chalk lines inscribed on the stone floor. It brayed in frustration when it discovered it could not pass.

The form dissolved and melted. It became a naked woman just burst out of girlhood. Her newly ripened breasts swayed as she stepped back. She caressed them enticingly, ran her hands down the curves of her body. Her soft, rounded arms lifted imploringly as she sank to her knees. Her white thighs parted. I surged toward her but was pulled up by a firm hand. I turned furiously to see Mr. Gaylord's impassive face. His eyes were veiled and dangerous. "You mustn't break the barrier." His lips pursed and he gave my arm a twist that wrenched a cry of pain from me.

Suddenly, I felt weak, drained of desire and will. I could scarcely stand. Behind me I heard cries of disgust intermingled with strange sucking noises. "You want to see what you would have embraced?" Gaylord grabbed my shoulders. "Then look!" And he spun me around.

In the center of the septagram lay a being out of a nightmare. It had no shape, but bulged and heaved with slimy caricatures of life. Here a head oozed forth, there a claw. The only permanent features were dozens of red mouths, alternately sucking and mewling with desire.

The object began to flow. It gathered itself into a foul-smelling pile. The putrid mass rose up until it was six feet tall. The mucuslike surface eddied and swirled. The lower half split lengthways and two pseudopods spilled out its upper half. A bulbous mass swelled from the top. With horror I realized it had become a grotesque parody of a man. The mouths opened and obscene laughter dribbled out of the creature as it mocked the very shape of humanity.

There was a scuffling sound and I heard Mrs. Pangbourne scream, "No!" Houdini shook off the hands on either side of him. He surged forward and his foot breached the septagram. There was a rush of hot air that smelled of an open sewer in the summer. I gagged; cries of disgust sounded around me. Then Houdini was inside the septagram. I have no idea what he intended, but I dashed in after him.

When I reached the thing, I stopped short. The gelatinous excrescence extruded a couple of tentacles. They reached for me. I felt a sluglike caress around my arm. With a cry I lurched backward in disgust and horror. The green light, the sounds, and the stench all vanished. By the light of the one candle I saw Houdini kneeling over the pale, motionless body of Maximillian Cairo.

Chapter 10
Clues from a Corpse

Later I blamed myself for wasting precious time, but at the moment I could only stare. What had become of the monstrous creature we had just seen? The other witnesses were in no better condition. Mrs. Pangbourne was on the verge of hysterics. Miss Luce tried to comfort her, but she herself was too shaken to be of much help. Mackleston stared as if hypnotized. Sir William looked as if someone had just struck him a blow.

Houdini looked up at me, fear on his face. "Conan Doyle," he called. "Come quick!"

I shook myself out of my daze and rushed to his side. I felt for Cairo's pulse. It was thready and weak. He was desperately pale. His flesh felt cool and clammy. This was no act.

Concern filled Houdini's eyes. "He isn't faking?"

I shook my head. "He is in shock."

Houdini looked appalled. "Did I do this?"

Obviously he had, but I saw no point in berating the man. The rest of our party crowded around. "Please step back," I begged. "He must have air." They responded slowly, as if numb.

Houdini sprang to his feet. "My God," he said, pacing back and forth. "How could I know?" In another moment, he was again at my side. "A cab! We gotta get him to the hospital."

Just then Cairo stopped breathing. I galvanized into action. First I pulled open his mouth to make sure his airway was not obstructed. Then I slapped his face until my palm stung. No response. I pounded upon his chest. It was all in vain. His feeble pulse had ceased. Houdini crept up behind me and stared over my shoulder in horror.

"Is he . . . ?"

"He is beyond reach of our help," I assented gently.

Miss Luce gasped in horror. The blood drained from Houdini's face; he was nearly as pale as Cairo. He threw his hands up in despair and clasped them over his head. "What have I done? What have I done?" he moaned.

I sensed a disturbance behind me and turned to see Mr. Gaylord elbow his way through the group. He knelt next to me and grabbed Cairo under the arms. "Help me get him upstairs," he said breathlessly. "I have prepared a room."

I nodded sadly and slowly rose from my knees.

"No, we must hurry!" he shrilled, heaving at the body.

"There is no need for that now," I said sadly.

"Oh, what do you know about it?"

"I am a doctor," I reminded him.

The man threw me a contemptuous look as he dragged Cairo's body toward the steps. "His condition is not of the physical plane," he panted. "We have only a very few moments to recapture his astral body." He paused to glare at Houdini. "If you have murdered him . . ."

Houdini did not speak, but the pain in his eyes was eloquent.

"That's quite enough of that," I said. "Whatever has happened here tonight, Cairo brought on himself."

Gaylord sighed in frustration. "You're fools, all of you."

He heaved at the body once more. The cadaver's heels bounced across the uneven stones of the floor.

"In a way, he's right," I remarked quietly to Houdini. "If rigor mortis sets in, getting him up the stairs will be most unpleasant."

Galvanized into action, Houdini shot forward and grasped the legs. The touch of the lifeless flesh gave him pause, but he pressed his lips together and lifted.

"Do cover him, please," Mrs. Pangbourne implored. Eyes averted, she held out the dead man's cloak. I grabbed it from her and flung it over his nakedness.

Gaylord and Houdini hefted the body up the narrow stairs. I followed. When they reached the kitchen, I hastened to support their burden at its middle. We proceeded awkwardly up a broader carpeted set of steps to the top floor. All the while, Gaylord exhorted us to hurry. The remainder of the group trailed along behind.

At the top of the steps was a bedchamber. We laid the poor unfortunate down on a magnificently carved four-poster bed. Centuries had darkened the oak to a deep maroon color. The rest of the party trooped in somberly. Gaylord hurriedly arranged the limbs and drew the red velvet hangings around the body. Then he turned to us.

"Out. All of you out." He shooed us with a flutter of hands.

When we were slow to move, he advanced on the closest, who happened to be Houdini. Jabbing at the magician with his fingertips, he insisted, "Out, out, out!"

Houdini looked despondent. "This is all my fault," he repeated to himself.

I took his arm. "Come," I said. "Let us leave him to his grief."

"He doesn't look grief-stricken to me," Miss Luce ventured as she followed us out to the landing. Despite her practical observation, I noted that her eyes were red-rimmed.

Indeed, Gaylord was a flurry of activity, opening drawers, setting out strange artifacts. He happened to glance up and see us watching. With a determined look, he hurried over to slam the door shut. A moment later, I heard a key turn in the lock.

Mrs. Pangbourne looked worried. "Do you suppose he's looting the poor man?"

"I don't think so," I replied.

The noises of large objects being dragged came to us through the door.

"What is he doing in there, do you suppose?" Mackleston asked.

"I suspect he is engaged in some pathetic ritual to resurrect his dead friend," I said sadly.

At my words the smell of incense wafted from underneath the door. Very shortly the muffled sound of chanting reached our ears.

Miss Luce pressed her ear to the oak panels of the portal. "It's no language I've ever heard," she whispered.

She backed away in alarm as a series of thuds and crashes reverberated through the door. It sounded as if large objects were being flung about the room.

"You don't suppose he means to defile the body?" Sir William asked.

"I'm sure he means no harm to the late Mr. Cairo." I sighed. "Possibly we are hearing his frustration at the failure of his rite."

Abruptly, all sounds ceased. In a moment a soft murmur drifted out from the room.

"One feels one should do something." Mrs. Pangbourne kneaded a handkerchief.

"We must call the police," Sir William asserted.

"What would we tell them?" Mackleston demanded. He looked around at each one of us. "Did you see what I saw?"

"I saw nothing," Mrs. Pangbourne stated virtuously. "I kept my eyes tightly closed the whole time."

"But you saw it, didn't you, Justine?" Mackleston's look was half hopeful, half fearful.

"Yes, Algy. I saw . . ." She chose her words carefully. "A

satyr. Then something like a nymph, and finally," she shuddered, "an abomination."

"Oh, God, yes," Mackleston agreed fervently. "Those mouths . . ." He turned his attention to me. "And you, Conan Doyle?"

"Yes," I had to confess. "That is what I saw as well."

"Has anyone a logical explanation for what we all observed?" Sir William asked as his eyes sought out Houdini. But the great magician did not respond. He stood a little way from us, wrapped in his own guilty thoughts. I was worried for him. He seemed so unlike his normal ebullient self. Obviously, beneath that cocky exterior beat a tender heart.

"What do you think, Conan Doyle?" Sir William called me from my musings. I scarcely knew how to answer him. My reason fought against believing in the occult. But if we had witnessed trickery, it was beyond my powers to explain what had occurred. I groped for words. "Could our imaginations have manufactured something out of the hysteria of the moment?"

"If so," Sir William said, "my imagination manufactured precisely the same objects as yours did."

"Point is," Mackleston said, "if we tell the police what we really saw, we'll all end up on the dock—or in Bedlam."

"Not if we stick to the basics," Sir William said practically. "After all, what really happened to Cairo? He overexerted himself during one of his rituals and suffered some sort of seizure."

Mrs. Pangbourne produced a handkerchief and dabbed at her eyes. "Poor Mr. Cairo."

Mackleston nodded. "We six are the only ones who know the entire truth."

"You're forgetting Mr. Gaylord," Miss Luce said sharply. "He has already accused Houdini. I imagine he will do so again in front of the police."

At this Houdini looked up, misery writ large on his face.

"But will they believe him?" Sir William pointed out.

"After all, they'll find no marks of violence upon his body. If we all stick together—"

Miss Luce glared at him. "A man is dead and all you can think about is protecting yourself from scandal!"

"We have no course but to tell the truth," I said. "Let them make of it what they may."

"You don't have to worry," Houdini spoke for the first time.

Everyone turned to look at him. He lifted his head defiantly.

"When push comes to shove, I'm taking the fall. After all, I was the one who . . ." But he couldn't finish.

It hurt me to see him so overwhelmed by remorse. Perhaps he had behaved impulsively, but not out of any desire to injure. "It is sad that a man has died," I said, "but nothing criminal occurred here tonight. Besides, there is a greater need than ours to consider now."

Miss Luce understood at once. "Mr. Gaylord," she said.

"Yes," I assented. "He and Cairo were close. Imagine the state he must be in."

As if in answer to my words, the door opened behind me and Miss Luce gasped. Turning around, I saw Mr. Gaylord framed in the doorway to the bedchamber. He slumped against the portal; his face was haggard. His hand shook as he raised it to smooth his tousled hair.

"He wants to see you," Gaylord said shakily. "All of you." He staggered aside for us to pass.

We stared at one another. Miss Luce looked startled, Mrs. Pangbourne frightened. Sir William merely shook his head sadly. I took his meaning. Investing a lifeless body with desires was a pathetic, if understandable, delusion. Who knew what had just gone on in that room— what feverish strivings and unanswered prayers? It was enough to unhinge any man's sense of reason. Clearly, our best course was to humor Mr. Gaylord. I tried to catch Houdini's eye, but he stood rigidly facing the open door.

"Let's go." Houdini expelled a breath and led the way. One by one we stepped into the room.

It was as if we attended a wake. The room had been straightened, the gas jets burned dimly, and the curtains of the bed had been pulled aside. The remains of Maximillian Cairo lay on the coverlet. Gaylord had wrapped the body in a lavender silk dressing gown. Cairo's hands were crossed upon his chest. In the pale yellow glow of the lights, the dreadful pallor of those cold cheeks was softened. The others filed in behind me, and we ranged ourselves around the body.

"He wants you to have these." We turned to see Mr. Gaylord bearing the lacquered box from last night. He raised the lid and moved to each of us in turn, allowing us to retrieve our valuables. It was obvious that with Cairo's malign influence gone, Mr. Gaylord's own innate spark of decency was kindling. I turned back to the occupant of the bed. What a strange man he had been; what a strange life he had lived; and now what a strange end there was to it.

"Shall I offer a prayer?" I asked.

"As long as it's not to that insufferable old bore Jehovah." Cairo's eyes snapped open. "You are most welcome to pray to any other god."

Miss Luce gasped; Mrs. Pangbourne shrieked. I stood rooted to the spot. Mackleston smiled in relief. Houdini's eyes bulged with emotion. Cairo struggled to sit up but collapsed in apparent exhaustion. Gaylord rushed over and with the aid of some pillows propped him up against the headboard.

Cairo surveyed us. "Your concern is most touching." His voice, though weak, had lost none of its ironic quality.

An angry voice rang out. "You fraud! You chiseler!" Houdini's face flushed a deep red. "I'm going to . . ." His fists were clenched. Shocked as I was, I moved to intercept him.

"Not now," I pleaded. "Let us hear his story first."

"I already know his story," Houdini muttered ominously.

I tried one last ploy. "Don't make a scene in front of the women."

He looked from Miss Luce to Mrs. Pangbourne. At last he nodded sullenly. "You're right. But he's not getting away with this."

Meanwhile, the topic of our whispered debate watched us with amusement. "Yes, do restrain him," Cairo urged. "Being murdered twice in one evening is more than even I could bear."

At that Houdini glowered but kept himself in check.

"Conan Doyle." Sir William's voice called from across the bed. "What led you to pronounce him dead?"

"His breathing had stopped. He had no pulse." I spread my hands helplessly. "What other conclusion was there?" I looked at Cairo, pale but alive on his bed. I could scarcely believe my eyes.

"Indeed." Cairo's voice was soft. "My soul, or more properly my astral spirit, had departed from my body." He drew a breath. "Without Mr. Gaylord's quick work I should have remained in the state which you call death indefinitely."

"What did Mr. Gaylord do?" Miss Luce demanded.

"Certain things may not be revealed to the uninitiated." Cairo closed his eyes and lay back on his pillows. When he continued, his voice was barely audible. "Suffice it to say that he performed certain acts and you see the result."

"But you feel all right?" I asked.

"A little weak, but other than that perfectly fine."

"What about the"—Mackleston fumbled for words—"the thing we saw?"

Mrs. Pangbourne looked away. Sir William's eyes filled with dread at the memory. Miss Luce stared straight at me. Suddenly, I was overwhelmed by the memory of the intoxicating female creature I had seen in the septagram and her powerful effect upon me. With mortification, I recalled the moment I had embraced Miss Luce. I flushed to the roots of my hair. After all my firm resolve, I had succumbed to temptation once more. I could not meet her gaze.

"Yes." It was she who spoke. "What did we see?"

"I invoked the god," he said simply. "He came unto me and allowed me to wear his mask."

"What exactly is it that you claim happened to you?" Houdini demanded.

At Houdini's words, Cairo's eyes opened. Anger glittered in their depths as he gazed at the magician. "To summon a deity, it is necessary that my astral body rise to the plane of his existence. When you so injudiciously interrupted me," Cairo continued coldly, "you severed the line of communication between my soul and body. In effect, you stranded my astral self far from home." He sat up. "And thereby you have put yourself and your friends in the gravest of dangers."

Houdini rolled his eyes. "You got a good racket here, Cairo. Don't push your luck."

"You irresponsible cretin!" The words exploded from Cairo. "You don't yet realize what you've done."

The exertion of his anger left him gasping for breath. Mr. Gaylord hurried across the room with a glass of water. He fussed over Cairo a minute until he was waved away. Cairo lay back down but continued just as intensely.

"Ordinarily, after a manifestation the power rises back up through the planes and resumes existence on a more abstract level. When you broke the septagram, you let it loose. It was as if you had summoned a demon and set it free."

"We'll take our chances," Houdini said with a sneer.

"You still do not understand. A being this subtle cannot survive on its own in our gross material world. It must have a host. I summoned you all in here to warn you. It fled me; therefore, it must have lodged in one of you. Someone in this room is under the absolute control of the god Dionysus."

Chapter 11
The Gift

A stunned silence greeted this revelation.

"Is it I?" Mackleston demanded. "How would I know?"

His eyes were wide and staring. I started toward him, but Miss Luce anticipated me. "It's all right, Algy," she said. She lowered her voice, spoke soothingly in his ear, and stroked an arm as one might console a nervous dog.

"You won't know—not for a while." Cairo smiled. He positively enjoyed the man's fear.

"Hah!" Houdini's contemptuous laugh exploded in the room. He pointed a finger at the occupant of the bed. "I, Houdini, will expose you for what you are—a swindler of the gullible and the unstable."

Cairo's voice was ice cold. "Just how have I swindled the gullible and the unstable? And, by the way, which of those two epithets describes you?"

"Yeah, make jokes, but you don't fool me. This whole thing was a setup."

The thought had crossed my mind as well. I waited to see how Cairo would respond. The man slowly sat up from his pillows like a venomous serpent rising above its coils. He fixed an unblinking eye on Houdini. "We had an agreement, did we not?"

"We sure did."

"All right, then. I intend to hold you to it." His expression was a frightening combination of anger and contempt. "I have given you a glimpse of the hidden workings of the universe. Either explain away what you have seen tonight or apologize and never again interfere with my work."

Clever, I thought, to lob the ball into Houdini's court. For the first time since I had met him, Houdini looked uncertain. But he drew a breath and said bravely, "Sure, it's easy. All the effects—the green light, the images— could have come from a magic lantern."

"But they moved," Mackleston interjected. "We saw them move."

"Yes," I felt compelled in fairness to agree. "And change shape."

"Which he did with one of Mr. Edison's kinetoscopes," Houdini retorted heatedly. "Mr. Gaylord snatched it away while our attention was drawn to Cairo's little act at the end." He looked around defiantly. "That's how he did it."

"And this machinery was concealed where?" Cairo inquired.

"Up on the ceiling or in a secret chamber."

"Gentlemen," Cairo looked to me and Sir William, "was there anything on the ceiling? Did you find a hidden room?"

I shook my head.

"We found nothing," Sir William agreed.

"You missed it," Houdini shot back.

This really was too much. "You are welcome to return there and remedy our deficiencies."

"I say, Cairo." It was Mackleston who spoke. "You weren't serious, were you? About a demon being inside one of us, I mean?"

"Of course I was," Cairo snapped. "And you can thank Houdini for the consequences."

"What consequences?" Mackleston insisted, his voice rising.

"After what you've put me through tonight, you can find out on your own." With that, Cairo withdrew into a sullen pout.

"Well, tell me," Mackleston begged. "I never spoke against you."

Cairo stared straight ahead. "Only if Houdini promises to keep his libelous assertions to himself."

"Ridiculous," Houdini snorted. "Blackmail."

I could see that Mackleston was becoming agitated. I decided to step in.

"Really, Houdini," I began, "I am as skeptical as you."

Here Mackleston groaned and Cairo sniffed.

"But without empirical evidence," I continued, "surely our hands are tied."

Then Miss Luce spoke. "After all, Mr. Houdini," she said in a conciliating tone, "it's not as if he were competition for you. Indeed, you have none; you remain supreme in your sphere."

The magician grew thoughtful.

"From what I've seen," Miss Luce continued, "you are too great a man to stoop to playing the bully. Surely you can extend a little professional courtesy tonight."

Houdini's face cleared somewhat. An expression of resignation crossed his countenance. "Okay, okay. If he doesn't rob Mrs. Pangbourne blind, I won't crash his racket."

Ah, woman, I thought, only your subtle ways can resolve the conflicts of this world. Again I upbraided myself for the liberties I had taken with her. But Mackleston interrupted my thoughts.

"For God's sake, tell us!"

"Very well," Cairo agreed. "I shall reveal all."

Houdini folded his arms and watched from his corner. He positively radiated skepticism.

Cairo smiled. "Even I cannot determine which of you he has inhabited. He lies dormant now."

"To do what?" Mackleston asked.

"He will give you great powers. Remember, this is the god of inspiration. You will burn with the white heat of creativity. He will drive you to better than your best."

"That doesn't sound like the influence of a demon," I pointed out.

Cairo frowned. "It wouldn't be, if that were the end of it. But he has another side, a dangerous side. This god knows no limits, for he is also the god of frenzy. In his power you will be, quite literally, capable of anything. No act will be too vile, no crime too heinous for you. He will leave destruction strewn in his wake."

Sir William looked dubious; Mrs. Pangbourne fanned herself with a handkerchief. Miss Luce appeared lost in her own thoughts. Houdini, of course, displayed open contempt. Could one of these seemingly normal people harbor a demonic spirit? I wondered. To my surprise, I caught surreptitious glances directed my way as well.

"What precautions can we take?" I asked.

Cairo's reply did not inspire confidence. "You will be powerless before him. Surrender to the moment and revel in it. It is a gift of the gods. Like all such gifts, it is both wonderful and awful." He yawned and fell back on his pillows. "I grow fatigued. Pray leave me to recuperate."

Before we knew what was happening, Mr. Gaylord was herding us out of the room. Once we were downstairs, I distinctly heard the sound of snoring issue from above.

At the entryway, Mr. Gaylord disappeared for a moment. He soon returned with our coats. Without another word, he held the door open and we found ourselves outside on a midnight street.

The rain had diminished to a fine mist. The wet streets shone in the yellow glimmer of the antique gaslights. We huddled together somberly.

Mackleston was the first to voice the question that I am sure occupied all of our minds. "Which of us do you suppose it is?" His eyes darted from face to face.

Resolutely, I pushed my own uneasiness aside. "I don't

suppose it's any of us," I said. "Mr. Cairo was simply having his little joke at our expense."

"Yeah," Houdini spat out contemptuously. "It's just a ghost story."

"But what about those things we saw?" Mackleston asked forlornly.

"I wonder . . ." Miss Luce mused.

"No one in this party," Mrs. Pangbourne declared, "is capable of such excesses."

Sir William was silent.

All at once Houdini's eyes widened and he snapped his fingers. "I got it!" he said. "I know how he did it."

We all clustered around him, imploring him to continue. He held up his hands for quiet. "Remember the Hindu fakirs I told you about last night? Well, that's the answer," he declared. "Cairo hypnotized us, like they do."

There was a shocked silence.

"Mesmerism. Of course." Sir William looked thoughtful. "It might do."

For the first time in an hour, Mackleston looked hopeful. "You really think that's it?"

"Yes," I agreed. "Remember his dance, the rhythmic movements he made? He might well have used them to put us in a trance."

Mackleston looked relieved. Unfortunately, I realized, an even greater threat loomed over us. "There is one thing we should be cautious of," I said. "Persons in a hypnotic state are extremely vulnerable to suggestion. It is possible that Cairo used this vulnerability. He may have issued commands of which we are at present unaware."

Houdini appeared thunderstruck. "I never thought of that."

Mackleston looked uneasy. "What could he make us do? Could he get me to kill someone?"

"I doubt it," I said. "You can't be persuaded into anything you would not normally do."

Houdini nodded. Miss Luce's expression was impossible to read.

Sir William gaped. "We might embarrass ourselves in public—that sort of thing?"

"It is possible," I admitted.

"Mr. Cairo would never do something such as that," Mrs. Pangbourne asserted.

Houdini spoke up once more, "Okay, here's what we gotta do. Any of you feels the urge to do anything strange, wire me. I'll snap you out of it."

"What about you, Mr. Houdini?" Miss Luce asked. "What if it's you who has an urge?"

"I make myself available," I offered. "My medical knowledge is at your service."

"Great," Houdini said. "Let's all exchange addresses just in case."

There was general assent. By means of the notebook and pencil I always carried, the deed was soon accomplished.

Mrs. Pangbourne spoke up. "Which of you arranged for a carriage?"

Houdini shook his head. Mackleston pulled his coat more tightly around him against the damp.

I looked about. Shabby brick buildings with high narrow windows fronted rough cobblestones. Several of the streetlights were dark and hung uselessly on their arched wrought-iron holders. Some half a dozen drunken men stumbled out from a pub down the street. They lurched toward us through the shadows.

Mrs. Pangbourne looked from one of us to the other. "Am I to understand that no one thought to procure transportation?"

"So it appears," I confessed.

Houdini shifted from one foot to the other in the cold. "Which way to the nearest big street?"

I pointed south. "Euston Road. But it's better than a mile away."

"I'll go," he said.

I looked at the narrow alleys that yawned ominously off the main street. Who knew what manner of creature lurked in their depths? The men from the pub rapidly approached us. "Perhaps we should all go together," I suggested.

By now the rowdies were close enough that we could hear their drunken voices raised in coarse jests. As they passed one of the few working gaslights, I saw that all were in their twenties. Their clothes were dirty and in need of mending. A couple wore cloth caps.

All at once they spotted us and huddled, talking among themselves. Houdini and I stepped forward to protect the women. To my surprise, Mackleston was right by our side. "Not so good, these odds," he observed. Sir William moved up beside Houdini, though he looked uncertain. We waited. With one accord, the men lurched across the street toward us.

The sound of horses' hooves brought them up short. A huge, four-wheeled carriage drawn by two sturdy bays rattled down the center of the glistening cobblestone street and scattered the ruffians.

Never in my life had I been more pleased with a sight. I leaped into the center of the road and waved my arms to flag him down. The driver pulled up in front of me. "Get in, get in," he urged. His horses stamped and shifted uneasily.

Before the hooligans could regroup, we hurried the ladies inside and leaped aboard ourselves. As the driver flicked his whip, Mackleston said, "Bit of luck, your showing up here."

"Twarn't no luck at all. Mr. Cairo, he hired me yesterday. Said he was entertaining a party without the sense to get out of the rain." The man chuckled. "Looks like he was right about that."

Chapter 12
A Fearful Decision

Before I left London, I managed to contact Dr. Burton. He was a young man with a confident air and he returned with me to Surrey. Despite Miss Luce's endorsement, however, he pronounced Louise's case too far advanced for him to help. Sadly, he departed. With him went all hope.

Louise's condition continued to deteriorate. Nurse and I fed her clear liquids when she was conscious, bathed her, and changed her fouled bedclothes. Kingsley asked to help, but his mother's decline took a dreadful toll upon him. I banished him from the sickroom except for those rare moments when she recognized us. Why didn't I leave all the unpleasant duties to Nurse?

Dear Touie, as I fondly called my wife, had married me back when I had to survive on twopence a day. Through her cheerfulness, her warmth, and her common sense we had somehow survived those early years, when patients were few and writing sales fewer still.

"A Study in Scarlet," the first of my Holmes stories, was not an immediate hit. Touie consoled me. Her small private income helped us survive. Not till three years and several stories later did Holmes finally catch on with the public. But she never complained, never suggested I abandon my writing. I adored her.

What matter that her once-pretty face had shriveled into a skull-like visage? What matter that her once-cheerful disposition had dwindled to semiconscious ravings? I could not abandon her to a stranger's care.

I strove to be cheerful in her moments of lucidity. When alone, however, I fell into the deepest depression. Days drifted into a week, then two.

Mindful of my promise at the Palace, I tried to produce a Holmes story, but my imagination had become as barren as my life. Wistfully, I occasionally recalled the excitement of my London adventure.

One morning a letter from Houdini arrived. It briefly lifted my spirits. He thanked me for my help and pledged to return the favor. Then I came to the letter's last sentence.

"You won't believe this, but that louse Cairo had the nerve to come to one of my performances. And guess who was with him? Justine Luce, that's who. No accounting for taste, as the fellow says."

At first I was shocked. How could she submit herself to the influence of such a man? Was she that desperate for company? If only I could have remained in London . . . Ah, but what use were regrets?

Such were my thoughts as I sat in my study that afternoon and strove to revive Holmes once more. How would I get him out of the Reichenbach Falls? Try as I might, no ideas came.

My wife had been restless in her fever all morning. My slightest attempts to make her more comfortable had evoked cries of pain. Eventually, I could brook her misery no longer. I abandoned her to Nurse and fled to the temporary study I had set up in the chamber next to her sickroom.

As the afternoon wore on, I grew angry—angry at my wife's illness, at my own impatience with her, and most especially at my writers' block. Here was the one area of my life that I should be able to control. I determined to stay in the room until an idea came, even if I starved to death waiting.

So there I sat. The minutes ticked by. Each time I set pen to paper, no words came. At last I could no longer stand to look at the empty page. I leapt from the chair and began to pace. Back and forth I went. Faster and faster grew my steps until I virtually ran from wall to wall. I panted from both my exertions and emotions. All at once, I paused in my frantic perambulations and stood stock-still. A small ember of an idea glimmered in my brain. I fanned it with silent questions. Miraculously, it flared forth; I saw everything. I raced over to my desk and snatched a fresh pen off its stand to begin "The Adventure of the Laughing Widow."

I was too excited to sit. I yanked open a drawer and grabbed a handful of paper. The story shrieked itself into existence. Yes, I was doing it! I was capturing the passion that lurked behind the cold mask of my consulting detective. For the first time in my life I had created a case wherein he had a personal stake in the outcome.

I had never experienced anything like it. I was merely the channel through which the white-hot words flowed. The nib slashed at the foolscap like a scalpel. The paper absorbed my ink as linen bandages absorb blood.

"Arthur."

Someone had spoken my name. I was jerked from my concentration. Angrily, I looked around. I was alone in the room. I dismissed the sound and bent back over my work.

"Arthur!"

The voice was more insistent this time. I threw down my pen. How could I work with such interruptions?

I dashed out of my chamber to silence the voice. I found myself in the sickroom, standing over Louise. Nurse had gone out for a moment. My wife tossed feverishly in her bed. Again my name erupted from her lips. It was not a summons—merely a delirious cry.

As I stood over her, I felt a surge of anger. The spell had been broken, the flood of story ideas had dried up. The plot that only moments ago had fired me now seemed dull and uninspiring. My ferocious energy had fled. I could have shouted with disappointment.

Unaccountably, my thoughts again turned to Justine Luce. I yearned for her strong character and sympathetic nature. A woman like that would have been a support rather than a burden. But she was not here. Indeed, I had forfeited forever the right to her friendship. The thought added shame to the seething mass of emotions that tumbled in my breast.

I was struck by the helplessness of my wife's wasted body. How beastly it was that such a frail being had so powerful a hold over me! I could make no long-range plans. I was a prisoner to her needs. I felt as if my very soul was wasting away along with her.

Outside, life went on in its infinite variety—people laughed, cried, loved. Within the confines of these walls existed only a pallid reflection of life. I could have howled with frustration. I despised the withered creature before me.

She looked repulsive. Dark circles from weakness and pain ringed her sunken eyes. Beads of perspiration dotted her pasty skin. All that remained to her was ever-increasing pain and debility. Each breath was an effort. Was such a life worth living?

An inspiration seized me. I would free myself and her too. I snatched a pillow off the overstuffed chair beside the bed. Just the briefest struggle and then there would be peace for both of us. I clutched the pillow tightly. My breath came in harsh rasps. I took a step forward and stared down at her emaciated body. Now! Before she could wake. Still, I hesitated. Had I the courage to end both our sufferings?

Her eyes opened. The light of reason, which had been absent for many days, flickered in them. She looked me full in the face. Her eyes strayed to the pillow in my hands. At first they widened in fear. Then, it seemed, a look of acquiescence settled over her face. "I have always trusted you to do what is best for us both," she whispered. I swear that a melancholy smile curled her lips as she closed her eyes, drew a long painful breath, and waited. With trembling hands, I brought the pillow down over her still face.

"Sir Arthur!"

The voice's high urgency pierced my soul. I spun around to face my witness. In the doorway stood Justine Luce, her hand to her mouth.

What had she seen? My body had shielded my actions from the doorway. Or had it? "H-how did you get in here?"

"I knocked at the front door and your son showed me to you."

Then, to my horror, Kingsley poked his head around from behind her skirts. He stared at me curiously. I looked down, saw the pillow in my hands, saw my wife slip once more into the grip of those fevers that so ruthlessly consumed her. My hands trembled. I felt groggy, as if awaking from a deep slumber. My God, what had I been about to do? The pillow fell from my nerveless hands. I heard no more, because for the first and only time in my life I fainted dead away.

Chapter 13
The God Dionysus

"There, he's coming round." It was Nurse who spoke. I lay on a sofa across the room. Nurse leaned over me and fanned my face with a magazine. Miss Luce and Kingsley stood beside her.

"I hope it wasn't I who— That is, I didn't intend—" she began.

"No, of course not," Nurse interrupted. "He's pushing himself too hard."

I struggled to sit upright, but Nurse flattened me with a shove to the sternum.

"You lie there a moment," she scolded. She looked up to Miss Luce. "Nursing his wife all day and half the night, just like he didn't have me to do for her. Then working in that study of his the rest of the time. He never sleeps, as far as I can tell. Picks at his meals."

"She's right, Father." Kingsley gazed down at me with a serious look in his large eyes.

I looked around. My wife lay comatose, as usual, on the bed. For a moment I hoped I had been dreaming. Then I saw the pillow lying on the floor where I'd dropped it.

Black despair overwhelmed me. I must be going mad. Soon I should have to agree to restraint, perhaps even incarceration—if I was not hanged first.

Kingsley approached my couch. "What were you doing in there, Father?" he asked.

Evidently, he hadn't seen my actions clearly. "I—I was trying to make your mother more comfortable," I said weakly.

He nodded, but his face wore a puzzled look. The sound of coughing from across the room distracted us. Miss Luce started in alarm as my wife disgorged blood upon the white counterpane. I rose and Kingsley dashed forward, but Nurse was there before either of us, lifting Touie's head and wiping her mouth once she could draw a breath. After the fit passed, Nurse made up some trifling errand to get Kingsley out of the room. Then she advanced upon me sternly.

"Can't you see what you're doing to yourself?" Nurse indicated the bed with a nod of her head. "I don't know why you keep me here at all. Mark my words: If you don't let me tend to my duties, you're heading for a breakdown. And there are people here who need you at your best."

I hung my head.

"I have come at a bad time." Miss Luce spoke in a strained voice. "Please forgive my intrusion." She fled for the door.

I looked to Nurse. "Yes," she said, "see what she wants. I'll tend to your wife. Then get some rest, for God's sake—for all your sakes."

I caught up to Miss Luce at my front door. She drew her shawl about her. I scarcely dared to meet her gaze. Had she seen my shameful actions?

"What—what is the matter?" I asked fearfully.

Her voice trembled. "I am so sorry to disturb you at a time like this—" she drew a shuddering breath and continued, "—but I am desperate."

Her face was in high color from the emotions seething in her breast, but she did not shy away in fear. Relief washed over me. She hadn't seen. "Believe me," I said, "I am most obliged for the interruption."

For the first time since she appeared in the doorway of the sickroom, I really observed her. She had come away without a hat; her hair was carelessly done up. Furthermore, her gloves matched neither her handbag nor her shoes. Clearly, she had bolted in a hurry.

"It's monstrous," she blurted out. "I know he's going to die, and there's nothing I can do." Her green eyes filled. "You are my last hope."

She broke into uncontrollable sobbing. I felt helpless. I dared not do what I longed to—fold her into my arms and comfort her. "Who's going to die?"

Miss Luce made a heroic effort and pulled herself together. "Algy," she managed to get out between gasps.

"Mackleston!" I cried. "What has happened?"

"His brother was murdered last night. Algy's been arrested. The police say he will hang."

This woman did not yield to tears easily. The case against Mackleston must be grim indeed.

"They let me visit him." She drew a breath. "I promised to seek your help."

"But why me?" I certainly was in no shape to help anyone. "What the man needs is a solicitor. I know you have contacts in London."

"So I thought," she admitted. "But none are willing to risk their reputations by involving themselves in such a scandal."

"Cairo will have no such scruples. Surely he has entries into society."

"Don't mention that name to me!" She looked up, her green eyes flashing. "Cairo is a beast! I cannot begin to tell you—" Here she paused to get hold of herself. If ever I had heard hatred in a human voice, I heard it then. "Cairo will not help."

Her devotion to her friend was touching. And I felt proud that she had chosen me in her hour of need. But what was I thinking? How could I forget what had occurred not ten minutes before? The horror of my actions once more overwhelmed me. How could I trust myself?

"I am afraid I cannot help you, either," I said.

Desperation flickered in her eyes. "Then an innocent man is doomed."

I was in agony at her look. "I am truly sorry," I said. "You are not safe in my company."

She strained toward me with the eagerness of a pointer. Her dainty, gloved hands clutched at my sleeve. Her eyes burned feverishly. "I thought so! You have felt it too."

"Felt what?"

"The touch of Dionysus. Just as Cairo said."

With a rush I recalled Cairo's words that night. "You will burn with the white heat of creativity. . . . He is also the god of frenzy. In his power you will be capable of anything."

With mounting excitement I recalled my fiery burst of inspiration and its abhorrent aftermath—as he had foretold. Had an outside force controlled me? The thought gave me hope.

I turned to Miss Luce. "Have you experienced it too?"

She nodded wordlessly. Her eyes stared into the past. Her face grew pale at some memory. "I cannot tell you the ecstasy I have felt, or the depths to which I have sunk—things I would never have believed myself capable of." She lowered her gaze in shame.

I shuddered at the thought of the depravities to which she might have succumbed in the company of a man like Cairo.

She weaved on her feet. I rushed forward and wrapped an arm around her shoulders.

She raised a hand to her forehead. "I am sorry," she mumbled. "I haven't slept."

The feel of her tender flesh beneath the fabric of her dress was like a jolt of electricity. It brought a frightful possibility to mind. Dionysus might still hold sway over my actions. Horrified, I steadied Miss Luce and withdrew my arm. "Shall I fetch you a chair?"

She smiled up at me gratefully but shook her head. "I shall be better in a moment."

I scrutinized my feelings, fearfully sought signs of madness. I felt concern and an undeniable attraction to this woman beside me, but thankfully nothing more. I seemed free of malign influence—at least for the time being.

Miss Luce struggled to smile. "Thank you. I am better now."

Were such a creature truly loose among us, it might well have made the rounds of everyone who had come under its sinister spell at Cairo's. "If you and I were overpowered," I said, "is it not possible that Mackleston also—?"

"You must believe he is innocent," she pleaded.

I shook my head sadly. "Your loyalty does you credit. But you must not let it blind you."

She chewed her lower lip in consternation. Finally, she looked up at me. "I shall tell you something that few people know. When my father died, I was thrown upon my own resources. Algy was the only friend who stuck by me."

Tears welled again in her eyes. "Without him I would have starved. I came to know his family intimately. I am certain that no power here on earth or in the heavens above could turn that poor, sweet boy's hand to murder."

My heart went out to her. However, she had left a critical question unanswered. "Then why do the police suspect him?"

"I do not know." She pressed her full lips together. "All they say is that they have proof."

"What explanation does he offer?"

"None," she replied unhappily. "He suffered a blow on the head and remembers nothing."

It certainly sounded bad for Mackleston. To hold out false hopes would be cruel. "Contrary to the conventions of fiction," I said gently, "the police are seldom mistaken in these matters."

"That is what torments him so. Not knowing the truth, you see."

She pushed herself from my grasp and gazed squarely at me with those arresting green eyes. "I am certain you can sympathize with the agony of not knowing whether one is a murderer."

My breath caught in my chest. Had she seen me with the pillow after all? She continued earnestly, "If you knew him as I do, you'd know he was incapable of killing."

I perched on the edge of an abyss. Was I really ready to admit that powers of this sort actually inhabited the world? If not, I was an attempted murderer.

"I must pursue the facts wherever they lead," I said, half to myself.

She looked up, her eyes pleading. "What if the facts prove that someone was under the control of an irresistible outside influence?" she asked.

She had touched the crux of the matter—for me as well as her friend. "Then that person was not truly guilty," I said. Could such things be? Or was I simply grasping at straws to assuage my own feelings of shame? The explanation was so tempting. If I could prove that Dionysus truly strode among us, I could exonerate myself—and Mackleston as well.

But I could not let my hopes blind me to the facts. Should we prove Cairo a charlatan, I would spare myself nothing. I would see to it I was locked away from decent society. I shuddered as I recalled my dreadful impulse in Louise's room. I had to know the truth.

"You may rely upon me to pursue the matter to its conclusion," I said.

Miss Luce sighed. Her whole body slumped with relief. Automatically, I reached out an arm to support her. She gave a wan smile. "I knew you would not refuse us," she said.

"Not at all," I replied. It was ridiculous: I had just committed myself to a well-nigh impossible task—proving to all officialdom that a demonic spirit was the real murderer. Yet here I stood, basking in the glow of her approval.

I had best quit mooning about and address the facts at hand. One thing told very strongly against our friend.

"There are times Mackleston is not himself. If you are a close friend, you have seen them."

She nodded sadly. "The opium. It's sure to come out at his trial. But you know it is a soporific. It could never drive him to violence."

"Unless he were deprived of it," I reminded her.

"Unfortunately," she said, "he has no dearth of supply."

My mind raced ahead. I was not without influence at the highest levels of the government. With official sanction I could certainly gain access to the murder scene. I might discover facts that others had overlooked.

And if the police would not listen to reason, I would take my case directly to the public via the newspapers. It was a course that had worked for me before. The disgraceful suppression of evidence at the Edalji murder trial came to mind.

It was imperative to begin at once. Even as we spoke, clues and memories were fading.

"We must meet at the train station at six-thirty tomorrow morning," I said.

She nodded gamely. "I shall be ready."

As I opened the front door, I fretted over how to broach the final issue that lay between us. She lingered on the stoop a moment. I got a good look at her in the lights coming through the big front windows of my house. She appeared absolutely exhausted. No doubt she was worn out with worry for her friend. I decided to simply plunge ahead.

"Miss Luce," I said, "before you agree to this expedition, you must hear me out. I have twice taken advantage of you. That I was not myself either time is no excuse. I most sincerely beg your forgiveness."

Her voice, when she spoke, was husky and her eyes were filled with indecipherable emotion. "Do you remember that evening when I called you medieval?"

"Indeed I do."

"Well, thank God I was right! If ever I needed a knight-errant, it is now." She pressed my hand briefly and was gone in a swirl of skirts to her waiting cab.

Chapter 14
Dionysus Again

Early next morning, I took Kingsley aside. "I must go away for a short time," I told him.

He looked unhappily up at me. "Is it another adventure?"

I hated to lie to him. After thinking a moment, I said, "With your mother's illness, I've not been myself. I know I have neglected you and the rest of the family. I'm going to meet someone who I think can help me. When I come back, I shall be a better father."

He thought that over. "Will you be gone long?" he asked.

"No," I said. "And when I return, we shall have adventures of our own—just we two."

"You promise?"

"I promise."

With that Kingsley was placated and actually helped me to pack.

The night before, I had sent a telegram suing for an appointment with a certain august personage. By the time Miss Luce arrived, I had still received no reply. Nevertheless, I determined to proceed as if my request had been acceded to. Accordingly, we boarded the first train that stopped at Windsor that morning.

My companion was looking much refreshed in a tucked and side-closed white blouse of cream-colored face cloth and matching full skirt. As for me, in my navy-blue blazer and trousers, it was not an easy ride. In addition to my uncertainty as to our reception, I worried that I might still be a danger to others.

My companion, too, seemed reserved. For most of our journey, she gazed out the window with an air of unutterable sadness. No doubt the rush of current events had left her shaken.

Fortunately, I detected no further signs of madness in myself. Perhaps whatever power had gripped me yesterday had fled. When we arrived at Windsor, I was cautiously hopeful.

I was relieved to find that my telegram had arrived and been perused. Fortunately, the one I sought was not unacquainted with Mackleston's family. Furthermore, he was in residence, having recently returned from grouse shooting at Balmoral. Suffice it to say, after a brief wait I was allowed to make my request. In a very short time, I obtained a letter that guaranteed us entry virtually anywhere the British Empire held sway.

And so we found ourselves once again at the Windsor train station. Every morning paper sported a headline decrying the murder of Reginald Mackleston and the arrest of his younger brother. None of them, however, added to my meager store of knowledge about the case.

"Where is Mackleston being held?" I inquired of Miss Luce.

"Holloway Prison." She added, "His trial is in a week."

Time was indeed of the essence. We decided not to wait for a train, but hired a carriage and driver to take us the twenty-two miles east into the city.

Once aboard, we passed Staines and followed the Great West Road to Chiswick. Suburbs of the metropolis alternated with vast open fields. The traffic changed from the occasional rider on horseback or farm wagon to an ever-increasing stream of horse-drawn carts, wagons, and omnibuses as we approached Hammersmith. Soon we were in the city itself.

We passed Hampstead Heath and drove south to the stone-faced Gothic pile that was Holloway Prison on Parkurst Road. Square towers and crenellated walls greeted us as we approached the reception ward. The whole appearance was of a medieval donjon keep.

Bearing my letter of introduction, we had no problems with the Chief Warder. In fact, he granted us a rare concession: Normally, visitors were shut up inside tiny, wire-covered visiting boxes with an officer present. We, however, were allowed to see Mackleston privately in his cell.

As we followed a guard through the maze of dark and narrow corridors, I thought about what courage and determination Miss Luce had shown.

"Mackleston has a rare friend in you," I said to her.

She pursed her soft lips. "If you knew what he has done for me, you would not think so."

My incredulity must have registered on my face, for she continued most insistently. "Over the years, he has endured a great deal of trouble for my sake."

I waited, but she did not elaborate. I wondered what trouble Mackleston had endured. It was difficult to imagine him in the role of a defender.

After a moment, she added, "You know, he's quite a remarkable artist."

"He has the temperament for it."

"He attended the Slade," she retorted.

I immediately grew more impressed with our client. The quality of that Bloomsbury art school was world-renowned.

"It was there he met Mr. Gaylord," Her expression hardened. "Which led him to Mr. Cairo." She turned to me. "I am certain that night at Mr. Cairo's is the origin of this crime."

I grew silent as I remembered the dreadful scene in my wife's sickroom yesterday. Could a demon have possessed me? The hopefulness of last night had given way to doubt. On the face of it, the idea was absurd. But there was the evidence of the half-finished Holmes story. Nothing so passionate had ever come out of me before.

My common sense resisted the thought of supernatural powers. Which was I—mad or possessed? Neither alternative gave much comfort. In addition to which, I was not used to suffering from indecision, and this disturbed me even more. Mackleston, too, was accused of behaving uncharacteristically. I became more anxious by the minute to hear his story.

Holloway Prison held people awaiting their trials. Therefore, it was not as mean as the prisons used for carrying out sentences. Mackleston's cell was a bit larger than the standard seven by thirteen feet. He had a real cot instead of the usual bunk with its straw mattress. Along the wall sat an old table and a couple of rickety chairs. A dirty brown drugget served as a rug.

Still, it was not comfortable. Rough stones ran from floor to ceiling. A single bare bulb suspended from the ceiling provided illumination. A stained chamber pot was mute evidence to the lack of amenities. When we entered, Mackleston lay on his cot, one arm flung across his forehead. At the sight of us, he sprang up and rushed forward.

"Justine," he cried, "you have come." Then he turned to me and pumped my hand vigorously. "Conan Doyle, good to see you."

At least he showed no signs of being mistreated. He had recently bathed and wore a clean set of prison grays. "Then let us begin," I prompted.

His pale face had developed worry lines between his brows and at the corners of his mouth. "They say I murdered my brother."

"We shall go over the facts and see where they take us. When did the crime occur?"

The poor boy pulled himself together enough to answer. "Two days ago, at about five in the afternoon."

"Miss Luce tells me you were in the room with him when he was killed."

"Yes."

"Can you remember nothing?"

"That's the problem!" Mackleston threw himself back down upon his cot. "I can't. I recall each moment of that day up to the time he arrived at my flat. From then on, everything's a blank until the police dragged me to this place."

"Do you mind if I examine you?"

He sat up. "Not a bit. Got a bit of a bump on the back of my head."

I went over every inch of his neck and skull with my fingers, as well as my eyes. Miss Luce hovered anxiously in the background. Mackleston winced as I touched the lower right side of the occipital. I found a thumb-sized swelling just above the mastoid process. Feeling around the center, I discerned a scab under the hairs. How had he received such a blow?

"I told the police a doctor should examine him," Miss Luce exclaimed when I revealed my discovery. "But they wouldn't listen to me."

I nodded and asked Mackleston, "You don't remember how you were injured?"

"No," Mackleston replied, puzzled.

Continuing, I tested his reflexes and checked his pupil response by covering his eyes with my hand for a minute and withdrawing it suddenly. All seemed normal. I straightened up. His injury gave me the first glimmer of hope I had discerned. The location of the wound was telling.

"Will I ever get it back? My memory, I mean?" he asked.

"It is possible. You may wake up one morning and recall everything in startling detail. You may get only flashes that gradually accumulate over weeks, months, or even years."

"And I may never recall anything at all, I suppose."

"That also is possible," I admitted.

Mackleston sighed. "Perhaps it would be for the best."

"Why is that?"

His eyes took on a hunted look. "When I came to, I was in the police wagon on the way here." He leaned over and sank his head down into his hands. "Thing is, I was positively covered with gore." His voice broke. "Pretty fresh, too." He began to weep quietly. Miss Luce hastened to him and laid a sympathetic arm across his shoulders.

"Never you mind, Algy," she said. "We'll explain that away."

I myself was not so sanguine. "Were you and your brother close?" I asked, though I thought I knew the answer.

"No," he sniffed. "Couldn't stand each other. But I wouldn't kill him. I wouldn't! They say I did, though— even the solicitor they appointed thinks so. Reggie would inherit, you see. They think I did him in to get the title. I don't want the damned old thing." He drew a sobbing breath. "M'father won't even visit me. I expect he thinks I'm guilty, too."

"Well, we certainly don't," Miss Luce said. "I shall arrange for your defense myself if your father doesn't come to his senses."

I added, "We shall do everything possible to determine the truth."

"Awfully decent of you," Mackleston replied. He wiped his eyes and raised his head. "Sorry about getting the drips. I'm a bundle of nerves."

"Anyone would be," I said brusquely. "Now I am afraid I must ask a difficult question.

"Did I kill him, you mean? Surely I couldn't do such a thing." Anguish filled his voice. "But, God, I wish I could remember!"

"No, not that. The question I must ask is how did your brother die?"

"Well, that's just it. They won't tell me."

"Won't tell you? Did they say why?"

He shook his head.

I considered a moment. "Perhaps you had better go over for us exactly what happened to you on that day up to the time of your memory lapse."

He nodded and began.

Mackleston's Story

I'm afraid most of that day is a gray fog. Just certain moments stand out vividly. It was only two days ago, yet it feels like a childhood memory. I do remember that I had stretched a new canvas the night before. In addition, half a dozen canvases lay drying about the room. Justine had been kind enough to sit for me and, if I do say so myself, I was especially fond of the creamy skin tones I had managed in the nude study. No, don't blush, Justine. If you recall, I had a ray of light highlighting your hair and bosom with a Rembrandtlike effect while your face remained in shadow. Anyone who recognized you from that wouldn't dare to admit it in polite company.

I'd left the canvases out because my brother Reginald was coming over that afternoon. Whistler had made some trifling praise of my work before he died last summer. It must have reached Reggie's ear, because he almost immediately began pressuring me to put together a show. He'd never even noticed my work before. I suppose he decided there might be some money in it. Always an eye for the family fortune, that's m'brother. Or, rather, that was him— Oh, damn it all, poor Reggie!

Oh, dear, where was I? Oh, yes. The canvas. I squeezed some colors onto my palette, but I had no idea what subject to paint. I recalled, however, an afternoon sky I'd seen the other day. You remember the storm of that night at Cairo's? Before the deluge, the sky had been just the color of putty. I had rather liked it, so I began to mix some colors, trying to capture that sort of pale gray-brown that I recalled. I had nothing definite in mind, simply an effect of the light.

When I finally reached the right mix of pigments, the hue reminded me of something else. The longer I stared at the paint, the more convinced I became that I was looking at flesh—but not healthy flesh. No, this was flesh untouched by the sun, the flesh of a corpse. I selected a brush and began to dab in an idle sort of way. I painted a hand, a young man's hand. I felt I needed red, so I squeezed a thick worm of pigment onto my palette and added it to the wrist of the hand. It looked quite like blood there.

I studied what I had done so far. It wasn't a bad hand, you know. Not half-bad. I crossed the room and looked at it from a different angle. I couldn't take my eyes off it. And then a strange thing happened. An entire scene blazed forth in my mind. I saw the whole painting—I mean colors, proportions, everything. To realize how thrilling that was, you must understand something. Usually, I'm quite methodical. I make sketches, tinker with the balance and composition before I set brush to canvas. Often I'll do a small study in watercolor to test my idea. Not this time. In a flash I saw the entire canvas as it would be.

I would paint the Daughters of King Minyas—a story I remembered from my Greek studies at school. Three sisters had rejected the teachings of the god Dionysus, so he drove them mad. They ended up tearing one of their own sons limb from limb. My painting would depict them at the height of their madness, dancing around a bonfire, holding up the pieces of their victim.

Fired with the concept, I snatched up my palette. Reds, I needed reds—the rich burgundy of blood, the orange glare of the flames, the scarlet of the son's cloak lying forlornly on the ground. Up until now I had always tried for a sort of heightened realism in my work. Not this time. I wanted the technique itself to reveal madness. Shapes would be distorted in insane ways. I'd use lines, thick lines, to emphasize their separation from reality. I would paint the visual equivalent of a shriek.

I attacked the canvas in a frenzy. My brush moved in a fury of strokes. I began by painting the subjects of my vision from above, as if I were the god himself looking down, enjoying his handiwork. The flames of the fire came first, twisting into life with bold brush strokes and a clash of colors. Then came the daughters. Their figures swirled like the flames they circled. I panted from the intensity of my vision. Never once did I step back to assess my work, but continued on, slapping brush to canvas like a fiend. Each of the dancers came out in a different perspective, making the whole a crazy, unresolvable point of view. Two of the women cavorted in an obscene tug-of-war with a part of the son's body. When I had the figures just right, I dug my fingers into the rich reds on my palette and smeared the mad, upturned faces with great gouts of blood. I was no longer the painter; I was in the painting itself, participating in the dreadful rite.

When I finished, hours had passed. The light was fading. I staggered backward in the dim room to see the entire canvas. It was like nothing I'd ever done before. Swirling black lines, riots of harsh reds, hideously misshapen figures leapt out at me. I flung down my brush and collapsed in a chair from exhaustion. I fell asleep and didn't stir until a knock at my door aroused me.

Mackleston looked up. "That's all I remember until I came to my senses in the police wagon."

Miss Luce and I exchanged glances. I am sure we shared the same reaction—what a ghastly subject for a painting.

"Who was at the door?" I asked.

"I can't recall, but it must have been Reggie," he said. "They tell me he was the only other person in the room when they found me."

I fell silent. How I could fail to recognize the similarity to my own experience? If I had come close to murder, why should Mackleston be immune from it?

Cairo's warning echoed once more in my ears. Here

was the second of our séance group involved in an act of wild creativity followed by violence.

Mackleston was in a terrible position. I could easily see what a jury would conclude when shown the painting he had described to us. Nevertheless, his head injury might be an indication of innocence. I had to visit the murder scene.

Mackleston said glumly, "I haven't a chance, have I?"

"Nonsense," I insisted more assuredly than I felt. "We shall pursue every avenue to determine the truth."

"But what if I did kill him? What if I can't remember because I don't want to?"

"It is premature to make those sorts of judgments," I said, rising. I was eager to pursue my slim lead. "What happened that night is a deep mystery. After all, there is still the blow to the back of your head to be explained." I refrained from revealing the train of thought that one fact had started in my mind. It was no use giving him false hopes.

He clutched at my sleeve. "Whatever you find out, you must tell me. Do you promise?"

"Of course," I assured him. "I will tell you the truth, no matter how painful."

He released his hold on me. "All right, then."

"We must be on our way," I said.

"Yes," Miss Luce agreed, "but first, tell me, Algy, is there anything you need?"

He looked sheepish. "There's an old suit of clothes I wear when I'm painting. You remember them, Justine. If you could bring them to me, I'd be ever so obliged."

"Those old things? Why, they're almost in tatters. Whatever do you want them for?"

"A touch of the familiar would be so comforting," Mackleston apologized. "They're in my closet. You can't miss them—they're khaki-colored and they smell of turpentine."

"Oh, all right," she said, and sighed.

"Be of good cheer," I said. "Things are not as hopeless as they appear."

With that we departed, leaving Mackleston with a puzzled look on his face.

Chapter 15
We Commence Our Investigation

I had earlier ascertained that Horace Woburn was the inspector in charge of the case. His name was familiar to me as that of one of the most successful officers in the CID. His murder arrests had always resulted in hangings. It had been written in no less prominent a paper than the *Times* that being apprehended by Horace Woburn was tantamount to a death sentence.

Therefore, it was with some trepidation that Miss Luce and I arrived at his office in New Scotland Yard on the Thames embankment. He chanced to be in. I was able to assess firsthand our adversary—for thus he soon proved himself to be.

We ascended to the CID offices. Above the second floor, the interior of the building resembled a rabbit warren, with cramped offices and piles of paper everywhere. Books, evidence, and various confiscated weapons littered the narrow corridors. One or two typewriters clacked away, but mostly the men scribbled their reports out in longhand.

We made our way through the maze and found him in an office scarcely larger than a closet. He sat at a desk awash with papers, laboriously copying over a set of notes. Upon our arrival, he rose to greet us. He was a person of great girth; with his beard and white hair, he resembled Father Christmas. Only his eyes, which were small and close-set, belied the comparison. They squinted suspiciously at me as I introduced Miss Luce and myself and stated our errand.

He sank back behind his desk and folded his hands across his stomach. "So the great Conan Doyle himself is takin' a interest in our little murder. Goin' to play at Sherlock Holmes, are you? Goin' to put it over on all the dunces at Scotland Yard?"

I was somewhat taken aback at this reception. Miss Luce, however, was not. "Actually," she said, "we are here on behalf of Algernon Mackleston. We hope to prove his innocence."

"You're wastin' your time," Woburn said. "He's guilty as Judas."

"Oh, how can you say that!" she cried. "If you knew him, you'd know he was incapable of a violent act."

Woburn looked at her with new interest in his eyes. "And might I ask what is your relationship to the accused?"

"We're friends."

He drew a notebook off his desk and flipped it open. The inspector copied down her name and asked for her address. "Were you close friends?"

"You could say so."

His expression grew sly. "How close?"

Miss Luce reddened.

"See here—" I began angrily. But she stopped me with a hand on my arm. Drawing herself up, she spoke calmly and purposefully.

"I despise innuendo. If you have a question, please put it plainly."

Woburn chuckled, but his eyes registered frank dislike. "Right, then. Were you lovers?"

"No."

"You're missin' a bet. With his brother gone, he comes into quite a load of nick."

She chose to ignore the loathsome insinuation and continued. "He does not appeal to me in that way. I would prefer the attentions of a gentleman with more strength of purpose."

Woburn rubbed his chin while eyeing her speculatively. "Strength of purpose, eh?"

"Yes," she said lightly. "The sort of a man who could commit murder."

He flipped his notebook shut. His small eyes glittered with anger. "Just what is it you came after?"

I spoke up. "Two things. First of all, we should like to know how the brother died."

"You sure?" he challenged me. "It's not pleasant."

"Perhaps you should wait for me in the hall," I suggested to Miss Luce.

"No," she insisted. "I must know everything."

"Right 'n' tight, then," he grunted. "Murder's all over this mornin's papers. Fleet Street's bound to get the details before much longer." He looked me straight in the eye. "Reginald Mackleston was dismembered." He leaned forward. "In all my years on the force I have never seen anything like it."

"Dear God!" The color drained from Miss Luce's face. She clutched at my sleeve.

Even I found the idea unnerving—especially when I recalled the subject of Mackleston's painting. Still, I forced my attention back to the matter at hand. After all, I had pledged my help. I hated to distress Miss Luce further, but I had to know the specifics. "You mean he was butchered?"

"No," Woburn said forcefully. "I mean he was tore limb from limb. Someone—or something—ripped him apart."

Miss Luce's appalled expression gave mute testimony

to her distress. As the horror of his words sank in, my mind conjured up Poe's "Murders in the Rue Morgue." "Might it have been the work of a savage beast?"

"I think it's the work of the devil himself," Woburn muttered. "In any case," he addressed us once more, "no zoos have reported escapes."

"Perhaps a private collection?" I suggested.

"Look." A note of desperation crept into his voice. "In the old days when criminals were drawn and quartered, it took four strong horses lungin' to pull a man apart. You tell me the animal what could do that."

It seemed to me that he had just given the best reason possible for freeing Mackleston. How could he hold a man for an act no man was strong enough to commit?

Miss Luce, too, had seized upon the fact. "Then how can you suspect poor Algy?"

He turned on her, fury in his voice. "You weren't in that room. You didn't see what I saw—the blood, the smell, the . . . the chaos. It took us hours to scoop up the remains. Organs was strewn around like Christmas wrappin'. And there lay young Mackleston, unconscious in a corner—drenched in his brother's blood."

Woburn pushed himself to his feet and paced the small room. "You ever see what a madman can do? I've seen some as ended up in Bedlam fling half a dozen constables about like scraps of paper."

He drew a breath. "That's the power that murdered Reginald Mackleston. Your boy was the only other bloke in the room. And he has the nerve to tell me he don't remember a thing!"

The man's eyes glittered with hatred. "That sort of trick might have worked in the old days, but we don't cover up for the gentry anymore. If he thinks he's goin' to get off because of his family, he's very much mistaken!"

All was silent in the room while Woburn struggled to recover his composure. Miss Luce appeared dazed. It looked bad for Mackleston—worse than either of them had suspected. I knew from personal experience that nothing was impossible for one in the grip of Dionysus—or whatever power had controlled my actions.

At length I spoke in what I hoped was a calm tone. "I should like your permission to examine the murder scene."

Miss Luce looked uncertainly at me. Woburn glared.

"Why?"

"There are one or two small matters upon which I should like to satisfy myself."

"Such as?"

I was not about to reveal the slender hope I had conceived in Mackleston's cell. It was not uncommon for evidence to disappear in cases when some official's pride was at stake.

"It is premature to speculate," I said.

Woburn's look darkened. He raised his head and called. "Oi, constable! Over here!"

A couple of uniformed men hurried up.

"Arrest these two," Woburn ordered. "They're charged with obstructin' my investigation and withholdin' information about a murder."

The two men blinked at each other, then leaped into action. One grabbed Miss Luce's arm. The other snatched at my coat collar and dragged it across my throat. I gasped as he hauled me backward.

Woburn trundled around his desk and glared at me. As I struggled for a breath, he gave me a smile that was little more than a grimace.

"I expect after a few days in gaol, you'll be beggin' to tell me those 'one or two small matters.' " He hissed at me, "I won't have a ruddy amateur second-guessin' me!" He stepped back. "Take 'em away," he ordered the policemen.

My chest heaved for air. I scrabbled at my outside coat pocket. My fingers dug inside and clutched at the letter there.

As the man dragged me backward, I waved the sheet futilely. My vision was blurring. Faintly, I heard Miss Luce's voice ring out calm and clear. "You had better read it—if you wish to remain employed."

The paper was snatched from my hand and someone shoved me upright. The pressure on my throat eased. I sucked air into my lungs, though it burned my raw throat.

I looked to Miss Luce. The other policeman had let her go. She appeared pale but resolute. Woburn opened the letter with a smirk. As he read, his countenance flushed red. When he handed the letter back to me, his hand was shaking. "All right, then," he said quietly. He yanked open his desk drawer and produced a key, which he flung in my direction. "It's Number Fifteen, Sutton Row."

I recognized the street as a Soho address. "Thank you," I croaked, scooping up the key. "May I have a glance at your notes on the case?"

"No, you bloody well may not!" Woburn glared at me. "I won't have my case mucked about by friends of the killer. I don't care who your little stories have impressed. This is not some game for fine gentlemen to play at."

He pounded the desk with a meaty fist to emphasize his point. "This is life-and-death. And I had better not even suspect you're getting in my way. No one is above the law—not even the great Conan Doyle!"

I did not deign to respond. I merely straightened my clothing, took Miss Luce's arm, and escorted her from the room. At the doorway, I paused and said, "Has Mackleston been seen by a physician?"

"A physician!" the man exploded. "What for?"

"Doubtless, it's just more of my amateurish second-guessing," I said. "Good day."

We found ourselves standing outside the granite facing of New Scotland Yard. Carriages and cabs clattered past us. "What an odious man!" Miss Luce said.

I wholeheartedly agreed with her. "Thank you for speaking out when you did," I said.

She dismissed my gratitude with a little wave. "I've run

into his kind before. He's like the school bully—jealous of his betters and vicious to his inferiors. I pity those who work under him."

Once again I reflected on the sad circumstances that had given her an intimate knowledge of such matters. I yearned to spare her further unpleasantness.

"Why not let me examine the room alone?" I suggested gently. "We can meet for luncheon later. I promise to relate everything I find."

Miss Luce was pale but adamant. "I should never forgive myself if I let Algy down."

"Really, I think—" I began, only to be cut off.

"You dare not exclude me." Her eyes flashed with anger. Then in a moment they softened. "You could not be so heartless. After all, were it not for me, you would be ignorant of the case."

It was true. If anyone had a right to participate, it was she. I sighed inwardly and escorted her to our carriage. She was not the Watson I would have chosen. Still, one admired her spirit.

Midday traffic was heavy up Charing Cross Road. Our cab took nearly twenty minutes to reach Soho. Mackleston's building was an unprepossessing three stories of brown brick.

We agreed it was best to let the landlady know we had the permission of the police to be there. In addition, I was eager to discover if she had been in the building at the time of the murder.

No one responded to our knock, so I tried the door. I was surprised to hear the jangle of a loud bell as we opened it. Through a clever cord-and-pulley system, opening the front door rang a bell hung beside it. The door of the first flat opened a crack. Through the narrow gap I heard the faint whistle of a teakettle. I could barely make out an eye glaring at us.

The door slammed closed. All was silence within. We approached, and I rapped on the portal with some force. The silence remained unbroken.

"What on earth!" I exclaimed, and raised my fist once more. To my surprise, Miss Luce took hold of my hand and gently lowered it.

"She's terrified," she whispered. "Imagine living downstairs from such a horrible murder. I should think twice about answering my door, too."

"Quite right," I agreed, impressed with her insight. "Perhaps we should simply find our own way there."

"Let me try." She stepped up to the door and called, "Won't you please speak to us? We're friends of the Mackleston family."

After a moment's pause, I heard the scrape of a bolt being thrown. A key rattled in the lock and the door opened a crack. We stepped back to allow the occupant a clear view of us. The door swung open and revealed a mousy woman in her sixties with a haggard face. Wisps of gray hair straggled down her neck. Her dark eyes roved over Miss Luce's figure, then snapped to me.

"You're not from the papers?" The question was half plea, half accusation.

"No," Miss Luce assured her. "As I said, we are friends of the family."

"Know him well?" the older woman asked.

"I did," Miss Luce said. "And Inspector Woburn has given us permission to examine the room in order to aid his inquiries."

At the name the landlady bristled. "Woburn, eh? I didn't fancy him very much. Right full of himself, he was." She backed off, as if to end the interview.

"That was our impression, as well," Miss Luce agreed quickly. Before the woman could shut the door, Miss Luce added, "This is Sir Arthur Conan Doyle."

The woman's eyes went wide. "What, the writer?"

I nodded. The landlady looked from me to my lovely companion. Miss Luce smiled encouragingly.

"Well, I never." She stepped back from the door and wiped her hands on her apron. "You're most welcome, I'm sure. Please come in. I was just making tea."

"If it's not too much trouble," Miss Luce said.

"Trouble?" The woman led us to a small but comfortable sitting room with red and white floral wallpaper. "I should say not." The room was scrupulously clean. Even the fireplace looked freshly scrubbed. She motioned us over to a horsehair sofa. Again I was indebted to Miss Luce's tact and gentle persuasion.

The landlady gave a furtive look down the hall and proceeded to relock her door.

As she poured tea, she kept up a stream of chatter. "Imagine me, Mary Finch, entertaining a literary gentleman. Wait till that Laura Elwood hears about this. And her so high and mighty about her daughter marrying a lawyer. Well, my goodness. We'll have biscuits, I think."

She ignored our protests and disappeared into her kitchen. I could not help but notice that every square inch of table, dresser, and mantel was filled with knickknacks. A bust of the late queen jostled for space alongside picture postcards of seaside holidays. Mementos of Victoria's first Jubilee stood shoulder to shoulder with tiny candlestick holders, carved animals, and cut-glass atomizers. Despite the clutter, not a speck of dust was to be found. When our hostess returned, she bore a plate with a dozen tiny biscuits.

We sipped and munched together. Miss Luce put Miss Finch at ease almost immediately. Soon we were on the best of terms.

"You know," the landlady confided as she refilled my cup, "I was very disappointed when Mr. Holmes went over that cliff. Very disappointed indeed."

I sighed. Here was another reminder that I had not fulfilled my promise at the Palace Theatre. "I believe many share your feelings."

I judged she was finally comfortable enough for me to introduce the topic uppermost on my mind.

"Was I at home?" she responded to my first query. "Well, I guess I was! I remember Mr. Mackleston had guests that night, which was unusual for him."

•

"Guests?" I interrupted. "You mean more than one person?"

"That's just what that policeman asked me. I'll tell you the same as I told him. I didn't see who came in that night. But I'll swear that there was more than two people up there arguing. Of course, Inspector Woburn would have it that I was wrong. He said I imagined it."

Miss Luce's glance at me was razor sharp. I nodded. "Pray continue," I urged. "Describe the argument you overheard."

"I didn't overhear nothing. I was down here getting dinner ready. I couldn't make out the words, but from the way they shouted each other down, it was a regular battle. Then suddenly I heard these high screams, like an animal in pain. They just went on and on. I couldn't believe one person could make that much noise. There was all this crashing around. It sounded like Judgment Day." She shuddered at the memory.

"At what time did this occur?"

"Let's see . . . I'd had my tea. It must been right around five o'clock."

"When you heard the screams, what did you do?"

"I ran out to find a policeman, that's what I did. My duties do not include catching murderers, thank you very much!" She paused to calm herself. "When we got back, there was this awful quiet. It gave me the gooseflesh almost as bad as the screaming had.

"The constable, he knocked and called out but got no answer. I give him the key. The door wouldn't open. Then I remembered. The gent had a bolt put on his door—at his own expense, mind. Said he didn't want anyone to disturb him while he was painting."

Miss Finch went on. "The constable kicked and kicked at the door. Finally, he broke the bolt and the door burst open. And what we saw—dear God, I'll have nightmares for years." She snatched a *London Illustrated News* off an end table and fanned herself with it. "There was blood everywhere. And pieces. Pieces of—" She swallowed.

"We are aware of the condition of the room," I hastened to assure her.

She nodded gratefully and intensified her fanning until her hand was a blur. Her face had grown pale. Her rate of breathing had increased alarmingly.

"Here now, I'm dreadfully sorry we have brought all this back to you," I said.

Miss Luce was up in an instant and rushed to the poor woman's side. "You lean right back," she said soothingly.

Meanwhile, I fetched an empty chair and we elevated her feet. "Nice, slow breaths," I encouraged her.

In a few moments, her respiration returned to normal. "I'm sorry," she said, "but if you'd seen it . . ."

"I doubt very much we could speak about it as bravely as you," Miss Luce assured her.

"I fainted dead away. But that constable, he was shaken too," Miss Finch added self-righteously. "When I came to, I found the poor man had been sick right there on the carpet." She struggled to sit up. "Anyway, after we could think, he stood guard at the door and sent me round to the Star and Garter. They've got a telephone, you see. Soon we had police all over the place."

Her color was returning. "He told me, the constable did, nobody come in or out of that room until Inspector Woburn got there." She snorted. "That's why they were so sure I had to be wrong about hearing three voices. In the room was just the dead gent, what was left of him, and my tenant, all passed out on the floor."

"I see what you mean," Miss Luce said thoughtfully. "Since the room had been locked from the inside, there was no way anyone could have got in or out."

"Might you have mistaken the screams for a voice of a different timbre?" I asked.

She shook her head. "I heard three voices," she insisted. "No matter what the police say."

Impulsively, Miss Luce clasped the woman's hand. "We believe you."

"What did the other voice sound like?" I asked.

"I couldn't really hear," she admitted. "They was all shouting at each other."

"One last question, Miss Finch," I said. "Have you cleaned the room yet?"

"Lord no, I haven't gone up there. I know I should. But I can't bring myself to do it yet."

I was immeasurably relieved. I'd feared the room had been scrubbed clean of all evidence. We thanked Miss Finch profusely and left. I steeled myself for what awaited us behind the door atop the stairs.

Chapter 16
A Gruesome Sight

Curiosity warred with trepidation as I mounted the steps to the second floor. Miss Luce followed closely behind. At the top I hesitated before the locked portal in front of us. If only those mute wooden panels could speak.

They clearly bore the marks of the constable's foot when he had forced the bolt. I turned the key in the lock. This room might hold the answer to the question that tormented me. Did the god Dionysus stride among us?

The door swung open slowly. Miss Luce gasped at the nauseating smell that launched itself at us. She put her hand to her mouth. Even I, used to the smells of the sickroom, had to quell my revulsion before proceeding inside. Woburn had not overstated matters in using the word "chaos."

The door opened onto the studio portion of the flat. Furniture was overturned and tossed about at random. Paintings had been strewn around the room. Half-empty tubes of paint littered the floor. Small rugs lay in crumpled piles. The very paper had been torn from the walls in places and hung in long shreds. Great, arcing sprays of blood had stippled the walls and splattered the gas fixtures. My eye was drawn to a large, rust-colored blotch that stained the center of the wooden floor. Flies buzzed everywhere.

Miss Luce stood just behind me, looking aghast.

With all the traffic the flat had seen, it was hopeless to look for footprints. I therefore pushed inside, intent on opening the bank of windows across the room. Miss Luce followed, taking in the details with wide eyes.

The windows would not budge. They were nailed shut. Another bank ran along on my left. They, too, were permanently fastened. These at least had transoms above them that might be opened. Nowhere, however, could I find the pole to spring their latches. In a far corner sat a stove and a sink. From the fine layer of dust upon them, neither had been used for many days. Evidently, Mackleston seldom ate in.

To the right was another doorway. I strode through it and was in the bedchamber. Since this room held no window, I spared it only a cursory glance. The tidy bed and great fireplace on the opposite wall stood in sharp contrast to the devastation in the room behind me. Another door led to the bathroom.

In there I finally found the window I sought—a small one on the left wall. The wood had swollen in its frame, however. It took much heaving to wrest it open. Grateful for a lungful of fresh air, I hung my head outside. The opening was barely large enough to accommodate this action. Certainly, I couldn't force even one of my shoulders through. By no stretch of the imagination could an attacker have escaped this way. Not even a child could squeeze through such a space. I considered animals that might be small enough to fit through the window. But no animal that tiny could have caused the mayhem we had seen.

And that was it for Mackleston's flat—three rooms in a row: a huge studio, bedchamber, and bathroom. I heard a noise behind me, pulled my head in, and spun around to see Miss Luce. She looked pale.

"Get a breath of air," I urged. She nodded and leaned out the window.

While she did so, I took the opportunity to pace off the rooms. Then I walked off the landing as well and wrote down the measurements in my notebook. I would compare them later with the outside dimensions. It seemed unlikely that a flat built this recently had any secret rooms or passages. Still, it was best to make certain.

When I returned, the smell had abated only slightly. Miss Luce stood dazed in the center of the studio. Her skin had a dreadful pallor and her eyes appeared sunken and dark.

"Do you see any way a third person could have escaped?" she asked in a strained voice.

"No." Nevertheless, I determined to exhaust every possibility for a rational explanation.

"Where shall we begin?" She looked positively ill at the thought.

"We examine every inch of this flat—furniture, walls, floor, and ceiling."

"What are we looking for?"

That was the question. It would take hard evidence to convince Woburn. "There is no way of knowing in advance. We must be alert for any detail which might bear on the murder."

She swayed on her feet. I rushed over and offered her my arm.

"Would you mind terribly if I examined the back rooms?" she asked weakly. "I find the atmosphere in here quite stifling."

"Certainly," I said. "Would you like to lie down for a moment?"

"I'll be all right," she insisted. "Just let me leave this room."

To be honest, I was relieved when she disappeared

into the far chambers with a swish of her skirt. I had been fearful she would inadvertently destroy some piece of evidence.

I began my investigation by examining the broken bolt. There was no blood on it. That seemed significant. Next, I slowly crossed the study. Aside from the large stain in the center, there was not much else to discover—merely traces of dust and soot, the inevitable concomitant of living in the industrial center of the world.

Eventually, I made my way across to the corner where Woburn said he had found Mackleston's body. Six inches up the wall I found a dark stain that appeared to be blood. It was, no doubt, where his head had struck, leaving the bruise and scab I'd noted in his cell. There was also a large dried stain on the floor beneath it. Considering how profusely scalp wounds bleed, this was not surprising.

I glanced through the open doorway into the bedchamber and saw Miss Luce energetically stripping the bed one layer at a time. Smiling at her thoroughness, I proceeded to examine the furniture, walls, and ceiling of the main room.

They added little to my knowledge. Mackleston had lived a Spartan existence. The central area, well lit by banks of windows, had been entirely given over to easels, now lying in a tangled mass of wooden struts. Clearly, this flat was for painting, sleeping, and very little else. Aside from a cupboard filled with paints and brushes, the room contained only the barest necessities—an inexpensive table and chairs, a set of dishes, a dish towel, and a teapot. It was sad, in a way. I found no family pictures, no letters, no books, no gifts. He must be a lonely young man.

The sole decorative touches were some portraits and a landscape or two that lay about. Mackleston's signature graced each in the lower right corner. All of the oils were competent but undistinguished. I found no portraits of his own family. They were not even close enough to him to sit as subjects.

I turned my attention to the distribution of stains. In the center lay one huge blotch. Smaller smudges radiated out from it more or less randomly. The primary stain lay as far from the door as from Mackleston's body. The inference was clear. There had been no attempt to flee. Either the attacker had swarmed over his victim with incredible rapidity, or else the victim had not recognized the murderer as a source of danger. Had the killer been an acquaintance?

The stains got fewer and smaller the farther they lay from the large central blot. The brother had not attempted to crawl away. Rather, he had dropped where he stood and his attacker had continued in a frenzy, dismembering the victim and tossing objects about the room until the fury that possessed him had abated. I could not help but be reminded of my own brush with madness. Resolutely, I forced the memory down and continued with my investigation.

I considered the position of Mackleston's body in relation to the corpse. Slowly, the sequence of events on that fateful night began to reveal itself to me. Yes, my slim hope back in Mackleston's cell had been justified. A third party had committed the murder.

But I felt no triumph. Rather, an increasing sense of frustration over came me. Major points eluded me. I looked around once more in bafflement.

"How is it coming?"

I turned to find Miss Luce standing in the doorway. Her color was much better and her eyes had regained some of their sparkle. "But you have ruined your dress," I said.

She looked down, abashed, at the soot on the hem of her garment and her sleeves. "So I have. It must have happened when I examined the fireplace." She looked up at me. "I wanted to be thorough."

"Excellent. What did you find?"

"Several stout bars have been set into the chimney," she replied. "I doubt a cat could get out that way."

I nodded, disappointed, but grateful for her initiative. At least she had done a proper job of searching.

"I am certain that Mackleston is innocent," I said.

"But that's wonderful." Her eyes glowed. "Why ever do you look so unhappy?"

"Because we need hard evidence to convince Woburn. It is all very well to know who didn't do it. But who did? And how did he escape?"

"Suppose Mr. Cairo was right," she ventured, "and a supernatural agency was responsible?"

That was the very question that still tormented me. Had the god Dionysus overwhelmed the third person in the room? I scarcely knew which was worse—to abandon my belief in a rational universe or to accept my own actions with no excuse. I went cold with the memory of the pillow in my hands and my rage. Was that what the killer had felt when he had slaughtered Mackleston's brother? Did he now feel the same remorse as I?

I looked up to see Miss Luce gazing curiously at me. I realized I had not responded to her question. "We shall never convince Woburn of a miraculous agent. Besides," I added, "according to Cairo, the being needs a physical body to function in our world. That body must have left somehow." I threw up my hands in despair. "The answer lies in this room, and I am missing it."

"Surely you're being too hard on yourself."

Little did she know that another doubt plagued me. Given what I had learned, I should have been able to reach a conclusion. A month ago I would have, I was certain. Could it be that my very reason had been damaged by a brush with the god of passion and anarchy?

She tried to offer some comfort. "You will come up with an answer, I am sure of it."

As it turned out, she had found nothing of importance in either of the other rooms. "Except for this." She held out a gold ring set with a large red stone. I examined it. The piece was one of the items of jewelry Mr. Gaylord had returned to us. It was not a particularly valuable stone—just a garnet.

"Perhaps we should bring it to him," Miss Luce suggested.

I shook my head. "Gaols are rough places." I explained. "Even such a trifle as this could cause trouble for him."

A plan began to form itself in my mind. I wanted to talk to Mackleston's father. Lord Vollmer, however, was notoriously standoffish. Returning one of his son's possessions might well provide the excuse I needed. "I'll return it to his family."

She readily assented. That settled, I was left with another problem. While I did not wish to insult Miss Luce, I had to have a look around the rest of the flat for myself.

"Why don't you go over my area," I suggested. "In case I have overlooked something."

Her expression showed she was not enthusiastic about the idea, but she set her chin and nodded. We had both grown accustomed to the smell by now, but it was still not a pleasant task. While she was thus employed, I examined the other rooms. To my dismay, I found Miss Luce had been correct—there was little information to be gained. They contained nothing other than the bed and a few toilet articles.

I verified that escape through the fireplace was impossible. I also noted that it had recently been swept. It was as clean as such nooks can ever get—a few sprinkles of ash, rather than the usual piles. That must have been done before the murder, since Miss Finch had not been in the room since. I was about to leave when I recalled the suit of clothes Mackleston had requested.

Upon looking into his closet, I was forced to smile. It was obviously the wardrobe of an artist. The outfits were arranged strictly by color, from brown tweeds through blues to blacks. However, I found no khaki-colored suit, much less one that smelled of turpentine.

I poked my head into the next room. "Miss Luce," I asked, "have you got Mackleston's suit—the one he asked for?"

"I'd forgotten all about it," she admitted.

"It's not in his closet."

She joined me in the bedchamber. "How odd." She gazed upon the row of neat outfits hung on the pole. "Has that horrid inspector made off with it?"

"More likely some underpaid constable," I said. "But why steal a ragged, smelly suit, when there are much finer ones to hand?"

Miss Luce shrugged. "*De gustibus non disputandum est.* Perhaps he thought it wouldn't be missed." She selected a comfortable-looking tweed and draped it over her arm. "This is much better than those old shreds he wanted, anyway."

Here was yet another mystery. Who had taken Mackleston's suit? "There's nothing more to be found in this place. Let us wash up and leave." I am afraid my voice reflected the discouragement I felt.

"Have you given up hope, then?" Her eyes were large with concern.

"Not entirely," I said. "We should revisit Woburn. With what we have discovered here, he must release Mackleston."

So saying, I led the way from the flat. Miss Luce followed. I trudged down the hallway unhappily. The most important part of the puzzle still eluded me. How had the murderer escaped? The answer would tell whether we dealt with a human agency or not.

So enmeshed was I in my own unhappy musings that I scarcely heeded my companion. Until, that is, her exasperated voice penetrated my ruminations.

"Well, at least tell me how it is you know Algy is innocent."

I gave a wan smile. "You saw the room as well as I. You observed the distribution of stains, the position of Mackleston's body. Ponder these clues on our way back to Scotland Yard."

She looked annoyed with me but said nothing.

Once outside, I tested one last possibility. I paced off the perimeter of the building before leaving. Miss Luce watched me curiously as I marked down the dimensions in my notebook and compared them with my earlier notes on the room measurements. As I had expected, the building contained no hidden rooms or passages. I confided this to her and we were on our way.

Despite our previous treatment by Inspector Woburn, I determined to lay my evidence before him. When we reached the great turreted tower of New Scotland Yard, I turned to Miss Luce. "There is no need for you to risk arrest again," I pointed out. "Why not wait here?"

She set her mouth most determinedly. From the look in her eyes I feared I was about to get another lecture on the modern woman. But all she said was, "I prefer to see this through."

We found Woburn at his desk. Given our reception last time, I was wary of how he would greet us. But his manner was mild in the extreme.

"Back so soon? Solved the case already, have you?" he asked in mock surprise at our return.

"No," I said. "Not solved."

His jowls quivered with suppressed amusement. "There now, don't take it so hard. Stories is one thing, but a real murder is quite another."

"Yes," I said, and sighed. "I have scarcely anything to add to the case. Except, of course, for the obvious facts that there was a third party in the room during the murder and that Mackleston was injured trying to save his brother's life."

At my words, Miss Luce gasped. The light of amusement faded from Woburn's small eyes and they narrowed. "Havin' your little fun at our expense, are you?" He rose ominously. "I won't have novices muckin' this up with half-baked theories. Oh yes, you go to the papers and get everybody to congratulate you. But behind the scenes, we do the real work."

"My good man," I said, "it is only to keep you from being made a laughingstock in court that I come here at all."

He glowered at me. "Right, then. Let's hear what we missed."

"I am sure you overlooked nothing," I hastened to assure him. "However, you may have been a trifle timid about drawing inferences."

A stony silence greeted this declaration. Miss Luce's eyes flicked from me to Woburn and back again. I confess, I was beginning to enjoy playing Holmes to his Lestrade.

I continued. "When you entered the room, Mackleston lay unconscious in the corner, is that correct?"

"That's what he wanted us to think," Woburn said.

"I assure you, he was senseless. His skull had been fractured. Or so I discovered when I examined him. By the way, did you ever call in a doctor?"

"One's comin' this evening," Woburn admitted.

"Then he will discover, as I did, a serious trauma to the back of Mackleston's skull—consistent with its striking the wall sharply."

"But what about the blood on his hands?" Woburn fairly shouted at me.

"Very well, then," I said. "Let us reconstruct the sequence of events as you believe they occurred. Mackleston and his brother have a falling-out. The argument escalates until Mackleston, in a fit of rage that gives him superhuman strength, attacks his brother. Then what? Before dying, his brother flings him across the room with such force that hitting the wall renders him senseless? And then, after being knocked out, did Mackleston continue to dismember his brother? Or alternatively, did his brother, after being completely dismembered, somehow contrive to throw Mackleston across the room?

"It won't do, Woburn! There had to be a third party in that room. Mackleston was trying to save his brother. He actually grappled with the bloody assailant, who tossed him aside. As he passed into unconsciousness, the real culprit finished his grisly task. That and that alone explains the positions of the bodies, it explains the blood on Mackleston's hands, and it explains the third voice the landlady heard in the room."

There was a moment of silence while my words sank in. Miss Luce's eyes glowed. Woburn, however, remained skeptical.

"That's all well and good, but his brother could just as easily have hit him in the head durin' the fight. Then Mackleston flopped down in that corner to play dead when he heard the constable kickin' at the door."

I protested, "But the trauma to his skull is consistent with—"

Woburn, however, never let me finish. "And there's one thing it doesn't explain." He struggled to rise from his chair. "It doesn't explain how this third party got out of a locked room. The constable swears he never left the door until I arrived. He's a good man with over a decade on the force, and I believe him."

He leaned across his cluttered desk. His small eyes glinted with malice. "Reginald Mackleston's father is a man of great social standin'. He has important connections—as good as your own, if I may be so bold," the man added with a sly smile. "It's all our necks, from the super's on down, if somebody don't swing for this murder, and quick."

"But his own son," Miss Luce protested, "surely he wants him freed."

"You'd think so, wouldn't you?" Woburn shook his head. "He disowned the boy, soon as he heard of the arrest. Just brimmin' over with family feeling, these Macklestons."

The man sank with a grunt onto his chair. "Unless you come up with some proof of your theory," and he pronounced the word with a decided distaste, "in ten days,

I'll send young Mackleston to the gallows, I promise you. And what a good lesson that'll be to the rest of them what thinks they're above the common herd."

And then the man tormented me with the very thing that had so far eluded me. "So how did he escape, this mysterious third party of yours?"

"When we have discovered that, we shall have solved the mystery," I said quietly.

"Oh, that's next on your little agenda, is it?" Woburn planted his fists upon his pudgy hips. "I suppose you are also a expert in escaping locked rooms."

"No," I replied, "but I believe I can enlist the services of a man who is."

Chapter 17
Reenter Houdini

I had one last question for Inspector Woburn before we left. "Have any items been removed from the flat?"

"No," Woburn said.

"Are you certain? No evidence taken, for example?"

"Yes, I'm certain. Why?" He glared suspiciously at me.

"A suit of clothes has disappeared."

Woburn's face contorted with anger. "If you think you can win over a jury by attackin' my men, you're wastin' your time. My constables don't steal. We left everythin' in that charnel house just as we found it."

On that note, we took our leave. I flagged down a cab and we climbed aboard. I had done my best. I could only hope that upon mature reflection, Woburn would see the logic of my arguments and release Mackleston.

We halted at Miss Luce's place of business on Moorgate. Her tiny office was squeezed in between the Northern Assurance Company and a chemist's. I climbed out to help her down.

"You are as good as your word," she said simply. "I shall never forget how you have put yourself out for a stranger."

"Not at all," I insisted. "Anyone would have done the same."

She smiled faintly and shook her head. "You can return to Sussex knowing you leave behind you a job well done."

"I am not returning to Sussex just yet."

"Why not?" She cocked her head to one side.

"There is a small matter of murder to be dealt with."

"But you have done your part." She spread her hands. "If you and Miss Finch testify at his trial, Mackleston is certain to go free. Surely the rest is the province of the police."

"When I have begun something, I prefer to see it through."

Impulsively, she lunged forward and grasped my sleeve. "But you mustn't," she insisted. "I am dreadfully afraid for you."

"Only a coward shies away from his duty because of risk."

"You mustn't involve yourself further." She stared me straight in the eye. "It is hideously dangerous."

There was something very close to terror in her look. I confess it sent a chill right down my spine. I believe women are, as a rule, more sensitive to things of a spiritual nature than are men. Therefore, I did not dismiss her concern lightly. Our foe, unearthly or not, was daunting indeed.

"I cannot leave the rest of you alone to face whatever it is," I said.

"You alone are a threat to it," she insisted. "You will be its target."

I was flattered by her high regard for my powers. And I was no stranger to adventure. My experiences in the Boer War and my stint as a ship's doctor among the rough-and-ready men on a Greenland whaler would serve me in good stead. One thing I have learned—self-reliance and a cool head will generally win through.

"More than that." She lowered her voice. "Your wife needs you."

Her words might have been cold steel piercing my heart. I had forgotten all about Touie. Was I not simply seeking an excuse to avoid her sickroom? I felt mean and selfish.

I thought of Mackleston. Was my testimony before a jury enough to set him free? Might they have the same reservations as Woburn? No, unless I discovered who had murdered Reggie and how he had escaped, Mackleston's life was in doubt. And the rest of our party, were not they and their loved ones also in danger? Touie or Mackleston—where did my true duty lie?

A great calm descended on me. I had my answer. To abandon this case was to put innocent lives in jeopardy. My wife was bound to die. But for Mackleston and the rest, there still was hope. As a doctor, I had sworn an oath to preserve the living. I must try to help.

Also, I needed to learn the truth for my own peace of mind.

I looked back to Miss Luce. She was actually trembling with fear. Surely, such acute terror came from something more than intuition.

I faced her squarely. "What happened when you felt the touch of the god?"

She shrank from me. For an instant, panic crossed her features and a flush spread up her throat to her cheeks. "No, it was too horrible. I cannot say."

She looked around, as if afraid the whole world could see the god's mark upon her. A tall, thin muffin man strolled past us, his tray of baked goods balanced on his head. In the street a cat's meat man pushed his two-wheeled cart in front of him. No one paid us the slightest attention.

I grasped her hand with both of mine. "I can tell you part of what happened. You had a moment of brilliant insight, didn't you? Followed by an act the very thought of which cripples you with remorse."

She gazed at me. Her wide, green eyes were unreadable. Gently, she withdrew her hand. "Yes, of course, I see.

It was the same with all of us, was it not?" She watched my face anxiously for confirmation.

I nodded. "Just so."

She drew a deep breath and let it out with a sigh that left her slumped. Her eyes closed a long moment. When they reopened, there was something of the old sparkle in them.

"If you care to confide," I offered, "I am the last person in the world to judge another."

"I scarcely know where to begin."

"Start with your inspiration," I suggested.

"Very well." Miss Luce pursed her lips in thought. "You know, of course, that throughout the city various small offices offer servants for hire."

I nodded.

"What I realized," she went on, "was that I could link them all into one central registry and assign territories. Do you see? By contacting me, anyone anywhere could find a suitable person for any task. And by fixing wages, all employees would benefit. Also, I would collect dues from the employees to provide a stipend in case of illness or to tide them over between assignments."

"An excellent scheme," I agreed.

She leaned forward as the idea fired her imagination once more. "I could charge a small percentage as a finder's fee from each client. And they would benefit as well, because any servant found unsatisfactory would be placed on probation. In the case of dishonesty, he or she would be barred from the group forever."

Miss Luce lifted her chin proudly. "I was going to be a wealthy woman. I felt invincible. And then . . ."

I waited.

Her voice was barely above a whisper as she continued. ". . . and then Cairo walked into my office."

I scarcely knew whether I wanted her to continue or not. But I could not have stopped her. Clearly, she felt compelled to confess. Her eyes did not see her surroundings. Her hands clenched into fists. They turned white with a little spot of red at each knuckle.

"I don't know why he arrived at that moment," she said lowly. "Was it coincidence? No, it couldn't have been. I shall go to my grave believing that somehow he knew. He knew I was not myself, that I was . . . suggestible. And he used that knowledge, God how he used it! The things I did that afternoon, the things I begged him to do . . ." Her voice trailed off.

She looked down at her hands and opened them. Her nails had left crescent-shaped dents in her palms. Her voice grew careless as she continued, but she avoided looking at me. "We were constantly together for a fortnight. If there is any depravity we did not commit, it is only because it did not occur to us."

She finally looked at me. There was a half-challenge in her eyes, as if she dared me to respond yet feared I might.

"However did you escape his influence?"

The look she gave me was one of pure gratitude. "It was when I heard Algy was in gaol. Somehow, his need gave me the strength to leave."

"There, you see?" I pointed out. "Your own innate goodness came to your rescue."

She bowed her head and put her hand to her forehead. "But you don't know—"

"You must not dwell on the past," I told her. "You bear no more responsibility than any other victim of a violent assault."

"But don't you see," her voice was soft but intense, "I know what he's capable of. I know what the dangers are—not just for your life, but for your immortal soul."

"All the more reason to stand and fight," I replied. "Fear is evil's best ally." I patted her shoulder and endeavored to put on a cheerful demeanor. "Don't you worry. You have done your part. Now it is time to pass the reins to a male hand. Return to your own domain—"

But I was not allowed to finish. Her eyes, which had heretofore avoided mine, now blazed with anger. Her color heightened. "How dare you patronize me!"

I was surprised at the fury in her voice as she went on.

"You really are no better than all the rest of them. A woman couldn't possibly know anything about the big world, could she? No, all she's good for is cooking your food, mending your clothes, and bearing your children. God forbid if she dares to think for herself!"

She was virtually shouting at me. With horror, I realized that she had misinterpreted my intent. A lanky ginger-cake seller across the street paused to listen to her tirade. A smile of amusement creased his features as he adjusted the neck strap that held his lap tray. A crowd of laborers around him turned to see what all the fuss was about. A chimney sweep hefted the long roll of cloth that held his brushes under his arm and gave me a wink. I flushed with mortification. I held out my hands and took a step forward. "Please, calm yourself."

"Oh, that's right! Just take it and shut up about it." In her anger, she thrust me away.

I stumbled backward and fetched up against the bricks with a jolt. There I slumped for a moment, catching my breath. When I found the strength to push myself away, I looked around for her. She had strode to the entrance of her building. Then a curious thing happened: She seemed to collapse. She sagged and had to clutch at the brass door handle to keep upright. At that moment, I was vouchsafed a brief glimpse of her face. To my amazement, tears streamed down her cheeks. She wiped at them angrily with the back of her glove, pushed herself erect, and hurried inside.

My outrage evaporated. She labored under some terrible emotional burden. Whence had come this mistrust of mankind? Sometime in the past she must have been extremely ill used by a man. I shook my head sadly and looked around.

The ginger-cake seller sauntered on. The rest of the crowd slowly dispersed, muttering to themselves. I caught a few glances of pity cast in my direction. I felt humiliated at being manhandled—if that is the proper phrase—by a woman. Of course, she had taken unfair advantage. How could I be on my guard in such a circumstance? I straightened my coat and tie. The movements caused a twinge of pain in my back. Doubtless I should have bruises tomorrow. I walked stiffly back to the cab that still waited to convey me to Houdini's hotel.

During the ride, I brooded on Miss Luce's unusual behavior. There was no other word for it—she had been irrational.

Of course, I thought! It was unlike her and she had shown unnatural strength. Had I just observed the return of Dionysus? I sat forward in my cab, stunned at the realization. I ought to go back and see what I could learn out about our antagonist.

Then I recalled the sad sequel to our encounter—the glimpse of her tear-stricken face. Her rage had already spent itself. The god had left her.

As I brooded over my missed chance, I was struck by something. If Dionysus had come back to her, might he not revisit me as well? Was the god going to keep attacking us over and over in an endless loop? What if Houdini was right and Cairo himself had planted these thoughts in our minds through hypnosis, like little bombs with long fuses? How many more such episodes lay in store for us?

Miss Luce, at least, believed Cairo's explanation. Her warning rang in my ears: *This creature is hideously dangerous.* For the first time, I wished I'd had the presence of mind to pack my service revolver.

I arrived shortly at Houdini's hotel, paid off the carriage driver, and dismissed him. In response to my knock, Houdini's wife answered the door. I was taken aback at her appearance. Her red, swollen eyes were proof she'd been crying. I was shocked to note that a purplish bruise ran from her cheek down to her chin. I had a terrible premonition.

"Thank God it's you!" she cried.

"Whatever has happened?" I demanded.

She ushered me in, talking in a high, frightened voice.

"I can't believe it. I've never seen him like this." She ran her fingers through her curly hair.

Two small dogs came up to sniff my hand timidly. Houdini was nowhere in evidence. Absently, I petted the dogs as I said, "Here, sit down and tell me what is wrong."

I guided her to the sofa in the drawing room of their suite and pulled up a chair opposite. She sank down onto the brocaded cushions. Wringing her hands, she cried, "He's left me."

"What?" I could scarcely believe my ears. "Why?"

Instead of answering, she shook her head. She looked dangerously close to breaking down entirely. "He's left me alone in a strange country." With that, the poor woman succumbed to her emotions. Tears flowed freely. "What'll I do? How will I live?"

The dogs left me to go nuzzle her legs in sympathy. "Do not worry about that," I said. "If need be, I can provide assistance."

She clasped my hands. "You're too kind," she said, weeping. "I'll pay you back, I promise."

I patted her hand. "Now now, it may not come to that. Do not despair. He may regain his senses. Where is he now?"

"I don't know," she gulped. I was glad to see her attempt to pull herself together.

"How long has he been gone?"

"Hours. He stormed out of here." She shuddered at the memory.

"Well, then, it's been less than a day—perhaps he'll be back."

"You don't understand," she wailed. "He's never done anything like this before. Anything. It's— I don't know. It's like he's gone crazy."

Those words chilled me to my soul. Had Dionysus struck again? I strove to put a bold face on the matter. "I know this city. I shall find him."

A flicker of hope crossed her face. "Can you?"

"Very likely," I said with more confidence than I felt.

"But you must help. I need to know exactly what happened."

She nodded bravely and drew a breath to begin. "I'd gone out shopping. When I came back, I didn't see him. So I went through the rooms. When I got to the bedchamber, I saw—" Here the poor woman broke down completely. "Oh, I can't say it."

"Another woman?" I prodded gently.

She shook her head.

"Not another woman?" I asked, confused.

"Two—hoo—hoo," she sobbed. The dogs at her feet looked up, alarmed.

"You found him in bed with two women?" I gasped.

She nodded miserably. "They were dancers from the Palace. But that's not the worst. When I came in and caught him, he invited me to—to—" But she could not go on. Another fit of weeping overcame her. In a moment she forced herself to continue.

"When I wouldn't, he jumped up and began shouting at me. Well, we were both shouting," she amended. "And then he—he hit me. I just stood there. I couldn't talk; I couldn't think. He stormed out. He hardly took time to dress." She buried her face in her handkerchief.

My heart went out to the wretched woman. I knew what had happened to Houdini.

"Tell me," I asked gently, "was this madness preceded by a burst of creative energy?"

She looked up, astonished. "How'd you know that?"

"Never mind that now. Please tell me everything."

"It started early this morning," she ventured. "He decided that our act was stale. He insisted on canceling the rest of our bookings unless we came up with a new trick. He was like a man possessed. Nothing I suggested was good enough. He yelled at me." She shook her head at the memory.

"Tell me," I asked, "did he actually come up with a new illusion?"

"Oh, yes. It's the best ever. But I told him it was too dangerous to try without practice. He insisted, but I held my ground. That's when he blew up at me. I decided to go shopping to let him cool down. So I did. He must have walked to the theater and . . . and met up with—you know!"

I looked around the flat. "What became of the two . . . er—"

"Hussies?"

"Ah, yes."

"I threw them out! And tossed their clothes out the window," she added. The poor woman gave way to her emotions once more. "They're just lucky it wasn't the other way around!"

I had heard enough. By now Houdini's rage had probably dissipated. He might be too ashamed to come home. He could even be a danger to himself.

I looked up to see Bess sobbing into her handkerchief. "I shall do my utmost to find him," I promised. "Yours is the infinitely harder task—to forgive."

"How can I?" The poor woman's tears flowed once more. "He was a stranger to me."

I leaned toward her. "Therein lies the answer." I thought how to proceed. "There is more to this than you know. Strange as it seems, he had no control over his actions. He was under the absolute sway of an outside force."

"That is how it seemed," she agreed doubtfully.

"Did he ever mention our adventure together?"

"Where you flummoxed the medium?" Curiosity began to tempt her out of her despair.

"It was far more than that," I informed her. "The man we pitted ourselves against is the most remarkable I have ever encountered. He has somehow caused disruption in the lives of at least three other members of our party that night. I myself have fallen prey to his vile influence."

"Did you . . . I mean . . . with other women?" she asked hesitantly.

"Certainly not!" I forced myself to continue more

calmly. "But my own trials have been severe. I do not yet know how this influence is exercised. But you must believe that your husband's actions, even his very words, were not truly his own."

"Bring him back to me," she said quietly. "Then we'll see."

"Very well," I said, and took my leave.

Despite my brave words to Bess, I had no idea where to begin. London was the largest city in the world. Houdini could hide for years in its byways and teeming millions. On the other hand, people tend to inhabit a fairly limited sphere. Most divide their time between home and employment. Accordingly, I made my way to the Palace Theatre.

I soon found the stage manager, a squat, balding man. There had been a matinee this afternoon and, he assured me, Houdini had performed.

"He was in quite a mood," the man said. "One look at his face and I was afraid to speak to him. Must have been something between him and the wife. Before he even said hello, he badgered me for an assistant. And when I took a minute to think, he like to bit my head off. But once he settled in, what a performance. Never seen its equal. He was a man on fire."

When I sought permission to go backstage, the man shook his head.

"Won't do you any good. He left right after the show."

"Do you know where he went?"

"No, but he seemed in a desperate hurry."

The man could tell me nothing more. I returned outside and searched the alley around the stage door for hangers-on. All had departed. Without a clue to Houdini's destination, I began interviewing the drivers queued up at the cabstand on the street. Not one had seen the magician.

I had practically despaired of ever finding him when I noticed a bootblack about eight or nine years of age across the street. He sat on his wooden box and fumbled with something in his hands. I approached and discovered that he was clumsily shuffling a shiny deck of cards. He was dirty, his coat was patched, and his battered shoes were two sizes too large. Where would such a boy get a brand-new pack of playing cards? At my approach, he jumped up and watched me warily.

"Practicing?" I asked.

He snatched the cards behind his back, as if afraid I would steal them.

"I'll bet I know where you learned that trick," I said.

"Yeah?" He glared up suspiciously.

"Mr. Houdini showed it to you, did he not?"

He nodded.

"Have you seen him today?"

The boy nodded again. "Mr. Houdini gives me a penny sometimes," he said pointedly.

"Did he give you one today?"

"Coo, no. He was all in a rush."

"Well," I said, "I shall give you two, if you can tell me which way he went."

"Two pennies?" He looked at me incredulously.

"Yes, indeed."

"Let's see 'em."

I produced two coppers and held them out to him.

He grabbed them. In a flash, they had disappeared into his pockets.

"Ask the gypsies," he said.

Chapter 18
On the Trail of a Madman

"The gypsies?" I repeated.

"O' course," he said impatiently. "Here's how it was. He comes out the back door there like water out a fire hose. Charges right through the crowd waiting for autographs. He looks around like he wants a cab. But they was all gone, wa'nt they? Taking the toffs home after the show, you see. He sees a gypsy caravan across the street."

The boy pointed with one grimy finger. "He runs over. I hears him promise them money if they take him somewhere."

"Do you know where he went?"

The boy shook his head. "All I knows is they took off like the devil was after 'em."

"Do you have any idea where the gypsies might be now?"

He nodded. "Cost you another penny, though."

I dug my hand into my pocket and came up with more change. I showed him a sixpence. "Here's half a shilling if you know. Tell the truth, now."

His eyes lit up. "By now they've set up in Hyde Park, telling fortunes."

I flipped the coin to him. He grabbed it in midair and was off like a shot—presumably before I could change my mind. As he scurried away, he shouted back over his shoulder, "By Marble Arch!"

I hailed a passing cab and soon arrived at Hyde Park. On the vast expanse of grass south of Speaker's Corner, I spied the parked caravan. It was painted a gaudy red with yellow and green trim. Its little chimney stuck up jauntily from the roof. The rear door was propped open. A crude sign offered, "Fortunes—ha'penny each." There were no takers.

What appeared to be three generations of the same family sat or lay around the tiny wagon. The older ones slept, their faces as brown and wrinkled as walnuts. The children wove baskets at the feet of a slim, middle-aged woman. A red handkerchief held back her glossy black hair. Her dark eyes were large and alert. Her skin was the color of undyed leather.

All their clothes showed signs of wear, but at least they were mended. As I approached, the woman handed a baby off her lap to one of the older girls. The younger ones charged up to me shouting, and I felt the tug of more than one little hand at my pocket.

"Here now," I said sternly. "Keep your hands to yourself!" I strode over quickly, the small mob trailing in my wake. I jammed my hands deep into my pockets and clutched my wallet firmly in one fist.

"Tell you' fortune, sir?" she asked. Her voice had a whisper of eastern Europe in the vowels. "I geeve you a good von."

I shook my head.

"Then shove off, mate. We're workin' here." I almost laughed at the speed with which her quaint accent vanished.

"I am looking for a friend of mine," I began. "You picked him up outside the Palace Theatre."

A short, stocky man whom I took to be her husband leaned over and whispered a warning to her. She responded indignantly. "Nah, this one ain't no rozzer! He's a gent. Use your eyes." She flashed me a smile. "Your friend was a generous cove. He crossed my palm with silver."

I sighed. This quest was like to break me. But I gamely fished around in my pockets once more and came up with another half-crown. "First tell me where he went."

Her eyes glittered at the sight of the money. "All will be revealed." She leaned forward confidentially. "Your friend was in a big hurry."

Her husband volunteered, "He looked like a crazy man." He threw out his chest. "I kept an eye on him, right enough."

"Yes, but where did you take him?"

The woman's eyes narrowed craftily. "First, let's see the money."

I gave the coin to her. She inspected it carefully.

When she had satisfied herself it was genuine, she looked up at me. "Where do you think we'd take a crazy man? We went to Bedlam." She cackled with laughter.

I registered her words with dread. "The asylum?"

"The hospital on St. George's Road." She held up her palms, absolving herself. "It was his idea. We told him we'd wait—for a fee, of course. But he said he wanted to stay."

The poor man. His surrender to that most famous of all mental hospitals, Bethlehem Royal, disturbed me deeply. I remembered my own tortured questionings of my sanity. Still, this news contained a glimmer of hope. Houdini had at least realized that he was a danger to society. Perhaps his true being could still be reached—especially by one who had suffered similarly.

The woman interrupted my thoughts. "You a want ride there? Cheap?"

"No, thank you," I said.

As I took my leave, the gypsy woman called after me. "Take care. Not all the madmen are in hospital these days."

* * *

On the cab ride to Bethlehem Royal, I pondered Mrs. Houdini's tale. Would I find a used husk of a man or a raving maniac? More critically, who next of our little group would be struck? Could it happen again to me?

Cairo had said that the god inhabited one of our party. Yet the creature appeared to leapfrog from one to another of us. I wondered if outsiders could be infected as well. Had they been, one would expect a rash of violence. However, none had been reported in the papers.

But here I was, taking Cairo at his word. Could I really accept such an explanation from such a man? I felt as if I stood upon quicksand and each step plunged me deeper into confusion.

The cab rattling across Westminster Bridge brought me out of my musings. Soon I was rolling up the large circular carriage drive in front of Bethlehem Royal. The six looming columns of its entry did nothing to soften the depressing effect of its dingy yellow brick construction. It saddened me to think of my friend even now imprisoned beneath its green copper dome. I paid the driver and went inside.

Fame has its drawbacks, but one thing I will say for it: It will get you an immediate audience with anyone below a prince in rank. So it was with Dr. Hyslop, the physician superintendent of the hospital. He was a dark young man with prominent nose and a quietly forceful manner.

Once I had shown my letter, our conversation was brief and to the point. Yes, Houdini was here; had been for nearly two hours. I wanted to visit him? Of course. Right now? Certainly, if I would wait until he could arrange for an escort. Houdini was down in the basement with the most severely disturbed cases.

Dr. Hyslop left and returned shortly with a steward who led me downstairs. The basement was still lit by gaslights. The wards were narrow and shadowy—a far cry from their more modern counterparts upstairs with their rows of cheerful arched windows, plants, pictures, and comfortable furnishings.

Down a dim corridor we stopped at a narrow wooden door with a small, barred window. Two attendants stood watch outside. The steward introduced me to them, explained my quest, and left. One attendant turned to me.

"That's 'im." He jerked his thumb at the bars.

The other man stood aside to allow me to peer into the room. As I did, I saw a sad sight. Houdini lay facedown on an iron bedstead with a canvas stretcher. He was wrapped tightly in a straitjacket. Thick canvas sleeves held his arms crossed against his chest. Large straps traversed his shoulders and buckled firmly to the back of the heavy garment. But he did not lie peacefully. Rather, he struggled vainly against the ties that held him so implacably. His trousers were wrinkled and soaked with sweat from his efforts.

As I watched, he gave a Herculean effort and wrenched himself from his stomach onto his back. He bent double and gnawed at the buckles with his teeth. His fingers clawed frantically at them from beneath the restraining canvas. Next, he flopped like a fish on a riverbank. His face was red and he panted from his exertions. I turned sadly to the guard.

"How long has he been like this?" I asked.

"Almost twenty minutes now." He smiled ruefully. "This 'ere's the third one we've 'ad on him."

"What?"

"That's right," my guide contributed, "he's got out of—"

But he was interrupted by a shout from within. I spun back to the window and saw Houdini fling his arms in triumph over his head. He had somehow managed to uncross them, and this gave him considerable slack in the jacket. In a moment he had shaken the canvas entirely off his body and flung it in a corner where two others lay.

Laughing madly, he sprang at the door. To my alarm, it swung open and Houdini charged into the hallway. When he saw me, his face registered shock. Involuntarily, I backed up a step. I was not eager for a confrontation with a madman, even if he had been a friend.

But his attention was diverted to the guard standing beside me. "How long is that, Thomas?"

To my astonishment, the guard pulled a watch out of his pocket. "Five minutes and seventeen seconds," he replied.

"Too short!" Houdini shouted. "People won't think they got their money's worth. On that style I got to stall a little."

The guard rubbed a whiskered chin and chuckled appreciatively.

Houdini finally turned his attention back to me.

"Conan Doyle, what are you doing here?"

I gaped at him. "Do you mean to tell me this was all a rehearsal for your act?"

"Yeah. What did you think?"

"But why come to an asylum?"

"Where else am I going to find a straitjacket? But tell me, is that trick worth paying money to see? Oh, that reminds me." Houdini dug into his pocket and came out with two pound notes. He handed one to each man. "I'd sure appreciate you boys keeping this little session to yourselves. Doesn't look good for the act if they know I practiced it."

"Right enough, guv'nor," the first guard said with a wink. The man who had led me here snatched his note, saluted with his forefinger, and the two were off—doubtless to plan how to spend their windfall. Houdini disappeared back inside the room. He returned holding his coat and tie, which he proceeded to don. He then smiled at me with a defiant cheerfulness. I determined to play along for a time.

He shrugged. "So, will it play?"

"It's marvelous. But isn't it a bit difficult on you?"

"Yeah well, the public, bless it, wants its thrills. Anyway, I can take it. I've got the stuff." He considered a moment. "I'm set for this season, but I still need a new idea for next year—to get me back on the front pages."

"You'll come up with something," I said.

"I'd better. Already some other weisenheimers are doing my handcuff challenge. I won't be able to use that much longer."

For the first time, he seemed to consider my presence. "What you doing here?"

"Your wife sent me."

His mouth dropped open. "Bess sent you?"

"She is quite concerned for you," I said.

At my words, all pretense of confidence dropped from his manner. He slumped, and a great sadness washed over his face.

"No," he said, "she can't love me anymore."

"Let us go somewhere we can talk," I suggested, taking his arm.

We strolled along St. George's Road toward Westminster Bridge. I was almost oblivious to the noises of traffic and the bustle of pedestrians as I spoke in a low voice to my companion.

"Return to her," I urged.

"How can I?" Misery filled his face. "If you knew what happened . . ."

We crossed Lambeth Road and continued on. "I do know; Bess told me. That is why I sought you out."

He shook his head sadly. "Even if she could forgive me, I could never forgive myself." Tears welled up in his eyes. "How could I do that to her?"

I waited until this flood of self-recrimination had passed before I spoke. "Perhaps it was not really you."

"Ahhh, what are you taking about?"

"Do you recall our last night at Cairo's?"

"That chiseler," Houdini growled through his grief. "What's he got to do with this?"

"I am beginning to suspect there is more to his claim than we have been willing to credit."

"You think some evil spirit is behind this?" When I saw the disbelief on his face, I knew I must reveal more.

I drew a deep breath. "I also have felt the touch of madness."

"You too? How?"

How could I reveal the horror of what I had done? In my mind's eye I saw the disgust that would transform his face, the inevitable denunciation. What decent human being would associate with me once he knew what I had done?

No, the details must remain locked within the dungeon of my soul. When I spoke, I could not keep the quaver from my voice. "I was inspired to write a story like none other I have ever attempted. But before I could complete it, I went mad and attempted to harm an innocent person." My hands were trembling. I prayed he would not ask for more details.

"And now you also," I continued, "have been visited by inspiration and brutality."

Houdini looked dubious.

I added, "Scant hours ago, I saw Justine Luce just so afflicted."

This gave him pause. "Her too, huh? That really is something." But at last he shook his head. "I can't buy it. Cairo's full of baloney, no matter how you slice it."

"Then how do you explain what has happened to us?"

Houdini ran his fingers through his hair. "I told you—hypnosis. I know a guy who can make people bark like dogs and cluck like chickens. He even gets people to do crazy things hours later, after the spell has worn off."

Unfortunately, I detected the flaw in his argument. "Doesn't the will generally rebel against doing something contrary to its basic nature?"

Conflicting emotions played across his face. Clearly, he was anxious for exoneration, but not at the price of acknowledging Cairo's claims.

"In any case," I said, "the important thing now is for you to go to your wife."

He shook his head miserably. "She never wants to see me again."

"Yes, she does."

For the first time, something like hope came to his face. "She said that?"

I nodded. "I explained that you were under a malign influence. She believed me. She will forgive you if you are contrite."

"Contrite? I'll kiss that woman's feet if she takes me back. Let's get going." So saying, he dashed into the street to hail a cab.

Chapter 19
Slash and Burn

We rode to Houdini's hotel, the Cavendish on Jermyn Street. It was a pleasant but not opulent establishment. At his insistence, I accompanied him as far as his door. He lifted a fist to knock and looked uncertainly at me. I encouraged him with a nod. He rapped lightly. The door swung open, revealing Bess standing there. Hope mingled with fear on her countenance.

"Bess," Houdini said. Hesitantly, he spread his arms.

At the sight she backed up, her expression wary. He followed her inside. Neither thought to close the door. Houdini dropped to one knee in earnest entreaty. Bess's lips were pursed, but her eyes grew moist. Neither one paid heed to the two dogs swirling about them in joy at Houdini's return.

The moment ought not to be profaned by outside eyes. I reached for the doorknob and pulled it softly closed. I would seek Houdini's aid another time. As I retreated down the hall, I did not regret putting aside my own affairs for their reconciliation.

But a grim foreboding filled me as I made my way

across the lush aubergine carpet toward the lift. Houdini, Miss Luce, and I had all given in to our worst impulses. Something, either a demon or Cairo's malevolent will, was infecting us.

I wanted no one else taken unawares as we had been. Both Sir William and Mrs. Pangbourne must be warned as soon as possible. As I reached out to summon the lift, I heard my name called desperately. I turned to see Houdini racing down the hall toward me.

"You have to come back," he panted.

I was alarmed. "Why? What has gone wrong?"

He beamed at me. "Nothing," he said. "We"—he flushed—"that is, Bess wants to thank you."

I resisted, but he would not be gainsaid. Reluctantly, I let him drag me back. Bess stood on the mushroom-colored carpet in the front room of their suite and made a very pretty speech. I endured it and tried to hide my embarrassment. Houdini hung back sheepishly until she had finished.

Afterward, he added, "Anything I can do for you, just ask—tickets, private shows for your friends, anything."

"I should never presume upon our friendship in such a way," I said. When he protested, I held up a hand for silence. "But there is one matter that you can help with."

"Name it—you got it," he declared.

Briefly, I outlined Mackleston's plight and my deductions concerning it.

Houdini shook his head sadly. "That poor guy."

"I am at an impasse in the investigation," I continued, "and desperately need the services of a magician."

"You mean you and me team up to solve the crime?"

"I do. We must discover how a third person could have left a locked room."

We settled into a couple of overstuffed leather chairs by the room's writing desk and he questioned me closely as to the door and windows in the chamber. The challenge obviously intrigued him. He sprang up. "Okay. I'll give it my best."

"Excellent." I rose as well. "I am in high hopes we shall find a human agency at the bottom of this."

"Of course we will," Houdini snorted. "There's no spooks in this. It's Cairo and his hypnotism all the way."

"But surely," I pointed out, "your hypnosis explanation has a flaw."

"Like what?"

"As we agreed," said I, "under hypnosis you cannot be forced to violate your sense of morals."

"Okay," he said patiently, "let me show you how to get around that. Say I hypnotize you. I give you a gun and tell you it's a magic toy. When you shoot it at somebody, it makes them happy. I tell you to take it home and make your wife happy tonight at seven o'clock. I wake you up. Bingo! Hours later, you shoot her and don't know why."

I stood there appalled. "What a hideous intent!"

"Don't I know it," Houdini agreed. Solemnly, he offered me his hand. As I took it, he said, "We're going to figure this out. And you know what? We're going to get Cairo locked up, too."

Before we departed, Houdini disappeared into one of the back rooms of his suite. He returned bearing a pry bar, a sharpened screwdriver, and a rule.

"Now we'll get down to brass tacks," he promised.

On our way down to the street, he refused to explain their uses. All he would say was "People take too much for granted."

Much as I itched to begin our investigation, I could not forget my concern for the others in our party. I put the matter to Houdini and he agreed we should take time to warn them.

To that end, we soon pulled up in front of Mrs. Pangbourne's home in Knightsbridge, just off Brompton Road. She lived less than a mile from the site where Harrods was erecting its splendid new dome.

At the entry to her opulent brick residence, we came upon a strange sight. The double front doors swung wide open and a mountain of furniture sat on the pavement.

Traffic had to detour around the ten-foot-tall heap of massive oak desks, tables, chairs, and plush red couches. As we watched, two panting servants staggered forth bearing a Gothic-style sideboard. They heaved it atop the pile. Houdini and I gazed at each other. This did not bode well.

We made our way around the heap of carved wood and rich fabric to peep in the front door. A frightened-looking young housemaid in black scurried like a huge beetle across the marble tiles of the front hallway.

"Excuse me, miss," I called.

She looked up, startled.

"We are friends of Mrs. Pangbourne. Is she moving?" I inquired.

The stout young woman shook her head. "No, sir," she said, and raced off on some desperate errand.

Houdini and I entered what appeared to be an unoccupied house. The halls around us were bare of furniture, pictures, or any other ornament. We heard grunts coming from the next room and flattened ourselves against a wall as four young men hauled a huge Jacobean bed past us and out the doorway. They leaned it against the pile in front and staggered back inside.

"What's going on here?" Houdini muttered.

I could only shake my head in bafflement. We moved farther into the house until we reached a large morning room. This, too, was nearly bare. The carpets had been rolled and lay against the walls. In a far corner of the vast, empty space stood Mrs. Pangbourne, energetically hacking at the red velvet draperies with a huge butcher knife. Trails of scarlet cloth littered the floor. The remaining fabric hung in ragged tatters at head level.

"Mrs. Pangbourne," Houdini called out.

She spun around. Instead of the frenzied visage I had expected, a cheerful-looking woman greeted us—albeit one puffing from her exertions. She had put off her widow's weeds and wore a plain blue housedress. Given her ample form, the dress's simple lines were quite flattering.

"Mr. Houdini," she said, setting the knife on a windowsill. "And Conan Doyle, how good of you to drop by. I shall be with you in a moment."

So saying, she turned back and gathered in an armload of hanging drapery. She clutched the folds of cloth to her bosom and lurched backward. Down came the whole pile with a soft thud that raised a chest-high cloud of dust.

Coughing, she fanned the air in front of her face and trundled over to us. "What brings you here?" she inquired good-naturedly. She tucked a stray lock of her salt-and-pepper hair behind her ear as she waited for an answer. A line of yellow threads trailed across the front of her dress. They ran horizontally across her bosom. She had ripped off some ornamentation—beadwork, lace, or some such.

"What are you doing?" Houdini asked her.

"Doing? Why, I am refitting this house. I had what I can only call an inspiration last night." She lifted her chin and drew a deep breath. "Yes, Mr. Houdini, an inspiration."

The look on Houdini's face spoke volumes. Mrs. Pangbourne caught sight of the carpet rolls lying against the wall. She frowned with distaste. "Would you be so kind as to remove those?"

Houdini held up his hands. "Sure, we'll help. But first tell me about your inspiration."

"Ah." She looked pleased. "It is so simple, I can't believe I didn't think of it before. We've begun a new century, have we not?"

"Two years ago," I reminded her.

"Exactly." She spread wide her arms. "High time for a new look, a new standard of design. I shall start it here." Her right hand swung to rest on her bosom. "In my very own house."

"What sort of a look?" I asked with some trepidation.

"Why, something totally new." She raised her forefinger in admonition. "Simplify! That has become my battle cry. No more gingerbread. It will be bold, clean—modern! Bright colors. Geometry! Angles and curves, curves, curves! Furniture like no one's ever seen before—low tables, black and red lacquers. All built from modern materials—glass, steel, plastic. I do not want just a chair, I want the soul of a chair."

Her smile broadened. "I have already contacted architects, workmen. They'll be here this afternoon." She paused to look around her. "So," she finished up, "it is imperative I remove these old things immediately."

She called to a passing butler. "Cowan, get matches from Cook and burn that pile of rubbish out front."

She looked around her. "Now, this room . . . ," she said thoughtfully. "I see new paneling on the walls—oblique angles, ray lines." She turned back to us. "It will be glorious, won't it?"

I finally found my voice. "You can't start a fire in the middle of the city."

"Can't I? I'll start a fire under the seat of everyone who has ever yearned for something fresh in her surroundings." In a flash, her voice shifted from grandiose to matter-of-fact. "Do get that carpet, won't you?"

She charged across the room, snatched up her knife, and had at the next row of draperies.

Houdini shrugged and led the way to a roll of carpet against the wall. I squatted down, grabbed at the stiff fabric, and lifted. My back gave me a slight twinge where I had fetched up against the brick wall when Miss Luce had shoved me.

I tried to ignore it. Down the hall and outside Houdini and I huffed and staggered with our burden. Dropping it on the pavement, we saw the butler leaning against the pile of furniture. He held a fist-sized box of sulfur matches. His long, horselike face wore a bemused expression.

I raced over to him. "You dare not start a fire here," I said. "The houses are too close. There'll be flying embers, sparks—think, man!"

He looked up at me. "Bless you, sir, I know that. But what am I to tell that sweet old dear when she asks me did I do it?"

"Tell her you tried but the furniture won't catch," Houdini suggested.

"State she's in, she'll probably come out and start it herself."

"Then," I said, "you must stay out of her sight and keep the matches."

"Yeah," Houdini contributed. "Just make yourself scarce. If this city's anything like New York, the stuff'll be gone by morning."

The man looked relieved. "I hope you're right."

"How long has she been like this?" I asked him.

"Since early this morning. She called us all together and said she was going to redo the house. She had a wild look in her eye. Nothing would do but that we rip out everything now."

I nodded sadly. "Take heart. Her mania will likely be over soon."

"I hope so," the man said sadly. "She's always been good to us as worked here."

As we left, he was sneaking around the house to find a side door. Back in our waiting cab, Houdini shook his head. "I wouldn't have believed it," he said. "Do we even want to go see Sir William?"

I sighed. "I suppose we had better."

Chapter 20
Another Victim

Checking my notebook, I learned that Sir William lived in Hampstead. Our way led into the country northwest of the metropolis. The land rose gradually but steadily. We passed fields and groves of trees in their autumn foliage. In about an hour, I was rapping a brass knocker against its strike plate in front of a modern house with tall front windows. White wood trim set off its brickwork.

A slim, middle-aged woman in a lavender morning dress greeted us. Her brown hair was done up in a soft bun at the nape of her neck. Worry had drawn tight lines along her open features. "Mrs. Bowers?" I asked.

"Yes?" She had a preoccupied air about her.

I introduced us. "We have come to speak to your husband."

"I'm sorry," she said, "but he is ill." She stepped back and began to shut the door.

I reached out my hand and held it open. "Sir William has not been himself lately. Am I correct?"

She flushed. "These are personal matters." She wrenched the door from my hand.

I continued rapidly, "He has just accomplished a startling breakthrough in his profession." The door hovered, half closed. "However, this breakthrough," I went on, "was followed by an act of madness that has nearly destroyed his personal life."

The door swung open. She thrust her face forward. "How did you know?" Hope and dread mingled in her expression.

"We've been through it too," Houdini explained.

She rocked backward in surprise.

"You must not give up hope." I urged. "Your husband is truly not himself. He has come under the sway of an evil influence."

"If only I could believe you." She threatened to burst into tears. Finding a sympathetic listener must have been almost more than her overwrought nerves could bear. But she gathered herself and asked, "What influence?"

"Mrs. Bowers," Houdini said, "the truth is we don't know. But some evil force has got to all the members of our party and we're trying to find a way to beat it."

"Your party?" Her eyes widened in comprehension. "You mean at that dreadful séance?"

"None other," I verified. "Has Sir William described it to you?"

She shook her head. "He told me little. Still," she added, as realization lit her face, "it was after his second visit that this horrible change came over him."

She came to a decision. "You shall see him. But I doubt that you will enjoy the sight."

We were escorted through a large, comfortable sitting room—done in burgundies and royal blues—to a short hallway. After a slight hesitation, she pushed open the door at the end. Houdini and I entered. Desks and bookshelves indicated that we were in a study. It was almost impossible to make out details, since the shutters were closed. The room was as dark as a cave. A foul odor assailed my nostrils. I did not see Sir William. Then a form stirred on a couch across from us. The man sat up and rubbed bleary eyes.

"Clarissa," he called, "is that you?"

"Yes, William," she answered behind us.

"Who are these men?" He blinked at us.

"It is Conan Doyle and Houdini," I said. "We have come to—"

"I don't want to see anyone," he complained to his wife. "And I'm out of wine."

As my eyes adjusted to the dim light, I picked out the silhouettes of bottles scattered about the room. Dozens littered the tables, the couch he occupied, and even the floor.

"Did you hear me?" His voice grew harsh. He rose unsteadily and lumbered toward us. He kicked bottles out of the way as he advanced. They rolled and clinked against one another. "I said I was out of wine."

"Yes, William." Her voice was neutral. "I'll have more brought up."

Sir William rubbed his cheeks, adorned with a stubbly crop of whiskers. The odor in the room was intolerable. Obviously, he had not shaved, bathed, or changed his clothing for many days. Dried pools of vomit fouled the rug.

"See that you do," he growled, and staggered back to his couch. Sir William flopped down with a grunt and grabbed the nearest bottle. He upended it to pour the few remaining drops down his throat.

His wife motioned for us to leave and pulled the door shut behind us.

"He's been like that ever since the night after the séance." She spoke softly. "He's not stirred from his study. At the rate he's consuming wine, our cellar won't last another three weeks."

"Have you tried to moderate his intake?" I inquired.

"How?" she asked. "You saw him. Could you reason with him?"

"You could lock the cellar door," Houdini suggested.

"I tried that the second day. His rage was dreadful to behold."

"Have you no relatives or friends to turn to?" I asked.

"You don't understand," she turned on me with unexpected vehemence. "He doesn't want to live any longer. And perhaps he's right."

Her eyes flashed defiantly at us as she spoke. Here, indeed, was a woman driven to desperation. The silence hung between us for a moment as I gathered my thoughts. "Do you recall," I asked, "how accurately I described your husband's emotional state?"

"Yes," she answered uncertainly.

"The reason I could do so is because—"

"Like I said," Houdini interrupted impatiently, "we've been through it too. If we came out of it, he can."

"But how?" She spread her hands helplessly. "If only you understood the magnitude . . ."

"Perhaps we can help if we know what has happened," I suggested.

The woman thought a moment. "Will you promise never to reveal what I tell you?"

"You have my word," I assured her. Houdini nodded vigorously.

"Very well." She appeared to draw up her courage. "Follow me."

She led us to a back parlor where a servant was dusting. "That will do, Meg," she said. "You may finish later."

Meg dropped a small curtsy and fled. Mrs. Bowers arranged herself on a scarlet velvet–covered chair and began her story.

"The day after the séance, William rose early and retreated to his study. He stayed there all day.

"My youngest daughter and her husband, James, came over that evening to give us our first look at their newborn daughter. William made no appearance.

"I bearded him in his study where he was making some

calculations. I said firmly, 'Your daughter has just arrived. Surely you can finish tomorrow.' He appeared not to have heard me as his pencil scratched feverishly across the page. All at once, he threw down the implement. There was an almost ecstatic look upon his face. 'I have proven it!' he shouted. 'An electron carries a negative charge. Not as a statistical mean, mind you, but as a definite constant! It's sure to mean another Nobel Prize.'"

"Of course, I congratulated him. 'Do you think you could join our guests now?' I asked hesitantly.

" 'What? Guests?'

" 'Yes, your daughter, James, and our new grandchild.'

"From his dazed expression, I wasn't sure he understood. Nevertheless, he arose and followed me from the room. He was still in a state of nervous excitement when he arrived among the company. The proud papa brought little Flora, as they had named her, over to her grandfather. William took her, it seemed, without noticing what he was doing. He glanced down at her pink swaddling clothes. A hideous change came over his face. I swear I have never seen such a look of hatred in all my life.

" 'What, another girl?' And then, to the horror of us all, he flung the baby to the ground.

"James was the only one who kept his head. He dived for the floor and managed to get his arms under the poor dear before she landed. Naturally, little Flora shrieked in terror. It took several moments to determine that she was unharmed. William had left the room in a rage. I apologized profusely and made what excuses I could, but my daughter and James left almost immediately. James positively shook with anger.

"That night William began drinking and hasn't ceased since. I believe," she finished, "if you interrogate him, you do so at the peril of your life."

Houdini and I sat silently after she had finished. Obviously, Sir William's current condition was a retreat from the horror of what he'd done.

"Others have recovered from states nearly as bad," I said.

"I'm not sure I care. Do what you will." She left with no further word.

Houdini shrugged. "Let's give it a try."

I opened the door to the study and we stepped inside. "Sir William," I called softly.

"Get out," a petulant voice snapped.

I plunged right in. "You are not to blame for what occurred."

"Don't know what you're talking about."

"Your granddaughter," Houdini said.

Sir William raised himself up from his couch. As my eyes grew accustomed to the dim light, I could see that his white, receding hair was tousled. A look of black rage twisted his face as he staggered to his feet. "I'll break your necks! I'll—"

"You'll listen to me." I braced myself and grabbed his wrists as he lurched forward. "Houdini, I, each member of the séance has gone through what you have."

He stopped in his tracks.

"We have felt your shame."

Sir William slumped. If Houdini and I had not grabbed him, he would have fallen.

"It's not you," Houdini said steadily. "It's Cairo."

"Cairo?" Confusion played over Sir William's face.

"Yes," I asserted. We half dragged, half carried him back to his couch.

Briefly, we sketched out our experiences as well as those of Miss Luce and Mrs. Pangbourne. By the time we had finished, he looked nearly rational.

"But how? What is the mechanism of such influence?" Obviously, he desperately wanted to believe our story. Houdini and I looked at each other. Could I tell a scientist my suspicions? No, he would dismiss them outright.

"Hypnotism," Houdini blurted out, with a warning glance at me.

Sir William leaned forward. "Could it be?"

Houdini explained the theory of a suggestion given while in a trance.

"But when could he have—?" Realization lit Sir William's face. "That dance of his. The music. His arm movements." He clutched my arms. "That was it, wasn't it?"

For his sake, I kept my reservations to myself. "What other answer could there be?"

Just then a servant peeped into the room. He held a bottle on a salver. "You ordered wine, sir?" he asked timidly.

"Take it away," Sir William ordered. The servant scampered off. The man looked at us. "I must see my wife." Tears formed in his bleary eyes.

We led the way; he shambled after us. In the drawing room Clarissa Bowers rose from an armchair, a stern expression on her face. It did not soften as he approached. We left the two of them alone in the drawing room and let ourselves out. Sir William was not going to have an easy time of it.

Chapter 21
The Mystery Deepens

When we reached Mackleston's flat, I purged my thoughts of the misery we had witnessed today. Houdini and I had work to do. Besides, I intended to rectify an oversight.

On my last inspection, I had given the paintings merely a cursory look. I needed to find the one Mackleston had painted during his frenzy. *The Daughters of King Minyas*, he'd called it. In the throes of his passion he might have included some clue as to the identity of the third party in the room. It bothered me that I had forgotten to look for it before.

I led Houdini up to the door and unlocked it. Before entering, he examined the keyhole from the outside. Though I had done the same, I kept silent. After all, he had a right to an unhampered inquiry.

When he opened the door, the reek that assailed us was at least as pungent as I remembered from earlier in the day. I gagged on the smell. Houdini coughed and turned his head to draw a breath of fresher air. "That's ripe," he announced.

In the room, flies swarmed like black confetti over the bloodstains. Houdini swallowed twice and went on to inspect the bolt. He held up a metal shank and pointed to the broken end.

"Really snapped," he said, "not cut through." I nodded but was a trifle disappointed. If he merely duplicated my investigation, our time here was wasted.

His next move, however, broke new ground. Houdini pulled his screwdriver from his pocket and applied it to the screws that held the bolt's housing in place. He removed half of them, eyed each one minutely, examined their holes. He even gouged deeply into the wood with the sharpened end of the tool. Then he replaced the screws.

Next he turned his attention to one of the windows. He jammed his pry bar under a nail head and levered down. With a screech of protest the nail slowly rose from its bed. Once it was out, Houdini examined it carefully. Then he searched the hole left in the window frame. He did the same with each of the other windows in the room. When he had finished, he frowned.

"You suspected the nails had been tampered with?" I finally inquired.

He nodded. "Or the screws. Like a box escape," he continued. "That's where the magician is nailed into a wooden box and appears at the other end of the stage. Most guys, they use short nails in one end of the box so they can kick a panel out. Later, they put the panel back and drive in real nails in case anybody checks the box."

"But this is remarkable. You were looking for counterfeit fasteners?"

"Yeah, and recent replacements. But these are all the real thing." He looked around. "Let's see what the rest of the place can tell us."

He began to pick up pieces of furniture and move them to the perimeter of the room. I followed suit, though I did not at once divine his plan. When all were stacked against the wall, Houdini called to me.

"Let's get this out of the way." He knelt at the edge of the carpet.

In a flash I realized what he was up to. He meant to check the floor for a trapdoor. I felt a moment of chagrin for not considering that possibility myself. We rolled the carpet up and went over every inch of the floor. When that availed us nothing, he climbed upon a chair and transferred his careful attentions to the ceiling. As he stepped down, he said with a sigh, "No traps."

My uneasiness had grown. "You assume advanced planning," I pointed out.

He turned impatiently to me. "To make an escape, you always rig the room. Always."

"You believe this escape was prepared beforehand?"

"Of course."

"But this is monstrous. It means that what happened to Mackleston's brother was premeditated."

The magician nodded glumly. "What's worse, I don't see how the guy did it."

"There is a fireplace in the next room," I offered.

His eyes lit up.

"But it has bars in the flue."

"Oh." His face fell. "Let's take a look anyway. You never know."

He strode briskly into Mackleston's bedchamber. I followed more slowly. If we were not on the trail of an actual demon, then surely it was a human fiend we searched for. I again recalled Miss Luce's warning, and I own it brought a chill to me. Such a creature must be brought to justice.

Houdini and I moved the bed, rolled up the carpet, and inspected the floor and ceiling. We had no better results than in the previous room. Our canvass of the bathroom produced the same unhappy dearth of evidence, except for one small thing.

In my desperation for some clue, I hung my head out the tiny window and looked down. The brick face of the building was smooth and offered no handholds. A small discoloration just beneath the sill caught my attention. A dark smudge clung to the bricks. The opening was so small that I had to withdraw my head in order to reach down with my hand. My fingers crept over the masonry and at last they found the spot. I felt a fine dust.

Withdrawing my hand, I studied the black and gray-flecked powder on my fingers. It felt greasy to the touch. Soot, I realized, mingled with ash—that's what it was. But how had soot got out the window? Clearly, it was from some fireplace.

Looking out again, I saw that the sill formed a windbreak that had sheltered this clump of dust from the autumn gusts. Could it have come from a neighboring chimney? I reached out again and felt along the underside of the sill. When I pulled my hand back in, it was coated with the mottled powder. Where had it come from? Surely a stray current of air could not have deposited so much. Did this oddity relate to the murder? If so, I couldn't, for the life of me, think how.

Puzzled, I pointed out my find to Houdini. He simply shrugged as he removed his coat and tie and unbuttoned his shirt.

"Keep an eye out, will you? I don't want anybody to walk in on me in my altogether."

I realized he meant to strip naked. He saw me staring at him and said, "Have to climb up the chimney to test those bars. I don't want to ruin these clothes. They set me back twenty bucks."

I closed the bedchamber door. As Houdini undressed and examined the fireplace, I noted the exceptional development of his musculature. I should not have been surprised, however. His profession demanded top physical condition.

"Well, this is clean, at least," he said, looking down at the hearth. He peered up the chimney. Then he rose and stood with his upper body hidden by the bricks of the stack. He gave a little hop, which must have put his hands within reach of the bars, for I saw his legs slowly rise up the flue. A small avalanche of soot preceded his reappearance. He dropped down, smudged with the grime from years of fires.

"Those bars, they're in there firm, all right," he admitted.

I nodded, impressed by his determination. Here was truly a good ally. As he crossed to the bathroom to clean up, he trailed little splotches of soot on the carpet.

We set to work returning the rooms to their original condition on his return.

"It looks bad for my theory, I fear," I said as we moved the furniture around.

"Boy, I'll say," he agreed. "But we got one more ace up our sleeve."

"What is that?"

"Come with me and I'll show you."

He went back to the door and picked up the ruler he'd left there. Houdini proceeded to measure every conceivable dimension of the keyhole and the bolt. With a piece of paper from my notebook, he made a precise sketch of the bolt and keyhole, complete with exact measurements.

At last he stood and said, "Okay. That's that."

"What next?" I inquired.

"We're going to see a friend of mine."

I begged his leave for a few moments in the studio before we departed. I was determined to find the painting Mackleston had described to us.

I soon found the empty stretcher bars among the tangle of wood that had been his easels. Obviously, the painting had been removed from its framework. Accordingly, I gathered up all the canvases in the room and laid them against the wall. There was the nude of Miss Luce with its marvelous skin tones and face obscured by shadow. I found a few still lifes, a landscape, and a more conventional portrait of Miss Luce. But that was all. The painting was gone.

Chapter 22
Some Bad News

"What are you looking for?" Houdini called out.

"The painting Mackleston did right before the murder. It's not here."

"No kidding?" Houdini said.

I devoutly wished I had remembered to look for the painting on my first visit here. During my last search, I had feared I was losing my logical faculties. Here was more evidence it was so. How could I have overlooked a missing painting? And who had taken it?

I had locked the room when Miss Luce and I had left. Could the landlady have a duplicate key? A painting by a notorious murderer might be valuable enough to tempt even an honest soul. I confided my suspicions to Houdini. We evolved a scheme to ascertain the truth.

Shortly, therefore, we knocked upon Miss Finch's door. When she opened it, I introduced my companion to her. She was thrilled to meet the famous magician. It took very little encouragement to have her produce a deck of cards. He soon had her enthralled.

As far as she was concerned, there was no one else but

Houdini in the room. I had free run of her flat. It comprised three good-sized rooms with several nice pieces of furniture. She was certainly not in need of cash. Furthermore, her rooms did not contain the painting. Returning, I motioned to Houdini behind the woman's back and he drew his entertainments to an end.

"Miss Finch," I asked, as we prepared to leave, "have you a duplicate key to the flat?"

She assented.

"Have you lent it to anyone since the murder?"

"I should say not!" she asserted. "The police was most insistent about that. No one gets in or out without their say-so."

Thanking her, we made our departure.

Out on the pavement, Houdini turned to me. "Still thinking about that painting?"

I nodded. "I wanted to make certain that no one else could have entered the flat and taken it." So saying, I flagged down a cab, and Houdini gave the address of his friend we were to visit.

My mind was wholly occupied with the question of the painting. Inspector Woburn had assured me he had removed nothing. I had no reason to doubt his word. That left one explanation. The only other conscious person in that room had been the murderer. Somehow he'd managed to get out with it. But why? Could it hold a clue to his identity? If so, would he not have destroyed it? He could easily have burned it in the fireplace—but the hearth had been clean.

I was so puzzled by this new mystery that I did not notice where our journey led us. Eventually, I realized we drove eastward. The large stores disappeared. We passed small shops in a maze of tiny, stone-flagged lanes. Women crouched on front steps surrounded by scrawny, filthy children. We found ourselves on a street of dark, abandoned buildings, gaudy gin shops, and stunted people.

"Slow down," Houdini called to our cabdriver. After a moment, he sang out, "Okay, here." Our cab pulled up at a small storefront squeezed between two tenements. A faded sign above the door announced it to be an ironmonger's. Houdini gave the cabdriver a pound note to hold him there until we returned.

A bell tinkled as we entered the tiny shop. The wooden cases that lined the walls held every conceivable shape of lock and key—from great, black medieval hasps to modern steel padlocks. Behind the rear counter was a pile of safes stacked against the back wall. We stepped up to the glass counter in the front of the shop. A wizened old man shuffled up to greet us. His glasses magnified his pale, rheumy eyes to twice their real size. He evidently recognized Houdini, for his face immediately broke into a grin that deepened the creases around his forehead, eyes, and mouth.

"Shalom, Ehrich."

"Shalom, Josef. How's business?"

The old man shrugged. "How should it be?"

They then exchanged a few short phrases in a language I did not recognize. From its gutturals, I deduced it was Yiddish. It did not surprise me that Harry Houdini was not my friend's real name. Many performers use a pseudonym. What did surprise me was that he was evidently a Jew. In the rush of circumstances I had not thought to wonder about his background. Now I grew curious.

Houdini turned back to me with a wink. "Josef knows every lock in this city. And in most of the rest of the world."

Josef smiled again. "I've got a set of five keys—they'll open any pair of handcuffs in America. Isn't that right, Ehrich?"

Houdini nodded. "Sure is."

"I hope the same cannot be said for British shackles," I said, alarmed.

Josef and Houdini looked at each other and burst out laughing. "You don't need keys to get out of English cuffs," Houdini explained.

"What? Then how—?" I began, but I was cut off sharply.

"Trade secret," Houdini said, and turned his attention back to the shopkeeper. "Listen, Josef, I need a favor."

"What? Another set of picks already?"

"No, this is something special." So saying, he pulled out his sketch of the bolt and keyhole from Mackleston's room. He handed the drawing to Josef and asked, "Could you build me a tool that would fit through this keyhole and let me close the bolt on the other side?"

Josef studied the sketch for several minutes. Then he looked up and asked, "What's the bolt made of?"

"Cast iron."

"This keyhole," Josef pressed, "it's just a simple three-tumbler lock?"

Houdini nodded. Josef peered again at the drawing. At last, he threw it down on the counter and announced, "It can't be done."

Houdini sighed.

"Well, look here," Josef said. "You have a span of at least a foot between the key and the bolt. Anything thin enough to fit through that hole isn't going to have the strength to do what you want. And how you going to get any side leverage at that angle?"

Houdini's face fell. "You sure?"

"Of course I'm sure. You haven't promised anybody you'll do this?" Josef asked, concerned. "I told you, come to me first."

"No, it's nothing like that," Houdini said, dejection in his voice.

"We are assisting the police with some inquiries," I explained.

Josef looked at me shrewdly. "Ah. The murder in Soho."

"Yes. How did you know?"

He shrugged. "It was in all the papers."

I realized how much this adventure had disarranged my life. Normally, I read the *Times* every morning.

"Yeah well, thanks, Josef." Houdini sighed and slapped a large banknote on the counter. Josef smiled in acknowledgment and wished us a good day.

Outside, we paused to reconnoiter.

"We seem to have run up against a blank wall," I said.

Houdini jammed his hands deep into his pockets and paced back and forth on the pavement. "I can't believe it," he said to himself. He looked up at me. "I was counting on Josef."

I nodded. "Have you any other suggestions?"

"I'm working on it!" he practically shouted. Then, more calmly, "There's no way a penny-ante crook like Cairo can fool Houdini."

"I am afraid only one course is left us," I sighed.

He paused in his angry promenade. "What's that?"

"We must return to the source of the mystery."

"You mean Cairo? Ask that chiseler for help?" Houdini hunched forward and folded his arms across his chest. "Not on your life! I can figure this out."

"Mackleston's time is running out. Have you an alternative?" I asked.

Houdini ran his fingers through his dark hair. "I wish I did," he admitted. Then his face lit up. "Hey, wait a minute. Maybe we're going about this wrong. Let's try it from the other end—find out if the dead guy had any enemies. Then we can trace their movements that night."

"A fresh start could be just what we need," I admitted.

"What about his father?" Houdini asked. "Wouldn't he be the best person to start with?"

I recalled the ring I had found in Mackleston's flat and how I planned to use it to gain entrée to Lord Vollmer. I explained to Houdini.

"Just the ticket," he agreed enthusiastically. "Let's go."

The sun was setting as our cab made its way west toward Lord Vollmer's house on Pall Mall. Our failure thus far to arrive at a solution to the murder had left me with a feeling of acute melancholy. I was more convinced than ever that I could no longer rely on my mental abilities.

To our left, through an occasional break in the buildings, I caught glimpses of the noble dome of St. Paul's some miles to the south. The dying light gilded it with crimson and gold. The building was lovely, but I found no consolation in the sight. Wasn't that what religion was supposed to offer—consolation? Instead of certainty and peace, I felt only foreboding.

I thought of the eight million inhabitants of this great metropolis, scurrying home for their well-earned suppers. Did even one of them have the slightest glimmer of the chaos that surrounded their predictable, well-ordered lives? What is our puny human understanding when compared to the great mysteries of birth, death, and desire that lurk forever beyond our control? I thought of primitive man huddled around his tiny circle of fire. All our thousands of years of progress seemed just a few more logs on that fire—so futile when measured against the vast darkness of the surrounding unknown.

I glanced toward my companion. He, too, had withdrawn into a contemplative mood. He was an odd little man, I thought—quick to take offense, yet capable of great generosity. "You were quite openhanded with Josef," I remarked.

Houdini shrugged. "What good is having dough if you can't use it to help people? Anyway," he added, "Josef's a regular guy."

"How did you become acquainted with him?"

Houdini smiled. "In my line of work, I have to know the best locksmith in town. I got contacts in Berlin, Paris, New York, Moscow. Remember, I told you how important a setup is."

"But your escapes look so spontaneous on stage."

"Yeah, and your detective stories all read real smooth and logical. But I bet you figure out the puzzle first and write it later."

"As a matter of fact, I do. I write my stories from back to front."

"Sure, like magic tricks. You use clues, I use distractions. We're in the same business."

I confess I had never thought of the matter in quite that

way. Houdini was more perceptive than I had given him credit for. However, I detected a flaw in his argument and couldn't resist teasing him.

"But Holmes always reveals his methods," I chided.

"And look how everybody treats him once they see how it's done," he shot back. "That guy'd rake in a lot more dough if he kept his mouth shut."

I chuckled to myself. Houdini, too, was smiling.

"That would do well for Holmes," I admitted. "But writing mysteries with no solutions would severely curtail my own income."

He laughed openly at that. The sun was almost gone, and the streetlamps were being lit.

In their golden glow I saw a young woman dash out of a dark alley. I leaned forward in my seat. She cast a look of absolute terror over her shoulder. A large, older man emerged, shouting, from the same darkness and made for her. He soon caught up with her and grabbed her roughly by one shoulder. Then he began to beat her mercilessly about the head and face.

"Holy cow!" my companion exclaimed.

"Stop the cab," I ordered the driver. He pulled up with a jolt, and I leapt from our conveyance. Houdini followed at my heels.

Chapter 23
A Familiar Story

"Stop, you!" I shouted at the miscreant.

The man stood a moment, legs spread wide apart, fist upraised. He was a stocky specimen with a bald head and long mustaches. Anger had contorted his face into a bestial leer with narrowed eyes and bared teeth.

When he saw the two of us bearing down on him, he dropped the girl and took to his heels. I watched him disappear into the night. Houdini chased after him while I made for the young woman who lay on the sidewalk.

By now people had trickled out of their doorways to see what the fuss was about. A small crowd of women in aprons and men with their pipes began to gather around her.

"Please let me through," I urged. "I'm a doctor." I raised the girl to a sitting position. She stared around wildly. She could not have been more than sixteen years old. Her hair was dirty brown, but her eyes were large and dark with delicately arched brows.

"You're safe," I reassured her. "He has gone."

She shrank from me. "I want to help you," I said.

She looked uncertainly up at me.

"It's all right, Kate," a middle-aged woman encouraged her. " 'E's a doctor."

"Let us see how you're doing," I said. "Kate—is that your name?"

"Y-yes."

Just then Houdini squeezed his way through the circle of onlookers. His face wore a look of chagrin. "Lost him," he panted. "That guy knows the neighborhood too well."

"Oh, 'e's a runner, John is," one of the women contributed.

As I examined the girl's battered face, I asked, "Do you know where you are?" I wanted to determine if she had a concussion.

"O' course I does," she replied indignantly. "I'm outside me 'ouse."

"That's very good," I said. Her lip was bleeding and her left cheek had already started to swell. "And can you tell me what time it is?" I went on.

"Don't know for sure, but it's after ten," she said. "Ain't you got a watch?"

I smiled. At least, she was coherent. Her nose and cheekbones appeared unbroken. Bruises and cuts seemed to be the worst of it. I noticed a small café across the street. Thither I sent a couple of women with some change from my pocket to inquire whether they had a beefsteak. They soon returned with a slab of meat wrapped in a rag. This I took.

"Hold this to your cheek. It'll bring down the swelling," I explained.

She winced at the touch but did as she was told.

"Do any of your teeth feel loose?" I went on. The girl obediently put her finger in her mouth and felt around. She shook her head.

"Good. You'll be all right, Kate." I smiled. "May have a bit of a headache in the morning."

Houdini knelt down beside her. "Did you know that guy?" he asked.

" 'Course I did," the girl said. " 'E was me da'."

"Your father?" I asked incredulously.

"That's right," an old man behind her agreed.

Kate's eyes were large with shock. She began to tremble. Houdini doffed his coat and we wrapped it around her.

"Why was he beating you?" I asked.

" 'E wanted money for beer. When I din't 'ave none, 'e commenced to hit me. I run away, but 'e cotched me." She looked up into my eyes. "What got into 'im?"

"I'm sure I don't know," I said.

"Never done anything like that before, has he, dearie?" a large woman with short, brown hair volunteered.

"Never," the girl agreed. "We was 'aving such a good day, too. " 'E'd come up with this grand idea. A stroke of genius, it were. And then 'e come over all crazy-like."

A small man in a worn sailor's cap snorted. "Genius, was it?"

The word "genius" put me on the alert. "Tell me," I asked the girl, "what was his 'stroke of genius'?"

Kate drew a breath.

"Shush, she's going to tell her story," a short woman in a dingy apron hissed. The rumble of conversation around us subsided. People crowded around to hear.

"It started this afternoon," Kate began, "when I was cleaning up our rooms. I was wishing I'd a bit of a biscuit to 'ave with me tea. In rushes me da' and says, 'I've just got a pip of an idea, I 'ave. My girl, we're going to make our forchune today.' You should of seen 'im. Wild-looking 'e was—with a strange light in 'is eyes."

"Is this unusual for your father?" I asked.

"I should say! 'E pulls me out of the house and drags me a mile to a street corner. I stand there, not knowing what to do. Then 'e tells me, 'Start singing.' "

"Singing?" I repeated. "That was his stroke of genius?"

Kate nodded vigorously. "See, I make up little tunes to amuse myself. Today was I singing one of 'em—'I'm Not the Girl I Used to Be'—just before 'e come in."

The man in the sailor's cap shook his head and gave a barking laugh.

"Now, then," the gray-haired woman scolded him. "She sang lovely. I 'eard her."

"Then what happened?" I asked Kate.

"Well, I never. I was so embarrassed, standing in front of everybody on the street. But 'e says, 'Start singing!' And there was that look on 'is face. I was scareder of 'im than of bein' embarrassed. So I just closed me eyes and opened me mouth. By the time I was done, 'e'd rounded up a crowd of people to listen. And then 'e said, 'Sing that other one.'

" 'What, "If I May Be So Bold"?' I asks 'im. 'That's it, girl,' 'e says. And so I did." She looked from one to the other of us. "And you know what? When 'e passed the 'at, we got over a quid, we did."

A gasp ran through the crowd around us.

"Was your father pleased?" I asked.

"I should say. 'E said tomorrow we'd set up farther west in the city where people got more money. 'You're going to make our forchune, girl,' 'e says again.

"I was so 'appy. I'd never thought people'd pay money to 'ear me tunes."

"What 'appened to the money?" the gray-haired woman put in.

"First 'e bought us a real dinner. We 'ad meat and potatoes—and even a pudding! Then 'e went to a shop and used the nick we 'ad left to buy me a dress. A brand-new dress," she said, wonder in her voice. "Said it was a hin-vestment."

"Did he have any more inspirations?" I asked.

"Oh, 'e was right full of ideas. Told me I was going to be famous. 'E'd get the newspapers to write about the East End Nightingale—that's what they'd call me. Said some-day soon I'd be on the stage of the Palace Theatre itself.

"And I was so 'appy 'cause I knew tomorrow we was gonna eat good again."

"And then, without warning, he went crazy?" I prompted.

She looked at me in surprise. " 'Owever did you know that?"

"Please, finish your story," I requested. My suspicion had grown to a certainty. Dionysus had visited these two. "We cannot help you unless we know precisely what happened."

She looked puzzled but continued her narrative. "Ain't much left to tell. When we got back to our rooms, 'e seemed to go crazy. Started 'ollering and carryin' on about 'is beer. And 'im all the time knowing where the money went, just like I did!"

I looked straight into Houdini's eyes. He shrugged almost imperceptibly.

The girl looked sadly up at me and lowered the beefsteak from her face. A tear trickled down her swollen cheek and left a track through the blood where the meat had lain. " 'E's gone off 'is 'ead. I've lost me forchune and I've lost me da' all in one night." She swallowed. "I'm scared to be here when he gets back. And I got nowhere to go." She began to cry in earnest.

"You can stay with us," the gray-haired woman offered.

"There, now," I said. I put my arm around her shoulder. "Remember when I told you I was a doctor?"

"Yes," she said, and sniffled.

"Well, there's a disease going 'round. It affects the brain. People come up with brilliant ideas, but shortly afterward, they go out of their heads."

"Like me da'?" she asked.

"That's right," I said.

The man in the sailor's cap spoke up. "I never 'eard of no disease like that."

"Sounds just like Tom, the baker, this mornin'," the gray-haired woman said. "Remember? 'E was all full of hideas for 'is shop. And then 'e went and chased Mrs. Sullivan with 'is carvin' knife when she complained about the price of oxtails."

"It's the full moon," a younger woman said.

"It's a new illness," I assured them. "My friend and I are the first ones to discover it." I glanced at Houdini.

"We're not sure what causes it," he said pointedly.

"So me da's sick?" Kate asked.

"Yes, he is," I said.

"Could we catch it from 'im?" the man in the sailor cap demanded.

"I honestly do not know," I replied.

The blood drained from the man's face. A rumble went around the crowd of spectators. People backed away from Kate. Some fled into the houses on either side of us. The rest appeared to remember urgent business down the block. In a few short moments, we were alone on the pavement.

Kate looked around at the empty street. "Now I am alone," she wailed. "And we ain't got no money to cure 'im."

"There I have good news for you," I told her. "The disease goes away all by itself."

"Does it?" For the first time, she looked hopeful.

"Yes, in just an hour or less."

"So by the time 'e comes back, 'e'll be cured?"

"I believe so," I said. "And he will be very sorry for what he's done."

She struggled to rise. "But what if 'e's not? What if it lasts longer with 'im? I'm scared. 'E like to kill me, 'e did."

"Don't you worry," Houdini said impulsively. "We'll stay with you."

Gratitude flooded her face. Just then a soft scrape sounded behind me. I looked around. A few yards away in the shadows stood a man.

"Kate," he called softly, "are you all right?"

The man advanced a step. I recognized him as the girl's father. She huddled closer to us. The man's face was stricken with remorse.

"My own dear Katie," he said, "I'm so sorry. I don't know what come over me."

She looked to me. I nodded my encouragement. She rose and hurried to him. He folded her in his arms and murmured to her.

Houdini approached the two of them cautiously. He reached into his pocket and handed the man something.

The two spoke earnestly for a moment. Then Houdini returned to my side.

"I gave him my card," he responded to my look of inquiry. "Told him to see the stage manager at the Palace. If they can't find a place for Kate in the chorus, they can get themselves a new headliner."

I beamed down at him, words failing me.

"Let's get going," he said gruffly and led the way back to the patient cabbie.

As we continued on to Lord Vollmer's, I turned to my companion. "The madness appears to be spreading." I was worried. Would it infect all of London?

The yellow glow of the gaslights we passed flickered across Houdini's features. He did not reply, but his brow was furrowed.

I let the matter drop for the time being. For the next hour we needed to concentrate on Mackleston's dilemma. Privately, I was not certain that my testimony would carry the day in court. To save Algy, we needed Vollmer's help. We had to learn who might have had a motive to kill Reggie.

I glanced at Houdini. His frown had faded to a thoughtful look. Without warning he blurted out, "You're a Sir, aren't you?"

It took me a moment to see what he was getting at. "Yes," I said finally, "I was knighted last year."

"I thought you had to be born noble to be a Sir."

"Sometimes that is true, but not always. In my case, it's largely symbolic. Merely His Majesty's way of saying thank you."

"Thank you for what?"

"Oh, just something I wrote." I did not want to go into it all. I had published a pamphlet defending my country's actions during the Boer War. I was glad to have been of service but had not wanted that sort of recognition. In fact, I had accepted it only to avoid offending the King with a refusal.

"I see." To my relief, Houdini relapsed into silence. His expression grew troubled, however. Finally, he could contain himself no longer. "I always heard that Sirs were snobs. But the way you went to help the girl—you're a regular guy." An idea appeared to strike him. "I bet you weren't born rich."

I couldn't help but smile. Earlier, I had been musing upon his character. Now he was doing the same with me. I wondered what I looked like through his eyes. "No, indeed," I agreed. "Finances were quite tight when I was growing up."

Houdini nodded. "Me too. I was shining shoes when I was eight."

This small revelation intrigued me. I ventured a timid "Well, you have certainly come a ways."

He snorted. "I was doing the act for ten years before anybody noticed me. Working the dime museums, six shows a day. Half the time we couldn't afford to have dinner. I was saving up to buy equipment for the act."

"How did you choose a career in magic?"

"At sixteen I was a cutter in a necktie factory. On the way home from work, a book in an outdoor stall caught my eye. It was a biography of Robert Houdin. He was French—the greatest magician who ever lived. Till me, I mean."

"Yes," I responded. "I have heard of him."

"I read that book over and over until it fell apart. From the first page, I knew that was for me. I even named myself after him. Houdin–i, see?"

He seemed so open about his past that I found the courage to ask one question that had been on my mind. "Josef called you Ehrich. Is that your real name?"

"Yep. Ehrich Weiss. My father was Rabbi Samuel Weiss. Never made a nickel for the family once we came to America. Even as a kid I made more money than he did.

"I knew I was going to be great," he continued. "It just took everybody else a little while to catch on." He frowned darkly. "I had to spend two years in Europe before I could

get a booking in New York. But now I got those weisenheimers where I want 'em. They pay me a thousand a
week or I go across the street to the other circuit."

This explained much. Here was a man who had to fight
all his life for dignity. I remembered his generosity with
Josef. My admiration increased. Despite his early poverty,
he had a naturally generous spirit.

I looked up to find him eyeing me quizzically. "What
about you?" he asked. "How did you start writing?"

"My father was not the best provider either. But my
mother managed to keep us clothed and fed. She was
magnificent and—"

"Mine too," Houdini interrupted excitedly. "She was an
angel. When I think of the things she did for us . . ." Tears
welled up in his eyes. He produced a handkerchief and
wiped at them. "Sorry. Go on."

"Well," I continued, "I promised her that one day she
should have a velvet dress and gold glasses and would sit
in comfort by the fire. Thank God it has come to pass."

"I can't believe it!" Houdini exclaimed. "I promised my
mother, too. I swore one day I'd shower her with gold.
And you know what? On this last trip to Germany I made
them pay me in gold deutsche marks. When I go home,
she gets them—right in her lap!"

He stared at me. Tears again brimmed in his eyes. On
impulse, he grabbed my hand in both of his. "We both
kept our promises to our mothers—our dear, sweet
mothers."

Although I approved of the sentiment, I found his
open show of emotion somewhat disconcerting.

"Yes, well, in any case, through the good offices of relatives I managed to attend medical school at Edinburgh
University. There I sold the odd story for spending
money. After graduating, I set myself up as a doctor at
Southsea but had no patients. With time on my hands, I
resumed my scribbling. My scribblings sold. I soon decided that it was better to be a paid writer than an unpaid
physician."

Houdini nodded and blotted once more at his still-damp eyes with his handkerchief. Looking out the window, I was startled to see that we had already reached the Vollmer house in St. James. For Mackleston's sake, I resolved to gather what wits remained to me and banish my other worries. I hoped Vollmer could throw some light on who might have wanted to kill his son.

Chapter 24
A Difficult Interview

We climbed down from the cab and ascended to the portico of the townhouse. Its fluted columns and carved pediment spoke of neoclassicism and the eighteenth century. I presented my card to the butler who opened the door.

"His Lordship is not receiving," he informed us.

Houdini glowered at the man. "Yeah? Well, you can tell that guy—"

"Please inform His Lordship," I interrupted, "that we bear some property of his son's that we wish to return to the family."

The butler blinked at us. Then he pinched a corner of my card between his thumb and forefinger. Holding it away from his body as if it were a dead rodent, he disappeared into the recesses of the house. Houdini watched his retreating figure sourly.

As we waited, I recalled what I knew of Vollmer. He was highly placed in the Foreign Office. Arrogance and lack of tact were his hallmarks. Would he see us?

After a moment, the servant returned at a somewhat

quicker pace. In a carefully neutral tone he informed us, "His Lordship awaits you in the library."

We followed him down a long hall into a large room ablaze with the very latest in electric chandeliers. Their light glittered off the gilt swirls and geometrical designs on the ceiling. The chamber itself was nearly two stories tall. Most of the wall space had been given over to dark oak bookshelves. I noted several medieval tomes among the mix. A few family portraits from various eras lent variety to the decor. The furniture was Hepplewhite and ornamented with carved urns and rams' heads.

"What a house," Houdini muttered under his breath.

Lord Vollmer himself sat at the far end of the room in an ornate chair—really almost a throne—upholstered in red velvet and positioned beneath the statue of an imposing seventeenth-century military ancestor. Beside the statue was a marble fireplace. Several logs the size of small tree trunks blazed away. A crystal decanter and a half-filled glass rested on the side table next his chair. He put down the copy of the *Quarterly Review* he'd been reading.

Vollmer himself was a tall, aristocratic gentleman in his sixties. He had a full head of white hair. Hollow eyes and gaunt features showed how much the death of his son had taken its toll.

As we approached, he called out brusquely, "Conan Doyle? You're that writer chap. I read 'The Hound of the Baskervilles' in the *Strand*. Hated it. Terrible way to treat a dog."

Evidently, I had not been misinformed as to his character. My companion took a step forward and announced, "I am Houdini." He stood, fists on his hips, awaiting a response.

"I daresay you are." Vollmer dismissed him with a glance and turned to me. "You have some of Reggie's things? How did you get them?"

Houdini bristled at being ignored. I could see the effort it took to keep himself silent.

"Not Reggie," I corrected Vollmer gently. "Your other son."

He stiffened. "I have no other son."

No wonder poor Mackleston had sunk into such despair. I could not allow that remark to pass. I held the ring out to him. "Lord Vollmer, your son, your living son, is in peril of his life."

The man stared at me. His face grew red. "What business is it of yours?" he exploded. "Ye gods, I've already seen the family name dragged through the mud. Isn't that enough to bear? Take your conjurer friend and leave!"

He seized a poker from the hearth and advanced upon us. Its point was white with ash. I shoved the ring into my pocket and fell back a step. Frantically, I tried to think of a way to calm the man. Houdini, however, charged forward. He stopped almost chest to chest with Vollmer. "What you going to do, huh?" He stared fearlessly up into the eyes of the enraged nobleman.

"If you do not leave my house at once—" Vollmer began.

"Sure, I'll go. I'll go right to the papers," Houdini promised. "You don't like bad press? Well, unless you listen to us, I guarantee you a bushel and a peck of it."

Vollmer stared in openmouthed surprise. I stepped forward, ready to enter the fray should Houdini need my help. The poker wavered in the air over Houdini's head. The magician ignored it and went on. "You been to see your son? Even once? You got him a lawyer yet?"

I suppressed a smile. My partner was certainly one for leaping into the breach.

"That's none of your affair," Vollmer sputtered.

"No? How's it going to look tomorrow when the papers report that his friends put up the cash for his defense because his own father wouldn't?"

"Don't tell me my duty," Vollmer snapped. "And don't threaten me." But from his expression I could tell Houdini had scored a hit. Vollmer lowered the poker.

I thought it time to intervene. "We wish no unpleasantness, either," I assured him. "Please, just listen to us."

"What can you possibly say to me that I care to hear?" Vollmer demanded.

I spoke quickly. "We have good reason to believe that your son is innocent."

Vollmer paused, a look of complete surprise on his face. Then his features hardened again. "Innocent," he snorted. "All right, who killed my boy? The police swore no one could get in or out of those rooms. They had to break down the door."

"That is true," I replied. "However—"

"Well, then," Vollmer interrupted, his voice rising once more, "how can he be innocent? Answer me that, eh?"

"I believe I can, if you will hear me out," I replied calmly.

Vollmer cocked his head skeptically and waited.

I briefly sketched out the conundrum I had presented in the police inspector's office. How could Algernon have murdered his brother if he himself was unconscious? Conversely, how could Reggie have knocked his brother unconscious if was already dead?

"In short," I finished up, "Algy was injured trying to save his brother's life. That I can prove."

"What's that? He tried to save Reggie's life? You're sure?"

"I have staked my reputation on it," I said. "And so I shall testify in court, if need be."

Vollmer's face went pale. The poker dropped from his hands and rolled along the Oriental carpet that covered this end of the room. Houdini picked it up before it could singe the pile and laid it on the hearth.

"You'd say so under oath? You really would?"

I nodded.

"If this is true, then he's a martyr." A look of hope came into his eyes. "The family's name is saved. And the papers, damn them—they'll eat their words!"

I glanced toward my companion. Houdini's face reflected deep disgust as he returned to my side. I could readily appreciate his feelings. We were more concerned with Mackleston's welfare than was his own father. In his position I would have moved heaven and earth to set my own child free. Perhaps Mackleston was better off relying on his friends.

"Lord Vollmer," I said formally, "I came here to return some property to you." Once more I withdrew the ring from my pocket. "I naturally assumed you would be interested in your son's plight. If I was wrong, forgive me."

Lord Vollmer took the ring from my hand. His brows drew together in thought. Finally, he looked up and asked, "Why have you interested yourselves in our affairs?"

"A friend of your son has asked for our help," I said.

"Friends!" he interrupted. "They're the ones that got him into this mess. Unwholesome companions, that's his problem. That fellow Cairo. Absolute rogue. Trouble was bound to come of it. I told him so."

"I am inclined to agree with you," I said. "We believe Cairo is involved in the matter and fully expect to prove it shortly."

"It's a cinch," Houdini said with more confidence than either of us felt.

Vollmer was silent a moment. Absently, he put the ring in his pocket. "Is there anything I can do to help you?" he asked finally.

Ah, at last, I thought. "You might answer a few questions," I ventured.

He nodded resignedly. "Very well. What do you wish to know?"

"Reginald was the older of the two?"

Vollmer nodded. "By seven years."

"Had he any enemies?"

"Every man makes enemies. Else, he hasn't accomplished anything in this world."

His evasions began to annoy me. "Can you think of any one in particular?"

Lord Vollmer flushed. "Yes, damn it—his brother."

I decided to pursue this line. The police were certain to

have done so. "How long has this antipathy existed between them?"

"Since the cradle, sir. Algy was jealous, I suppose. Reggie was worth ten of him."

"And what were Reginald's feelings toward his brother?"

Lord Vollmer blinked at me. "How should he feel? Young pup underfoot, always a bit of a pest. Growing up, Algy never took an interest in the finer things—like hunting or sport. Always mooning about the museums or going off on some queer notion or other."

Mackleston had an artistic temperament, I knew. I shuddered to think what his life must have been like under his father's thumb. "So the dislike was mutual?"

"It wasn't Algy's place to like or dislike," the man snapped. "Reggie was going to be head of the family. Algy's responsibility was to obey without always coming round to whine."

I struggled to organize my thoughts. Could the man tell us nothing to help?

It was Houdini who spoke next. "Was Reggie married?" he asked.

"No. He'd been engaged, but it had been called off six months ago."

"Why?" Houdini pressed.

Lord Vollmer drew himself up and peered down his magnificent nose at the little man before him. "The woman proved unsuitable."

"What was her name?" I inquired as I pulled out my notebook.

"I fail to see what possible import—"

"Come on, Conan Doyle," Houdini interrupted, taking my arm. "He doesn't want our help. Let's leave this guy to stew in his own juices."

As Houdini escorted me across the long room, he gave me a slow, solemn wink. I could hardly suppress a smile. Really, he was right. Without Vollmer's willing help, we were just as well on our own. We were scarcely halfway to the door when his voice boomed across to us.

"Bowers, that was the name. Gwendolyn Bowers."

We froze in our tracks. I turned back. "Not one of the daughters of Sir William Bowers?" I exclaimed. Was another one of our group linked to the murdered man?

"Yes, I believe that was the father's name," Vollmer said. "Dull fellow. Spent all his time mucking about in some laboratory."

"His mucking about was sufficiently interesting to garner a Nobel Prize last year," I said.

"As you say." Vollmer was obviously not impressed with scientific achievement. My thoughts swirled at this revelation. Why had the engagement been called off? And why had Sir William failed to mention the fact?

I named the rest of people who had made up the party at Cairo's. Vollmer shook his head at each one.

"Never heard of any of 'em," he asserted.

Next I inquired whether Reggie had any business associates we could speak with. Here, too, Lord Vollmer was vague. He thought Reggie might have been involved in some financial scheme or other last year, but could give no details. Apparently, he thought preparing to become the next Lord Vollmer was occupation enough for any man.

I asked whether Reggie had any friends we might interview. Once again the man failed to come up with a single name.

"Do you really think you can help Algy?" Vollmer asked.

"We already have." I then added, "As you would know, had you contacted the authorities."

But the man was once more off on his own set of musings. "If we can get him out of this, I'll see that he lives a healthy life. No more mixing with those decadents. No more nonsense with paints and brushes. He'll hunt, he'll play at sports—all the manly pursuits."

It was time to leave. Vollmer knew little about either of his sons. As I turned to go, I noticed a marble-topped side table nearly hidden in an alcove behind Vollmer. What caught my eye was a framed photograph draped in black crepe. A shock of recognition ran through me. I lurched forward a step to verify what I saw. The portrait was of a man's face. Dark hair, close-set eyes, and a generous nose sat above thin lips with a supercilious smirk. I could never forget those features.

"Is that your son?" I asked, pointing to the photograph.

"Yes, that was Reggie." Vollmer studied me keenly. "Did you know him?"

I scarcely knew what to say. "I played cricket against his team," I finally said.

"What? You played against the Chevaliers?" A smile illuminated Vollmer's stern features. "What's your team's name?"

"I play on James Barrie's team, the Allahakbarries."

"How'd you do against Reggie's bowling?" he demanded.

"We lost."

He chuckled. "Yes, they were hard to beat. Reggie had several centuries, you know."

Vollmer waited for torrents of praise to spill forth. Though I could not in all conscience comply, I put the best face on things that I could.

"I remember him as a dedicated player," I said, "with an iron determination to win." I almost added, "at whatever cost."

"Yes, that was Reggie," the man agreed happily. "He played all out."

"Indeed," I said.

For the sake of courtesy, I looked at the photograph again. Then I made our excuses. Before we left, I gave him both our London addresses in case he recalled anything further. Then we departed. I couldn't get out of that house soon enough. Reggie's picture had stirred up distasteful memories.

Chapter 25
Reggie

On our way home I was not good company, sunken as I was in my own thoughts.

Houdini, to his credit, kept silent until the cab pulled to a stop. Looking around, I saw we were at Houdini's hotel. He hopped out. "You look like you could use a home-cooked meal."

I protested, citing the hour, until he finally said, "Please. I don't know how else we can thank you for—you know."

After that, how could I refuse? He virtually dragged me from our conveyance, paid the cabman, and sent him on his way.

Once in his suite, I was welcomed warmly by his wife and the two dogs that scurried over to renew my acquaintance. They were strays, she told me, that Houdini had found roaming the streets. "Always picking up strays," she said.

At her words Houdini blushed, evidently recalling the two other creatures he had picked up during his temporary madness.

If his wife had intended to remind him of it, she gave

no outward sign. "Well, you two'll be wanting some food." I saw an old alcohol-burning stove on a sideboard. She lit it and to my surprise proceeded to fry a huge mass of scrambled eggs. From Houdini's look, this was a treat.

"That's the stuff," he chortled, rubbing his hands.

He could have afforded to dine anywhere in London. Apparently, however, he still relished the simpler fare from his days of struggle.

While Bess worked, Houdini opened the door to their rooms a crack to let out the smoke. Then he regaled her with an account of our day. His telling transformed our unproductive search through the flat into a tale of clever deduction. Bess listened patiently while she turned the eggs and encouraged him at appropriate intervals. Our trip to Josef's shop assumed the status of the quest for the Holy Grail. Finally, he described Lord Vollmer's reluctance to confide in us. "But when he realized that it was Houdini who stood before him," the magician concluded, "he came across with the goods."

"So you met your friend here on the way home?" Bess asked innocently as she ladled huge portions of scrambled eggs onto our plates.

Houdini looked confused for a moment. Only then did he realize that in telling the tale he had managed to omit me from it entirely.

"Why, we were in on this thing together," he said, looking to me for confirmation. "Like Holmes and Watson, right?"

I am afraid I could not keep a twinkle out of my eye as I said, "Quite." There was no doubt in my mind which role he had reserved for himself. I looked up to find Bess standing behind her husband. Love and amusement mingled on her face. Her eyes traveled up to me and she shook her head.

"You're wonderful, Harry," she said quietly as she filled our plates. Houdini nodded in happy agreement as he began to shovel eggs into his mouth with a spoon. She served herself a plate and sat beside her husband to eat.

The crucifix glinted at her neck. Clearly, the difference in their faiths mattered not one whit to them.

Though it was not what I would have chosen for a meal, hunger drove me to attack my plate with gusto. The eggs were steaming hot, and we finished them in no time. Afterward, Houdini pushed back from the table while Bess cleared away the plates.

He fixed me with a stare and asked, "The dead guy. You didn't like him, did you?"

"Was I that transparent?" I asked.

"Nah. I make my living reading crowds, remember." Houdini leaned forward. "What happened between you two? Something to do with a game?"

"Yes." I had to tell him. If we were to work together, he should know everything.

"It was about five years ago," I began. "We were playing against his team. The winner would go to the Test Matches."

"This is cricket you're talking about, right?" he interrupted. "Sort of like baseball?"

"Rather like, except that our 'pitchers' bowl the ball stiff-armed. It was the second day and I was batting well. In fact, I was well on my way to a century."

"What's a century?" Houdini interrupted.

"One hundred hits in a row without being called out," I explained. Then I continued, "Lord Vollmer's son Reggie was bowling. It had been a dry spring. The ground was hard and the ball began to take odd bounces on the green. I sustained several painful hits to my shins and knees. Though the padding gave some protection, by late afternoon of the second day I had to limp over to my base."

"This ball," Houdini interrupted again. "Is it like a baseball?"

I cast my thoughts back to my last lecture tour of America. On it I had satisfied my curiosity as to their game. "It is smaller, harder, and slightly heavier," I said.

Houdini nodded, and I continued. Or at least I would

have, had Bess not pleaded, "Wait a minute. I have to fill this pan, and I can't hear when the water's running."

I smiled and waited until she had filled a dishpan from the tap in the loo. She returned carefully so as not to spill suds on the carpet and set the pan on the sideboard. "Okay," she said.

I went on. "It was about four o'clock and I had eighty-nine hits on my century when one ball hit me in the shoulder. It caused no little pain. I believe it was then I realized that all the bounces had been deliberate. Reggie was trying to injure me. Despite the blow, I tightened my grip on the bat and waited. He smiled at me in that same supercilious way we saw in his photograph.

"His next pitch was fast and strong. That's the last I remember. It struck me in the head and knocked me unconscious. I am told I was carried off the field.

"I remember awakening that evening in hospital with James Barrie standing over me. He revealed that if the ball had struck me a couple of inches to the right, it would have hit my temple and killed me.

"We discovered later that Reggie often boasted no one would ever get a century off him. It seems he would go to any lengths to make good his claim. In any case, we lost the game. My century had been sorely needed. There was a protest, but it came to nothing. His father was too important."

Bess, who had been listening the whole time, pulled her hands from the water and jammed soapy fists on her hips. "That's terrible!"

Houdini was silent a moment. "Were you okay?" he finally asked.

"I suffered a concussion but made a complete recovery."

His face darkened. "If that had happened in my neighbourhood . . ."

". . . you and your friends would've taken him out behind the clubhouse," Bess finished for him, as she plunged our table service into the water.

"There was considerable uproar at the time," I told

them. "The next time our teams played, someone else bowled."

"Too bad," Houdini snarled. "You could've put one down his throat."

"The thought did occur," I admitted. "As I am sure it had to him."

Anger gave way to consternation on Houdini's face. "This could make it tough," he said.

"Indeed. If he lived his life the way he played cricket, we shall have suspects queuing up around the block."

"No kidding," Houdini agreed. "When Sir William's doing a little better, we have to talk to him. A guy dumps his daughter, he's going to be upset, don't you think?"

"Yes. Remember his anger? He, too, was infected by Dionysus—or Cairo's hypnotism," I amended quickly.

Houdini gave a pained look at the mention of Dionysus. But what he might have responded I was never to know, for at that moment the door burst open and Lord Vollmer stood framed in the portal. The man positively bristled with rage. He blew like a racehorse. His eyes were wide with fury. I sprang to my feet as he strode to the table and fixed me with a fierce stare. Reaching into his pocket, he pulled out the ring I had left with him earlier that evening. He shook it under my nose.

"Here now, sir! What does this mean?" he shouted.

Chapter 26
A Lioness Defends Her Cub

"What are you talking about?" I asked.

"Where did you find this bauble?" Vollmer roared at me.

"In your son's room in Soho. We thought it too valuable to—"

"I'll wager you did not!" he bellowed. "The stone has been switched. It is a cheap imitation." He grabbed my hand and thrust the ring into it. "Look at it. Such a shoddy copy, it's ludicrous." Vollmer looked from me to Houdini. "What have you done with the real one?"

"Let me assure you—" I began. But Vollmer interrupted me.

"I'll have you both horsewhipped!" he thundered. Pointing to Houdini, he continued, "I'll have you run out of the country! You'll never be welcome in Europe again."

"Let me get this straight." Bess's voice cut across the room. "You're accusing my Harry of stealing?"

Something in her voice drew everyone's gaze in her direction.

"They're both going to—" What Lord Vollmer saw caused him to stop in midsentence. Gone was the spatula

I had last seen in her hand. In its stead was a long butcher's knife still dripping with suds from the dishpan. She held it like a dagger as she walked to the center of the room. The blade gleamed silver in the light.

Vollmer moved back a step. Houdini rose to his feet and sauntered over to the door. He pushed it shut. The look in Bess's eyes was that of a lioness protecting her cub. Vollmer's face turned ashen. He stared longingly at the shut door. Houdini leaned against the portal with elaborate casualness.

"You bust in here without knocking," Bess said ominously and took a step forward. "You interrupt our supper." She took another step. "You accuse my Harry and his friend—"

"My good woman—" Lord Vollmer remonstrated, looking down in shock at her diminutive form.

"—and you don't even let them get a word in edgewise," Bess interrupted. "My Harry never stole anything his whole life." She looked His Lordship up and down. "Is this the thanks he gets for trying to help your son?"

Vollmer held his hands up in front of him. "Er—perhaps I was a bit hasty."

"Yes, you were. You were real hasty."

"As you say," he agreed, his eyes on the knife.

"Okay, then," she nodded. "You three work this out. I have to get back to my dishes." And with that, she returned to her dishpan and plunged the knife back into the soapy water.

"That girl of mine," Houdini said, his voice admiring. "What a tiger." He pushed away from the door and brought up a chair to Lord Vollmer. "Take a load off," he offered.

Vollmer sank down gingerly. "Yes, well," he began. "There appears to be—ah—" He kept a wary eye on Bess as he spoke, but she never looked back from her dishes. "—a serious misunderstanding."

"Really," I said, standing over him. "Had we wanted to

loot your son's room, we would hardly have come to you afterward."

"Especially since you'd never have known," Houdini contributed. "Before we came by, you weren't even going to see to your boy."

For the first time since we had met him, I saw sadness overwhelm his features. "Your point is well taken."

"Are you certain this stone is not the original?" I asked.

"Yes, yes," he said impatiently. "It was an heirloom—a ruby. Been in his mother's family for years. She gave it to him shortly before she died." After a moment's contemplation, he added, "But who could have substituted that tawdry counterfeit?"

Houdini leaned forward eagerly. "Cairo," he said. "That chiseler."

He quickly detailed how on the evening of the séance we had removed our jewelry. Vollmer was all for dashing off immediately to confront the man.

I, however, was not certain. Cairo'd had our jewelry for only twenty-four hours. That was hardly enough time to manufacture a replica—unless he had planned the substitution beforehand. There was a more likely solution to the puzzle, and I determined to pursue it. "Might not your son have sold the ring himself to procure funds?" I asked Vollmer.

He looked outraged at the suggestion. "Algy had a generous allowance."

I grew annoyed with the man as I remembered the Spartan furnishings I had seen. Neither Vollmer nor Reggie, I was convinced, would have considered such surroundings generous.

"Perhaps a sudden increase in expenses," I suggested, remembering the opium.

"All he had to do was ask," Vollmer insisted. "But he had no vices. Didn't even gamble. Hadn't the stomach for it."

It saddened me to realize how little Vollmer knew or cared about his son. A sudden doubt assailed me. I glanced down at my hand. With relief I recognized my familiar ring. Of course, it was a simple gold band and not worth stealing. But if I had not thought to question its genuineness until this moment, might not Mackleston have been equally careless? It appeared that we had several issues to raise on our visit to Cairo.

To my dismay, Vollmer stridently voiced his intention to call on the man. I feared Cairo would be angered beyond all reach of reason. Hastily, I cautioned Vollmer, "If he is guilty, he might not admit you. Unless," I added, "you wish to involve the police."

"No!" I was relieved to see him blanch at the thought. "If they go, Fleet Street won't be far behind. Our name's been bandied about enough as it is."

"Perhaps we can gain admittance," I ventured. "If not, we shall inform you and you may take whatever steps you see fit."

"Very well," he agreed.

I gestured at the ring in his hand. "May we keep this for the evening?"

He readily acceded and urged us to resolve the mystery as soon as we could. As he was leaving, I recalled one question that had slipped my mind in our first meeting.

"Lord Vollmer," I asked, "have you any of your son's paintings at your residence?"

He stopped up short and cast me a disdainful look. "Algy's daubs? Whatever would I want with one of those?"

"I was thinking of something he had done quite recently," I prompted. "All full of red swirls. *The Daughters of King Minyas*, he called it."

Lord Vollmer shook his head. "Sounds like just the sort of idiotic thing he would paint, though. I told him, if you want a subject, why not paint your brother? Then at least we could hang it in the family gallery. Young pup didn't even have the courtesy to answer me."

He shook his head at his son's insolence. Then, sparing a wary glance at Bess, Lord Vollmer took his leave of us. I stood a moment, considering. The whereabouts of the painting remained a mystery. I made a mental note to check with Inspector Woburn tomorrow, in case the police had impounded it as evidence after all.

Houdini's rooms fronted on the street. My gaze strayed out his window and I saw a young couple down below strolling home from a late supper. Their arms were linked. His head was bent and he spoke softly into her ear. Her face wore a knowing smile. I could not but compare their situation to mine. What had I to look forward to at home?

I was at once stricken with remorse. How selfish it was for me to dwell on my own misery. I should be thinking of Touie, who would shortly face the great unknown. What was I doing here? My place was at her side.

But dared I trust myself in her presence? No, I could not return until I had rid myself of whatever influence had taken hold of me. Besides, I had given my word to see Mackleston set free.

But how to do so? I was at my wit's end. In my despair, I could see only one recourse. Cairo had set these events in motion. Only he could halt them—if indeed it was still possible. But how to persuade him? That was the question.

I was rudely pulled from my musings by Houdini's intruding voice and his none-too-gentle grasp on my arm.

"Conan Doyle," he said. "Are you okay?"

"Of course. Why?" I responded—a trifle brusquely, I'm afraid.

"I've been talking to you for a whole minute. You heard anything I said?"

"Sorry, no. I was lost in my own thoughts."

"Yeah? Well, I been thinking too." He let go of my arm and strode to the center of the room. "I bet I know how the ring ties in with the murder. Hypnotism again." He lifted both hands, like a conductor leading his orchestra.

I saw where he was tending. "You think he hypnotized Mackleston?"

"Bingo!" Houdini pointed a forefinger at me. "Like what happened to us that night at Cairo's. Why we all saw the same thing."

"It would explain much." I remembered my tentative theory after Cairo's "death" and resurrection. "A posthypnotic suggestion could account for my own violent behavior as well."

"Yeah," he continued excitedly. "I bet Cairo was in the room with Mackleston when the brother came in. Say Cairo's got Mackleston hypnotized for some reason or other."

Bess carried the dishpan into the loo, and I heard the gurgle as she emptied it into the sink. "Anyway, let's say the brother sees the ring and realizes it's a fake. He figures out Cairo substituted it. So he threatens to expose Cairo as a thief. Cairo orders Mackleston—still in a trance, you see—to help him kill the brother. Cairo leaves and has Mackleston lock the door after him. Mackleston wouldn't remember anything about it afterward."

It did not explain the blow to Mackleston's head, but I supposed we could work that out. What really interested me was Houdini's tacit admission. Heretofore, he had stoutly denied seeing anything strange that night.

"What did you see at Cairo's?" I asked.

Houdini looked away. "I'm not sure," he muttered.

"Something not human?" I prodded.

He merely shrugged.

"Something that appeared to change shape?"

He took a moment to answer. "I guess so." His eyes flashed up to my face. "That's why it's got to be hypnotism. Don't you see, it all fits?" A note of insistence had crept into his voice. The look on his face was almost defiant.

"We must find another hypnotist to undo the damage," I exclaimed.

Houdini shook his head. "I don't know anybody who's even close to Cairo's league," he confessed. "Besides, somebody as good as he is would bury the suggestion too deep. There'd be nothing for another hypnotist to find."

"Then he is indeed the only one who can help us—the only one who can save Mackleston's life!" I exclaimed.

Houdini shook his head. "He won't do it. He'd have to admit to planning the murder himself."

How does one induce a murderer to confess? The glimmer of an idea came to me. It was a desperate plan, but the only one left to us. "Perhaps we can use his arrogance against him."

"Good trick," Houdini said glumly. Bess returned to the sitting room and dried the dishpan with a faded blue towel.

"No, listen," I insisted. "What is his weakness? Why, his vanity, of course."

Houdini cocked his head to one side and looked up at me. "Yeah? So what?"

"So we appeal to his pride. If he is anything like the man I think he is, he will not be able to resist."

"How do we do that?" Houdini asked suspiciously.

"We approach him humbly. We admit he has bested us. Mark my words: If we can get him boasting, he'll not be able to resist giving the game away."

"You mean Houdini goes begging for help?" There was a dangerous glint in my companion's eye. "I won't do it," he growled. "Anyway, once he knows we're onto him, he'll have to get rid of us."

"That's what I am counting on," I admitted. "But first, he won't be able to resist taunting us. We must provoke him into revealing enough for us to thwart him."

"Then what?" Houdini demanded.

"I'm hoping that the two of us together can either outsmart or overpower him."

Houdini shook his head. "It's too risky."

He was right, of course. But I was desperate. With a sinking heart, I bowed to him. "I shall miss your company very much. Good evening, Houdini, Mrs. Houdini." So saying, I strolled to the door. I had not gone three steps before I felt a hand at my elbow.

"You mean you're taking him on alone?"

"I am."

Fierce emotions played across my friend's face. At last he said, "No, you're not. Let's go."

Relief flooded through me. "Stout fellow," I said gratefully.

"Yeah, yeah," he replied as he led the way out the door. "But when it comes to crawling, you go first."

"Wait a minute," Bess called to him. "You're going back to that man? The one you said hypnotized you into . . . into . . ." But she couldn't finish the thought. Tears welled in her eyes.

Houdini was at her side in a moment. "Bessie," he said tenderly, "you got to trust me. I'm onto that guy now—I can handle him with one hand tied behind my back. Besides," he added, "I can't let Conan Doyle go all by himself."

"I don't see why either one of you has to go."

"Bess," Houdini looked her full in the face. "If you say so, I won't go." He gestured toward me. "But think what he's done for us."

She leaned closer to him. I looked away. After a moment of silence, I felt a tug on my sleeve. When I turned around, there stood Houdini, hat in hand. "Let's get cracking," he said.

As I pulled the door shut, I saw a worried Bess blow a kiss at her husband's back.

Once outside, Houdini dropped the mask of confidence. "We have to be real careful tonight. If Cairo hypnotized us once, he could do it again."

I nodded my agreement. Even if Cairo had not used hypnosis, Houdini was right about the danger. Somehow the man was capable of exercising his evil influence over great distances.

"Pay attention to his voice," Houdini warned. "Listen for a singsong tone or repeated words. That's how they get you. The right sounds can put you under before you realize it."

I tried to remember the evening at his flat. During the

ceremony itself he'd not spoken at all. What I did recall was his shocking dance.

"I think we should be on the alert for any rhythmic movements, as well."

"That's the ticket!" Houdini agreed. "And don't drink anything in case he tries to drug us."

In a trice we hailed a cab and headed east once more. My companion lapsed into silence and I was left to my own musings. Unaccountably, my thoughts turned to Miss Luce. Was she at a soirée tonight, her musical laugh ringing out above the merriment? Or perhaps the evening found her alone in her room in a pensive mood. Did she spare a thought for me?

My attention was distracted by a raucous noise outside our cab. It came from one of the houses we approached. We passed two policemen running toward the sound. Without warning, a man in full evening dress flew from the doorway and landed on the portico. He lay against one of the fluted columns and looked for all the world like a character from some Buffalo Bill penny thriller.

When we pulled even with the Georgian home, I shall never forget the brief glimpse I was vouchsafed inside. A dinner party had degenerated into a brawl. Down the long, marble hallway elderly men in evening jackets swung fists. Women in pale silks shrieked and clawed. One young woman rode another like a horse, tearing at a graceful white chiffon gown to reveal the stiff-fronted corset underneath. Some people were on their knees. Others flailed their arms drunkenly, knocking delicately carved mahogany furniture this way and that. Several guests howled in pain, blood trickling down their faces.

As I watched, a young man on his knees lunged at a woman's train and proceeded to rip it from her dress with his bare teeth. I could not take my eyes from his face, which was twisted with madness. The cloth tore free and he shook it in his mouth like a terrier. With horror I recognized the man. It was none other than Dr. Burton, the specialist who had examined Louise. The swirl of pandemonium around him could have come from the halls of Hell itself. It reminded me of one of Hieronymus Bosch's paintings—grotesque figures, monstrous torments, and helpless souls.

An instant later, we passed the melée and the sounds receded behind us as the policemen, truncheons drawn, waded into the home. I grew aware of Houdini beside me. He, too, looked appalled by the brief scene we had just witnessed.

"What was that?" he demanded.

Though I did not answer, I had seen just such a frenzy before—in the face of Kate's father as he beat her. I realized with a sinking feeling that Houdini's explanation must be wrong. Cairo couldn't possibly have hypnotized the frenzied people we had encountered tonight. Something was abroad in London—something malign and insidious.

A dreadful thought sprang to mind. What if our group from the séance were to blame for this rash of lunacy? Suppose I had transmitted the madness to Dr. Burton and he to the others in his party—like a spiritual infection? The idea left me shaken. Could we then be reinfected?

Were Kate's father and Dr. Burton but the advance guard of the tide of lunacy sweeping across the land? If so, how could we prevent it? Thoughts of enforced isolation, exorcisms, even calling in the army all tumbled around in my head. It was hopeless. I could not pursue a course of action until I knew more about our adversary.

The cab came to a stop in front of Cairo's house.

"Let me take the lead," I reminded my companion.

Houdini nodded his agreement and I steeled myself to the task at hand. The stakes tonight were even higher than I had thought.

Chapter 27
Cairo Poses a Riddle

A sullen-looking Mr. Gaylord answered our knock. He eyed us superciliously from the doorway. "He's busy," he said, and pushed the door shut in our faces. Before the portal could close, my companion charged forward. He shoved the door open and sent Mr. Gaylord sprawling.

Houdini barged across the dark entry and stood over the man, now lying in the shadows on the floor. "Tell your boss this: If he doesn't see us, I'll drag him out by the scruff of his neck."

Mr. Gaylord scrambled to his feet and fled. I closed the door and sighed. Houdini might just have ruined my plan. I placed a warning hand on his shoulder.

"I know, I know," he said. "I went overboard."

Cairo appeared in the doorway of his study. Light at his back illuminated him. He was clad in a lilac smoking jacket with black embroidery over gray flannel trousers. His expression was forbidding. "How dare you force your way in here?" He folded his arms across his chest. "Leave at once, or I summon the police."

Houdini's eyes bulged with suppressed anger. I thrust myself in front of him.

"Please do not," I begged, the words bitter on my tongue. "We need your help."

Cairo's face went blank with surprise. Then he looked from Houdini to me. "My help?" he purred. "Now, how could I possibly help two such august personages?"

Here was the delicate moment. I must incite him to indiscretion without putting him on his guard.

"Dionysus is running amok in the world!" I exclaimed.

Cairo motioned us over to him. "What have you seen?" He could not conceal his excitement. "Tell me."

We stepped through the darkened hallway to his well-lit study and he closed the door behind us. Without revealing names or specific details, I outlined in a general way the creative and destructive frenzies that had overcome all the participants at the séance. I finished with the two instances of madness we had witnessed on the streets this evening.

"Magnificent." Cairo nodded in approval. "It is just as I predicted."

Now was the time to press him. "No, it is not," I asserted. "You said he would inhabit only one of us. In fact, he is spreading his influence among the general population. How could you have been so mistaken?"

Cairo bristled at my words. "You question me?"

I remained alert for rhythmic movements of his hands or body, ready to avert my eyes. His form remained still, however, with his hands clenched at his sides.

"Yes," I said. "The being you loosed upon the world has escaped even your control. You are as powerless as we are before it." I held my breath. Had I gone too far?

Cairo drew himself up to his full height. "The being I loosed upon the world?" His brown eyes smoldered like chunks of ebony on a fire. "Of all the . . ." Words failed him for a moment.

I felt a tightening in my chest. I couldn't get my breath. The enormous force of his will seemed to descend upon me like a shroud. A scent of sandalwood clogged my nostrils. The room took on a greenish hue. My vision blurred. I gasped for breath.

Then, as quickly as it had come, the suffocating close feeling was lifted from me like a blanket. I gasped for air. My knees wobbled and I struggled to keep standing.

I looked anxiously at Cairo. His gaze no longer rested on me. Instead, he stood and pointed an accusing finger at Houdini. My companion looked pale and struggled for breath. "There stands the man responsible," Cairo thundered. "If you had not broken my protective septagram, none of this would have happened."

Houdini swayed on his feet.

Cairo eyed him scornfully. "What's the matter?" he spat, "Could you not bear to stay out of the limelight for even one evening?" Houdini tried to speak, but only a small croak emerged from his throat.

"Stop it!" I shouted, and lunged for Cairo.

He turned his attention from Houdini and brought me up short with a wicked little smile that burned like a smoking poker. I felt as if a red-hot ice pick had been driven into my brain. I cried out and stumbled in agony.

"Do not think you have fooled me," Cairo warned.

Somehow I managed to keep on my feet. The waves of pain slowly receded. I tried to put up a brave front but felt too weak to speak.

"You came expressly to trick me into revealing the secrets of my creation. Your souls are too small to appreciate the gift you've been given, so you seek to destroy it."

"No," I protested weakly, desperate to save something from the disaster of this encounter. "We merely wanted—"

But he would not let me finish. "This alternately currying my favor and then baiting me," he said with contempt. "You are so transparent."

I looked to Houdini. His color was returning and he breathed more easily.

"But there's been a murder," I said.

Cairo leaned against one of his stuffed bookshelves. "I'm not surprised," he answered. "There will be more. And you have only yourselves to thank. Now leave me." The man strolled across the room toward the hidden door we'd seen on our first visit.

Was he dead to all decent feeling? "An innocent man will hang!" I called after him.

To my surprise, he paused and turned. His expression was unreadable. "Innocent? Who?"

"Algernon Mackleston," I responded.

He showed no surprise but merely asked, "And whose murder is he innocent of?"

"His brother Reginald," I replied. "Two days ago."

"Reggie murdered?" Cairo inquired blandly. "Dear me. I know he deserved it, but I hardly thought any of his victims were up to it."

"You knew the guy?" Houdini blurted out. He flinched involuntarily as Cairo's gaze found him once more.

"We were in school together," Cairo said briefly. "The world is a much happier place without him."

I staggered over to a small chair against the wall and sank down onto it. Cairo pulled a pipe and matches from the pocket of his jacket. He proceeded to light the pipe's contents. "How do you know Mackleston is innocent?"

His tone of voice was too casual, especially since my revelation had halted his exit in midstride. Somehow, we had found a chink in his armor. Now, if only I could puzzle out how to exploit it.

"The inferences were clear enough for anyone who had eyes," I stalled.

"Don't trifle with me." The man's voice was silky. "Tell me what you know and who else knows it." He looked down at his pipe so I could not read his eyes.

Here was my chance at last. But to take it, I had to defy Cairo. I remembered the excruciating pain of short moments ago. Resolutely, I put the thought aside. I said, "I shall be happy to—if first you tell us what sort of power we are up against."

Cairo's hand tightened around the stem of his pipe. The tendons on the back of his hand stood out like cords underneath the skin. "I warned you—" he began.

"Anything happens to us, you got big trouble," Houdini interrupted. His voice was not as strong as usual, but he was convincingly defiant. "You think we came here without telling people—lots of people?"

Once more I was glad fate had given me such a comrade in arms. Cairo's hand relaxed. He sighed.

"I suppose it's fair to trade for the information I want." His tone was careless. "And you did bring good news— that Reggie is dead." He leaned back against the wall and appeared to come to a decision. "Tell me what I want to know."

I hesitated. Would he keep his word? I looked up to see him smiling at me. He shrugged as if he had read my mind and was amused at my quandary.

There was nothing for it. Briefly, I described the circumstances of the murder and my own conclusions. As I continued, he moistened his lips and rubbed his hands together. He seemed to derive an almost sensual pleasure from hearing the grisly details. When I finished, he turned to Houdini.

"And what do you think, little man? Now are you willing to concede that there are more things in heaven and earth than are dreamt of in your philosophy?"

Houdini gave a noncommittal grunt, turned, and flung himself down in a burgundy club chair in front of a row of shelves.

"Who else knows of this?" Cairo asked.

"Only the police," I said. I had no intention of putting Miss Luce in danger of further attentions from such a man.

"Of course," Cairo mused. "An honest citizen such as you would go straight to the police."

"Now, keep your word and help us to free Mackleston."

"Yeah," Houdini contributed. "First of all, tell how you hypnotized me without my knowing it."

Cairo turned toward him and blinked. "Hypnotize you?

Is that what you think?" A laugh bubbled up from his depths. "My dear mountebank, I have hypnotized no one. I wouldn't even know how to begin. I told you the truth from the start. Your interference has set loose the god Dionysus—with predictably tragic results."

He poked the stem of his pipe in my direction. "I tell you what I'll do. I'll pose you a riddle. If you can solve it, I shall offer what help I can. If not, I won't."

I was outraged. "Is that how you keep your word? This is playing with human lives!"

"Yes," Cairo agreed cheerfully, "it is. But at least you'll be no worse off than before. So, do you accept the challenge?"

I looked over to Houdini in his chair. Disgust was writ plainly on his face. He shrugged and looked away. Though it galled me, I said, "We have no choice."

"None," Cairo agreed cheerfully. "Are you ready?"

I nodded.

Cairo began, "I tell you that Dionysus inhabits only one of you. You counter that you've seen him control several other people. Here is the riddle—both statements are true."

"But how can that be?" I asked. "They contradict each other."

"Nevertheless," his smile was maddening, "both are true."

My face must have registered the frustration I felt, for he continued, "Well, I told you it was a riddle. If you can solve it, you will have earned my help."

"But this is impossible," I protested.

Houdini finally spoke up. He lurched to the edge of his well-stuffed chair. "What kind of baloney are you trying to feed us? He's in one person; he's in everybody. What do you think we're talking about here? Santa Claus?"

A glint of amusement twinkled in Cairo's eyes. "Oh, very well," he said. "I shall give you a hint. But do pay attention, because I shan't repeat myself." He looked upward and sighed. "I swear I am too generous."

With that, Cairo strolled over to a large leather chair across from me and settled himself comfortably. He smoothed the shoulders of his lavender smoking jacket with a palm and asked, "Do you know why, of all the gods, Dionysus alone is called the twice-born?"

He waited for an answer. When I shook my head, he continued. "He was Zeus's favorite son. Next in line to inherit, like dear, departed Reggie. After Dionysus was born, the jealous Titans lured him away from his mother. They dismembered him and devoured all the pieces of his body, except for his heart, which Athena rescued and preserved."

He folded his arms and leaned forward confidentially. The man might have been relaying a current tidbit of gossip. "When Zeus found out about their little prank, he was, as you can imagine, quite incensed. In his anger, he flung a thunderbolt at the Titans that blasted them to ashes. From these ashes a new race, the race of Man, was formed."

He sighed and continued rapidly, as if the rest of the story bored him. "From the heart of Dionysus was brewed a love potion which was given to a mortal woman. She was soon with child. The story goes on from there with typical Greek lust and violence, but the upshot of it is that Dionysus was born a second time." Cairo nodded with satisfaction. "That is—or should be—all you need to solve my little conundrum."

He looked from one of us to the other. "Does anything present itself?"

We both stared back, speechless. I struggled for a response. "If he's not mortal," I hazarded, "then he can appear in two places at once."

Cairo smiled. "That's clever," he approved, "but wrong. For his manifestations in the physical world, he is largely bound by its limitations. Care to have another go?"

I grappled with my thoughts, seeking another answer.

"No?" He stood up and sauntered over to open the

door to his study. "Well, don't bother me again until you've solved it, for I shan't receive you." Cairo ushered us down the dark hallway to his front door. "But feel free to drop by as soon as you have—any time, day or night."

Chapter 28
Encounter in the Fog

We stood outside on Cairo's front steps. The slam of the door still rang in my ears. The click of a latch gave proof that Mr. Gaylord had locked it behind us. Feelings of indignation and helplessness warred in my breast. Evidently, a friend's life meant nothing to Cairo.

Outside his house the street was absolutely deserted. The murky night was still. I turned to my companion and saw he was stiff with anger.

"Riddles!" he fumed. "He tells us riddles, like we're a couple of schoolkids." He tossed his head back and threw his arms wide. "I'm going to get that guy," he promised the cold night air.

I entirely sympathized. Moreover, I was vexed at my inability to solve Cairo's conundrum. After a moment, I mused, "The answer must have to do with some form of transformation or rebirth."

"Ahhh." Houdini waved the thought away. "It doesn't mean anything. He's just trying to confuse us." He set his jaw as he hunched against the cold.

To avoid an argument, I said nothing more. Privately,

however, I thought a session at the reading room of the British Museum was called for. I needed more information on the god Dionysus.

Houdini's attention suddenly snapped back to me. "Hey, you know what? We forgot to ask him about that ring—the one you found in Mackleston's apartment."

It did not look as though we could rectify that lapse tonight. Cairo would not see us until we solved his little puzzle. Therefore, we set off to procure transportation home.

As we strolled along the tiny cobblestone lane, there was not a cab in sight. Not that we could see far. The damp fog off the Thames had worked its way north to this neighborhood. A thick patch of it rolled in quickly. In a few minutes, we could barely see across the street.

A little chill ran down my spine. I had a distinct feeling of being watched. I turned to look behind me. The gaslights had become faint glows that hid more than they illuminated. Movement at the corner of my eye caught my attention. There, had something behind us just flitted into the shadow of a doorway? Or was it merely a swirl of mist? I felt alone and quite vulnerable. I was grateful for the sturdy companion at my side. Houdini spoke in a low voice.

"Let's get out of here," he said. "I'm getting the creeps."

We picked up our pace and made south for Euston Road. The fog thickened and thinned around us in pale, cottony patches. We encountered no other soul. At its densest, the fog could have concealed armies. Indeed, it played strange tricks on one's ears. I thought I heard footsteps shuffling along behind us. Perhaps it was the lateness of the hour or the disturbing events we were investigating, but the sound made me uneasy. We continued on even more quickly. Then, suddenly, we were in the clear. We could see the entire block of flats behind us. I paused, and restrained my companion with a hand on his arm. Here was our chance to get a good look at our pursuer before the murkiness descended upon us again. I could not be sure, but I thought I heard a foot scrape the stones of the road before silence surrounded us. I looked to Houdini.

"I heard it too," he said softly. He jerked a thumb over his shoulder. "Back there."

Why his confirmation filled me with dread, I cannot say. The person behind us was almost certainly a weary pilgrim such as we, eager for his own sitting room and a warm fire.

I saw that Houdini had drawn the sharpened screwdriver out of his pocket and held it like a dagger. We turned to face whoever was following us.

Halfway down the street a single gaslight glowed feebly. At the end of the lane a figure approached. It jogged along the walls of the buildings. I got an impression of a manlike shape with an impossibly lean body and grotesquely long limbs. It loped along in an odd, loose-jointed way. I could have sworn I heard soft, animal-like moans. It was as if some savage beast were hot on our trail. I felt Houdini clutch my shoulder.

"What is it?" he hissed in my ear.

I could only shake my head. It was like no creature I had seen in all my travels. The thing's unnatural form filled me with loathing. Its huge shadow, magnified by the streetlamp, flitted along the bricks of the buildings.

I stood, my eyes riveted on the gaslight down the street. What would I see when the thing stepped full into the glow? As if in answer to my thought, it paused and sniffed the air. The misshapen head swiveled until it pointed precisely in our direction. Its eyes glittered in the faint light. Their malign emerald glow recalled the supernatural radiance that had bathed us that night at Cairo's. The beast took a step forward. Then an absolutely unexpected thing happened. Just before it stepped full into the light, the creature swarmed straight up the sheer wall. I gasped at the speed with which it scaled the bricks. It climbed until it was lost in the shadows. For a moment, all was silent. Then I heard a sound that chilled me to my soul—the faint sound of claws scrabbling across the roof tiles high above us. And the sound was approaching rapidly.

"Come on," Houdini hissed, grabbing my sleeve.

We took off down the street at a run. My shoes slipped on the flagstones. I wheeled my arms to catch my balance. On and on we raced. The blood beat in my temples. We careened into abrupt turns and doubled back on ourselves. Soon we were back in another patch of fog. My breath sounded harsh in my ears. At last I felt Houdini's grasp on my arm as he pulled me to a stop.

I sagged against the cold bricks and gasped for air. Silence surrounded us. My heart pounded in my chest. Had we given our pursuer the slip? The alley next to us was dark. We huddled in its shadows and peeped around the corner. We could barely make out the walls of the tenements that loomed over us. The stones beneath our feet were rough and uneven. The cold air seared the back of my throat as I caught my breath. I scarcely dared look back for fear of seeing something.

Houdini whispered. "I think we lost—"

The unmistakable sound of scrabbling above us cut him off.

"Run!"

The cry echoed off the walls. We plunged into the blackness of the street before us. I was racing at full speed before I realized that it was I who had shrieked the command. Our feet pounded the pavement as we dashed through the darkness. We both flung our arms up to protect from an overhead attack. The thing that pursued us—was it what had murdered Mackleston's brother?

The street turned out to be a long, curving one with no side alleys. But at the end I thought I discerned a glow of light.

"At . . . end," Houdini gasped beside me. "Stop . . . set ambush."

I thought of what the creature above us had done to Reggie and shivered. How could we defend against an attack that could come from any direction? But each breath

I drew felt like a stab in my side. I couldn't run much longer.

Not three yards from the end of the street a huge figure loomed out of the lowering fog in front of us. We skidded to a stop and barely avoided colliding with it.

"Here now, what's the rush, lads?" a loud voice boomed.

Two hands the size of hams clutched at our lapels and hauled us into the street. "Let's get a better look at you," the voice declared.

We found ourselves under an electric light on Euston Road. The figure looming over us revealed itself as a frowning giant of a policeman. The fog had lowered again. Little droplets had condensed on the brass buttons of his uniform. They glittered like gems under the lamplight. Though I continued to gasp for air, my relief was palpable. As he saw how we were dressed, a look of surprise registered on his face and he loosed his hold on us.

"I beg your pardon, gentlemen," he said. Then he noticed the sharpened screwdriver, still clutched in Houdini's hand. "Now what—"

"Constable," I panted, "someone or something is after us." I pointed into the blackness behind us.

Houdini nodded vigorously as he leaned over to suck in air. "Tried to lose him . . . chased us a good two miles."

"Oh, he has, has he?" The officer drew his truncheon out of his belt and turned to face the yawning darkness. "We'll see about that."

I could not let him face the demon alone. "Whoever he is . . . he's gone mad," I warned between breaths. "You must . . . get reinforcements."

The policeman turned back to us and smiled. "One man only?"

"At least wait . . . until we catch . . . our breaths," I urged. "We'll accompany you."

The policeman seemed not to have heard me. His face lit up in anticipation. William the Conqueror's face might have looked the same as he led the charge at Hastings. "I hope he tries to resist arrest. I truly do."

So saying, he picked up a little black lantern from the ground beside him. He lifted it to head height and plunged into the unlit street.

"Like Custer at Little Bighorn," Houdini muttered to himself. Neither of us had fully recovered, but we straightened up and staggered after the man.

"Wait up!" Houdini called. We chased the watery glow of light from his lantern as it floated through the foggy darkness. Before we had gone six steps, the light appeared to dance wildly. We heard a shout, a feral screech, and finally a shrill scream, like a soul in torment. The shriek rose and fell. Abruptly, it cut off. The lantern fell to the street with a clatter. It glowed brightly for a moment and then winked out. A terrible silence followed.

We advanced cautiously to the black tin lantern. Beside it lay a rounded shape. In the dim light from the streetlamp behind us, I recognized the officer's helmet. When I picked it up, it was slippery with blood. I let it fall in disgust. Peering into the darkness in front of us, I could see no trace of the man.

Without warning, the creature dropped in front of us. It landed lightly twenty yards away. Fear rooted me to the spot. In the dark I got a confused impression of pale, wiry limbs, dripping claws, and hooves. A smell like rotting flesh wafted over. I dared not breathe. What had it done to the policeman? In that moment I truly expected to die.

The being launched itself forward. We spun and fled for our lives. Its hooves scrabbled on the stones behind us as we reached Euston Road.

Out of the fog I heard hoofbeats and the telltale creak of wheels. The clatter of the creature's hooves behind us drew ever nearer. We redoubled our efforts and flew toward the sounds of the cab. Houdini dashed into the street first. The hansom nearly ran him down.

The cabman gave a shout of surprise.

"Open the doors!" I yelled, hearing footsteps not ten feet behind us.

The cabman looked puzzled at our panic, but he complied. We tumbled inside and Houdini pulled the door shut behind us.

"Drive," he shouted.

The little window in the roof slid open. "Where to?" the man called down. The footsteps were right beside the cab.

"Just go," Houdini yelled. "Go like the devil!"

The cabman whipped his horse as the door on Houdini's side flew open. The magician grabbed for it and hauled it shut. The cab jolted, almost as if it had run over something. The horse gave a whinny of terror and broke into a full gallop down the foggy street. From above us came a high, keening wail.

An object, something like a rugby ball, fell past my window. We bounced and jostled against each other. I pulled up and steadied myself on the open window just in time to see the driver's headless body fly past and bounce onto the street. A font of blood bubbled from the open neck. The horse careened on and the sight was mercifully lost in the fog.

Cold air blasted us from the open front of the cab. The roof window slid open. "Look out!" I cried, as a long arm reached down. I pulled Houdini back into the seat. The arm was long and wiry with stiff brown hairs. Its hand ended in talons dripping with blood. No doubt drawn by the sound of my voice, it took a swipe at us. I hunched away from it. One of the claws sliced my cheek. I felt a warm wetness run down to my chin. The hand whipped left and right. We scrambled in opposite directions as the claws raked the air around us.

In the midst of its flailing and our dodging, the claws somehow came into contact with Houdini's hair. It immediately clutched and grabbed a handful. Then, amazingly, Houdini rose with a shout straight into the air.

"Nooo!" he hollered.

Slowly, the creature lifted him toward the small, square opening in the top of the cab. Houdini twisted and clawed at the arm, trying to scrabble free, all the while howling like a banshee.

As Houdini struggled and yelled, an object dropped to the floor. The screwdriver! I scooped it up and drove it into the beast's arm.

I realized I was yelling, "Let him go!" over and over.

The cab lurched so violently that I fell to my knees. Somehow, I managed to keep stabbing at the creature's arm. Blood dribbled down the rangy limb. At last, with a cry of rage and frustration it let Houdini drop. He landed next to me in an awkward heap. The arm withdrew through the top window in a shower of red droplets.

For a moment, all was quiet in the madly careening cab. Houdini struggled to sit up despite the jolting ride. Without warning, an attack came from another quarter. While our horse galloped freely, I heard a scrabbling sound to my right. As I watched, five claws punctured the thick leather of the roof over our heads.

"Look!" Houdini pointed as another five holes punched through the leather farther down the side of the coach. I caught a glint of talons. The creature was making its way hand over hand down and around to the open front of the cab. In a second or two, it would be inside with us. I saw a sinewy arm reach for the window in the door. I yanked the shade down across it and hung on it with all my weight. The claws penetrated the thin leather. They gripped fiercely and wrestled with me to jerk up the shade.

The cab gave a lurch that nearly jerked it from my hands. Another set of claws scrabbled for a hold on the open front of the vehicle. The creature was hanging by the shade and trying to swing itself around to get a purchase on the open front. From there it could easily draw itself inside.

I still clutched Houdini's screwdriver in my hand. In a frenzy I slashed over and over again across the top of the leather shade. The carriage jerked from side to side. Desperately, I fought to maintain my balance. The creature redoubled its effort to get hold of the front lip of our cab. The hand stretched and clutched. Finally, it got a purchase. Houdini flung himself to the floor and kicked savagely at the hand. It let go just as my screwdriver slashed through the shade. The flap of leather tumbled away and dumped our unwelcome passenger onto the street. Leaning out, I strained to catch a glimpse of the thing's face. All I saw was a rapidly diminishing lean body in a jumble of sinewy arms and legs, scrabbling to right itself. A howl of frustration echoed down the street and terrified our horse to even greater speed.

Looking ahead, I saw that we had entered a more congested area. The fog had once again lifted and the faces of startled pedestrians flashed past us. Other vehicles scurried from our path. I turned around to see Houdini clambering out the window.

The cab swayed as he climbed hand over hand up to the top. I learned later that, fortunately, the reins were looped over the driver's seat. He gathered them up easily. The horse's head jerked back as he pulled. The cab had so much momentum that it was another fifty yards before we rolled to a stop.

I climbed out on shaky knees and helped my companion down from his perch. We both stared behind us but caught no sign of our pursuer. Had we truly lost him?

Chapter 29
An Appalling Conclusion

Our wild ride had deposited us only a few blocks from my rooms at the Langham Hotel. The stares of passersby recalled me to myself. The cut on my cheek still bled. I drew out my handkerchief and wiped my face as best I could. A small crowd began to gather around us. Houdini looked nervously this way and that. His scalp wound had bled freely onto his face and neck. At the sight of him, people gasped and backed off.

"We can't stay here," he said.

"My hotel's right over there," I said, and gestured in the direction of Regent's Park. He nodded and thence we hastened.

Up in the suite, my first action was to lock the door behind us. Next I raced from room to room securing windows. I prayed that the creature had not followed us. For all I knew, it could punch through a solid door.

Meanwhile, Houdini turned on every lamp in the place. I also ardently craved light. Only when every window had been checked and every single lamp glowed brightly did we pause to consider what to do next.

"I don't suppose you have a gun," Houdini said.

I shook my head. I had even managed to lose Houdini's sharpened screwdriver.

"We have to find something to defend ourselves with," he insisted.

A frantic search of the rooms turned up no weapons other than a couple of scalpels from my medical bag. I snatched them up and gave one to my companion.

We stood back to back in my sitting room, flourishing the surgical instruments. The minutes ticked by. It dawned on me how woefully inadequate the inch-long blade in my hand was.

"You know," Houdini began tentatively, "if he was still after us, he'd be here by now."

"Doubtless our fearsome display of weaponry frightened him off," I observed.

Houdini guffawed behind me. That was all it took. I, too, exploded with mirth. We could not stop. Tears rolled down Houdini's cheeks. My sides ached. It was minutes before the hysteria drained away and I could get a breath.

"I could use a bracer," I announced at last.

"For once, I think I'll join you," Houdini replied.

I strode to the sideboard and poured us each a shot of brandy. In spite of our smiles, both our hands shook perceptibly as we raised our glasses to our lips. I downed mine eagerly. Houdini's gulp left him red in the face and gasping.

"I'd rather eat fire any day," he asserted after his breath came back.

As the liquor stretched its soothing fingers through my body, I remembered that we both had wounds to be tended. My medical bag yielded up a bottle of disinfectant. I made Houdini sit still while I bathed his scalp and face with a towel from the bathroom. After I had finished with him, I used a fresh towel to cleanse my own cut. It was not deep.

I began to feel peculiar. The room seemed to go in and out of focus. My stomach heaved. I dropped the towel onto the carpet, staggered over to an armchair, and collapsed in it. Houdini remained slumped in his chair. Evidently, he too was having a reaction to our narrow escape.

"My God," he said. Neither of us was laughing now. "It lifted me like I was a doll."

Scenes flashed upon my inward eye. Again I saw those slashing talons and the headless body of the cabman.

Houdini roused himself enough to look at me. "What do you think it was?" he asked.

I swallowed with an effort. "I think it was the thing that killed Mackleston's brother," I answered. "A manifestation of the god Dionysus."

Houdini slipped back into his chair with a groan. "Don't tell me that."

I had no strength for debate, so I let silence reign. My mind drifted back to Cairo's riddle. The clues hinted of rebirth and transmutation. An unspeakable idea came to mind. I sought to dismiss it, but I could not.

I shivered even though several logs blazed fiercely in the fireplace. I rose to make my way to the couch opposite the fire. On my feet I felt light-headed and nearly stumbled. My gorge rose again. I staggered to the couch and collapsed. I lay there weakly and breathed deeply in an attempt to quell the upthrust of nausea. The symptoms were unmistakable. I was in shock.

From across the room Houdini's voice came to me, low and urgent. "We have to do something about this, and quick."

I struggled to sit up, but queasiness overwhelmed me once more. I sank back onto the cushions. "Yes," I agreed weakly.

"That Cairo guy," Houdini said. "He sent that thing after us."

"The truth may be even worse than that," I said. "Remember his riddle."

"The riddle?" Houdini sounded doubtful. "What's that got to do with anything?"

I could hardly bring myself to speak. But my companion had a right to know. "According to Cairo's story, the god has the power of transformation."

"What are you getting at?" Houdini's voice was querulous.

I heaved myself upright so I could see him. The effort left me light-headed. "Remember how it scrambled up that sheer wall?"

Houdini lifted a hand. "Don't remind me."

"The place it chose to do so was most suggestive."

"I don't get you." My companion frowned.

"It fled out of sight just before it reached the streetlight."

Houdini's mouth pursed as he puzzled over my words. Then his face cleared. "You mean it didn't want us to get a good look at it."

I nodded. "Eight people were there the night of the ceremony."

"You think they're in danger too?"

"No," I said. "I think the creature who attacked us is one of them."

Chapter 30
No Rest for the Wicked

A dead silence emanated from the other corner of the room. At last Houdini spoke. "You really think one of them turned into that—that thing?"

I nodded soberly.

The heat of the fire finally began to warm my cold bones. I shifted my position to better see Houdini. He leaned forward on the edge of his chair.

"If Dionysus got to all of us, why don't we all turn into monsters?"

He had a point. "If we solve Cairo's riddle, perhaps we shall understand that as well."

"Riddle, shmiddle," Houdini spat. "We got no time to play his games."

I was afraid he was right. "Let's see how things look in the morning," I suggested wearily.

Houdini's brow was furrowed with worry. "Listen," he said, "the, uh—whatever it is—it's after us, right? Nobody else?"

I nodded. "I believe so. It attacked only those who stood between us and it."

"Then would it be okay if I stay here tonight? I don't want that thing anywhere near Bess." He added apologetically, "I could sleep on your couch."

I readily acceded. "If you're sure you'll be comfortable."

"Don't worry," Houdini assured me. "I've slept worse."

I accompanied him downstairs to the telephone in the hotel's lobby. I kept a lookout for our pursuer, while Houdini left a message with the clerk at his hotel.

"I told her to keep the door locked until I come for her," he confided upon hanging up. "He promised he'd take it right up to her."

On our way back up the lift, we puzzled over why the creature had not followed us to my hotel. Perhaps it had lost our track in the teeming millions of London. In any case, back in the room we determined to risk getting some sleep. I lent Houdini a dressing gown and saw him settled on the couch with plenty of blankets before I retired.

Sleep was long in coming. It was not pleasant to lie in the darkness and know that out on the streets a malevolent being hunted for us.

I passed an uneasy hour before exhaustion finally won out over fear. It seemed I had just closed my eyes when I awoke with a gasp. Someone was shaking me violently. Houdini's white face hovered above me. "Get up," he whispered urgently.

A terrific racket sounded from the next room. I bolted upright. Were we under attack? I stared around wildly. Pale pink light leaked around the curtains across my window.

"Something's at the door." Houdini's eyes were wide, his face white. Paralysis gripped me for a moment. Had the frightful beast finally tracked us down? The pounding reached a furious crescendo. Out of the cacophony, a voice shouted. "Open up in there."

At least our disturber was human. Houdini relaxed. He helped me into my dressing gown. We padded over to the door. Cautiously, I opened it. In the hallway stood, of all people, Inspector Woburn with two policemen.

"Let us in—it's official business." He caught a glimpse

of Houdini over my shoulder. "Oh-ho, so you're together, are you? How handy."

"What is it you want?" I asked sharply.

"Oh, we'll get to that, don't you worry," Woburn assured me. I stepped back as he forced his considerable girth into the room. I felt self-conscious in my nightclothes.

Woburn waddled to the center of the room, muttering under his breath. The policemen followed him. One was long and lanky with a mournful expression. The other was stocky with a face like a side of beef. He touched his hat to us as they entered. Woburn was in a state of considerable agitation. The policemen arranged themselves behind him. From the looks that passed between them, they were obviously uncomfortable intruding upon us.

"What is the meaning of this?" I demanded.

Woburn's expression was not pleasant. "Tell me what you were doin' last night."

For a moment I was taken aback. Then I thought of the two murders we had witnessed—the policeman and the cabman. No doubt we should have reported the killings. But we had been fleeing for our lives.

I looked at Houdini. He shrugged. "Tell him," he said simply.

Woburn's eyes glittered. "Yes, tell me," he said.

As briefly as I could, I recounted the details of our flight through the streets last night. When I was finished, I waited for his reaction.

For a moment he regarded us silently. His eyes bulged with some emotion. When he finally spoke, his face was rigid and his voice strained. "Three nights ago, I investigated the most horrible murder I've seen. Two days later, you and your lady friend come pokin' around and want to know all about the crime."

His face had grown red as a tomato. "Last night, we had two other murders—just as savage. A policeman in the area has disappeared. And a cabman was decapitated. Witnesses place two men, who looked very much like you and your friend, at the scene. You admit you were there.

But for some reason, known best to yourselves, you didn't report these deaths."

I saw where his thoughts led and drew myself up. "I hope you do not mean—"

The man cut me off. "You told us to look for a criminal who escaped from a locked room. And this mornin' what do I find? Why, I find you with the most famous escape artist in the world." He practically trembled with rage. "And for an alibi, you tell the most amazin' cock-and-bull story I ever heard in my life."

Woburn practically roared at me, "If you was me, what would you make of all that?"

"Well, I sure wouldn't try to make flapjacks out of hot air and hope," Houdini cut in.

Woburn's eyes widened as they sought out my companion. "What did you say to me?"

Houdini bounced to his feet. My dressing gown was so large on him it hung almost to the floor. He had rolled the sleeves, but they still dangled below his elbows. "It means you got nothing and you know it." His expression darkened. "We been straight with you and this is how you thank us. Come in here, threatening us like we're a couple of lowlifes." The hem of the long red dressing gown flopped around Houdini's bare feet as he strutted over to Woburn. The magician did not stop until he stood chest to belly with the larger man. My companion once again resembled a bantam rooster. This time, however, he seemed like a bantam rooster challenging a bull.

The policemen hurried around the chair to defend their superior. It was time to intercede. Before I could reach Houdini, however, he lifted a hand. "Ease off, boys. There ain't gonna be any trouble here. Right?" he asked Woburn.

Woburn, angry as he was, backed up a pace from the sheer force of Houdini's personality. I stood behind Houdini, ready to pin his arms should he go too far. The two constables looked at each other uncertainly.

Houdini stared up defiantly at Woburn. "You going to

arrest us?" he demanded. Before the man could answer, Houdini cut in with "Can you make it stick? You got no witnesses who saw the crime. And you got two murders that would take an animal the size of a gorilla to pull off."

Woburn looked as if he was about to burst. He tried to sputter out a response, but my companion did not give him the chance. "And for suspects you pick two of the most famous guys in London. Guys with powerful friends. And one of 'em's a Sir, on top of it. Oh, this'll look real good in the papers tomorrow." Houdini thrust himself forward, his jaw jutting truculently. "What about it? You going to put your money where your mouth is?"

The inspector blinked and looked down at his diminutive antagonist. "Well, I—er . . ."

I could scarcely restrain a smile at the frontier spirit that burned so fiercely in my friend.

Houdini nodded, satisfied at Woburn's response. "Good." He strolled back to his chair and threw himself in it. " 'Cause you ain't got a jail on this whole island that can hold Harry Houdini." He folded his arms and stuck his chin out defiantly. I smiled to see how any chair that Houdini occupied took on the characteristics of a throne. "Now, get outta here so we can solve your case for you," he said. "You treat us real good, we'll see you get your name in the papers."

Woburn's face flushed nearly purple. At last he found his voice. "This is not over. Not by a long shot." He raised a hand and shook a chubby finger at us. "You slip up once more, we'll collar you," he vowed. "And you'll hang beside your friend Mackleston." With that, he lumbered from the room, the policemen in tow.

The shorter one hung back just long enough to whisper. "Please forgive him, gentlemen. He's not hisself. It's like the entire city's gone crazy. You wouldn't believe what we been through." With that he fled to catch up with the others.

After they had left, Houdini's look of confidence dropped like a discarded mask. He slumped in his chair.

I seated myself on the sofa across from him. "Did you hear the policeman?" I asked. "About the entire city going mad?"

Houdini sighed. "Yeah, I heard him."

The implication was dreadful. Were we up against a monster that could corrupt all of humanity? Houdini interrupted my thoughts.

"I've been thinking about that thing that chased us." Gingerly, he touched the top of his head where the creature had hoisted him by his scalp.

"So have I," I assured him. "I am convinced it was a horrible transmutation of one of our party." I fixed Houdini with a steady gaze. "We both know who."

"Cairo." He made the name sound like a curse.

An idea grew in my mind. "None other. It was he who changed shape during the ritual."

"Yeah." Houdini drew the dressing gown tightly around him. "He wants to do us in, but he doesn't want a mess in his own rooms. So he follows us." Despair surged over his features. "Only—knowing this doesn't help much, does it?"

"Oh, yes it does," I said. "It is the first ray of hope we've had."

Houdini looked incredulous. "How do you figure?"

"Consider." I sat forward on the cushions. "We visit Cairo. He refuses to even talk to us—until I reveal that we're close to solving the murder. Once he finds out how much we know, he attacks us with deadly intent."

"You're saying he thinks we know more than we do?"

"He must. Why else would he need to eliminate us?"

A kind of wonder filled Houdini's face. "He's scared of us."

I stood. For the first time in many a long hour, I felt a shred of hope. "Mark my words, Reggie's murder is the key." I hurried into the bedchamber to gather my clothes.

"So what's next?" Houdini called after me.

"Our main obstacle is that we have no idea how the creature escaped," I called back as I dressed myself. "And that really is your specialty."

Houdini appeared in the doorway to the bedchamber. His trousers were on and he was buttoning his shirt. "I know, I know," he said unhappily. "But I can't figure it out."

I inserted my cuff links. "Together, we shall. Tell me how you make your escapes."

"All kinds of ways." Houdini leaned against the doorjamb. "The thing is misdirection. Take a box escape. Remember I said that I use short nails in one end?"

"I certainly do."

"Well, if I really want to sell it, I lie down in the box with the lid off and have six guys come out of the audience to nail the top shut. Down comes my curtain. Presto, I kick out the end—which I rigged like I told you—and wiggle out. Then I shove the tailpiece back in place. If the same guys want to come up and inspect it, I let them. I got everybody thinking about the top, so they don't look anywhere else."

I detected a flaw in his explanation. "But you also put the box on display in the lobby for people to examine. Wouldn't someone discover your ruse?"

"Oh, that," he shrugged dismissively. "First I take the box up to my dressing room and pound real nails into the end. See," he added, "I can rig it either before or afterward."

"Afterward," I repeated thoughtfully. "By God, that is it!"

Houdini started. "What?" he demanded.

My fingers were making a hash of my cravat. I gave up on it. "We were looking for someone who left before the police came. What if he didn't leave?"

"Didn't leave?" Houdini looked puzzled.

"What if he hid until everyone else left?"

"But where could he—" Houdini's eyes widened. "The fireplace!"

"Exactly," I agreed excitedly. "The killer hid up that huge chimney—"

"—holding on to those bars," Houdini contributed.

"When his arms grew tired, he braced his back against one wall and his feet against the other until it was safe to descend," I finished.

Houdini strode across the room, hand outstretched. "Put 'er there, partner," he exclaimed. "You got it."

I grasped his hand. For a moment I felt almost giddy. At last, we were making progress. My happiness was short-lived, however. "Unfortunately, we have no proof to take to Woburn."

Houdini's joy faded as well. He relapsed into a thoughtful mood.

"We must determine how he got out of the building," I continued. "Remember, Miss Finch swore no one left that day."

"Yeah," Houdini said. "And with that bell, she'd have heard."

"Perhaps he disabled the bell," I suggested.

"Nah. I checked on that while you searched for the painting. She swears it was fine."

I cudgeled my brains. We were so close and yet a single fact eluded us.

"Hah!" Houdini lurched upright. "Ha-ha-ha!" He threw his hands in the air and danced a little jig.

"You've solved it?" I asked.

"Oh, yeah." He grinned from ear to ear. "Remember what I said about misdirection?"

"Of course."

"That's it. We asked her the wrong question. We only asked if anybody left. We never asked her if anybody came in."

"How would that—"

But Houdini had no more time for talk. He spun around and dashed off. I barely had time to snatch my coat off the chair and follow him as he fled out the door and down the hall.

Chapter 31
Hot on the Trail

It was just after seven-thirty in the morning when a cab deposited us on the pavement outside Mackleston's flat in Soho.

At the door, Houdini turned to me. He could barely restrain his enthusiasm. "If I'm right, she saw Cairo here—just after the murder. That's enough to put him away!"

"If you're right about what?" I demanded.

He wagged a finger in my face. "Just wait," he said. "You'll see."

I felt a momentary rush of exasperation. His occupation had made deception second nature to him. I wondered if he was capable of giving a straight answer to anyone.

I forced myself to put my feelings aside. In many ways, he was simply an overgrown child. If he needed to spring the solution on me like one of his stage illusions, I would allow him to do so. Besides, his excitement was contagious.

Houdini swung the heavy front door wide and charged inside. The overhead bell, connected by its cord-and-pulley system, announced our presence with a jangle.

Miss Finch's door opened a crack. It swung wider as she saw who strode across the brown rug of the entryway.

"Well, I never," she beamed her appreciation at seeing us and dried her hands on her apron. "Any earlier and you'd have caught me at breakfast. Have you solved the mystery yet?"

She stood away from the door and waited in her maroon and white striped dress with its eight-inch ruffle at the bottom. Houdini did not even wait to be seated, but began as soon as he was inside the flat. "We're getting there," he said, "and you can sure help us."

There was a strong smell of soap powder about the place. I shut the door behind me as the small woman combed a wisp of gray hair back into place with trembling fingers. She looked from one to the other of us. "You mean you know what happened inside that awful room?"

Houdini nodded. "And we need to ask you just one more question."

She leaned forward. "Was it—?"

Houdini lifted a finger for silence. "You said nobody left the building after the murder."

She nodded vigorously. "Just the police. I'm sure of it."

Houdini cast a brief glance in my direction. "Ah, but did anyone come into the building?"

She stared at him as if he'd gibbered at her in a foreign tongue. At last she shook her head. "No. Nobody."

Houdini looked startled. "Are you sure?"

"Of course I'm sure," she snapped. "I'll never forget one second of that day. No matter what a certain police inspector may think."

Houdini looked crestfallen.

"Perhaps a tradesman?" I suggested gently. I had no idea what my companion sought, so I was clutching at straws.

Miss Finch turned to me, a stout denial on the tip of her tongue. But no words issued forth. Rather, her mouth slowly closed. "There was one." She dismissed the thought with a wave of the hand. "Oh, but he was only here for a moment."

"Who was it?" Houdini demanded.

"Just a chimney sweep."

"How did you know he was a chimney sweep?" Houdini's face flushed with anticipation.

"Well, he was all covered in soot—"

"Soot from a fireplace," Houdini interrupted with a triumphant look in my direction.

"Yes, of course." She gave Houdini an exasperated look. "Where else?"

Excitement filled me as I saw where his thoughts were heading.

"Go on," he encouraged her. "What did he look like?"

She shrugged. "He had on some old clothes—"

"Were they khaki-colored?" I blurted out.

She turned to me, surprise on her face. "Why, so they were. However did you know that?"

"Tell me everything." Houdini leaned forward. "Everything."

She put her hands on her hips and stared at him. "He was just a chimney sweep."

A question occurred to me. "Was he carrying anything?"

"Well, he had his brushes," she answered impatiently. "They were all wrapped up in a canvas bundle under his arm."

"This bundle," I asked hopefully, "was it in the form of a long roll?"

She nodded. "It was. Very long. That's how I knew it had to be his tools."

"The painting!" Houdini said gleefully. "That's what happened to it."

Miss Finch stared at him wordlessly. She leaned over to me. "Is he all right?" she whispered.

"He's fine," I assured her. "Please tell us exactly what happened when you saw the chimney sweep."

The older woman looked dubious. "What happened?"

"Yes," Houdini urged. "How did you know he was here?"

"Same as always," she responded. "I heard the bell ring.

When I opened my door, he stood there in the entryway, just as bold as you please." Her voice grew stronger at the memory. "Had the nerve to ask if I'd any work for him. I sent him straight away, I'll tell you."

Houdini leaned forward intently. "Would you recognize him if you saw him again?"

She looked doubtful. "I don't know. . . . He was awful dirty. And his cap was pulled low on his face. I don't think so."

My companion's countenance registered his disappointment.

She turned to me. "What's so important about a chimney sweep?"

"That chimney sweep was the killer," I told her.

She sighed with exasperation. "I told you, he came in the front door—after it was all over."

"But you didn't see him come in, did you?" Houdini insisted.

She looked puzzled.

"You heard the bell ring," Houdini said. "That was the killer—in disguise—on his way out. As he heard your door open, he spun around and stepped toward you. All you saw was the open door and him walking forward. You thought he'd come off the street."

"The khaki suit he wore was stolen from Mackleston's closet," I added.

As our words sank in, she went pale. "Oh, my goodness." The poor woman staggered to her overstuffed sofa and sank down onto it. "I could have been murdered."

I inclined my head toward Houdini. "You'd best fetch a glass of water."

He sprang to the task while I hastened to her. "We always seem to be upsetting you."

She didn't even hear me. "Fancy," she said, "me not ten feet away from the murderer."

"What can you recall about him? Was he tall? Brawny?"

"I'm not sure."

"Try to remember," I pressed her.

"Oh, I don't know! With those baggy old clothes on, it was hard to tell anything."

Houdini returned with the glass of water, which Miss Finch gratefully accepted with both hands. "Did you notice his hair color?" Houdini asked as she drank.

She lowered the glass and shook her head. "Like I told you, the cap covered everything."

"How old was he?" I asked.

"Well, he wasn't a child, but on the other hand . . ." Her voice trailed off. "He was so dirty, you see," she added apologetically. "And all I wanted was to get shut of him."

"Of course," I said. Inside I roiled with frustration. Our only living witness to the killer was proving useless.

"Just one thing." Her voice was a little stronger now. "If he really was the killer, why didn't I hear him when he came in? He'd have rung my bell."

Houdini and I traded swift glances. She had hit upon the one flaw in his theory. Moreover, that was exactly the question Mackleston's prosecuting attorney would ask. Could Houdini's solution be wrong, after all? No, it explained too many things—the soot, the missing painting, Mackleston's stolen suit.

Houdini looked to me, a silent plea in his eyes. From the disarray of my thoughts, an idea emerged. "Perhaps the killer came in with Mackleston."

"Hah!" Houdini's face filled with admiration.

Miss Finch sat upright and clutched at the water glass on her lap. "He could have, you know. When Mr. Mackleston came back from lunch, I was in the middle of my ironing. I didn't want to stop, so I just called out, 'Is that you, Mr. Mackleston?' When I recognized his voice, I didn't even open the door."

I nodded gravely.

One hand flew to her mouth. "Oh, my. That means he knew his killer."

"We think so," Houdini agreed.

"And I let him leave." She turned to me. "What if he

comes back for me?" Her hand shook so badly that water sloshed over the top of her glass.

"Why should he?" Houdini asked with a touch of asperity. "You can't identify him."

"That's right." Gently, I removed the glass from her hand. "You mustn't take on so," I said. "The last thing he wants is to return here."

She looked up at me doubtfully. "If you say so . . ." She grabbed the sleeve of my jacket. "But you'll catch him, won't you?"

"We shall exert every effort."

"Should I tell the police?" From her expression I could tell she did not relish another meeting with Woburn.

"Not until we have proof. And," I added with a smile, "I rely upon you to back us up."

She solemnly promised to do so. We stayed another fifteen minutes simply to calm her down. I made tea in her tiny kitchen. After a cup, she was talking more easily. Finally, we left with promises to keep her informed of any developments.

Outside the flat, I turned to Houdini. "You realize she has just exonerated Cairo."

"How do you figure?"

"Her description—"

"If you could call it that," he interrupted.

"—sounded nothing like Cairo," I finished patiently. "Mackleston's suit would not have appeared loose on him."

Houdini flung up his hands in frustration. "Maybe the clothes were torn or—I don't know." He faced me. "Look, as scared as she was just then, I wouldn't believe her description of her own nose."

I frowned. He had a point. Still, it bothered me that her description did not resemble Cairo.

Houdini folded his arms. His expression was glum. "Ah, what does it matter? We're no closer than we were yesterday."

"On the contrary," I said. "We have another important lead."

"Like what?" Houdini demanded.

"We have discovered that the killer stole the painting." I lifted a forefinger. "Why would he do such a thing?"

Houdini shrugged.

"The only possible explanation is that there was something on it he did not want us to see."

Houdini clapped his palm to his forehead. "My God. You don't suppose Mackleston painted his portrait?"

"It may well be," I said earnestly. "Why else would Mackleston bring him to the studio?"

"I don't see how that helps us," Houdini complained. "He'd just destroy it."

"Then why bother to take it away? Anything powerful enough to rend a human being could easily have torn the canvas to shreds."

"You got a point," Houdini rubbed his chin thoughtfully. "What kind of a guy would keep evidence like that around?"

"A vain and arrogant one," I replied.

"That's Cairo all over."

I nodded. For a moment, each of us was lost in his own thoughts. Perhaps even now the painting reposed in Cairo's flat. It may have been hidden in the very room where he toyed with us, asking riddles. Houdini interrupted my musings.

"We're forgetting something."

"What?"

"We saw the killer, right? Last night?" He looked around nervously. As he spoke, I could not help doing the same. The pale sunlight of an autumn morning shone on workmen, vendors, cabmen in the street, and housewives with wicker market baskets on their wrists.

I felt a tiny frisson. I realized I half expected a rangy shape to come loping out of the crowd.

Houdini's voice was urgent. "If I saw what I thought I

saw, it could do anything, appear anywhere—right next to us, even."

Now was no time to give in to panic. "I do not think so," I said. "Remember what Cairo said. When it manifests itself in the physical world, it is bound by those rules."

"If we can believe anything that guy told us," Houdini replied fretfully.

"I think we can. To him this is a game. He enjoys taunting us with just enough truth to frustrate us." I cast my mind back to last night. "Besides, we saw it was so. The creature can bleed; it can be knocked off a hansom cab. It can be thwarted."

"That's right." Hope dawned in Houdini's eyes. "We beat it once, didn't we?"

I nodded. "We certainly did. If only we can prove what we know, we can have Cairo locked up. I'll wager one of our stout British gaols will keep him where he can do no further harm." Privately, I also hoped he could be persuaded to counter the madness that seemed to be spreading across London.

"Jeez," Houdini said. "Wish we could find that painting. I bet it's in his house right now."

In a flash I saw what had to be done. "I am sure you're right," I said. "There's only one thing to do."

My comrade looked up at me, appalled. "You mean—?"

"Yes. We must search his house."

Chapter 32
Unexpected Revelations

Houdini held up his hands in protest. "He won't even let us in until we figure out his riddle. Remember—it's in one of us, it's in all of us?"

"I certainly do. And I propose to solve it."

"How?" Houdini looked doubtful.

"Here in London we have one of the most extensive libraries in the world. The reading room of the British Museum must hold a clue somewhere in its voluminous stacks."

"Yeah, then what?"

"Then I shall go in alone and engage him in conversation. Can you pick the lock to his house?"

"Of course, I— Ohhh, I get it. While you keep him busy, I search the house."

"It is a desperate scheme," I acknowledged.

To my surprise, he laughed out loud. "You said it, pal. This is really risking the farm." Houdini's mirthless smile faded. He chewed on his thumbnail. "How about we talk to Mackleston first—see if he remembers who came up with him that afternoon?"

"A good suggestion." I did not like to think what might occur should Cairo catch us in his house. "If Mackleston does not recall, however—"

"Then I'm with you," Houdini said with finality.

I clapped my hand on his shoulder. "Stout fellow," I said.

He grinned at me. "I like you, Conan Doyle; you got guts."

Mackleston's guard recognized me from my last visit and admitted us straightaway. We found Mackleston himself practically bursting with nervous energy—possibly from being deprived of his opium. No doubt the closeness of his plain white walls and the daily monotony had taken their toll on his artistic temperament as well. The tweed suit Miss Luce had brought him hung in loose folds on his body as he strode back and forth in his tiny cell.

He stopped pacing to greet us. A worn volume of Blake's poems had been flung facedown on the threadbare coverlet. He shook our hands briskly. His flesh was warm and he spoke in clipped sentences.

"Good of you to drop by. Sorry I can't offer any refreshment," he added wryly.

"How are you holding up?" I asked.

He shrugged. "Passed through despair sometime yesterday afternoon. I'm working on resignation now. How's the investigation getting on?"

"It's coming along," Houdini said, with a warning glance at me.

I quite understood. We needed to bolster Mackleston's spirits without giving false hope. "Though perhaps not as rapidly as we had hoped," I added.

He nodded and threw himself down onto his cot. The boards creaked. The mattress sagged under even his slight weight. "My trial's in less than a week. I haven't a chance."

What would London look like in a week? I wondered. Would madness have spread to the entire population? I kept these fears to myself, however, and attempted to buck him up. "Here now," I said. "You mustn't lose heart."

"I'm just being realistic. Woburn means to have me up for it."

"He won't," I said. "I have proven that it was impossible for you to commit the murder."

Mackleston sat up. "Justine dropped by yesterday. Said something of the sort. Quite decent of you. But they'll get me anyway, you know."

"Nonsense!" I exclaimed. To ease his mind, I proceeded to relate our deductions. "So," I concluded, "there was a third party who escaped via a clever ruse."

Mackleston strode to the wooden doorway of his cell and pulled a cigarette case from his pocket. He opened it and offered it to us. I shook my head. He took a cigarette, replaced the case, and pulled a lighter from his pocket. "It won't matter. Woburn's uncovered certain secrets."

The lighter clicked again and again as his fingers fumbled with the mechanism. "The jury will convict me out of spite."

"The narcotics?" I asked.

Mackleston shook his head impatiently. "No, not that." Finally, he produced a flame and lit his cigarette. He took a grateful draw on it.

What was he hinting at? Had he been goaded to violence in the heat of youthful passion?

"Holding back," I said, "could hamper our attempts to help you."

He ran his fingers through his hair. "Well, that's just it, you see." He smiled bitterly from me to Houdini. "Once you know, you won't want to help me."

"Your friends will never desert you," I asserted.

He dismissed my words with a wave of his hand. Cigarette smoke curled in the air behind it. "After the way people treated poor Oscar Wilde?"

I well recalled Oscar Wilde. We had dined together one evening at the Langham Hotel with the American publisher Joseph Marshall Stoddart. That night he had commissioned both "The Sign of Four"—my second Holmes story—and *Picture of Dorian Gray.*

Six years later, the Marquess of Queensberry learned of Oscar's liaison with Queensberry's son. There was a trial that ended with Wilde being sentenced to two years at hard labor for the crime of homosexuality. By all accounts, he died a broken man, impoverished and alone.

But what had that to do with—? Unbidden, my hand flew to my mouth. I saw everything. Mackleston was one of those who indulged in the love that dare not speak its name. A quick glance at Houdini revealed consternation on his face, as well.

I am afraid I retreated a step from the boy when the realization hit me. He smiled wanly. "You see? That is how everyone will respond."

Now I understood what Vollmer had meant by the words "unwholesome companions." I felt a wave of revulsion pass over me. How could I help someone whose basic desires were anathema to everything I believed in?

"You need help that I cannot give you," I said. "Perhaps your family should seek the care of a nerve specialist."

"Yeah," Houdini contributed. "They might let you off, if the court sees you're trying to get cured."

"I don't want to be cured," he snapped.

When next he spoke, his voice was lower, but passion surged beneath the surface. "I just want to be left alone. I don't hurt anyone. God knows, I've had to live a life of hypocrisy as it is."

He took another draw on his cigarette. "Once this gets out, I'm done for. Even if I'm acquitted, everyone will shun me."

"But not those with whom you have been . . . intimate," I pointed out.

"Especially them. Do you think they'd risk exposure?"

He looked so desolate that I could not help but feel sorry for him.

"I shan't have a friend left in the world. Except for Justine, of course."

"Miss Luce knows about your—habits?" Houdini asked.

"Well, of course. She doesn't care a fig about things like

that. Best friend a chap could have. She's the only one who understood what a beast Reggie could be."

He was right. Justine Luce was just the sort who would fly in the face of propriety for the sake of a friend—even if it threatened her livelihood.

Mackleston's voice recalled me to myself. "You're fond of her, aren't you?" he asked.

"I count her among my friends," I said uncomfortably. I shot a quick glance at Houdini, who regarded me with frank curiosity.

"No, I mean, you've really got it for her, haven't you?"

"Certainly not!" I replied hotly. "Remember, I am a married man." Annoyance swept over me. How dare he, of all people, chide me? I glared at him. His reaction utterly surprised me. A weary smile illuminated his features briefly. It was as if my own agitation had calmed him.

"It's all right, you know. She is a pip. And no one really knows what goes on inside another man's heart." He sighed. "Anyway, I'm certainly in no position to judge others."

As the import of his words sank in, a sense of shame overwhelmed me. I was doing to him the very thing he refused to do to me. I was judging him—I, who not long ago had given in to my own basest passions. Miss Luce, on the other hand, would surely support a friend and not count the cost. Had I a lesser soul than Justine Luce?

"Well," he straightened up and moved from the door, "there's no point in prolonging this. I'm sure you've done your best." He squared his shoulders. "I shall just have to muddle through."

When I saw him like that, manfully refusing to succumb to despair, I could not suppress a feeling of admiration. Here was a fellow facing at least public excoriation, and possibly the hangman, as bravely as any soldier ever faced an enemy charge. It was unfair for any man to suffer for a crime he did not commit, no matter what his proclivities. And, after all, I had given my word to help him.

"If I don't see you again . . ." He held out his hand.

I grasped his hand firmly. "Nonsense, my dear fellow," I assured him. "I am still in your corner."

Houdini charged forward and slapped his own hand down on top of our two. "That goes double for me," he said.

"There, you see?" I told Mackleston. "If we've not given up, neither should you. In fact, we intend to devote our full time to the murder."

"Do you really mean that?" The poor fellow looked astonished.

"Of course I do," I assured him.

"Awfully decent of you." He blinked back tears as he struggled to continue. "No matter how this all works out, I'll never forget those words."

"Justice shall triumph, don't you doubt that," I said with more certainty than I felt. "In fact, we are hoping you can help it along." I then asked the question uppermost in my mind. "The day of the murder, did anyone accompany you back to your flat after lunch?"

Mackleston shook his head. "If someone did, I don't remember. So much of that day is a blank, you know."

"Have none of your memories returned?"

He looked surprised at my question. "No," he said forthrightly. "Not a thing."

The silence stretched into nearly a minute.

"Let's retrace your thoughts of that day," I suggested. "Perhaps if you were to recap your actions for me again—"

"It's no use!" The words burst angrily from his lips. "Do you think I haven't tried?" He looked at the rough stone walls of his cell, up to the ceiling, and down to the bricks of the floor. So might a trapped animal have measured at its cage. "Over and over until my head swims."

Houdini and I traded looks. Evidently, he was on the ragged edge. After a time, Mackleston collapsed back onto his mattress.

As I waited for him to calm down, I recalled the information Lord Vollmer had inadvertently revealed about

Reggie. After a minute or two, I asked, "Do you know why your brother broke off his engagement to Sir William's daughter?"

"He didn't," Mackleston said matter-of-factly. "She did. Or rather, Sir William did."

"What happened?" Houdini wanted to know.

"How shall I put this?" Mackleston mused. "Reggie was not—er—gentle with women. In fact, he preferred to take them against their will. I believe he gave his bride-to-be a foretaste of what their connubial bliss would be like."

I was appalled. "You mean he—"

Mackleston nodded. "Bragged at his club about how she struggled. Of course, Sir William broke off the engagement immediately. Very difficult for pater, keeping the whole thing quiet, so I heard." A sad little smile twisted his mouth. "And m'father calls me a pervert."

"Why did you not tell me this before?" I expostulated. "Don't you realize it gives Sir William a strong motive for the murder?"

"I suppose," Mackleston agreed doubtfully. "Doesn't seem the type, though."

I did not answer. I remembered Sir William's rage when under the sway of Dionysus. But his wife had sworn he'd not left his study since the night of the ritual. I hardly knew what to think.

"Reggie could be a swine," Mackleston admitted sadly. "But he didn't deserve to die like that." He swallowed. "I heard the body was so mangled, the only way to identify it was by the clothing." His eyes had grown red-rimmed. "It was new, you know," he said wistfully. "A lounge suit in blue serge. He'd just bought it that morning. I suppose they called in his tailor to verify it."

His hands clutched at the dingy coverlet he sat on. "I haven't got a chance. I'll hang just so the jury can be shut of the case."

I stared directly at him. Feelings of annoyance built in my breast. "You must be absolutely frank with us," I warned, "if we are to help you."

"I have been," he assured me desperately.

"No, you have not."

For an instant he looked stricken. Then he looked away from me and set his lips. Houdini stared at me in puzzlement.

"You are certain you have nothing more to tell us?" I asked brusquely.

He avoided my gaze as he said, "No."

I spared him not another glance, but moved over to the door, where I could see the guard standing a few feet away. The man was built like a small barrel. I motioned through the barred window for him. "Good-bye, Mackleston," I said. The key rattled in the lock and the door swung outward.

"That's it, then?" he asked.

The guard ushered Houdini out. I paused just long enough to say, "We shall continue to work for your best interest. See that you do the same." I left without looking back.

"What was that all about?" Houdini asked as we accompanied the guard down the hall.

"Mackleston's lying to us," I replied sotto voce.

Chapter 33
On the Trail of Dionysus

Houdini gaped at me. I turned to the guard. "May we speak with you a moment?"

"Certainly, sir."

He led past the cell doors down to the central corridor. We entered a small room containing several pairs of stalls, each with a wire mesh window communicating between them. We were in the prisoners' visiting rooms. Wire mesh also roofed the stalls to prevent anything from being thrown over the top.

The tiny rooms were deserted. He led us into the last one before the big folding doors that opened upon the reception area. A rough bench sat underneath the window. On the floor in front of it lay a small pile of ash. The faint smell of old cigar smoke hinted that here was where our guide relaxed when his duties permitted.

The guard offered me the seat, but I declined. Houdini threw himself down on the bench. The magician's eyes never left my face. The guard shut the door and stood in front of it.

"Did you tell Mackleston about his brother?" I asked the guard.

The man laughed nervously. "Well, I guess I did. It were probably the wrong thing to do. You won't tell the Chief Warder, will you?" He looked anxiously at me.

"Not if you answer all of my questions honestly," I responded.

"That I will, that I will," the rotund man promised. "Young Mackleston's such a pleasant sort. I got him paper, pen, and ink. You know what? He drew pictures for my daughter. Horses, all kinds. I told him she loves horses. She put 'em on her—"

"Did you tell Mackleston what sort of suit his brother was wearing when he died?" I asked impatiently.

The guard looked at me, surprised. "Bless you, sir, how would I know that? I just told him what the room looked like, which I got from reading the papers, same as anybody."

Houdini could contain himself no longer. He jumped to his feet. "What do you mean the kid was lying?" he demanded of me.

The guard looked to my companion. When his eyes returned to me, they held the same question.

"He described exactly the suit Reggie was wearing," I reminded Houdini. "And told us his brother had bought it that very day."

"So?"

"How could Mackleston know about the new suit if he remembers nothing of that day?"

"Holy cow!" Houdini slapped his forehead. "His brother had to have told him. He remembers their conversation."

"Precisely," I said. "I believe he remembers the murder, as well."

"Then why wouldn't he tell us?"

I turned to the guard, who had been following our conversation with no little interest. "Has anyone visited the prisoner in the last day or so?"

"Yes," the man admitted. "That woman who came with you, sir. And later there was a tall, dark fellow. Dangerous-looking, if you know what I mean. His eyes give me a fair chill, they did."

"Did you catch the man's name?"

" 'Twere like a city, I remember. Now, what was it?" He rubbed his vast belly as he concentrated. " 'Twarn't Paris. Nor Delhi."

"Cairo?" Houdini spoke the name with distaste.

"That were it," the man agreed excitedly. "The young gentleman called him Cairo. Seemed fair surprised to see him, too."

"I'll wager he was," I said.

"What did they talk about?" Houdini wanted to know.

The man shook his head. "Couldn't say. Whispering the whole time, they was."

"How did Mackleston look when you let the man out?" I asked.

"Well, now that you mention it, the young fellow did seem real quiet. Wouldn't look at me." The guard rubbed his grizzled jowls thoughtfully. "You know, he ain't been the same since." After a moment, the man volunteered, "The dark gent, he didn't stay long."

"Just long enough," I muttered to myself.

The guard leaned forward eagerly. "He was that spiritualist bloke, wa'n he?" He looked excited. "What was he—?"

"He's a friend of the prisoner's," I interrupted.

The man was bursting with curiosity. I moved toward the door. "You've been quite a help. You needn't worry about the Chief Warder." His face fell as he realized I intended to tell him no more. I handed him a half a crown from my pocket. "Have a pint on us tonight. And please keep our conversation to yourself."

"Thank you, sir. That I will." The guard managed a smile, but it was obvious he would have preferred explanations to money.

* * *

Outside the prison, Houdini pulled me to one side of the pavement, out of the path of the pedestrians who hurried past us. "You understand what's going on?" he demanded.

"At least partially," I said. "Cairo came here to see if Mackleston's memory had returned. When he discovered it had, Cairo said something—something that terrified Mackleston into silence."

"But the poor guy's going to hang," Houdini protested. "What could anybody threaten him with that's worse than that?"

"That's the question, isn't it?" I said.

A silence lingered between us. Finally, I spoke the thought that must have been on both our minds. "I'm afraid we must proceed with my plan."

"You mean, you keep him busy while I search his house for the painting?" He looked almost ill at the thought.

"Yes. I shall start researching Dionysus immediately," I vowed. "I hope I may quickly solve Cairo's riddle."

Houdini jumped to his feet. "While you're at the library, I'll cancel my performances." He added, "I'll tell the stage manager I hurt myself on an escape. I'll lose a lot of money." He shrugged philosophically. "But what good's dough if you're not alive to spend it?" His face went serious. "Then I have to get Bess out of town."

Houdini's concern for his wife reminded me of my own family. I had been so enmeshed in the events of the last twenty-four hours that I had neglected all concern for their safety. "And I must determine that my own household is safe," I said.

We hailed a passing cab and bade him take us to the nearest wireless office.

There I sent an emergency wire to my household in Surrey, asking Nurse if anything unusual had occurred in my household or the surrounding neighborhood. I requested an immediate reply. We waited for the answer, which came within half an hour and reassured me that all was tranquil in town and that Louise was not yet at a crisis.

"Evidently," I said to Houdini, "the madness has not yet spread that far. If you like, you can send Bess there."

His eyes glowed with gratitude. "If I know that she's safe, at least for a while, I can think what to do about the rest of it."

He immediately went off to make his arrangements and I wired Nurse to alert the staff to expect a houseguest.

The hansom I had summoned to take me to Bloomsbury deposited me shortly at the columns of the British Museum's noble portico. I applied to the reading room's director for a short-term ticket, which I was granted. Soon I was ensconced at a desk under the reading room's magnificent blue dome. The pile of books around me exuded their marvelous stale-vanilla smell of old paper. I delved into mythology, philosophy, and even archaeology in my quest for knowledge.

I began with high hopes. Information about Dionysus was plentiful. I knew him as the god of wine. Dimly, I recalled that Greek theater grew from primeval rites devoted to his worship. And since our own theater came directly from the Greek forms, very nearly all our popular entertainments flowed from the same ancient source.

I learned a little more from my researches. According to legend, the Amazons, those doughty female warriors who removed their left breasts to better wield a bow, followed him. For a time they were his own personal army.

The facts were interesting, but they helped me not one jot. I learned that Dionysus was indeed god of wine, ecstasy, drama, and battle. He epitomized all forms of emotional excess. He seemed to exercise a particular fascination for women. I shuddered as I remembered the sight of Justine Luce on Cairo's arm.

Story after story was the same. Mortals pitted themselves against him only to go down in utter defeat. Not even one tale showed Dionysus being bested.

In desperation I turned to his chief rival, Apollo. All I could discover was that this god presided over order and reason, medicine, and music. How could these attributes possibly help us? I was no closer to solving Cairo's riddle than when I started.

My restless eyes strayed from the white and gold decorations on the papier-maché dome of the ceiling down to the lines of desks that radiated out from the center of the room like spokes of a wheel. All was quiet save for the rustle of pages and the occasional soft clearing of a throat. But for how long? It was only a matter of time before Dionysus' influence made itself felt, even in this bastion of civilization.

With an increased sense of urgency, I delved into my few remaining sources. I verified that the details Cairo had given us were essentially accurate. Dionysus was indeed called the "twice-born." The Titans had devoured him and their bodies had been reduced to ashes, from which was formed the race of Man. But his heart had been the chief ingredient in a love potion fed to a woman who subsequently gave birth to him.

All at once, I came across a tantalizing clue. King Perseus waged war against Dionysus. The god punished him by driving the women of his kingdom mad. Only when the repentant king built a temple in the god's honor did the violence cease.

Here was something—a man had actually won, if not a victory, at least an uneasy truce with the god. Unfortunately, the discovery did little to elevate my spirits. I was well-to-do, but I had nowhere near the means to erect such a structure.

On second thought, perhaps I was being too literal. Ancient myths often masked their insights by means of metaphor.

Primitive peoples saw vegetation die off in the winter and miraculously come back to life in the spring. Each culture embodied this wonder in the story of a god who died and was resurrected. The Egyptians had Osiris, the Roman soldiers had Mithras. Even Jesus Himself could be seen as a manifestation of this universal story.

Looked at this way, "built a temple to Dionysus" might not mean an actual structure. It could refer to some purely symbolic act. But what? I turned to the other books for clues. Once more I was disappointed. Not one of the volumes shed any light on what the word "temple" might be a code for.

A shadow fell across my open copy of *Apollodorus, Volume I.* I looked up to see Houdini standing by my shoulder.

"You done?" he asked lowly.

I nodded grimly.

"Got anything?" he asked.

I shook my head. "Nothing that will help us."

"I was afraid it was a waste of time." Houdini's voice rose. "And we don't have time to waste."

Heads around us were raised. The clerk at the central desk arose from his chair, stepped down from the dais, and walked purposefully toward us. I led Houdini from the room.

As we descended the broad steps in front of the museum's Ionic colonnade, I asked, "Has something happened?"

"It's Bess," he responded unhappily. "She won't leave."

I could scarcely believe my ears. "You explained the danger?"

"I did everything but pack her bags for her. No soap. She says if I'm in trouble, she stays. Just in case there's some way she can help."

We made our way down to Great Russell Street. "Perhaps if I were to speak with her . . ." I offered.

Houdini shook his head. "When her mind's made up, it's made up," he said.

"Then you must stay away from her at all costs."

"Don't I know it," he agreed. "I never thought I'd say it, but I wish she wasn't so loyal." He looked at me with something akin to desperation in his eyes. "What if that thing hurts her?" His face darkened. "We have to get Cairo. The quicker the better."

My mouth went dry. The blood pounded in my throat.

There was no mistaking my companion's grim meaning. We would have to put my plan into operation after all.

I breathed in the crisp air of the fine autumn weather. The trees on Bloomsbury's broad avenues and elegant Georgian squares were just losing their foliage. Pale yellow and brown leaves lay scattered over the pavement and parks. All around I heard shouts of laughter and murmured conversations. I wished with all my heart I could simply enjoy the day. But the entire scene was rendered fearful by the specter of the task that awaited us.

Houdini drew my attention with a grunt. He shook himself all over like a terrier arising from a nap. He looked up at me. "Ready to start?"

Before I could answer, my ears were assailed by shrill cries. Voices howled with pain and anguish. They appeared to come from Russell Square to the north. The sounds swelled until it seemed that dozens of people were being tortured. My companion and I looked at each other and without a word raced toward the cacophony.

Chapter 34
The Caress of the God

When we reached Russell Square, a scene of madness greeted us. Someone had unlocked the wrought iron gate that excluded entrance to all but residents. It swung loosely on its hinges. We entered cautiously. I saw at a glance that I had mistaken the sounds I'd heard.

A doctor witnesses many strange things in the course of his practice. But in all my years, I had never observed such a sight. We had stumbled upon an orgy on a vast scale. People ripped off their clothes. They tore at the clothing of anyone near to hand. The dying grass of the shady lawns was awash with a mass of bare flesh. Moist tongues thrust and private parts flailed. Here a stout nanny hiked her black skirt up around her hips and coupled with a man who looked for all the world like a university professor. There, beneath a broad plane tree, an elderly lady wrapped her aged legs around the flanks of a young tradesman.

People from all walks of life copulated without regard for propriety or station. White thighs flashed in the morning light. Bare buttocks bucked and heaved. Hands clenched at exposed flesh. Grunts and sighs pierced the air. The bodies were so closely packed that it was impossible to tell where one grouping stopped and another began. Two women on one man, two men on one woman, men with men, women with women—the combinations surged and re-formed on the lawns. They spilled over into the brown canes of the autumn rose beds. The scene was a nightmare of grunts and squeals. The musky smell of rutting bodies was almost overpowering.

With horror, I felt a fullness in my loins that warned my own body was responding to the primitive call. Was I once more succumbing to the god?

One of the men rolled off his partner and took no heed for the state of his revealed manhood. He lay panting beside the woman—a busty, young flower girl. She lolled her head about and noticed us. A slow smile crept across her features. Lazily, she motioned us forward. "Here, now. Let's see if one of you can go better than what old Tom did," she called.

I could not take my eyes off her pale thighs as they parted invitingly. I found myself taking a step forward. With a surge of will, I wrenched my gaze away. I forced my unwilling feet back a step, then another. Grabbing my companion's arm, I gasped, "Come away."

"Huh? Oh, yeah." Houdini flushed a deep red. We spun around and bolted off. The young woman's scornful laughter followed us.

We ran until the cries and groans had faded from our hearing. I was consumed with embarrassment. Clearly, Dionysus still had some power over me.

Our pace slackened. Neither one of us spoke for a long time. We passed Bloomsbury Street and Tottenham Court Road. The appearance of French and Italian restaurants around us signaled our approach to the exotic Soho district. I looked about apprehensively but saw no evidence of extraordinary behavior in the crowd of foreigners around us. Houdini evidently could keep his thoughts to himself no longer.

"What was that?" he asked.

"I fear we have once more witnessed the influence of Dionysus," I answered. "It is spreading, just as Cairo said it would."

Houdini halted. "You're saying that guy was being straight with us?"

"What other explanation is there?"

"I don't know—maybe something in the water . . ." His voice trailed off.

Despite our experiences last night and this morning, I almost smiled.

He must have read my expression, for he sighed. "All right, all right, I know." He spread his hands in a forlorn gesture. "Say he's for real. Where does that get us?"

I considered. Pale intimations drifted through my mind, like faint lights glimpsed through heavy fog. Around me smells of garlic and exotic spices drifted from the open restaurant doors. Workmen, shop girls, and well-to-do matrons eddied around us. Their shoes clattered, clumped, and scraped along the pavement as they made for their luncheons. Why did the madness strike some and pass others by?

"We have seen upper-class dinner parties and working-class ghettos equally affected," I mused aloud. "The god clearly is undeterred by education, refinement of mind, or social status."

"Maybe it goes after people with no willpower," Houdini contributed.

"But you and I both have strong wills," I countered, "or we should not have risen to the heights of two highly competitive professions."

"So it only attacks people with strong wills?" Houdini demanded in frustration.

"No. It affected Mackleston strongly. I scarcely consider his an indomitable personality."

Houdini flung up his hands. "We're right back where we started."

Finally, the dim idea that had flitted around the back of my mind came to the fore. "There is something in the physical world that acts in the same way," I said, excitement mounting.

"What?"

"Mr. Marconi's radio waves. They radiate invisibly and penetrate all strata of society. Anyone with an appropriate receiver can pick them up."

Houdini looked interested. "What kinda receiver you talking about?"

"Artists—creative people and those with intense or unstable personalities. They function as better 'listening devices,' if you will."

Houdini nodded thoughtfully.

"If I am right, once you have been infected by Dionysus, you also become a transmitter. As more people are influenced, the signal will grow stronger and stronger until every single person in the world will be contaminated."

He took hold of my coat sleeve. "Maybe we should get our families away somewhere safe—until this thing, whatever it is, works itself out."

"Where? It will soon be universal. Consider the appalling deeds that will occur." My imagination ran wild. "People will commit acts of violence over something as trivial as a sporting event."

Houdini grew thoughtful. His hand fell away from my garment.

"No segment of society is proof against this infection," I continued. "Think what might happen when the plague reaches the highest levels of government."

He frowned in consternation.

"Imagine," I urged, "lunacy on a global scale. Countries will find themselves immersed in war before they realize what has happened—the whole world swept up in a global conflict. Soldiers will savage helpless populations. Why, the world could lose an entire generation."

I looked around at the shoppers hurrying by us, the

workmen on their way to their next job, the children swinging on a lamppost down the street. I tried to picture the street empty of them—all gone in a fury of bloodlust.

Houdini pursed his lips as he pondered my words.

"And you mustn't forget," I added, "we also carry the infection. Wherever we go, we spread it."

His hand rose to his mouth in horror. One agonized word issued forth. "Bess!"

I nodded soberly. "All our loved ones are in jeopardy."

Houdini clenched his fists. "We have to put the quits to it."

He talked on, but I wasn't listening. I pondered Cairo's riddle. Dionysus was in only one of us, yet in all of us. I thought of the legend—how Dionysus' ashes had formed the race of Man. How he had been reborn himself, and how his influence resembled a radio-wave transmission.

"That's it!" I exclaimed.

Houdini stared at me. "What's it?"

"The answer to Cairo's riddle."

"You figured it out? Tell me!"

I recalled how my companion had teased me when he'd solved the killer's escape. That still rankled a bit. Desperate as our situation was, I could not resist paying him back in kind.

"Just wait," I said. "You'll see."

Houdini jammed his hands on his hips in exasperation. "What kinda deal is this?" he demanded. "We got serious—"

He stopped in midsentence. Evidently, he realized that I had merely repeated his own words to him. "A taste of my own medicine, huh?" he asked. "Okay, okay. I guess I deserve it." He looked at me grimly. "But I hope you know what you're doing."

A short cab ride took us to the Palace Theatre, where Houdini retrieved his lock picks and scooped up an electric torch. Then we set out. I had the driver drop us off a couple of streets away so the noise of the cab would not give away our arrival. As we made our way toward Cairo's house, I told my companion, "After I have entered, wait a good five minutes."

When we reached the right street, we parted company. Houdini hung back and I continued on alone. It was now midafternoon. The sun was still high in the sky. My footsteps sounded forlorn to me as I clumped over the stones of the street. At Cairo's door I paused and looked back. Houdini shifted nervously from foot to foot. He lifted his arms over his head, clasped one fist in his other hand, and silently shook them at me. I waved back, smiling bleakly at his little encouragement. Summoning all my courage, I knocked upon the door.

As I waited for an answer, the pilasters on either side of the portal seemed to glare back at me sullenly. A minute passed. No one responded. I knocked again, harder. Still no answer. A wild hope began to grow in my breast. I pounded on the panels of the door until the sound of my blows echoed off the brick fronts of the houses across the street. There was dead silence from within. I turned to gesture to Houdini and found him already racing up the street to meet me.

"Can you believe it?" he panted when he arrived. "Nobody's home."

He produced two slim pieces of metal from his pocket and knelt down in front of the door. Thank God he had come prepared. I turned around and examined the street. So far we had it to ourselves. Houdini inserted the tools into the lock of Cairo's door. His face grew hard with concentration. He manipulated his implements delicately, like a surgeon wielding a scalpel.

"Cairo might return at any moment," I cautioned.

"Don't I know it," Houdini replied without looking up from his task. "This is a real good lock. Better even than the ones in jails."

I positioned myself as best I could to screen his actions from casual passersby. I held my breath. A faint click drew my attention. I snatched a glance, but still he labored on.

I heard a faint call. Down the street a Hokey Pokey seller pushed his ice-cream cart toward us and chanted his singsong cry:

Hokey Pokey, penny a lump;
That's the stuff to make you jump.

A doorway opened and three small children spilled out. Soon they were joined by their mother. Houdini continued to tinker with the lock. More house doors opened as the seller slowly pushed his hand truck toward us. When he'd gathered a crowd, he stopped to make his sales. One child tugged at her mother's dress and pointed in our direction. The mother ignored her for the moment, but the child persisted. I glanced back at Houdini in time to hear another click. He yanked down on one of his tools. The lock turned and the door swung silently inward. We hurried inside, pushing it shut behind us.

We found ourselves standing on the blue and tan Oriental rug in the small entryway. All was silent. We stepped into the hallway that ran along the left side of the building. Dust motes drifted in shafts of sun from the fanlight over the door. Our previous visits had been at night and the hallway had not been lit, so this was the first real look I had got of the passage. A strange gallery of figures decorated the white plaster walls. Most were a foot high or less and sat on shelves jutting out from the wall. Other, larger ones sat on the smooth oak planks of the floor itself.

One of the statuettes I recognized right away. Anubis, jackal-headed Egyptian god of the dead, stood at eye level opposite me on the wall. A few of the images obviously came from sub-Saharan Africa, but the majority were unknown to me. They ranged from primitively carved wood to the most delicately tooled marble. Some were feathered or bejeweled. One Buddha appeared to have been carved from a single, foot-high crimson gem.

We stood in the midst of foreign gods—no doubt souvenirs of Cairo's travels. I could not help but wonder what bizarre rites these icons had witnessed. Did any of them figure in the loathsome rituals Cairo himself held behind these walls?

Houdini spared the figures but a cursory glance. "If we split up," he whispered, "we can search faster."

I shook off the eerie feeling that threatened to overwhelm me. "We can also be trapped more easily," I replied softly. "I believe one should search and the other keep watch."

"Good idea," Houdini nodded. "First off, we have to find out if this place has a back door—so we can get out quick if we have to."

We crept along the hallway, past a stairway on our left that led to the upper floors. The closed doors of the study and the séance room lay to our right. At the rear of the house was Cairo's small kitchen. As we had hoped, a back doorway gave out onto the alley behind the house.

"Okay," Houdini said, rubbing his hands. "Where do we start?"

Haste was essential; Cairo could return at any moment.

"Since we're here," I suggested, "let's search the cellar where he held the ritual."

Fortunately, the door to Cairo's "Holy of Holies" was unlocked. Houdini lit his electric torch. We descended the stone steps and looked around. The tiny room was completely bare. Even so, the dank stones brought back unsettling memories.

"Now what?" Houdini asked.

"Let's try to locate the hidden room Cairo disappeared into on the night of the séance," I said. I could not bring myself to speak above a whisper. "It would make a perfect hiding place."

"Good idea," Houdini agreed softly.

Accordingly, we returned up the steps and tiptoed to the door of the séance room. As we passed the foot of the stairs, I heard something that sent a chill down my spine.

It was a muffled groan. We both froze. Was Cairo still in the house? The noise came from upstairs. I heard the sound again, this time louder. There were no words, only an inarticulate moan—a soul in torment. After a pause, the sounds continued, muted as if from behind a closed door. They came in short bursts. Higher and higher they rose. The hairs on the back of my neck rose with them.

All the rumors of Cairo's dreadful rituals came back to me. Was he sacrificing a poor innocent in some nameless rite? The cries conjured up visions of hideous torture. Houdini and I stared at each other in wild surmise. Despite my fear of Cairo, I could not allow such torment to continue. With one accord we charged up the steps. The sounds, now almost shrieks, came from the door to Cairo's bedchamber. We thundered over to it. The shrieks merged into one long howl that I feared was a death agony.

The door handle yielded to my frantic twist and the door itself swung open. We burst into the room. The scream blasted our ears.

What I saw is forever burned in my memory. On the floor was Justine Luce, naked, on her hands and knees. From her mouth were wrenched the cries we had heard. Her eyes clenched shut, her face was contorted—but not in pain. No, for on his knees behind her loomed a nude Maximillian Cairo. One hand clutched at her thigh, the other reached around to plunge into the shadows of her nethermost femininity. Sweat glistened along his muscular shoulders and powerful arms. His chest heaved from the exertions of servicing her in his vile, abnormal way.

Cairo looked up at our arrival but did not pause in his rhythmic motions. Rather, he increased their tempo as he stared, with a triumphant smile, directly into my eyes. We stood as rabbits hypnotized by a snake. The woman gave a final wail of fulfillment and Cairo ceased his movements. She collapsed sideways onto the floor. Her bosoms heaved as she drew a series of long, shuddering breaths. At last, she lifted her head. Her eyes slowly opened and came to rest on me.

"Oh, my God!" she exclaimed, and buried her head in her arms. Cairo wiped the sweat off his brow with the back of his hand. A wicked grin twisted his features.

"Gentlemen," he panted. "How may I be of service?"

Chapter 35
Cairo Produces an Alibi

The woman began to weep softly. As we stared, dumb with shock, Cairo rose and snatched a pale green silk dressing gown off the dark four-poster bed behind him. He dropped it carelessly over her prone form. His well-muscled body still gleamed with the dew of his exertions.

"Allow me a moment to attire myself more conventionally. Then I shall receive you downstairs in the library."

It took a moment for his words to sink in. Annoyance flickered across his face. "Downstairs, gentlemen," he insisted, taking a step toward us across his thick burgundy carpet.

That broke the spell. Blushing furiously, we backed out of the room. Before I closed the door, he added, "Should you chance upon Mr. Gaylord, send him up."

He jerked the door from my hand and slammed it shut. I felt like a schoolboy who had just endured a visit to the headmaster.

We made our way downstairs without speaking. On the first floor, I felt myself redden once more at what I had witnessed. I remembered Miss Luce's confession to me outside her office. Evidently, the influence of Dionysus was too powerful for her to fight off every time.

"What are we going to do now?" Houdini whispered hoarsely.

"I am afraid there is nothing for it but to make ourselves comfortable until Cairo joins us."

He looked doubtful. "I don't like the idea of sitting around and waiting for him."

I could not have agreed more. Truly, I had no wish to face the man—or Miss Luce, for that matter. But it was clear where my duty lay.

"Cairo promised he would help us if we solved his riddle. I intend to hold him to his word." I wished my voice were steadier as I spoke.

The door to the library was unlocked. I trudged inside; Houdini followed. A couple of gas sconces gave a dim light. My companion muttered something about a "last chance," but I was not paying attention.

Clearing a chair of its books, I collapsed into it with scarcely a glance about me. That appalling scene upstairs kept repeating itself in my head. The sheer animalism of their coupling left me shaken. I had thought Cairo shared Mackleston's proclivities. Clearly, he cared not where he took his pleasures.

I recalled Miss Luce's soft touch, her forthright manner. How could any woman of sensibility sink to such degeneracy—and with such a one as Cairo?

Or were more subtle forces at work here? Perhaps she was not herself. I recalled the orgy in Russell Square we had witnessed. By God, that was it! She must still be under the sway of Dionysus, even as I had been. Perhaps her sex did not fight off this influence as rapidly as mine. It was the only explanation possible. Nothing but the grip of a mad frenzy could drive a decent woman to such acts. Cairo was exploiting her vulnerable condition.

The heat of anger suffused my face. He would pay dearly for taking advantage of her. I did not know how, but I swore I would see to it.

A faint tinkling sound across the room drew my attention. To my dismay, I saw Houdini on his knees, picking the lock of the séance room door.

"For God's sake!" I started to my feet.

He glanced at me. "Don't worry. The condition that guy's in, he'll take his time getting down here." He returned to his work. His tools clinked in the lock. "We find the painting, we don't have to hang around and face him."

"But we don't know that it is in there," I protested.

"This is the only locked door we've found," Houdini replied. "I'm going with the odds."

I understood his desperation. I was not looking forward to the encounter with Cairo. I glanced toward the door of the study. How long would we be alone?

"Come away," I whispered urgently.

With a click the séance door swung open, revealing a dark, empty room beyond. Houdini grinned. "Inside doors are a cinch," he said. He was rising to his feet when a haughty voice sounded behind us.

"Really, is there no limit to your trespasses?" At the words we spun around to see Cairo standing in the doorway. He wore a lemon-colored silk dressing gown with black embroidery around the hem and cuffs. He was still barefoot.

For once, Houdini was speechless. He stood sheepishly beside the open door.

"At least now I know how you gained entry to my home," Cairo observed.

What could I say? My brain scrambled for an explanation. Mr. Gaylord had left the front door unlocked and—No, it was no use. No excuse would serve.

Strange to say, I felt a sense of freedom. If no excuse was possible, I need not attempt one. Another thought struck me. Cairo had not so much as mentioned summoning the authorities. No doubt he had his own reasons for avoiding official notice. A bold front might just win through. I drew myself up and took a deep breath.

"I have solved your riddle," I announced. I held my breath and waited for his response.

"Have you, indeed?" Cairo sauntered across to the room's blue and white tiled fireplace. He threw himself down on the armchair beside it. Smoothing the yellow folds of his dressing gown across his thigh, he murmured, "I shiver with anticipation."

I glanced at Houdini, who stood by the open door of the séance room. Cairo's back was to him. Houdini lifted his brows and cocked his head toward the dark, beckoning space beyond. My God, I thought, he intends to search the room under Cairo's very nose. I looked to Cairo. His attention remained fixed on his own lap. My eyes flicked back to my companion. Almost imperceptibly, I shook my head. My lips formed the silent word *no*.

My eyes remained on Houdini as I spoke to Cairo. "On the night of the ritual, you said that Dionysus had lodged inside one of our party."

With relief I saw that Houdini had not moved to enter the room. I looked to Cairo. He gave no sign of having heard me. "The riddle," I continued, "was that though he inhabited only one of us, you swore he was in all of us, as well."

Cairo inclined his head ever so slightly.

"According to the myth, Dionysus was eaten by the Titans, who were jealous of him. Zeus blasted them to ashes and brewed a love potion from his heart. This he had given to a mortal woman. Nine months later, she was delivered of Dionysus—his second birth."

"So much I have told you," Cairo reminded me acidly.

His smugness nettled me. "The solution is elementary," I said airily. "The ashes, harboring his essence, were used to create the race of Man."

Cairo lifted his head and stared straight at me. I could not read the expression in his eyes, but I carried on.

"Therefore, every human contains a bit of Dionysus. The god ignites his dormant part within them, much as a cold, charred log will glow anew when a flaming brand is brought near."

Cairo slumped back in his chair. "You have it," he said in surprise. "You actually have it. I misjudged you, Conan Doyle. I never dreamed you would solve my little puzzle."

Now was the time to strike. "Then help us rid London of this menace."

He sat upright. "Menace? You still think him a menace?"

"How else would you characterize a being that visits madness upon the population and bids fair to destroy civilization itself?"

He dismissed my words with a wave of his hand. "Fool. You are not worthy of the gift you have been given."

I summoned all my courage. "You made me a promise. I expect you to keep it."

He looked at me. I braced myself for an attack, but none came. Instead, he craned his neck to look behind him. "Where is your partner in crime?" he inquired mildly.

Startled, I looked around. Houdini was nowhere in sight. With an inward groan, I realized he had sneaked into Cairo's séance room after all.

An unpleasant mirth lit Cairo's eyes. "Shall we find him?"

He rose from his chair and led the way through the yawning door. I followed unhappily.

Inside the dark room I caught a glimmer of light in one corner. To my dismay, Houdini emerged from the secret room. His electric torchlight played about the séance room and happened to catch me in its beam. "False alarm." He sounded disappointed. "The painting's not in there."

"What?" Cairo's voice exploded behind me. He pushed past us and into the secret room. A volley of oaths trailed behind him. A moment later, he emerged. Houdini's torch lit a face suffused with rage. He advanced upon my companion. "What have you done with it, you little thief?"

Houdini backed up a step. "I told you, it wasn't there."

Cairo stood where he was and fixed Houdini with a stare. In the torchlight I saw my companion's face turn white. He gasped for breath.

"Where is it?" Cairo demanded.

"Haven't . . . seen it," Houdini choked. The torch dropped from his fingers and clattered to the floor. As it rolled, its light threw crazy shadows on the walls around us.

I could only imagine what hideous torment Cairo was inflicting upon my companion. In the dim, indirect light I made out that Houdini's eyes were closed and he swayed on his feet. His hands clawed at his chest. The only sound was his gasping for breath.

"Release him." My voice rang out in the quiet room. I have no idea how I found the courage to speak. "Do you think you can cover up one murder by adding another to your roster?"

Cairo faced me. "Another murder?" Hatred had transformed his face into a snarl that was less than human. I stood my ground, but the hairs all over my body stiffened. Were we about to face the demon again?

In a flash I realized how bad our position was. No one knew we had come here. Why had we not gone to the police with our deductions? I cursed the false pride that had dared us to keep this information to ourselves. We might well pay for our vanity with our lives.

Our only hope was a bluff. I prayed I had the fortitude to carry it off.

"It's over, Cairo." I spoke as boldly as I could. "We know everything—and so does Inspector Woburn of Scotland Yard." I anxiously awaited his response.

"And just what is it you all think you know?"

The malevolent gleam in his eyes made my heart sink, but I plunged ahead. "You've all but admitted you had the painting—the one that disappeared from the murder site."

Houdini staggered upright. "You had to be in that room," he gasped.

Cairo retrieved Houdini's torch from the floor and

shined it directly into my eyes. I squinted and brought up my hand to shield my face. The murderer took a step toward me, then another. I moved to the side, but the light followed me. I spoke hurriedly. "The police know you came in with Mackleston. They know you escaped disguised as a chimney sweep." I prayed my voice did not give away that I was dissembling.

Abruptly, the light switched off and darkness surrounded me. I was blinded and felt utterly vulnerable. Cairo drew so close I could hear his breathing.

"The landlady can identify you." I flung up an arm in defense. My hand encountered nothing but empty air. I fairly shouted at him, "If we disappear, you are the first suspect."

To my surprise, Cairo's footsteps continued into the study. Had my bluff worked? Groping, I found Houdini's arm. "Are you all right?"

He grunted his assent. "I felt his . . . his . . . hand," he gasped, "his icy hand . . . on my heart. He was squeezing it. Trying to stop it from beating."

"Can you walk?" I asked.

Houdini nodded. "Let's get out of here," he said shakily.

I wholeheartedly shared his desire. It had been madness to break in. "He's waiting for us in the study," I whispered. "It is our only way out."

In the darkness I felt rather than saw Houdini straighten up. "Let's get it over with."

We staggered through the doorway. After the utter darkness, my eyes watered in the dim gaslight. I wiped them with my sleeve. When they cleared, I saw the man leaning against his fireplace. He seemed in control of himself once more. He regarded us coldly.

"My property is missing," he began.

I braced myself as his eyes found mine, but I felt no attack, psychic or otherwise.

"You tell me you don't have it. Yet you have virtually admitted that you broke in to steal it." His gaze left me and traveled to Houdini. "What am I to make of this?"

I could not think of a thing to say.

Beside me Houdini glared back defiantly. "If we had got it, we sure wouldn't wait around to run into you." His voice was a little stronger now.

Cairo lifted a finger to his lips and pressed on them thoughtfully. "Oddly enough, I am inclined to believe you."

His gaze turned inward. He was silent a moment. Questions swirled inside my brain. Was this all an act for our benefit? No, his surprise and anger had been genuine. Someone had indeed stolen the painting from this house. But who? And why?

Cairo gathered his lemon dressing gown more tightly about him. "You say the police know all your suspicions. If this is true, why have I not been arrested?" I felt skewered on his gaze. "Why have they not searched my house?"

It was a telling question. How could I answer it? "I said I informed them." I tried to assume a stiffness of manner. "I did not say they believed me."

"But if anything happens to us, this is the first place they'll look," Houdini put in.

A wisp of a smile played across Cairo's lips. "And that's why you came here? To find proof that I killed Reggie." Then he threw his head back and laughed. "How delicious!"

Houdini and I looked at each other. Had his contact with Dionysus unhinged his reason? His laughter died. "I must decide what is best to do," he mused aloud. "I can't have you going around accusing me of murder."

Cairo pushed himself off the mantel. Houdini and I instinctively raised our fists in a futile attempt at defense. Cairo's attack, I was sure, would not come on the physical plane. To my surprise, he ignored both of us and walked to the room's doorway. Through it I could see the flight of steps leading up to his bedchamber.

He called out the door, "Justine, dear, will you join us for a moment?"

"There is no need to bring Miss Luce into this matter," I said shortly.

"Oh, I very much fear you are wrong."

The woman must have been waiting at the top of the stairs, for she descended immediately. She was clothed in the pale green silk dressing gown he had tossed over her body. Somewhere she had found matching slippers. Her eyes were cast down. Even so, I could scarcely bear to look at her. Whether the humiliation I felt was for her or for myself, I could not have told you. In any event, she bore no sign of Dionysian possession now. She held her hands folded demurely at her waist; she did not look up or speak.

Cairo turned his attention to me again. "What day was Reginald murdered?" he inquired.

"Sunday last," I replied, "roughly at around five in the afternoon."

"Justine, where was I Sunday afternoon?"

"You were here," she said softly. The woman still refused to look up.

"And how do you know this?"

Her response was muted. "Because I was with you."

"For how long?"

"All day."

"In fact, you stayed the night, didn't you?"

"Yes." The words came in a low monotone, as though rehearsed.

I could stand no more. "Miss Luce!" I expostulated. "Think what you're doing. You are shielding a murderer."

My words broke through whatever reserve had held her. Slowly she raised her head. Her eyes blazed with indecipherable emotion.

"He's not a murderer, you great bloody fool!" She shrieked with such vehemence that I backed up a step. "He never left the house."

Cairo smiled thinly at me. "Ah, a woman in love. So volatile."

His words cut me to the quick. In that instant, she shot

him an indescribable look. Love, hate, gratitude, and despair all mingled in her eyes. Her hands flew to her face to hide the tears that coursed down her cheeks.

A great sadness welled up within my breast. In the battle for her soul, Cairo had won. The poor girl was completely under his spell. More than that, she was tormented by her helplessness. And we were as far from knowing the truth about his actions as ever.

"Leave us, Justine," Cairo said gently. To his credit, there was no triumph in his voice.

As I watched her trudge out the door, I grew hot with anger once more. Cairo was using that poor, innocent girl to sate his base appetites and escape a murder charge. She lacked the will to resist him.

But I did not. My wrath gave me courage beyond all bounds of sense. Houdini and I were still in his power. At the very least, he could have us arrested. But what he had done to Miss Luce blinded me to all danger.

I found myself blurting out words before I knew what I was saying. "We had a bargain, Cairo," I spat. "Now keep your pledge. Or are you as careless with your promises as you are with lives?"

Chapter 36
Unexpected Help

For a moment the man was struck dumb. He struggled to master his emotions. I met his gaze steadily. Do your worst, I thought. We shall see who leaves this room alive.

It was Houdini who spoke first. "Forget it, Conan Doyle. He's not going to help." My companion's voice was nearly like its normal self. He turned to Cairo. "You win." He shrugged. "You got an alibi for Reggie's murder and we got no proof. Just let us go."

"Not yet, I think."

Cairo's words, spoken so casually, hung in the air. He moved toward us. I shifted my weight onto the balls of my feet, determined to charge him, whatever the price.

Houdini broke the silence. "Don't even think about it," he warned Cairo. "We're two of the most famous guys in the world. We disappear and you're in big trouble."

The man's response was curiously mild. "You misunderstand. I have no intention of harming you."

I was surprised at the conciliatory look on his face. "You mustn't leave before we discuss how I am to help."

I did not let down my guard. "You agree to rid the earth of this demon?"

Cairo winced at the word "demon." "I suppose so. At first it was fun. But, really, things have gone too far. And you must believe me—I had no hand in Reggie's death."

What game was he playing now? Houdini evidently shared my skepticism. He stood, arms akimbo. "You didn't, huh?"

"No. Why should I?"

It was true we had not discovered a motive. But that proved nothing. "If the god had driven you mad, you would not need a reason."

Cairo sighed. From his expression we were trying his patience. "Have you learned nothing about him? He brings forth only what is already within you—as your own analogy of the glowing log so aptly showed. 'Though this be madness, yet there is method in't.'"

Could he be right? Each violent act we had witnessed—had it been merely an expression of a deeply buried desire? Memory of my own shameful attack upon Touie bubbled up within me. My God, were we all savages underneath the thin veneer of civilization? I sank down into a chair.

Cairo interrupted my thoughts. "If you want someone with a motive, interrogate Mrs. Pangbourne."

"Mrs. Pangbourne?" The very thought was outrageous.

"Yes. Reggie talked Mr. Pangbourne into backing a business venture." Cairo strolled over to his armchair, seated himself comfortably, and crossed his legs. "Reggie pulled out before the company collapsed, but Mr. Pangbourne lost thousands of pounds. Imagine the emotions of his widow—entirely dependent upon her husband's much-diminished fortune. That's why she has to sell her property in Brighton, you know. She can barely afford to keep up her London house."

Houdini folded his arms across his chest. "How do you know this?" he demanded.

"Young Mackleston, of course. We were close at one time. Quite close."

I ignored his indecent insinuation. "You don't expect us to believe that monster is Mrs. Pangbourne."

"I cannot say. All I know for certain is that it is one of your party."

I recalled the horrible way Sir William's daughter had been used by Reggie. He and Mrs. Pangbourne and Mackleston each had a motive to kill the man. Only Miss Luce and Cairo had none. Was it possible I had misjudged the man in front of us?

Houdini brought me back to the present. "If you don't know who Dionysus is inhabiting, how you can send him back to where he came from?" he demanded.

Cairo interlaced his fingers and stretched them over his head. "That's why I shall need your help," he admitted.

"What help?" I demanded.

"You must contact everyone who was at the séance. Tell them to assemble tonight at the murder site."

"Wait a minute," Houdini said. "You want us all at Mackleston's flat in Soho?"

Cairo nodded. "It's where Dionysus made his strongest manifestation. It will be easiest to recall him there."

"We do not want to recall him!" I expostulated. "We want rid of him."

"Yes," Cairo said with the attitude of one explaining long division to a slow child, "but I must get him to show himself first, mustn't I? Unless, of course, you are prepared to murder every single member of your party and kill yourselves when you've finished."

I glared at him in outrage. We were fighting for humanity itself and he sat there mocking us. "Really, Cairo—"

"Oh, I don't recommend that solution," he said soothingly. "But it is an alternative. No host, no Dionysus. No Dionysus, no more intoxicating influences on humanity." He spread his hands. "C'est fini."

"You said everyone had to be there," Houdini said. "Mackleston, too?"

"Of course. Dionysus could be in any one of you."

"But Mackleston is in gaol," I reminded him.

"I've told you what I need. It is up to you to accomplish it." He grabbed the arms of his chair and pushed himself upright.

Did he really expect us to attempt a gaol-break? Houdini threw his hands in the air. "You're asking the impossible!"

"A few weeks ago, you'd have said it was impossible to summon a Greek god," he replied.

I regarded the man. He smiled blandly from one of us to the other. What game was he playing now? To test him, I offered a suggestion. "What about building him a temple?"

Cairo blinked. "Build a temple? Where did you get that idea?"

"Through my researches. King Perseus won a truce with the god by building a temple in his honor."

"You have been busy," Cairo said, and sighed. "And how do you propose we do such a thing?"

"I do not know," I admitted. "I assume it refers to some symbolic act."

Cairo smiled. Strange to say, he looked almost rueful. "You continue to surprise me, Conan Doyle," he admitted. "Why, you scarcely need my help at all."

"Don't play with us, Cairo," Houdini growled.

Cairo smiled indulgently at Houdini before he faced me again. "Yes, building a temple to Dionysus will allow humanity to coexist with him. But that's not what you want, is it? You want him gone."

Reluctantly, I acknowledged his logic with a nod.

"Very well, then." Cairo rose. He gathered his pale dressing gown about him and strode to the door of the library. "I have extensive preparations to make. But I shall meet you at Mackleston's flat at midnight."

It was useless to prolong this interview. I got to my feet.

"What if we can't get Mackleston?" Houdini asked.

"Then the entire world will go mad." Cairo spoke lightly, as if predicting rain for tomorrow. With that, he nodded to us and left the library.

"Aren't we leading all those people into trouble?" Houdini called after him. "Won't your ritual be dangerous?"

Cairo poked his head back into the room, an exasperated look on his face. "My dear conjurer, we propose to summon the god of passion and madness. Then we shall attempt to banish him from the world where he's been having so much fun. Do you suppose he will go without a struggle?"

Outside Cairo's house the sun was low in the sky. It bathed the shabby buildings around us in an orange light. The street vendors were all gone, and the other denizens evidently did not come out until dark. We had the pavement to ourselves. Except for the odd wagon rattling by, there was scarcely even any traffic. I set a brisk pace west down Phoenix Road. Cairo's behavior pointed to one inescapable conclusion.

Houdini was furious as he stomped along beside me. "Break Mackleston out of jail," he railed. "Who does he think we are, Jesse James?"

"Oh, he does not expect us to succeed," I said.

Houdini stopped up short. He looked at me in surprise.

"Suppose," I said, pausing as well, "we try to sneak Mackleston past the authorities. What happens?"

"We get caught and put in jail ourselves," Houdini answered.

"Precisely. And thus we are neatly disposed of without Cairo's having to lift a finger." I continued walking.

Houdini hurried to catch up. "He was lying the whole time."

"I expect so," I said. "We were lucky to get out alive."

Houdini rubbed his chest, no doubt remembering the pain he had endured. "Don't I know it. Why didn't he finish us off?"

"It must have something to do with Mackleston's painting," I replied. "Did you note how frightened and angry he was when it turned up missing?"

"Yeah," Houdini agreed. "It has to reveal something. When he figured out we didn't have it, he pretended to help us. Why?"

"To put us off our guard," I replied.

"Why?" Houdini repeated.

I could only shake my head. "He is playing a deep game."

We had to face the truth, bleak though it was. Cairo was a ruthless murderer, and he had the might of Dionysus behind him. Our one hope to prove it—finding Mackleston's painting—had failed us.

"However are we to vanquish such a being?" I felt something akin to despair. "It has cunning, overwhelming strength, and powers we can only guess at."

"Get rid of Cairo and we get rid of it," Houdini made a gun with his hand and forefinger. He pulled an imaginary trigger.

Could I murder a man in cold blood—even to save lives? I was not sure. "Suppose we do kill him. The creature might well leap to another host," I said. "You or I would be the nearest to hand."

"Oh, jeez," Houdini said. "Hadn't thought of that." He relapsed into a brooding silence.

I looked up at the dingy brown bricks of the houses we passed. I had the uneasy feeling of being watched. I caught Houdini scanning the tiled roofs above us, as well.

"You feel it too?" I asked lowly.

He shivered as if with the cold. "Yeah. Let's get out of here."

We picked up our pace. I couldn't stop glancing behind me. I was unpleasantly reminded of our last mad dash through these very streets. All at once, Houdini clutched at my coat sleeve. "There!" His index finger stabbed at a third-story rooftop over my right shoulder.

I spun around to look. I could have sworn something flitted behind a chimney. The glare of the setting sun made a clear view impossible. But the thought of what might be following us chilled me to the bone. I thought I heard a faint scrabbling overhead—as of claws on roof tiles. With one accord we took off at a run.

Neither of us spoke until we reached Eversholt Street and merged into the crowd around Euston Station. Instinctively, I made my way to the majestic Doric arch at the station's front. We sought the shelter of one of its four pairs of massive limestone columns. Here we tarried a moment to catch our breaths. At least in the open area in front of the station we could see what was coming.

"You think we lost it?" Houdini panted, as he scrutinized the bustling crowds around us.

I canvassed the throng for any sign of the beast. "I hope so," I said doubtfully.

As the moments passed and no stubbly, lank figure burst from the multitudes, I felt more at ease.

"What are we going to do now?" Houdini asked.

I had been considering that very question. "I believe we should continue on the trail of the missing painting."

"How? Even Cairo doesn't know where it's gone."

I moved closer to my companion and lowered my voice. "We must ask ourselves who has access to the secret room—aside from Cairo himself and Miss Luce."

Houdini's face lit up. "Gaylord!"

I looked around to see if anyone was paying attention to our conversation. None of the travelers who shoved past us showed the slightest interest. "Just so," I agreed softly. "He is one of Cairo's intimates."

"But why would he take it?"

I considered. "Perhaps he has grown to fear Cairo as much as we do."

"Maybe," Houdini conceded. "Or else he's jealous of Cairo's affair with Miss Luce."

I cringed inside at this reference to the scene of passion we had so unwillingly witnessed.

"But I don't see how knowing this helps us," Houdini continued.

I put aside the debasing memory and posed Houdini a question. "If you had stolen the painting, what would you do with it?"

He shrugged. "Give it to the police?"

"Perhaps. But, remember, they believe they already have their killer. Are they likely to welcome evidence that would threaten their case?"

"You're right," Houdini agreed. "And who'd believe that story, anyway?"

"Who, indeed?" I said. "He would have to find someone who had actually seen the beast."

"Somebody like us!" Houdini reached up and grabbed my lapels. "He'd contact us."

"I hope so." I gently removed his hands. "We might well be his only hope to fight the creature. I should not be surprised if a message from Gaylord awaits us at our hotel."

I noted an ominous aspect to our cab ride west to our hotel. Small knots of people had gathered on street corners and muttered among themselves. Each group eyed the others suspiciously. Occasionally, voices were raised in taunts or threats.

Is it starting? I wondered. Has Dionysus taken hold of the general populace? But we had more immediate worries. Throughout the drive my partner's glance darted from building top to building top, as if searching for a sniper. His knee bounced up and down with nervous tension. Nor could I shake the feeling that we were still being watched. At several points on the journey, I leaned out my own window and scanned the roofs of the shops we passed. Once I caught sight of a shadowy form, but it could have been a flock of pigeons settling down to roost. In any case, we soon pulled up at the two-story stone arches that surrounded the entry to the Langham.

I led the way into the lobby. We entered between the sandstone columns and crossed the white marble floor with its red carpets. A right turn at the palm court took us to the reception desk.

I sensed a flurry of movement behind me. "Conan Doyle," a voice called urgently.

I turned to see Gaylord stagger over to us.

Chapter 37
Trapped!

"Thank God," Gaylord said breathlessly. "I've been waiting in the bar for hours."

From the smell on his breath, he was not exaggerating. I took his arm and steered him toward the palm court, out of earshot of the people at the desk. Houdini followed closely.

Gaylord was scarcely recognizable. Gone was the black attire from head to toe. In its stead he wore a tweed suit with a brown patterned tie. His thinness was not so pronounced as I recalled. Evidently, his emaciated look had been helped along by clever stage makeup. In normal clothing he seemed an unremarkable young man with short, dark hair and a nervous manner.

My companion could not contain himself. "You got the painting?" he blurted out.

Gaylord nodded. His pale face was even whiter than usual. "I don't know what to do." On closer inspection, I saw blue-black circles under his eyes. "It's been horrible," he added.

"What's been horrible?" I demanded.

Gaylord's encampment at the hotel bar must have muddled his thinking. He scarcely seemed to hear me. "You won't believe it." He raised his long, slim fingers to his mouth. "I can hardly believe it myself."

I realized that his hands were empty. "Where is the painting?"

Gaylord gave a start as a uniformed bellman approached the desk. "Not here," he begged.

I led him toward the lift. He kept looking back at the bellman, who appeared oblivious to the scrutiny. It was the same fellow who'd brought tea the day Miss Luce had visited me.

"What is it?" I asked. Gaylord threw another glance over his shoulder. "That man." He indicated the bellman with a nod. "He's one of Cairo's."

The lift doors opened and the three of us crowded inside. "One of Cairo's?" I repeated as the lift door closed.

"A spy," Houdini explained as the lift rose. "The big-time mediums pay a guy in each major hotel to keep his eyes and ears open."

We arrived at our floor and the doors slid open. As we hurried down the hall, Houdini added, "They go after unhappy servants, too."

"Cairo does this?" I asked Gaylord.

"He has sources all over town," the man confessed.

This revelation started a train of thought as I unlocked my door.

"That's how they come up with their 'miraculous' knowledge," Houdini added. "You'd be surprised what you can find out by listening at doorways."

The others entered, but I stood, overwhelmed by a revelation. "That would explain the wire!" I blurted out.

"What wire?" Houdini asked.

"The one Cairo sent. You remember—the day we all met to discuss strategy."

"Oh, yeah—the one where he called you an old goat."

I blushed at the memory. "The servant must have listened though the closed door," I explained hastily, "and—er—misconstrued what went on between Miss Luce and me."

"Sure," Houdini agreed easily. He turned to Gaylord. "Cairo got a telephone?"

"Yes, of course." Gaylord put his hands on his hips. "Probably the only one in the neighborhood."

"There you go," Houdini said. "The spy races to the hotel phone and feeds Cairo the information while your guests show up. Cairo runs out and sends us a telegram before everybody leaves. No magic, see?"

I was shaken at such a simple explanation.

Houdini addressed Gaylord again. "Let's get down to brass tacks. Where's the painting?"

Gaylord clutched his arms to his chest. "Close the door," he pleaded.

I did so and locked it. But first I checked to make sure the hallway was empty.

"It's cold," Gaylord complained, hugging himself even more tightly.

"The maid must've left a window open," Houdini said. "Now, quit stalling. Where's the painting?"

Gaylord leaned toward us. He weaved a bit on his feet. "I hid it in Mackleston's flat."

"Where the murder was committed?" I realized I had inadvertently lowered my voice. We three huddled closely in my drawing room. Our shoes made a shallow nest of crushed pile on the thick red and blue patterned carpet.

Gaylord nodded. "He'll never look for it there."

"How'd you get in?" Houdini asked suspiciously.

"Cairo had a key. Here." He dug into a coat pocket. The man shivered as he handed me the large brass key. "I never want to see the inside of that room again." He pulled his coat closer about him.

"Cairo had a key to Mackleston's flat?" I repeated.

"So that's how he got in." Houdini slapped his thigh in disgust.

"Not if Mackleston had thrown the bolt from the inside," I reminded him.

"Oh, yeah." Houdini looked disappointed.

"Why did you take the painting?" I asked Gaylord suspiciously. Cairo might have sent him over to dupe us. As fast as Dionysus' influence was spreading, we couldn't afford a false lead.

A hint of pain glimmered in Gaylord's eyes. "He's leaving tonight. And he's taking that woman with him."

Houdini shot me a significant look. "No wonder he wants us out of the way."

"And you were not invited," I finished for him.

"He doesn't even know I overheard their plans." Gaylord's sadness deepened. "I thought he loved me. Or, rather, I didn't," the man corrected himself. "I wasn't quite that stupid. But I thought he cared enough at least to say good-bye."

"Where is he going?"

"Italy. I found a map in his bedchamber. But he won't leave without the painting."

"Why is he running away?" Houdini wanted to know.

"Don't you see?" Gaylord said impatiently. "Flight is his only recourse. He's tried to dispose of you once and failed. You're too close to the truth."

"What is the truth?" I demanded.

"I'm not sure." Gaylord slowly shook his head from side to side. "When I first met Max, I thought all his occult trappings were just an act. To keep the money coming in, you see. But now . . ." Wonder filled his voice. "I don't know if I can believe my own eyes."

He clutched at my arm. "There's something you must understand: He's a master hypnotist."

"Hah!" Houdini cried. "I thought so."

There was genuine fear on Gaylord's face. "He's so good at it, he can put people under with just the rhythms of his voice."

"What about suggestions?" Houdini interrupted. "You know, after he's put you under? Can he do those?"

The man nodded. "He's brilliant at them. He can make you remember things that never happened."

Houdini and I stood silently a moment as we digested this information. "My God." Houdini turned to me. "You see what this means? The monster, the people going crazy around us—maybe it's all an illusion."

My very soul rebelled against the suggestion. "The policeman was dead," I asserted. "Woburn's visit this morning proved it."

"If Woburn was really there," Houdini said. "What if he was a figment, too?"

I was staggered. Surely it couldn't be true. But a voice in the back of my mind whispered, *All madmen believe their hallucinations.*

I felt dizzy. What could I be sure of? Was Gaylord really standing here? Were we really at the hotel? After all, there were madmen who wandered the halls of their asylums convinced they trod the Palace at Versailles or a savage jungle.

My thoughts began spinning out of control. I had tried to murder my wife. Had that been the beginning of my madness? Perhaps even now I lay comatose in a small, dingy room in an asylum, spiraling ever deeper into fantasies of fear and danger.

A prosaic comment from Gaylord pulled me out of my maelstrom. "It's really cold," he complained. "Couldn't you find that window and shut it?"

Illusion or not, the temperature was beginning to bother me too. The cold air seemed to come from my bedchamber. I made for the door.

Behind me, I heard Houdini ask Gaylord, "Does Cairo ever use drugs on his clients?"

Gaylord answered, "Oh, yes. Something he gets from South America."

I entered my bedchamber. The window was indeed open. I took a step to shut it.

"I knew it," Houdini cackled. "The wine we drank at the ritual. Was it—"

I heard no more. For at that moment I saw what crouched behind the door. It was the dreadful beast that had attacked us.

I froze. Hissing at me, the creature rose to its feet. I stood rooted to the spot between it and the door. We stood face-to-face. The bristle of hairs over its body stuck out like quills. Its face was almost foxlike, with sharp bones and slanted eyes. Its foul breath brought a scent of rotting flesh. But the most horrible aspect was the malignant intelligence behind its green eyes. It saw my fear and reveled in it. A hideous smile lifted its features into a leer that was a dreadful mockery of human expression.

"Look out!" I shouted. The creature gave a yowl and launched itself forward. I hit the floor with a thud that knocked the wind out of me. I had a confused impression of a weight on my chest. Claws like thorns pierced my belly right through my clothing. Then it was gone. The thing had literally run right over me.

Shouts issued from the drawing room. I lurched to my feet and staggered through the doorway.

I shall never forget the sight. Gaylord stood nose to nose with the beast. Houdini lay stunned against the wall, where he had evidently been flung. Gaylord lifted his hands—but whether as a plea or a defense, I shall never know. The creature became a burst of shredding talons. Its howls of angry glee nearly drowned out its victim's shrill cries. It flayed at the poor man's body with its claws. It dug bloody talons into his chest and raked upward with the claws on its feet. It slashed him to ribbons. When Gaylord's body slumped to the ground, the beast followed it down, pulling and twisting. In my nightmares I still hear the dreadful cracking as joints gave way. Fountains of blood arced and sprayed.

At last the creature stood over the poor lumps of bloody meat that had been Gaylord. It lifted its head and looked at me. I stared directly into its emerald-green eyes and again saw hatred. It took a step toward me.

Its gaze enveloped me. I should have been horrified. I

suppose some part of me was. But at that moment what I felt mostly was a fascination—no, almost an awe—for the sheer power of the beast.

I had hunted; I had felt the triumph of besting an adversary on the playing field. Here in the pools of blood on the floor was the wellspring of all sport—glorying in power over your prey. And the only power that truly mattered was the power of life and death.

In that moment I understood the emotions that had driven our primitive ancestors to human sacrifice. I also felt the ecstasy of the victim. I was powerless before this creature. But more than that, I yearned for that force, to merge with it. Only one way could I be a part of its hideous strength. I dropped to my knees in supplication and waited.

The creature paused in its advance. I heard a commotion outside the door. Footsteps pounded down the hall. Shouts sounded. The beast glanced around, then leaped clear over my kneeling body and into the bedchamber. I heard it scrabble up the sill of the open window just as the door burst open and Inspector Woburn lumbered into the room.

Chapter 38
Arrested

Woburn recoiled at the sight I presented. "Dear God," he whispered.

Cries of despair and horror burst from the two constables behind him. I looked around. Gaylord's remains lay before me. I knelt in a pool of his blood. Somehow my hands and my clothes had become stained with it. I was unable to move or speak. I scarcely knew where I was.

Houdini staggered to his feet and slumped against the wall. He held his head in his hands. His shirtfront was stippled with gore. Slowly, he raised his eyes and took in the sight before him. "Oh, no," he moaned.

Woburn lurched forward. I felt myself roughly grabbed. They hauled me to my feet. Each constable clutched one of my arms.

"What kind of a thing are you?" Woburn hissed in my face.

I could not speak.

Woburn gestured and the constables heaved me toward the door. I stumbled and would have fallen had their grip on me not been so tight.

Woburn's voice followed me. "You have some fancy theory to explain this away?"

What could I say? I felt irredeemably vile. I had not committed the violence, but I'd worshiped at the feet of the creature that had.

"Cuff him." There was distaste and horror in Woburn's voice.

I was in a daze. I scarcely felt it as the two men yanked my hands behind me and shackled them with black iron gyves.

"I'll get his partner," Woburn growled.

He manhandled Houdini around and tore off his coat. My companion was too stunned to protest. I watched, my arms pinioned behind me, as the men expertly patted Houdini down. When they were finished, Woburn grunted in satisfaction. "No hidden keys on this one," he announced. All three of them avoided looking at Gaylord's remains.

Under their rough treatment, Houdini came to his senses. "You're making a mistake," he protested. "The thing's getting away!"

"The thing?" Woburn said with a leer. "Oh no, nothin's getting away from me."

I finally began to gather my wits. "What are you doing here?" I asked.

"We had a visit from a friend of yours. Gent named Cairo. He said Gaylord admitted to seeing you leave Mackleston's flat after the murder. The man had swore to come here and confront you. Mr. Cairo was quite worried over his friend's safety."

Woburn glowered at me. "If Cairo'd told me ten minutes sooner, we could have saved that poor devil's life."

"Cairo!" Houdini spat out the word. He looked at me. "He set us up good, didn't he?"

"None of that," Woburn said savagely. "You two are alone here. The corpse is still warm. You're for it, gentlemen. You have an appointment with Miss Hemp."

Houdini spoke. "You have to believe us. There was a

creature here. It knocked me out and . . ." his gaze strayed toward the remains of poor Gaylord, "did that."

One of the constables, the large, beefy one, cleared his throat. "We 'aven't searched the rooms, sir," he pointed out.

Woburn stared at the man like he wanted to throttle him. But the inspector's voice was controlled. "Very well," he said. "We'll make sure there's no accomplice hidin'."

So saying, they went through my rooms thoroughly.

"We didn't do this," Houdini called out to them. "Look at that body. How could we? How could anything human?"

None of the men deigned to answer.

They returned shortly and Woburn thrust his face next to mine. His jowls quivered with emotion. "You're alone in here. I suppose you're goin' to tell us this monster of yours jumped out the window and flew away."

"He didn't fly," Houdini corrected the man sullenly. "He climbed down the wall."

"Of course he did," Woburn said in mock sympathy. "Let's go."

"At least check the sill for smears of blood," I begged.

Woburn ignored me and pushed us out the door. We found ourselves surrounded by a crowd of curious hotel residents. No doubt they had been drawn by the screams. Woburn left one constable to control them. He and the other officer then hurried us along the hall, down the lift, and through the luxurious lobby. Heads turned and I heard our names whispered as the men thrust us out into the night. A police van waited in front of the columns that flanked the Langham doorway.

As a constable unlocked the rear door of the van, I turned to Woburn. "Please," I begged, "you must listen. The real murderer, Maximillian Cairo, plans to flee the country."

The inspector paused in his progress toward the van and relaxed his hold on my sleeve slightly. Encouraged, I continued. "At the murder site is a clue—Mackleston's painting, the one that disappeared. That poor devil in there"—I nodded my head back over my shoulder toward the Langham—"came to tell us where he hid it."

Woburn's eyes narrowed as he listened. They almost disappeared into the folds of flesh of his cheeks. I went on desperately. "I honestly do not know what is on the canvas, but it is enough to kill a man for. Please take us there. I am sure it will clarify the whole mystery. If it does not, I shall come along without another word, I swear."

Woburn planted his fists on his huge hips and rocked back on his heels. "Sir Arthur," he said. "This week I've seen an orgy of crime—public indecency, robbery, fathers beatin' daughters, women attackin' men. It's as if the devil himself was loose. And it gets worse every day."

His voice rose. "Prisons are full; police stations are stuffed to burstin'. Only orders from Downing Street has kept it out of the papers. And you want me to take time out to help you cobble together an alibi."

He leaned forward and bellowed into my face. "I saw you kneelin' in that poor devil's blood. Your fame won't save you now. The government has granted us special powers until the crisis is over. By God, I'll enjoy exercisin' them on you."

With that he and his constable shoved us into the waiting police van. It was an ancient vehicle that should have been retired years ago. Its wheels sagged outward sadly and the side panels were warped.

The two men slammed us down onto the hard wooden benches. The constable climbed up front and took the reins while Woburn locked the rickety back doors. He lowered himself to the bench opposite us and glowered as the van lurched off.

Far away I heard shouts and the crash of breaking windows. Riots had started. Woburn hunched lower on his bench. "Mad. They're all going mad," he muttered to himself.

We rode on in silence. The close atmosphere smelled of old sweat. If the madness had spread as far as Woburn said, could anyone stop it? The van creaked and swayed on its worn-out springs. Houdini and I were constantly thrown against each other and had to struggle to right ourselves without the use of our hands.

During one of these lurches Houdini whispered to me, "We have to get away. This road—it goes past the Palace Theatre, doesn't it?"

Looking out through the tiny barred window in the rear door, I caught sight of the Whitefield Tabernacle Church in the electric streetlights. I realized we were headed down Tottenham Court road. "Yes," I breathed.

Houdini nodded imperceptibly. "It's a long shot," he muttered. "But I have to try." Then he righted himself. His lips barely moved as he said, "Tell me when we're close."

"No talkin', you two," Woburn grunted across from us.

I had no idea what my companion was planning, but our situation was desperate. We had to get to Mackleston's flat and find the painting. If Cairo wanted it so badly, it might hold a clue as to how to defeat him and prove our innocence. At the very least, it would be a bargaining chip to force him to banish the demon from our midst. When we passed New Oxford Street, I nudged Houdini with my elbow.

To my surprise, he started laughing. "What are we worried about?" he said. "This isn't real. We're still under Cairo's suggestion. It's all a . . . a whatchamacallit. A figment."

"I warned you, no talkin'," Woburn growled.

Houdini ignored the man. "He can't hurt us," he giggled. "He's part of the figment." And he began to laugh even harder.

Woburn pushed himself to his feet and staggered over to Houdini. I looked on in alarm. Did Houdini know what a dangerous game he played?

Woburn raised his pudgy hand to deal my companion a blow. The laughter died on Houdini's lips. He curled up in fear, knees tucked into his chest.

Just then, the van jigged again and Houdini shot his legs straight out in front of him. Woburn staggered back. His great bulk hit the frail rear doors with a slam. They burst open. With a bellow Woburn clutched at the sides of the van and frantically tried to regain his balance. At his cry, the wagon lurched to a stop. Houdini leaped to his feet and charged like a bull. His lowered head took Woburn right in the waistcoat, and the two men pitched backward over the edge. They landed in the street. I sprang up and ran to the open door. Woburn lay gasping on the macadam. Houdini struggled to his feet and raced for the theater. Craning up to look, I saw the constable drop his reins and leap from his perch.

I spied Houdini's destination. He headed straight for the bootblack who had directed me to the gypsies yesterday. The youth again played with the deck of cards Houdini had given him. The boy looked up in openmouthed astonishment. What a sight it was—the great magician, hands manacled behind him, racing with an angry constable in pursuit. When Houdini reached the boy, the magician turned to offer his trouser pocket to the lad. The boy reached in and dug out every farthing my friend had. Houdini gasped out only a few words before the constable was on him.

He grabbed Houdini's collar and yanked it across his throat, then dragged the magician, gasping and choking, to the van. I heard Houdini wheeze over his shoulder: "Get Bess. Tell her, 'Remember Moscow.'"

The boy hesitated only a moment before he took off at a dead run.

By this time Woburn had regained his feet. His face was suffused with crimson as the constable hauled my friend up. The two men thrust Houdini back inside the van. He tumbled to the floor in a heap and gasped to get his breath back. I saw a rough, red band of skin across his throat where the constable had collared him. As Houdini struggled to his knees, they climbed in after him. Between the two of them, they tore his clothes right off his back.

"That ought to hold you," Woburn muttered as he pulled the doors shut.

Then they threw Houdini back down to the floor. He hit the boards with a thud and the men began kicking him. He tried to protect himself by curling into a ball with his cuffed hands sticking out behind him. He grunted as their boots struck him.

I sprang from my seat. "Stop!" I shouted. Though my hands also were pinioned, I threw myself at the constable. We fetched up in a heap against the far wall. He swung an elbow that knocked me to the floor. I landed heavily on the wooden boards beside Houdini.

My head throbbed from the blow. I felt the splintery wood against my cheek. At any moment I expected to feel their boots slam into my body.

The two men stood panting over us. The constable grabbed my collar and hauled me back onto the bench. I coughed and gasped for breath. The man grabbed Houdini under the arms and heaved him up beside me. The bench rocked as my friend's body landed beside me. A rivulet of blood trickled from Houdini's forehead and down his cheek. His left eye was swelling shut.

"Give it up," Woburn said. "Where you're goin' there's no rescue."

The constable left without a word to climb aboard the driver's seat. Woburn threw himself down on the bench opposite us. He panted from his exertions and avoided my gaze. We started off again. Houdini's labored breathing slowly returned to some semblance of normalcy. I did not dare speak. But it was clear to me that Dionysus' influence had spread to the police.

Eventually, the van slowed to a stop. Woburn opened the back. As the doors swung wide, I saw we had pulled up at the grim stones of Holloway Prison. Evidently, this was what Woburn had meant by the government giving him "special powers." We were to be imprisoned without a trial or even formal charges being filed.

Woburn and the constable hauled Houdini to his feet. They half carried, half dragged his naked body through the doors of the prison. I followed.

The Chief Warder greeted Woburn without a word. He was a tall, slim man. In his black suit and mournful demeanor, he looked like a mortician. If he recognized me from my previous visits, he gave no sign. The man tossed a set of keys to the inspector and wandered back to wherever he had come from. There was no attempt to take our names or assign us a cell. Should something untoward happen to us in here, no one would be any the wiser.

Woburn led us through the double glass doors and back into the cells. It was a scene of madness. Prisoners were crammed two, three, even four to a cell. Some of the men pounded on the walls of their tiny rooms. Others fought until all parties fell to the floor from sheer exhaustion. The air was rife with yells and groans. Interspersed among the cries of rage were the unmistakable sighs and moans of passion. As we staggered down the hall, I stared straight ahead. I had no desire to witness such scenes. The air was humid and rank from the exertions of anger and lust.

Arms reached through the small, barred windows at us. Houdini walked under his own power now. His eyes had swollen nearly shut. The men hooted and made obscene offers when they caught sight of his nakedness. One prisoner managed to grab hold of my hair. Woburn ignored it all. With my hands still cuffed, I had to lunge and twist to get away.

Eventually, Woburn paused at a cell door and unlocked it. He turned just long enough to grin at me. I could only wonder at the sort of company we were to join. What would be our reception? Woburn opened the door and thrust Houdini inside. I followed cautiously.

The small white room had only one other occupant. With great surprise, I recognized Mackleston. He rose from his cot in astonishment.

"That's right," Woburn said. "You fiends can share a cell. With any luck, you'll tear each other apart before mornin'. And I won't have to clear a space in the docket." So saying, he slammed the door shut and I heard the key turn in the lock.

Chapter 39
An Angel of Mercy

Houdini and I were still helpless with our hands manacled behind our backs.

"Our handcuffs," I called after Woburn. There was no answer, except for a few mocking calls from men down the hall. "Our handcuffs, our handcuffs," I heard repeated with much rough laughter.

With some trepidation, I faced Mackleston. Had he, too, gone mad? We were totally at the mercy of whatever use he cared to make of our bodies.

I turned to see him gently easing Houdini down upon the small cot against the far wall of the cell. Mackleston's face was filled with concern. "Those brutes," he muttered. I was instantly ashamed of my fears. There was nothing but sympathy in his bearing.

"I'm okay," Houdini insisted through his bruised lips.

"You're the doctor," Mackleston addressed me. "What can we do for him?"

With my hands cuffed, I could do little more than look Houdini over. The injuries to his face and head appeared superficial. The kicks, I recalled, had been aimed at his midsection. I leaned over and listened at his chest. His breathing sounded normal. At least he didn't have a collapsed lung. I straightened up and instructed Mackleston how to feel for broken ribs. Houdini winced once or twice under the pressure of Mackleston's fingers but did not appear to be in great pain.

"I shan't be able to say for certain until the swelling goes down," I said. "But it appears that none of them are broken." I addressed Houdini. "Spit on the floor."

"What?"

"Just do as I say. And be sure you miss the rug."

He sighed and complied. I leaned over and looked at his sputum upon the pale stone. The saliva was clear. "There's no sign of blood, so perhaps you have escaped internal injuries, as well," I said.

"Yeah, I'm tough," Houdini responded with a rueful smile.

"What on earth has happened to you?" Mackleston asked, eyeing my blood-spattered clothing.

Briefly, I recounted our adventures since we had met Gaylord at our hotel.

"Poor Gaylord." Mackleston shook his head.

"That Cairo," Houdini said through clenched teeth. "He figured Gaylord would try to get ahold of us. But how did he know it would be in your hotel?"

"He didn't," I replied. "Remember our nervousness after leaving his house? He was following us as the beast. When we met Gaylord, he fled to the police, resumed his human form, and delivered his warning to them. Then he raced back as the creature and timed his attack just before they arrived."

"You mean we led him straight to Gaylord?" Houdini looked stricken.

"I am afraid so." How could I have been such a dupe? We ought to have sequestered Gaylord. But where? Was there a safe haven in a world gone insane?

Despair threatened to overwhelm me. Civilization itself

was falling apart, the beast was on the loose, and we were trapped in prison.

I regarded Mackleston. If we were to witness the collapse of civilization, at least I would know the truth. "We have told you everything. Now it's time you were frank with us."

"What do you mean?" His expression was innocence itself.

"Your memory of the murder returned. Several days ago," I said bluntly. "Tell us exactly what you saw."

"No, I say—" he protested.

"Come, come," I cut him off. "How else could you have known that Reggie wore a new suit the day he died?"

Mackleston's face went blank in surprise. After a moment, he set his chin defiantly and looked at the wall over my head.

"We know Cairo came to see you," Houdini contributed.

Mackleston's face was rigid as he stood up and walked the three short steps to the door of the cell. The man stood looking out the window. The bars cast vertical shadows down his face.

"He threatened you with something," I said. "Something that frightened you into silence. Tell us!"

Mackleston remained silent.

"You saw Cairo change into the beast, did you not?" I prompted.

The man bowed his head. The shadows wavered and flowed along the contours of his cheek. "I'm sorry. I just can't."

"He's running away. To Italy," Houdini said. "And he's dragging Miss Luce with him."

"Don't you see?" I implored. "It's not only for our sakes, but for Miss Luce's as well. You called her your friend. You can't want her in that devil's power!"

Mackleston spun around. His face was filled with misery. "I can't. I gave my word."

I could scarcely believe my ears. "He has murdered

twice and contrived to have us blamed for his crimes. Surely you can no longer protect him."

The man would only shake his head. "I can't explain. I'm sorry. Please, don't ask again."

I was speechless. To continue shielding such a one was beyond comprehension.

"Ah, forget it," Houdini said. "Whatever he saw, it won't help us fight that thing."

"He's right," Mackleston confirmed. "I swear it."

His sincerity was palpable, and I had run out of ideas. I sank down on the cot beside Houdini. "It looks as though we're up against it," I admitted.

"I know." He writhed to find a more comfortable position. "We'll hang just on Woburn's testimony."

"If enough civilization remains to hold a trial," I replied gloomily. "By tomorrow all of humanity may well perish in a squealing orgy of violence."

No one said another word. It was only a matter of time until the guards themselves went totally mad. They might begin killing prisoners. Or perhaps they would flee to join the throngs in the streets and leave us to starve.

Houdini wriggled around on the cot to face Mackleston. "I have to tell you," he said, "one thing still bothers me. Why would Cairo go nuts at the sight of Reggie? He must've had a reason."

Mackleston turned to face us and lounged against the wall. Oddly enough, a wistful smile lit his features for a moment as he looked down at Houdini. "As it happens," he admitted, "you're right. Max had a reason to hate Reggie."

"You might as well tell us," I said. Further knowledge could not possibly help us now. Even so, I was curious to learn the genesis of all this havoc.

Mackleston strolled over and settled himself comfortably on the cot beside Houdini. "Cairo and Reggie were at Eton together," he said, crossing one leg over the other. "When Reggie was in sixth form, Max was his fag. I believe Max developed an attachment to Reggie. One of those schoolboy-crush things. I'll say this for Reggie: He was a good-looking devil."

Mackleston shook his head ruefully. "One day Reggie sent Max down to buy tobacco. That was strictly against the rules for a younger boy, but Max would have done anything for Reggie."

Mackleston's fingers plucked at the worn brown blanket as he continued. "Max returned to find the Assistant Master waiting in Reggie's rooms. Reggie was there and so were half a dozen of Reggie's friends. Max had been set up. Well, there he was, caught with the tobacco in his hand. The punishment for smoking was flogging. Reggie made him drop his trousers right then and there. Two of the older boys held him across a table. While the Master looked serenely on, Reggie gave him twelve strokes with a birch rod across his bare buttocks. Max told me they beat him till blood ran down his naked legs. All the while, the other boys laughed and made fun of his body. He hadn't yet developed sexually, you see."

Mackleston shook his head wearily. "Max never forgot the humiliation and he never forgave Reggie."

An old school hatred had triggered all this devastation? From such little seeds grow the tragedies of the world.

My ruminations were abruptly shattered by a commotion in the hall. Far off, I heard catcalls and whistles. The inmates were raising another howl. The sounds traveled from cell to cell, louder and louder. The voices grew more distinct. "Hey, darling," someone called. Another man made kissing sounds with his lips. Someone was approaching. Houdini's head came up, like a hound on a scent. The glitter of excitement in his good eye surprised me.

"Help me to my feet," he grunted.

Mackleston heaved him upright. Houdini tottered to the door. The window was too tall for him. He looked back at us. The cries had been taken up by the people in our wing.

A high, desperate voice called, "Harry, where are you?"

I recognized Bess's voice. How had she found us? What was she doing here?

"Hoist me up, boys," Houdini pleaded. His urgency forestalled further questions. Mackleston grabbed an arm and lifted. I got my shoulder under his naked backside and heaved with my legs.

"That's it, that's it," Houdini grunted. "Here, Bessie!" he shouted.

"Harry!" The voice was louder now. I heard the pounding of boots on the floor. By craning my neck up, I could just see out a corner of the window.

We waited. My legs trembled from supporting Houdini's weight. The door felt cold and rough through my tweed suit. Mackleston was panting.

"Just a little longer," Houdini implored.

Footsteps clattered up to the door. From the rumble of boots, a crowd of men was right on her tail. Voices called "Stop!" and "Get her!"

"Harry," the woman gasped.

Her face appeared at the bars. She must have leaped and grabbed for them. "I was afraid I guessed wrong. But from what the kid said, I figured this was the closest jail."

No further words were exchanged. Instead, through the bars the two engaged in a long, lingering kiss. Abruptly, Bess disappeared with a gasp.

My legs gave out. Houdini, Mackleston, and I tumbled to the floor in a heap. I heard a key turn in the lock. The door swung open and the Chief Warder appeared in the doorway. Behind him crowded half a dozen guards in their pale-gray uniforms.

I watched from the floor as two of them held Bess while the rest charged into the room. They dragged Houdini to his feet.

"What did she slip you?" the Warder demanded. He panted from the chase. His long, slim body was all elbows and knees, like a huge, dark insect looming over my companion.

Before Houdini could answer, one of the men wrapped an arm around Houdini's head and held it immobile. Another pinched his nose shut, while a third pulled down his jaw.

"Let him go." Bess struggled against the two men who held her.

The Warder ignored her and peered into Houdini's gaping mouth. Still not satisfied, the man jammed his slender fingers in. He rooted around, over and under Houdini's tongue. He went so deeply down the throat that Houdini choked.

The Warder pulled his fingers out and wiped them on his trousers. "All right, let him go," he said. "She didn't pass anything to him."

"Of course I didn't," Bess replied. She looked scornfully from one to the other of her captors. Her powder-blue walking dress was sadly wrinkled. "I just wanted to see my Harry." She spoke to Houdini. "Are you okay?"

"Yeah, I'm fine," he gasped.

She looked accusingly at the Warder. "He's hurt. Has he been seen by a doctor?"

"There hasn't been time," the man said.

"Why is he handcuffed in a cell? And what happened to his clothes?"

While they talked, Mackleston surreptitiously helped me to my feet.

The Warder shrugged. "You'll have to see Inspector Woburn as to that. He's taken a personal interest in the case."

"I most certainly will see him. What are they charged with?" she demanded.

"The Home Secretary has declared a national emergency. We're locking criminals up as fast as we can. We'll sort out the charges later."

"My husband isn't a criminal," she insisted. "I'll see the American Ambassador about this."

"Be my guest," the warder said. "He's in the next wing over."

Words failed her. I looked at Mackleston. His youthful face was impassive.

"When we get around to charging him," the Warder continued with obvious relish, "it'll be for assault, public fornication, and other things I can't describe in front of a lady."

Bess digested this bit of information, then resolutely faced her husband once more. "Harry, do you need anything?"

Houdini shook his head. "Go home, Bessie," he said. "Be careful on the streets and lock your door."

Bess said, "I can take care of myself." She spoke to her captors. "Kindly let go of me." The men looked to the Warder. When he nodded, they released her. She drew herself up to her full five-foot height, straightened her blue dress, and said calmly, "Harry, I'll see you in the morning."

With that, she turned on her heel and strode down the hall, pausing only to slap away a hand that reached through the bars at her. The warder looked down his beaklike nose at one of his guards. "Make sure she leaves the building," he said. The guard touched his finger to his hat and took off after her retreating figure.

"What a gal." Houdini laughed, then winced at the pain in his ribs.

The Warder faced us. "Laugh while you can. Tomorrow you hang at sunrise."

"But we've not even had a trial," I protested.

He glowered at me. "There's no time for trials. We're full up, and more coming in all the time. We've got to get rid of dozens of you to make room for the rest. I just got a wire from the Home Secretary ordering summary executions as long as the civil unrest continues. And damn if I don't think it's a good idea."

The Warder then slammed the wooden door shut and locked it. We heard his footsteps fade off down the hall.

Chapter 40
The Last Chance

I could not speak. Even Houdini looked shaken. It had finally happened. The influence of Dionysus had spread to the highest levels of government.

Houdini staggered over and sank down on the cot. I tried to shift the position of my arms behind me. My wrists and shoulders ached.

We had less than eight hours to live. I looked to Mackleston. He stared numbly at the stone floor. Here was the only one who had any idea what we were truly up against. He had seen our adversary change into the thing. And by his own admission he knew Cairo intimately.

"Mackleston," I entreated, "you see how desperate our situation is."

His face contorted in anguish. "Do you think I want to die?" It was as if the words were wrenched from him one by one. "Telling what I saw—it wouldn't help."

In my frustration, I blurted out, "At least tell us why Cairo visited you in gaol."

Mackleston heaved a resigned sigh. "He told me he had

contacts in the government. He swore to get me out and smuggle me to the continent if I kept quiet."

"Obviously, he has no intention of keeping his word," I pointed out.

Mackleston shrugged. "It doesn't matter."

Despite the hopelessness of our position, I couldn't give up. "Did he not say anything that might aid us?"

Mackleston grew thoughtful. "There was one curious thing. I asked him—wasn't there any way to lay the demon to rest?"

I hunched forward. "How did he respond?"

"He said the only way was to build a temple to it."

There it was again. I felt a thrill at hearing my own deduction confirmed.

"Yeah, fine," Houdini said. "But what's it mean?"

Mackleston shook his head. "He wouldn't explain. But he told me one other thing."

"What was that?" I enjoined him.

"He said that one of our party already had."

Houdini grimaced. "Oh, that's a big help."

I thought furiously. Obviously, Cairo was referring to some symbolic act. One of us had made peace with the god. But how? I ransacked my brain. The answer was so close. Which of our party had been unaffected by Dionysus?

Houdini interrupted my thoughts. "You were face-to-face with it," he reminded me. "Did you see anything, any weak spot?"

The very memory made my gorge rise. "No."

Houdini frowned. "I don't understand—it had us; we were defenseless. Why didn't it kill us too?"

"Cairo wanted us alive to take the blame for the murders," I replied.

"I guess that's right." He sounded disappointed.

Unwillingly, vivid memories of that event overwhelmed me. Again I stood in that dreadful room. Again I faced the thing over the shreds of Gaylord's body. I saw malevolence in its eyes as it took a step toward me. And then—

"That's it!" I exclaimed.

"What?" Houdini asked.

"I do remember something. After the beast destroyed Gaylord, it intended to attack me too. I saw the bloodlust in its eyes."

"The police showed up. They must've scared it away," Houdini asserted.

"It has murdered a policeman before," I pointed out excitedly.

"Then what stopped it?" he demanded.

I hesitated. I knew the answer. Moreover, I owed it to my comrades to reveal my deductions. But the words refused to come.

"Conan Doyle," Houdini pleaded with me. "If you know, you have to tell us. Before Bessie goes nuts, too."

He was right. I had to put aside my own shame and confess. Red-faced and halting, I began. I explained my emotions in facing the beast. I detailed the fear and exultation that had swept through me—sparing nothing. "It stopped," I explained, "when I went down on my knees before it. When I had acknowledged my kinship with it."

Houdini looked doubtful.

"Remember Cairo's riddle," I prompted. "We all share a spark of Dionysus within us. That is the truth behind the myth."

"Yes," Mackleston surged forward and sat next to me. "That would make sense. 'Build a temple' means to acknowledge the part of the god that is within you." His eyes were alight with comprehension. "Otherwise, it will overwhelm you—as it has with the beast."

I looked at him with a dawning respect. "It is you!" I said. "You are the one Cairo meant—you have built a temple to Dionysus."

He blinked at me.

"Consider," I urged. "You alone have been untouched by the madness that has swept through all of London. Houdini, even I, have both been caught up in it. You had your ecstatic experience, but you did not pay for it with an act of savagery."

"Oh, I say . . ." He dismissed my words with a wave of his hand.

Despite his protestation, I continued. "The beast did not attack you. You had earned your reprieve by accepting your true nature. You have faced your desires honestly. Therefore, you exist in harmony with them."

Mackleston dropped his gaze. His expression grew hooded.

"Let's say you're right," Houdini interjected. "Can you use it to beat that thing?"

"I believe so." Fear and hope mingled within my breast. "But only if I can come face-to-face with it once more."

Houdini looked appalled. "Are you sure?"

"No," I admitted.

Mackleston spoke soberly without looking up. "You'd be taking a dreadful chance."

"What choice have I?"

My companions fell silent. Houdini was the first to speak. "I think you're crazy. But count me in."

"Of course I'm with you," Mackleston chimed in.

I smiled warmly at them. With two such men at my side, I could face any fate.

"Oh, what are we saying?" Mackleston cried in frustration. "We're trapped in here."

"All we have to do is break out," Houdini said impatiently.

Mackleston laughed hollowly. "As if that were possible."

"As if?" Houdini repeated, anger flashing in his eyes. "You're talking to Houdini, kid!"

I stared incredulously at him. "Do you really think you can get us out?"

Houdini snapped his fingers behind his back. "Like that," he said.

"Then why haven't you?" Mackleston demanded.

" 'Cause there was no point," Houdini explained. "Till

we came up with a plan, we were safer behind bars than out on the streets."

"Then do so and hurry," I urged him.

"Okay," Houdini said. He squared his shoulders. "Both of you, close your eyes."

"What?" Mackleston asked, eyes wide.

"I have to use my best tricks." He shrugged. "Can't let anybody see."

Mackleston crossed his arms. "Am I hearing you right? The world is facing Armageddon and you're worried about us revealing your act?"

"Well . . ." Houdini looked embarrassed. "Yes," he finally admitted.

"Harry," I said gently, "we are about to plunge into mortal danger together. I think you might give us the benefit of the doubt."

His brow furrowed. He pursed his lips for a moment. "Okay," he said, and sighed. "But promise me you'll never ever tell anyone what you see here."

"I promise," I said.

"On your mother's life?"

"Yes, yes," I said impatiently.

"Say it," he demanded.

I groaned. "I promise on my mother's life."

"You, too," he said to Mackleston.

The young man rolled his eyes, but he, too, said, "I promise on my mother's life."

"Okay." Houdini's brow cleared. "Down to brass tacks."

He stood and backed up to the cell wall. "One thing about British handcuffs," he said as he angled his hips out. "If you hit 'em just right—" He whipped his arms against the wall. I heard a clatter and the cuffs fell off his wrists as if by magic. "—they pop open all by themselves."

Mackleston and I stood in openmouthed astonishment. Houdini swung his arms around a few times to limber them. Next he took hold of his cuffs by their connecting chain and spun me to face the wall. Out of the corner of my eye I saw his elbow cock back and whip around. There was a clang, I felt a jolt, and my wrists, too, were freed.

"But this is marvelous," I told him. My shoulders felt stiff. I worked them up and down with difficulty.

"That's nothing," he advised. "Watch this."

So saying, he plopped down on the cot and slumped forward. His stomach muscles contracted. In waves they traveled from his abdomen up to his throat. Houdini gagged. He choked and coughed. Finally, he gave a retching sound and spat into his hand. In his palm lay a slim metallic object. A pick.

In a flash, I understood. "Retroperistalsis," I said excitedly. "You can actually reverse the action of the muscles of your throat?"

"Yep." His voice was gravelly from the effort of bringing up the tool. "Learned it from a Japanese guy when I traveled with a circus."

He swallowed to soothe his throat. Then he dried the pick by wiping it on the brown drugget covering the floor. "I was just a kid. I used to tie a string around a piece of potato, swallow it, and practice pulling it up."

"Your wife passed it to you when she kissed you?" Mackleston guessed.

"That's it," Houdini agreed, clearing his throat. "Just like in Moscow. They had me locked in one of their big prisoner's wagons—the ones they sent people to Siberia in. They searched me too good and got all my picks. So Bessie came through for me, just like she did tonight."

He jumped up. "Enough gabbing." Houdini strode confidently to the door. He rubbed his hands briskly, no doubt to help his circulation. Delicately, he inserted the pick in the lock and worked it a few seconds. There was a click. The door swung open. Mackleston and I looked at each other, joy in our eyes.

But Houdini was not finished. He stepped outside and looked in at the next cell. I heard a startled cry and two rough faces vied for a place at the door's barred window.

"You want out too?" Houdini asked.

"Bloody right, I do," one of the man called.

"Please, gov'nor," the other entreated.

Down the hall, prisoners were beginning to realize something was up. I saw faces pressed to their bars and heard the mutter of conversation grow in volume.

"You want out, give me your clothes," Houdini demanded.

"You're crazy," the first man said.

"Mine! You can have mine," the other promised.

"Hand 'em over," Houdini demanded.

I heard a brief scuffling. A hand shoved a shirt and trousers through the bars. Houdini quickly donned them. They were too large, but he rolled up the pant legs. The belt was too long to buckle. He wrapped it around his waist, cinched in the pants, and tied a knot.

Good as his word, Houdini inserted the pick in the lock of the cell. In a trice he had the door open. Three men rushed out, one in only his smallclothes and shoes.

As they fled, Houdini tackled the rest of the locks in our wing. Evidently, he had divined their secret, for he raced from one to another, snapping them open with a flick of his wrist.

Soon the hall was filled with men dashing for freedom.

Houdini grabbed my arm and thrust me into the crowd. "Good camouflage," he said.

Mackleston followed us as we shoved our way into the center of the mass of fleeing men. Other prisoners bellowed and pleaded for freedom. Arms reached out to us. We ignored all and kept going.

The crowd bunched up ahead of us. I jolted to a stop against the man in front of me. The ruffians behind shoved and yelled. The crush of bodies made it difficult to breathe. I raised my head and saw the top of a door, evidently locked. The men groaned and cursed. Houdini, beside me, dropped to his knees. I feared he would be trampled, but he wiggled his way between the tangle of legs. In a few seconds, the door burst open and we all tumbled forward.

We landed in the central hallway. I scrambled to my feet with the others and we thundered down the wide corridor between its stone walls. Here we surprised one of the guards. He was a stocky young fellow and tried to raise an alarm, but went down in front of the tidal wave of humanity before he could so much as draw a weapon.

Several other guards came out from side corridors. Some laughed and cheered us on. Many were the worse for drink. A couple of them looked bruised and disheveled. Obviously, they'd been fighting.

Our feet pounded on the tiles of the hall as we surged through the inner gate, which had been abandoned. We passed the Porter's lodges, the gardens of the Governor's house, and pushed through the huge double glass doors. And so we burst onto Camden Road.

Free! The chill night air smelled of freshness and liberty. Crowds took no notice of us as they shoved past. The men dispersed into the night. I looked behind me. No one chased us—no one seemed to care. The poor guard who had been run down slowly dragged himself to his feet and limped off into the depths of the gaol. Houdini—in his bare feet—Mackleston, and I stood alone at the entrance to Holloway prison. I paused to look up at the sky. The stars glittered like tiny white beacons. Tonight would decide my fate and that of humanity. I looked around.

All London seemed to have gone mad. Couples fornicated in alleys or right out on the pavement. Fistfights arose spontaneously between crowds of people. Men swung their arms at one another like clubs. Cries of anger and desire filled the night. One young woman came at me, her white dress in tatters, lace hanging from her shoulder. Her face was twisted in savagery. She charged, her fingers crooked like claws. I threw my hands up to cover my face and leaped to one side. She stumbled past me into another crowd, where she clawed at anyone to hand.

Down the middle of the street surged a crowd of nude men and women. They chanted an incomprehensible rhyme over and over in singsong tones. Some clapped out a rhythm. All were dancing. People leaped in the air or spun around like dervishes. Many of them held tree branches, ripped no doubt from nearby Caledonian Park. Some used these to beat time. Others whipped themselves about their bare arms, thighs, backs, and buttocks until rivulets of blood dripped off their bodies and spotted the street. I heard cries of pain and ecstasy. The people around us greeted the passing throng with rapt expressions. They tore off their clothes and rushed to join it.

"Holy cow," Houdini said beside me. Mackleston stared, entranced. I would have made bet that his painter's eye was composing the scene for a canvas.

For a moment we three watched as the vast, obscene parade sang and gyrated and howled and flogged into the night. It left us alone on the street.

I was the first to come to my senses. "We must get to the flat."

"Why," Houdini demanded.

"The painting," I said. "I need it to verify my theory." What I did not want Mackleston to know was that I intended to use the painting as a lure.

Mackleston came to himself, reluctantly I thought. "I don't want to go back there."

I understood. He did not want us to see what he had painted. "Either you're with us or you're not," I said.

Mackleston chewed his lip and did not respond.

"You see a cab?" Houdini asked. We looked around.

"There!" I pointed to an abandoned vehicle. God alone knew where the driver had gone.

The horse shifted uneasily when it spied us. The animal's eyes were large and round. It ducked its head and danced from one side to another as we approached. Mackleston lifted his hand slowly. It tossed its head suspiciously, but his quiet words and gentle stroking soon calmed it.

"Can you drive that?" I asked, gesturing to the cab.

Mackleston looked from me to my companion. At last

he sighed. "I don't see why not. It can't be any harder than m'father's carriage."

I beamed at him. "Then make haste."

We all climbed aboard.

That ride through London streets was a nightmare. Some neighborhoods were deserted. Others were filled with frenzied people indulging in every excess imaginable. The repeated scenes of lust and violence eventually numbed me. I had lost all sense of shock or outrage. I leaned back in the seat and prayed that my deduction about the creature's weakness was right.

"Conan Doyle," Houdini said. I barely made out his silhouette beside me.

"Yes?"

"What if that thing is following us again?"

"I'm sure it is," I said. "In fact, that's what I am counting on." Cairo, I believed, would follow us in hopes we led him to the painting.

He opened his mouth to ask another question, but the sight ahead of us stopped him. We had caught up with the nude parade that had passed us outside the prison.

The throng of chanting, dancing flagellators had swollen to vast proportions. They filled the street in front of us. Some caught sight of our cab. With excited cries they rushed us. Hands grabbed our vehicle and heaved at it. All the while, the chanting continued. The cab rocked on its two wheels. The faces that pressed in around us looked mad with excitement. Some were smeared with crusted blood. The cab tilted precariously to one side, then the other. Finally, it toppled over, spilling Houdini and me onto the street.

Chapter 41
What the Painting Revealed

We lay there a moment, stunned. The horse, freed of its traces, wheeled around, looking for an escape. People yelled and stumbled over one another to get out of its way. Seeing our chance, I jumped to my feet. I grabbed Houdini and helped him stand. We looked around for Mackleston.

"There," Houdini said, and pointed. The fellow was pushing himself off the pavement after the spill he had taken from the top of the cab.

We dashed over to him. He looked up, startled. We hauled him upright. He had holes in the knees of both trouser legs.

"Can you walk?" I asked.

He nodded.

To avoid the horse's plunging hooves, the crowd fled back against the buildings on either side of the roadway. With a clatter the animal galloped off down the street.

The three of us dashed through the pathway it had cleared before it could close again.

We kept going. Mackleston limped along by my side. Houdini's bare feet pounded the pavement next to us. He ignored his swollen eye and bruises. Behind us, we could hear the chanting and fighting start up again. Fortunately, we had reached Soho before taking the spill. Mackleston's flat was only a few streets away. We soon arrived at his doorway.

In the rush of events, Woburn had neglected to search me when he arrested us. Therefore, I still carried the key Gaylord had given me. I unlocked the door to Mackleston's building. Houdini grabbed my arm before I could open it.

"The alarm," he whispered.

"Let us hope that Miss Finch is a sound sleeper," I said quietly, and slowly pulled the door open. When the bell tinkled, it sounded like a fire alarm in my ear.

Houdini and Mackleston and I squeezed through the narrow opening. We needn't have worried. The door to Miss Finch's flat was wide open. Apparently, she had left in a considerable rush—no doubt to join the mad throngs sweeping through the city. I tried not to think what she might be doing now. Cautiously, we climbed the blue-carpeted steps to Mackleston's flat.

Gaylord's key opened Mackleston's door as well. For the first time in days, Mackleston stepped over the portal to his home. The interior had been cleaned—the walls scrubbed, the carpets changed. Still, a faint odor like that of rotting garbage remained behind.

As soon as the door shut behind us, I asked Mackleston, "How big was the painting?"

"Fairly large—about three feet by four feet."

That made sense. Miss Finch had confused it, when rolled up, with a satchel of tools. We searched the rooms. I looked up the fireplace. Nothing but soot. We stripped the bed and checked underneath it. We looked on the floor and in all the corners of the closet, even shoving the clothes from one side to the other. We opened every drawer and pulled up all the rugs.

I flipped through the paintings stacked against the wall of his studio. Halfway through, the nude of Miss Luce caught my attention. Her face was hidden in shadow. Once again, the marvelous golden-pink skin tones enchanted me. She was truly a beautiful woman. I wondered if I would ever see her again. Was she even now running amok in the streets with the other debauchers? The thought made me sad.

In the end, our search proved fruitless. We sat about the studio and tried to think. "Gaylord was an artist too," I said to Mackleston. "Where would an artist hide a painting in an artist's studio?"

"I suppose he could have painted over it," Mackleston suggested. With one accord the three of us raced to the stack of paintings against the wall. We divided them and checked each for wet pigment. All felt dry.

Our brief hope turned to frustration once more.

"You know," Houdini said, "he could have hidden it under one of the others."

"You mean take off the canvas, tack *The Daughters of King Minyas* to the frame, and stretch the old canvas over it?" Mackleston asked.

Houdini nodded.

Back we trudged to the stack of paintings. But nowhere did we find one with a double layer.

Thoroughly discouraged, we ended up sprawled about the studio again. Houdini sat on the floor, his back against a wall, his bare feet stretched out in front of him. He tapped his chin with a forefinger. I slumped on a chair. Mackleston lounged on the couch against the opposite wall and blew on his skinned knees. He, too, was deep in thought. I caught the gleam of tears in his eyes. Possibly, he was reliving the last horrible moments of Reggie's death.

My ruminations were shattered by the tinkle of the downstairs bell. Up I jumped. Had the monster finally tracked us down? To my surprise, I heard two sets of footsteps pounding up the stairs.

The door burst open and Inspector Woburn pushed his great girth through the portal. Behind him stood Maximillian Cairo in a trim black suit. Woburn had a pistol in his hand. He shifted it from Houdini to me. The barrel looked as huge as a drainpipe.

He spoke over his shoulder to Cairo. "Here they are, like you said."

Cairo gave a smile that was little more than stretching his lips.

Woburn swung the pistol to point at me. "This is twice tonight you two haven't been so clever, isn't it? You should have skipped the country while you could."

He sidled over and swung the revolver to point at Cairo.

"And you, get over there beside them."

Cairo looked annoyed. "Are you mad? I'm the one who led you here."

"Yes," Woburn agreed, "and you're the one who knew there was a murder goin' on at the hotel. You knew the victim and the killers. You even knew the room number. You know a little too much about this whole affair to suit me, Mr. Cairo." He gestured with the gun.

Cairo fixed the rotund inspector with a gaze of pure malice.

Woburn's face drained of blood. His free hand grabbed at his chest.

"Stop it, Cairo," I said. I had seen enough pain and death for one night.

Cairo looked to me, a faint smile curling his lip.

Woburn's eyes flicked over to me in puzzlement as he got his breath back.

They flicked back to Cairo just as the man fixed the inspector with his gaze again. Woburn gasped and his eyes widened as he realized that Cairo himself was the source of the pain. Woburn's gun hand sank. His knees buckled, but somehow, through sheer will, he forced himself to stay upright. He squinted with the effort as he lifted his free hand off his chest to support the pistol. "Ease off," he gasped. "I'll put a slug in your belly." His finger tightened on the trigger. "I'm no gentleman," he warned hoarsely.

Cairo dropped his eyes. Woburn sagged with relief, but his gun never wavered from Cairo's middle. He staggered back until he could lean against the wall. He gulped in air. As color returned to his face, Woburn gestured with his pistol. "Over there—next to your friends," he panted.

Cairo strolled with apparent unconcern and stood beside me.

Woburn kept his revolver aimed in our direction. "Outside," he inclined his head toward the open door, "the world's gone mad." He licked his lips. "I've had a touch of it myself." His eyes flicked to Houdini. "Sorry about—well, you know. Back there in the wagon."

Houdini shrugged. He looked around, everywhere but at Woburn's face. "Forget it. You aren't the first cop who ever worked me over."

Woburn swallowed before speaking again. "You gentlemen know what is going on. Before I take you back to Holloway, you'll tell me all."

"If you don't leave this room soon, none of you ever will," Cairo said languidly.

Woburn's eyes narrowed. "And what's that supposed to mean?"

"It means, you insufferable little bureaucrat, that there are powers loose tonight you cannot even comprehend."

"Don't play with me." Woburn gripped the pistol tightly.

Cairo ignored the man. Instead, he turned to me. "Have you found the painting?" His voice was businesslike.

I shook my head. "How did you know we were here? Did you follow us?"

"No, I deduced it." He shot me a wry smile. "Gaylord was gone. When I realized the key to Mackleston's flat was missing, I put the two together."

Woburn broke in. "You three broke out of gaol, and let

a couple of dozen prisoners loose on top of it, for a painting?" He sounded outraged.

"Well, there was the small matter of a hanging," Mackleston interjected dryly from his place on the couch.

"Hanging? What hanging?"

"We were going to be summarily executed in the morning. To make room for more prisoners," I informed him.

"Rubbish," he declared. "Typical gaol-yard rumor. Who fed you that nonsense?"

"The Chief Warder," Houdini answered.

Woburn lowered his pistol in surprise.

"He said the orders came from the Home Secretary," Mackleston added.

Woburn could only shake his head. "My God," he said. "My God. It's gone that far?"

Cairo stepped forward and addressed the inspector. "We have a more immediate problem. Shortly, a creature will be joining us that you do not wish to meet. You four would all do well to be out of here."

Woburn did not respond. He looked truly at a loss. His pistol hand hung limply at his side. "What's to do when there's no one to give orders?"

I ignored him. "Can you not control the monster?" I asked Cairo. I had visions of his transforming into the beast before my very eyes.

"Only in a limited way. I've pacified it for a time."

Our conversation appeared to rouse Woburn from his preoccupations. "What's this about a monster?" he demanded.

"It's the thing that killed Reggie and the cop," Houdini said.

"And Gaylord," I added.

"We've all seen it," Mackleston contributed.

Woburn's gaze traveled from one to the other of us. He looked suspicious. "You've all seen a monster?"

"Not a monster," Cairo corrected him. "The monster. The little bit of nastiness that lurks in the sewer of everyone's soul."

Woburn jerked his thumb over his shoulder. "Then what's going on out there . . . ?"

"Yes," Cairo verified. "All due to its influence."

Woburn raised his revolver. "Not very good, gentlemen. You're stayin' until I hear a story I can believe."

"All right," Cairo said agreeably. "What would you believe? That I did the murders all by myself? Or possibly the four of us go out and rend people limb from limb after a jolly night together at the pub?"

Woburn advanced on Cairo. His eyes were narrow. He clenched the pistol in his fist. "Shall I prove to you I'm not joking?" he asked in silky tones.

Cairo stood his ground. "Shall I?"

Of its own accord Woburn's hand flew to his chest. The memory of the pain there gave him pause.

Cairo faced me. "Help me find the painting and I shall take the beast away with me."

I shook my head. "And have it infect the entire world? No, I must confront it."

"Always the 'parfit gentil knight,'" Cairo sneered. "You're a fool. It'll slash you to mincemeat."

I did not reply. I hoped I had discerned the beast's weakness. I was not about to reveal that to its host.

Cairo grabbed my sleeve. "You don't understand. This is not what you think it is."

"I understand that civilization is coming to an end," I replied stoutly.

"Oh, spare me." Cairo rolled his eyes skyward. "I suppose you've cast me as the villain of this story."

I did not deign to reply.

"Look," he said, "I had no idea—I never wanted the deaths. Reggie was an accident."

"An accident!" Mackleston expostulated. "You call what I saw an accident?"

"What are you talking about?" Woburn's voice was almost a shriek.

All four of us ignored him. "Don't be such a hypocrite," Cairo snapped at Mackleston. "You had no love for him. Remember the insults? Having to beg for money to eat?" A sly look came over Cairo's features. "Remember the letters?"

Mackleston gasped. "How did you know about that?"

"We were in school together, remember? He used to boast about how he put one over on you."

"What letters?" Houdini asked.

Mackleston said sheepishly, "I'd written a love letter to a school chum. Left it in the hall for the servants to post. Reggie found it and read it. I never dreamed he'd open a sealed letter. Anyway, he threatened to tell m'father unless I turned m'self into his bloody slave. He made my life a hell for months."

"You stole it back?" I asked.

"Lord, no. He was too clever for me. He'd hidden it in a trouser pocket. Justine found it one day in his room."

Mackleston clapped a hand over his mouth in dismay. I stood there, stunned at what he had just revealed.

Cairo gave a tiny smile. "I am afraid you just gave away the game."

Woburn surged into the middle of us. "You . . ." He waved his pistol at each of us in turn. "You will explain all this to me now!"

As he glared at Cairo, Houdini deftly snatched the pistol from his hand.

Woburn grabbed at Houdini. The man was too agile for him, however, and twisted away from his outstretched arms. Woburn turned and charged. Mackleston casually stuck out one leg from the couch where he sat. Woburn tripped and fell to the ground. In a flash, Houdini was on top of him. The magician grabbed one beefy arm, wrenched it up into a hammerlock, and deposited himself cross-legged in the middle of Woburn's back.

"Go on," Houdini said to Mackleston. "You're giving me an idea." The magician ignored Woburn's thrashing and grunting underneath him.

Mackleston's disclosure had opened up startling possibilities. "Miss Luce lived in your household?" I asked.

"How . . . ?" I began to understand. "You were the one who gave her employment after her father died."

Mackleston looked stricken. "I talked m'father into it," he admitted.

"No wonder she felt indebted to you." My mind raced ahead. Could it be? No, it was impossible!

"Hey!" Houdini shouted.

We all turned to look at him. "I got it. Somebody come take my place."

"Got what?" Mackleston asked.

"Just get over here," Houdini ordered. Dutifully, Mackleston replaced Houdini on Woburn's back. By now the man had stopped struggling and was trying to speak. The weight on his back kept it to little more than a series of gasps.

Without another word, the magician dashed into the bedchamber. In a moment he returned with the rolled-up canvas in his hand.

"Where on earth . . . ?" Cairo asked.

Houdini strutted like a drum major in a parade. "Mackleston's story clued me in."

"Which part?" Mackleston asked.

I scarcely paid them heed. Unspeakable thoughts filled my mind. What a fool I had been.

"You said Reggie hid the letter in a pants pocket, remember?" Houdini continued triumphantly. "Well, guess what? We looked though your closet, but we never checked your clothes. I found a pant leg with a knot tied in the bottom. This," he said, flourishing the painting, "had been stuffed into it."

He took hold of the canvas top. "Now we'll see what's the big deal."

Cairo lunged for the picture, but Houdini danced out of reach and continued to unroll it.

Just then the bell below sounded again. Everyone in the room froze. I held my breath, waiting. Mackleston sprang to his feet. With the weight gone, Woburn lurched to his knees. I heard a muffled scuffling as of hooves skittering across a rug. Footsteps slowly mounted the ten steps to Mackleston's room. I counted them silently in my head. One, two.

As Woburn gained his feet, understanding dawned on his face. He looked at Cairo. "Is—is that—?"

Cairo nodded.

Three, four, five.

"Wait a minute." Houdini lowered the painting and stared at Cairo. "The monster—it isn't you?"

Six, seven.

Cairo shook his head, a sad smile on his face.

Houdini's gaze dropped to the unrolled painting in his hand. It took a few moments for him to register what he was seeing. "Holy cow," he said to me. "Look at this."

Eight, nine.

"I don't need to," I replied calmly. "I know what is on the canvas."

Ten.

With those words, I stepped to the door and flung it open. Before me stood the beast. Its green eyes narrowed. I heard Woburn give a gasp. The creature's vulpine features leered at me.

It flexed its fingers. Its talons clicked and a cruel smile animated its bony, pointed face. It reached and ran a razor-sharp talon down my cheek. I flinched but held my ground as I felt a sting. A warm trail of wetness dripped down to my chin. The thing cocked its head to one side and examined its work critically. I was shaking in every limb. I wanted to turn and run. Instead, I leaned in and lifted my head, baring my throat.

I felt the blood throb in my carotid artery, scant inches from the beast's claws. The creature looked uncertain at my boldness. I took courage from this and actually leaned forward. I was less than an inch from its snout. I could smell its fetid breath, feel its bristly hairs against my cheek.

"I wanted you," I whispered to it. "I almost killed my wife to possess you. I freely admit these things."

The beast gave a snarl of rage and backed up a step. I sensed movement behind me. Houdini had dropped the painting and stepped forward. Though his eyes filled with terror, he refused to let me face my fate alone.

"Keep back!" I warned. "I know what I'm doing."

A surge of power coursed through me. I was doing it, I was building a temple to Dionysus. I must not deny, but rather accept that side of humanity, of me.

Even so, I was not sure I had the courage for my next move. "You are indeed powerful." I reached out for it. Its spiky hairs tickled my palms. Its reeking breath scalded my slit cheek. It was loathsome. It was irresistible. Gingerly, I embraced the beast.

I hugged its wiry form to my breast. I heard a howl of frustration in my ear that set my head ringing. I echoed its howl again and again. I sang the rising notes like a song.

The beast squirmed and pushed at my chest. Converting its cry into a melody had upset it. I had transformed chaos to order. I clasped my hands behind its back and held on. The beast twisted and writhed. It was like hugging a sack of serpents. Miraculously, the thing did not use its claws.

We toppled over and fell to the floor. The fall broke my hold and the beast sprang free of me. There was a flicker, as if the universe itself had blinked. In an instant the creature changed. It became a satyr.

I launched myself at it. I dug my fingers into its soft, dark pelt. Cloven hooves kicked at my shins. I cried out in pain but clutched even tighter. Its short, stubby horns beat against my forehead as it bayed its displeasure. Still I held on.

Under my grip, I felt it changing again. The hair disappeared under my fingers to be replaced by tender skin. The figure softened and lay still. The nubile, young maenad nestled in my arms. Her long blond hair fell coyly over one eye. Her soft breasts flattened themselves against my chest. Her arms encircled my neck. Her mouth opened invitingly. Her legs parted and she pressed her warm loins against mine.

I felt my manhood rise in response. But I felt no shame. At this moment, I was not a prisoner to any of my urges. It was merely the animal side of my personality responding—natural and innocent. If I didn't deny it, it had no sway over me. I held her gently and planted one kiss in the hollow of her throat.

She stiffened in my arms. Her lips twisted and she bared her teeth in a snarl. Her eyes blazed with anger and disappointment. With a burst of energy, she flung me away. I landed on my back and lay there panting.

The outlines of the figure melted and flowed. The maenad seemed to dissolve on the rug in front of the door.

What was left was a corpse-green pool of liquid. It was the slime I had seen at Cairo's. Mouths bubbled out of the ooze, crying and sucking and sputtering. They gave off the stench of rotting flesh. Foul liquid dribbled out of some of them. The muck surged toward me. It roiled as if seething in a giant cauldron. I rolled away in disgust, and the mouths tittered in high-pitched laughter.

What was I doing? I could not give up my advantage. Though I shuddered at the thought, I steeled myself and crawled toward the mass. The pile of sludge paused and quivered at my approach. I rose to my knees. I wanted nothing more than to flee the sight.

No, it had to be done. Closing my eyes, I launched myself into the muck. Greasy slime enveloped me and seeped into my nostrils. I rolled in the reek of decay. The mouths fastened onto my cheeks, my neck, my hands, and sucked on my flesh. I embraced the foulness that I had rejected at Cairo's house weeks ago.

Suddenly, it was over. The slithery embrace disappeared. The smell vanished. I opened my eyes. In my arms I held a nude, desperately sobbing Miss Luce.

"There, there." I stroked her honey-blond hair.

The others stood, frozen in place. Houdini gaped. Mackleston watched unhappily. Woburn had retreated to a corner of the room, where he stood shaking his head over and over as if in denial. Cairo lounged against one wall, arms folded, and frowned his disapproval. Abruptly, he disappeared into Mackleston's bedchamber.

I turned my attention back to the woman in my arms. Her weeping had abated. "You're all right now. Your torment is over."

To my astonishment, she shoved me away. "Damn you!" she gulped.

Ignoring her nakedness, she pushed herself into a sitting position and glared at me through tear-drenched eyes. "You ruined everything," she accused. "For once in my life, I felt strong. I wasn't afraid—I made others afraid." The woman leaned toward me. The scent of her body was intoxicating. "I made you afraid."

Her intensity was overwhelming. I found myself leaning away from her. Oblivious to me, she broke down once more, this time in despair. "How can I face a life of being ordinary?"

She turned her face from me and wept for what she had lost.

Chapter 42
Conclusion

I rose shakily to my feet and staggered back into the room. Mackleston handed me a handkerchief, which I held to my bleeding cheek. Cairo reappeared, a forest-green dressing gown in his hands, no doubt from Mackleston's closet. He pushed past me and knelt to slip the gown over Justine's head. Then he gathered her in his arms to console her.

After a moment, he looked up at me. "Fool!" he spat. "You think you have saved the world? You haven't. You have condemned it."

"Listen," I replied.

For the first time, the night was quiet. No distant cries of rage or rapacity sounded. With the incarnation of Dionysus gone, people were freed from his spell. Even now I imagined them all over the city, waking as if from a bad dream.

"Humanity is safe," I replied.

"Oh, yes," Cairo's voice dripped with irony, "the world will continue to run in your image—decency that is but a mask of repression, pride that merely cloaks prejudice, confidence that disguises naïveté."

"How can you mock me?" I expostulated. "Look at the violence, the pain, the deaths you caused."

"I caused?" Cairo looked outraged. "Had you not broken the septagram, he would have remained imprisoned, able to work only through subtle suggestion. But you two set him free to occupy a human body. That was when the murders began."

I had no answer for him. Was this all our doing?

Angrily, he continued, "Think back. Except for the beast's few killings, what terrible things did you see? People acting out their deepest desires—sex, a fistfight or two, a little sadism. No one was permanently injured."

My face must have betrayed my incredulity, for he said, "Don't believe me? What has happened to you? You have accepted a side of you that had been suppressed all your life. And thereby you found a reservoir of courage you didn't even know you had. And what was the cost? Some humiliation, a little sadness. A small price to pay."

"But if I had not acted—" I began.

He would not let me finish. "Had you let the 'madness' run its course, humanity would have purged itself of these desires and awakened tomorrow sane and at peace."

Cairo shook a finger at me. "That was the Great Work I attempted—nothing less than a spiritual cleansing for all humanity. That was the outcome you have destroyed."

"Yeah, you say that now," Houdini weighed in. "You didn't know how it would end up. You were just a little kid playing with fire."

Cairo ignored the magician. "You have banished him before he could complete his work. But you have not destroyed him. He still exists as a spark in every living soul on this planet.

"He is just waiting to burst free. The more people repress him, the stronger he'll become. In a decade you'll see an eruption of worldwide carnage. I hope you can live with yourselves when it comes."

His tirade over, Cairo helped Justine to her feet. The look she gave him was indescribable—equal parts of loathing and joy. He gave her a wry smile in return. Neither one looked back at us. She leaned shakily on him as they faded into the darkness of the landing. I heard their footsteps descend the ten stair steps and cross the carpeted entry. The bell tinkled as the front door opened and they fled into the night.

A few evenings hence, Houdini, Mackleston, and I relaxed in the high-backed chairs at a table in Simpson's in the Strand. We sipped our port after a fine dinner of roast beef. Dark paneling surrounded us. Waiters in chef's hats and red-checkered neckerchiefs hovered nearby. The chandeliers and sconces on the plaster frieze around the room gave off a gentle glow. Normalcy was returning. Most people went about their business as they always did, albeit with a dazed look.

The morning after our adventure, I'd arranged a hasty meeting with His Majesty. As a result, the government suppressed all news of the matter. They must have been quite persuasive, as no newspaper or magazine or book ever mentioned the Night All London Went Mad. People seemed only too willing to forget, if they even remembered. Perhaps, as the years passed, they would convince themselves that it had simply been a nightmare.

All charges against us were dropped. Woburn was in no condition to press them. I believe he retired to the Cotswolds, where he ran a small pub in Lower Slaughter for the rest of his life.

Mackleston reached for the decanter and refilled our glasses with the dark ruby liquid. Even Houdini joined us in imbibing tonight. I sucked meditatively on my cigar. Our injuries were healing. The cut on my cheek was only a thin pink line. The bruises on my shins and forehead from wrestling with the satyr had faded to yellow stains. Houdini's ribs scarcely troubled him.

Outwardly, we were simply three friends enjoying a meal. But inwardly, I was troubled. Though I had deduced much, several details still eluded me.

"When Justine was in your father's employ," I said, "did Reggie attack her?"

He nodded sadly. "It was all my fault. If I hadn't brought her to my house, he'd never have had the opportunity."

"You were just a boy. What could you have done?" I pointed out.

"I'll tell you what I did," he answered fiercely. "I came upon them in her room, just as he was . . ." Mackleston hesitated and took a big gulp of wine. "Anyway, I found one of Reggie's own shotguns and ran back to the room. I fired a blast into the ceiling and told him if he ever touched her again, I'd kill him."

"No wonder she was so loyal to you," I observed.

He shrugged.

"You could have told your father," Houdini pointed out.

"I tried, but he wouldn't believe anything against Reggie. Neither one of them ever forgave me. As soon as I came of age, m'father threw me out."

That answered one question, but I had another. "On the afternoon of the murder," I said, "why did Reggie drop in?"

"Oh, he did that every once in a while. I think he liked to assure himself that I wasn't living too well."

When I had finally seen the painting, it was as I knew it would be—a work of genius and madness. Swirls of color and crazy perspectives jostled one another. One daughter of King Minyas held center stage. Justine. She had been in the room, posing one more time for Mackleston.

I gestured toward him with my glass. "Reggie interrupted you while you were painting?"

"Just as I finished, actually. Justine was still nude. Reggie barged in and she scrambled into her dressing gown.

I'll never forget the smug look on his face as he said, 'Don't worry, my dear, I've seen it all before. And it's nothing special.'"

Mackleston stared straight ahead of him, seeing, I should imagine, not the restaurant but the room in his flat. "Both of us were"—he searched for the *mot juste*—"in a rather heightened state. She flew into a rage. I tried to pull her off him, but she wasn't herself anymore. She'd turned into . . ."

"Yes, I know," I said. "That is why she was so desperate for me to prove you innocent. She couldn't bear to see you hang for a murder she had committed. She hoped I would find traces of a third person in your flat but wouldn't realize who it had been."

I realized how very clever Justine had been. "When I took her to your flat, she used her time to remove all traces of her stay there. She even cleaned up the ashes she had tracked across the floor when she climbed down from the fireplace. That is why I found ash outside on the windowsill."

No doubt about it; she had managed me quite skillfully. I sighed with self-reproach. "I overlooked so many clues, simply because it never entered my head that a woman could do such a thing."

And Miss Luce was not the only woman who'd surprised me. Had it not been for Bess Houdini's defiant courage, we should never have left Holloway Prison alive.

I would have to rethink my opinions of the "gentler" sex. Could it be there were fewer differences in ability and inclination between us than I had always supposed? The thought was profoundly disturbing.

"One last thing," Houdini asked Mackleston. "What happened to the stone in your ring?"

Mackleston looked puzzled a moment.

"The garnet," I explained. "We found it in your flat. Your father accused us of stealing the real gem."

"Well, isn't that just like him," Mackleston said, disgustedly. "Originally, it was a ruby." He shrugged. "I sold it to buy brushes. Had the jeweler substitute a cheap stone."

And that answered that last of our questions about those remarkable events. The rest of the evening we spent trying to decide whether Cairo had been trying to suppress the beast in Justine Luce or incite it to ever-greater acts of madness. We never reached a conclusion.

My wife lingered for several months before she passed on to the other planes of existence. Eventually, I married again—a woman of considerable intellect and a skilled conversationalist. I had lost my desire for a life partner who was entirely submissive. I have never forgotten Justine Luce. I often wonder: Had I been a little more astute, a little less close-minded, could I have won her away from Cairo?

In due time, Mackleston succeeded to his father's title and worked valiantly behind the scenes to ease the oppression of those who shared his proclivities.

As everyone knows, Cairo's dreadful prophecy came true. On midnight, August 4, 1914, after a comedy of errors, the Great War broke out. It devastated Europe. Almost an entire generation perished. I lost many things to it, including my son Kingsley. He died during the final weeks of fighting in October 1918.

Was that, too, my doing? Had Cairo told the truth about his plans to save humanity, or was it all a pack of lies designed to save face? I shall never know.

Over the years, Houdini managed to convince himself that everything we saw could be explained away by hypnotism or drugs. We argued about it more and more frequently. Ultimately, it destroyed our friendship. In later years, he made a living exposing spiritualist frauds. It was his boast that no occultist had ever gotten the better of him. No one but he and I ever knew otherwise.

As for me, I spent the rest of my life probing the forces that lurk beyond the physical world. I also wrote "The Adventure of the Empty House" and gratified the world by bringing Holmes back from the dead. But I never again attained the heights of inspiration of the Holmes story I left unfinished.

And what of Justine and Cairo? I finally traced them— ironically enough—to the ship the *Saxon Warrior*, which left port the night they fled Mackleston's flat. The ship went down with all hands off the coast of Spain. There were no known survivors.

DOUGLAS CLEGG
NIGHTMARE HOUSE

There are places that hold in the traces of evil, houses that become legendary for the mysteries and secrets within their walls. Harrow is one such house. Psychic manifestations, poltergeist activity, hallucinations, and other residue of terror have all been documented in Harrow. It has been called Nightmare House. It is a nest for the restless spirits of the dead.

When Ethan Gravesend arrives to inherit Nightmare House, he does not suspect the horror that awaits him—the nightmare of the woman trapped within the walls of the house, or the endless crying of an unseen child.

Also includes the bonus novella *Purity*!

DEEP IN THE DARKNESS
MICHAEL LAIMO

Dr. Michael Cayle wants the best for his wife and young daughter. That's why he moves the family from Manhattan to accept a private practice in the small New England town of Ashborough. Everything there seems so quaint and peaceful—at first. But Ashborough is a town with secrets. Unimaginable secrets.

Many of the townspeople are strangely nervous, and some speak quietly of legends that no sane person could believe. But what Michael discovers in the woods, drenched in blood, makes him wonder. Soon he will be forced to believe, when he learns the terrifying identity of the golden eyes that peer at him balefully from deep in the darkness.

Dorchester Publishing Co., Inc.
P.O. Box 6640   5314-4
Wayne, PA 19087-8640 $6.99 US/$8.99 CAN

Please add $2.50 for shipping and handling for the first book and $.75 for each additional book. NY and PA residents, add appropriate sales tax. No cash, stamps, or CODs. Canadian orders require $2.00 for shipping and handling and must be paid in U.S. dollars. Prices and availability subject to change. **Payment must accompany all orders.**

Name: _____

Address: _____

City: _____ State: _____ Zip: _____

E-mail: _____

I have enclosed $_____ in payment for the checked book(s).

For more information on these books, check out our website at www.dorchesterpub.com.
_____ *Please send me a free catalog.*

FEARS
UNNAMED
TIM LEBBON

Tim Lebbon has burst upon the scene and established himself as one of the best horror writers at work today. He is the winner of numerous awards, including a Bram Stoker Award, critics have raved about his work, and fans have eagerly embraced him as a contemporary master of the macabre.

Perhaps nowhere are the reasons for his popularity more evident than in this collection of four of his most chilling novellas. Two of these dark gems received British Fantasy Awards, and another was written specifically for this book and has never previously been published. These terrifying tales form a window into a world of horrors that, once experienced, can never be forgotten.

Dorchester Publishing Co., Inc.
P.O. Box 6640
Wayne, PA 19087-8640

5200-8
$6.99 US/$8.99 CAN

Please add $2.50 for shipping and handling for the first book and $.75 for each additional book. NY and PA residents, add appropriate sales tax. No cash, stamps, or CODs. Canadian orders require $2.00 for shipping and handling and must be paid in U.S. dollars. Prices and availability subject to change. **Payment must accompany all orders.**

Name: _____

Address: _____

City: _____ State: _____ Zip: _____

E-mail: _____

I have enclosed $_____ in payment for the checked book(s).

CHECK OUT OUR WEBSITE! www.dorchesterpub.com
_____ *Please send me a free catalog.*